ISLANDS OF FIRE

THE SICILY CHRONICLES: PART I

DICK ROSANO

Illustrated by
KARI GILLMAN

HOW TO READ THIS BOOK
NOTES AND ASSISTS

This book is a work of historical fiction. The events chronicled here are derived from archeological evidence and historical records, but some of the names, characters, places, and specific incidents are the product of the author's imagination and are used with actual people and places in Sicily to illustrate the history of the island and bring it to life. Any resemblance of these characters to actual events, locales, or persons, living or dead, is purely coincidental.

The time frame for *Islands of Fire: The Sicily Chronicles, Part I* begins in the era referred to as B.C.E. or "Before the Common Era," which is the generally accepted scientific reference to the time before the birth of Christ (formerly written as B.C.). In later parts of the book, the reader will note the use of the term C.E., or "Common Era," to refer to the time since the birth of Christ (formerly written as A.D., for *Anno Domini*). The use of B.C.E. and C.E. is a religion-free nod to today's world of science; however, Vito Trovato, the old man in the story who is mentoring Luca, hasn't accepted the modernization of the term yet and, so, in his quoted passages the reader will still see B.C. and A.D.

The Ancient Place Names list attached at the end of the story describes the names of islands, villages, towns, and cities as they evolved over the millennia. The Vocabulary is an aid in deciphering the words used in antiquity, along with the modern meaning. The List of Characters includes those individuals, both historical and fictional, for each era and portion of the story in which they appear.

This volume, *Islands of Fire: The Sicily Chronicles, Part I*, is followed by the next volume, *Crossroads of the Mediterranean: The Sicily Chronicles, Part II*.

LIST OF ILLUSTRATIONS

PREFACE

To have seen Italy without having seen Sicily is to not have seen Italy at all, for Sicily is the clue to everything.

JOHANN WOLFGANG VON GOETHE

SICILY IN THE 21ST CENTURY

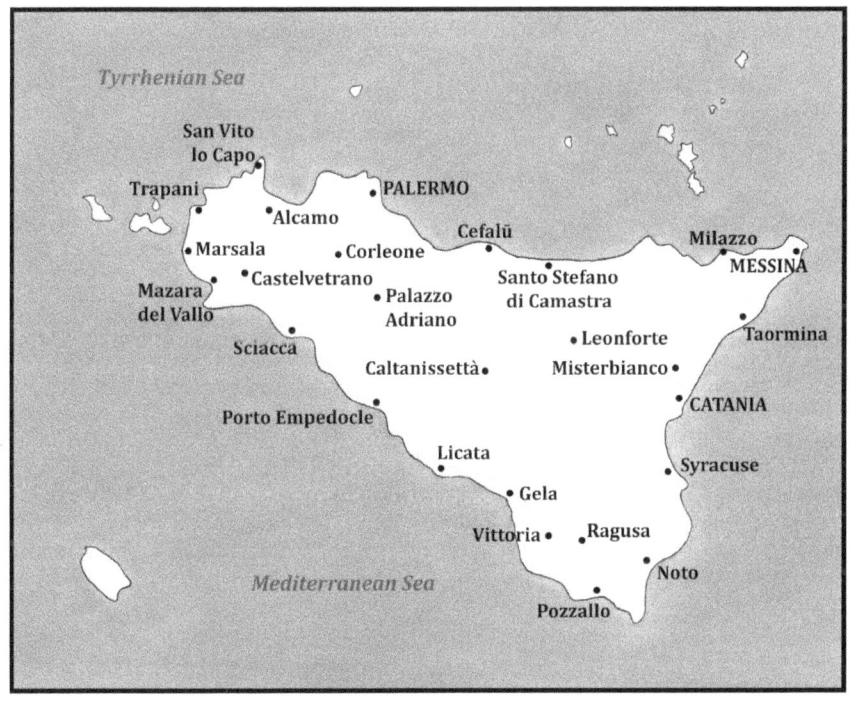

Tyrrhenian Sea

San Vito
lo Capo
Trapani
PALERMO
Alcamo
Cefalù
Marsala
Corleone
Milazzo
Castelvetrano
MESSINA
Santo Stefano
di Camastra
Mazara
del Vallo
Palazzo
Adriano
Taormina
Leonforte
Sciacca
Caltanissettà
Misterbianco
CATANIA
Porto Empedocle
Licata
Syracuse
Gela
Vittoria
Ragusa
Noto
Mediterranean Sea
Pozzallo

1943

FEBRUARY 1943
NORTH AFRICA, WAR JOURNAL

Another chilly night. The moonless sky is hauntingly black and a thin sheet of clouds obscures the stars overhead. The air is still; the only sound I hear in our encampment on the edge of this mountain is the murmur of a passing breeze winding through the trees. Scores of exhausted soldiers are bivouacked around me in this pass through the Atlas Mountains in Tunisia. We wait for orders from our German commander or, worse, a sudden attack by enemy forces.

We have no firepits to warm us, only the red glow of a cigarette to light the ruddy cheeks and coarse hands of the men. We know that burning cigarettes is discouraged, but the pop of a flaring match is worse, so we have adopted the practice of chain smoking, lighting each butt from the one before to avoid the signal given off by the sulphurous burst of a new match.

"Shhh," one man whispers to some others sitting in a cluster near him. Sound is also discouraged, but my fellow recruits from Sicily have little of home left in them except the stories they share on these dark nights.

"Silensu!" the man says again. "Ira infernu!" he spits out in Sicilian argot.

These men were recruited by the local authorities in their towns, mostly from Gela, Agrigento, and Mazara del Vallo on the southern coast of our island. The Italian government thought it expedient to bring young Sicilian men into the conflict, men who had a local connection and who would commit to the fight to preserve their homeland. We didn't count on being shipped to North Africa though, even when the German commander told us that this was the way to keep the Americans and British far enough away from attacking Sicily itself.

I sit behind these squabbling men, understanding their disappointment and pain, but I am also disappointed to be defending this mountain pass in Africa rather than my beloved Sicily. I shift my position and arch my shoulders to stretch them, then lean back into the shallow wooden chair that I have provisioned. It is not very comfortable, but I can rest on the burlap sling seat and back of the sparse furniture.

The stiff neck of my starched sand-colored uniform chafes at my skin, so I poke a finger into the collar to pull it from my neck. Lifting the stubby cigarette to my lips, I draw in deeply and hold the breath for a moment before letting the smoke drift slowly out in a silent whisper between my lips. But I should write more about the war, not just my discomfort.

It's doubtful that anyone will read this journal, even if it survives the war. Even if I survive. But the bloodshed, devastation, and terror all around us convinces me that I should put my thoughts on paper.

I am Vito Trovato, from Mazara del Vallo. I was drafted into the Italian 131ˢᵗ Armored Division Centauro. Most of the 'recruits' – we're encouraged to report that we volunteered – are from my part of Sicily in the province of Trapani on the western side of the island. The German Army built up its reserves by recruiting divisions of Italian conscripts to defend our land. But, more importantly to the Third Reich, we are here to serve as a defensive line against attempts by the enemy to use Sicily as a staging area for an attack on the European mainland...and, from there, to the Fatherland.

They think of Sicily as a barrier island, a battleground between Africa and Europe, and they treat us like cannon fodder. They know we will fight to protect Sicily and our people, and that should be enough to satisfy their goals.

My country has been thought of that way for a long time...a barren ground on which the peoples of the world staged their battles. If it's not the Greeks taking over our cities and taking our women, then it's the Romans stealing our grain or the Spanish or Byzantines or Normans vying for domination over us.

No one believes that the Nazis care about Sicily itself, or the Sicilians. But I am a Sicilian, and any invaders coming to my country must be sent back.

We haven't been very successful in sending back the invaders, though. Now, or in centuries past. Maybe we should just regard each new aggressor carefully and choose which ones we should surrender to.

We – the 131ˢᵗ Armored Division recruits – assembled in the square of our city in November of last year and we were later ferried across to Tunisia to fight the Allies who had landed there. I have a good education from the university at Palermo and I returned to my home in Mazara to teach Italian literature to secondary students. The German hierarchy thought I should become an officer and lead men of lesser status.

I had to laugh at this. I am true to my occupation, but it's hard to find a profession of lower status to a German general than a teacher of literature. But, these are unusual times.

We landed the next morning and the Germans quickly set up their camp. We Siciliani were left to ourselves, an armored detachment in defense of a German operation that, otherwise, pretended we weren't here. They say the place is called the Kasserine Pass, but all I know is it's cold, dark, and unfriendly.

We're in a trail through the mountains and they say it has some importance to the war, but the war itself lacks meaning for most of us. We hear that our Prime Minister, Il Duce, is fighting against the Americans and British, but while leaders declare wars, real men fight them. This pass, this Kasserine, matters for some reason that Herr Rommel, the most honored German field marshal, decides. But will he die along with us?

I would rather be back in Sicily, in Mazara del Vallo, but I suppose defending my country against these attacks here in North Africa keeps the threat farther from my people. Sicilians have had too much conflict throughout our history; we could use a break.

———

It is now the evening of the following day. We were told at daybreak that Rommel was moving his 10th Panzer Division against the Allies defending the Kasserine Pass. He was relying on a combined push by the German Afrika Corps Assault Group and our Armored Division to overpower the Allied positions. It appears to have worked, and we pushed the American and British contingents into a panicked retreat from the mountains in North Africa.

The commander reports that the Allies lost many men and much military equipment in the rush to abandon their positions, and he bravely predicts that the enemy can no longer take over the North African theatre.

Once again, we are assigned to sit and wait. All around me, in small clumps, tired soldiers sit around the muddy roadway, leaning against the worn tires of the trucks we drive, and smoke cigarettes. One of the new recruits – we can always pick them out by the relative cleanliness of their uniforms – seems dazed. When I walked over to him and offered him a cigarette he smiled wanly. He looked like he was lost, or confused, or maybe just scared.

The Nazi commanders tell us about the great generals – Montgomery, Dunphie, Patton, Kesselring – but the names mean nothing to us. We're soldiers who fight in the trenches, in the dust, in the hills. We can't see farther than the sights on our rifles, or the smoke and cinder that erupts when one of our shells lands on enemy lines. Dry clothes, a pocketful of cigarettes, and a little to eat...that's all we hope for.

We drove the Allies from North Africa, but then something happened. Herr Rommel changed his mind. I heard rumors but couldn't tell what was true and what was not.

All that mattered was that we were pulling back, giving up the pass and the land we had died to hold. The survivors were thankful to let go and retreat to safer ground, but we were also dejected to leave behind our friends who had died for nothing.

―――

Another day has passed. In the early morning hours, we shipped back to Gela, on the southern coast of Sicily. We retreated from North Africa, although the German officers told us we had just conquered North

Africa. Most of my men are uneducated farmers, but they can tell that there was no victory over there. So, in shipping out, we moved the battle lines backward across the water, back into Sicily, all the while keeping our eyes and scouts focused on the coastline of the continent we were abandoning. If we had conquered it, we wouldn't have to keep watching it.

'We've run before the enemy,' he said to us. I knew the German officer's mastery of Italian was weak, which meant that his mastery of Sicilian was probably non-existent. He might have wanted to say that we escaped the clutches of the Allies, but to say 'we've run before the enemy' sounds – to the ears of the exhausted foot soldiers assembled in the piazza – more like 'we lost, and so we ran.'

Siciliani are a proud people and running from the enemy leaves a stain on the man's soul, his family, and the community. Over many years, many centuries, we've been overrun by people from Europe and the east, but surrender is ugly.

'We've run before the enemy.'

Herr Traubel couldn't have worded it any more poorly.

The Germans told us to plan to regroup on Sicily and establish a line of defense against the advancing Allied forces. But their strategy failed almost immediately. American General Patton landed with his Seventh Army on the shores of Sicily near where we had landed, outside of Gela. Rumors are the news bulletins for soldiers at war, and we were no exception. I heard from a German sergeant that Patton was heading west away from us, although that didn't make sense. Why quit the battle when they seemed to have us in retreat?

We also heard that British General Bernard Montgomery was heading due north, right into the path we had been ordered to take as we backed up through the island. We were given a short pause in the march and the men slumped to the ground to rest their backs and legs.

We were pushed back again, at the instruction of the Germans. They didn't want to confront the British on the southern shore of our island and they didn't know where the Americans were headed by their swing to the west. All this meant for the soldiers in my command was to put themselves in between the two armies, the Allies advancing and the

Germans backpedaling from the confrontation. My men asked what to do, and I could see desperation in their eyes.

I had been put in charge to lead these soldiers, and I intended to do so. But I couldn't tell what the Germans would do, and I was becoming afraid of what the British and Americans could do.

———

Another day of light fighting and a rapid retreat, and now we are camped out near a stream on the eastern part of Sicily. The Allies are advancing toward us and have already won battles in the south between Gela and Ragusa, and the west around Agrigento and Licata. Many small towns in Sicily have been transformed from quiet hamlets to killing fields in an afternoon.

We are being driven back into the north-eastern corner of Sicily with only the water and Straits of Messina behind us. The Germans have no option but to stage another retreat across the strait to the boot of Italy and try to reorganize there and make a stand against the Americans.

We Siciliani are being dragged along with the Germans as they pull back from the south. The campaign is going terribly for all to see, and my men don't need my summary of events to realize that we are losing.

Some men have left the ranks, never to be seen again. Some have been found ahead of our division, with a single gunshot below the chin. Some have merely sunk into a sullen depression, forced into losing a battle they had not chosen to fight.

'I know we fight for our country,' Adolfo told me one morning. 'But the Germans don't care if we win it.'

I have to agree with him. I don't need to remind him of the history of our country, how people from everywhere have fought for domination of Europe and the entire Mediterranean region using Sicily as the battleground. Adolfo has had enough fighting. He doesn't need to be reminded that this has been the plight of our island ever since it was first inhabited by primitive people.

———

This morning was bright and crisp. The sun rose and brought a soothing warmth to my skin. The air was still, except for a light breeze that tickled the leaves of trees. It is a new day and I have come to a decision. Lifting my pack by a strap and throwing it over my shoulder, I looked once more at the camp around me. My six-month contract had ended weeks ago.

Adolfo sat with lowered chin nearby, but when I stood he turned in my direction. He looked up with sullen eyes and nodded. It was as if he knew what was in my mind.

I held his gaze for a moment, then I turned and walked toward the edge of the encampment. And when I made it that far, I continued walking. I am heading home for Mazara del Vallo.

ANCIENT PEOPLES

9230 B.C.E.

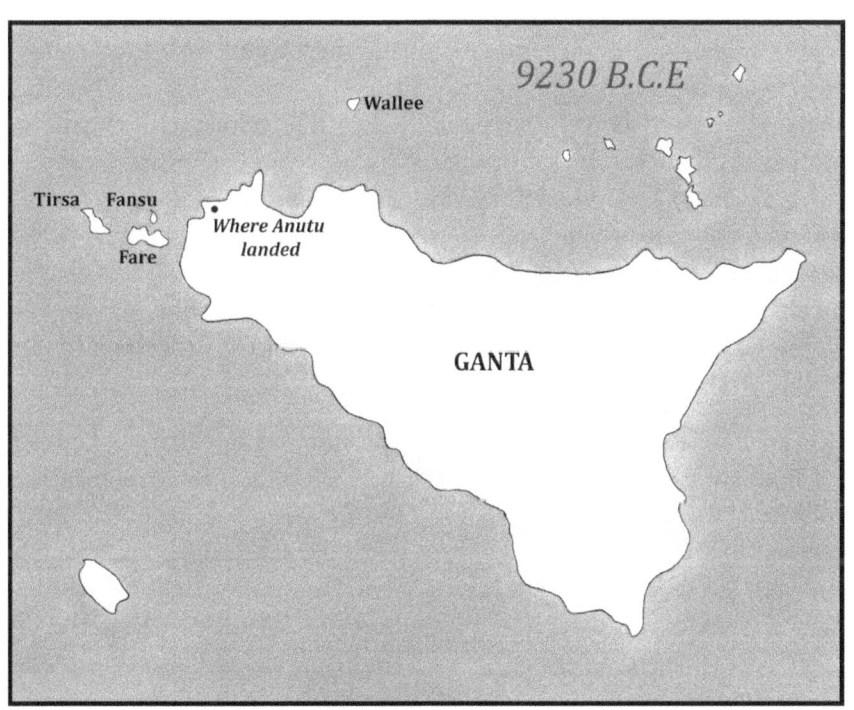

9230 B.C.E.

ISLAND OF FANSU

Anu's eyes openly slowly as he rolled from his right side onto his back beneath the soft weight of the animal skin covering his body. He peered out of the small shelter that he slept in, a lean-to pushed back into a crevice in the rock and covered with more animal hides to shield him and his family from the cool air of early spring. Through the narrow gap between the leather flaps at the opening to the outside, he could see the first hint of sunrise as the dark sky was chased up into the heavens by the yellowish orange glow of the sun on the horizon returning from its own short slumber on the other side of the world.

Baia lay beside him and her soft breathing let him know that she had not yet been awakened. Anu rubbed the heel of his left hand against the crust of sleep that clung to his eyes and let out a soft sigh as the day dawned upon him. Blinking his eyes twice, he reached up with his left arm and stretched to loosen his muscles. He didn't want to move his right arm yet; it was wedged between him and Baia as they shared each other's body heat.

Anu blinked his eyes again to clear his vision, then brushed his left hand across his brow and the bridge of his nose. Another long sigh escaped from his lips as he adjusted to the dim light coming in through the opening of the hut. He was reluctant to leave the warmth of the hide that protected him and Baia from the crisp morning air but, with a resigned heft onto his left shoulder, he hoisted his sturdy body up from the grassy mat that had cushioned him against the sand and rocky surface of the shelter's floor.

The cool air greeted him once he slipped out from under the hide. It wasn't much of a shock to his bare skin, not for a man who had lived many winters on the coast of this small island. As Anu rose to his feet, he pulled another animal hide over his shoulders, enough to cover his upper body and reach the waistline of the soft pelt that covered his loin and legs.

A slight shiver shimmied down his back, an action that provided momentary warmth as he stretched his arms above his head and prepared for the day ahead. His feet were covered with sewn hides taken from the toughest animals, stitched together carefully by Baia's deft hand with animal sinew and twisted fibers serving as thread. His britches were similar, though composed of softer material, and the hide that covered his upper body still held the fur of the animal that had been sacrificed to provide this covering to Anu.

The people of Fansu, a tiny island in the middle of the great sea, respected the animals that they hunted and the plants that they gathered for sustenance. The existence of his people would have been impossible without the hunting and gathering that was a daily necessity for the tribe, and they thanked the animals and plants for giving themselves up to them. They paid homage to the animals especially, because they moved about on four legs or two just as the people did, and the tribesmen believed that the earth mother had given these creatures to them for nourishment. So, the people carved the animals' images on the walls of sacred caves in solemn appreciation.

It was to one such cave that Anu was going today, to render features of ritual art on its walls to honor his father who had died the day before. Carving images of the animals and humans was reserved for the sacred caves found nearby and kept for privileged ceremonies such as Anu planned for the day.

The tribe had long ago chosen this particular cave because it was angled toward the sun that fell from the sky at the end of the day. The opening of the cave let in the radiant red light as the fiery ball settled into the water on its trip around his world, to reappear on the other side of his little island after they had slept.

Anu stepped toward the opening of the shelter and turned slightly back to survey the people who made up his world. There was Baia, whose fluttering eyelids and twitching smile reminded Anu of the amusing and confusing dream his head had conjured in the dark of night. There was also his young son, who recently had learned to go about on his feet but was now cuddled in the crook up Baia's right arm, nestled in the warmth of her body and the animal hide that was big enough to cover them both. On her stomach, and pressed closely to Baia's breast and armpit, was the latest addition to his world, a tiny newborn girl whose gentle babbling suggested that she might be awake and angling for her mother's nipple.

Anu looked out at the sun, squinting now that its light was growing stronger, then glanced back once more at his people. Baia's eyes were now open, probably brought out of her sleep by the needs of the baby. She looked up at Anu and blinked recognition. She knew that her man had a duty to perform for the elder who had died, and he would soon be out into the sunlight. Baia would remain in their cave to take care of the children.

Anu looked beyond this cluster of bodies to another person. His father, Anutu, was composed with crossed hands and feet, curled up on his left side and resting in death at the rear of the shelter. After Anu had carved the animals on the cave wall that morning, he would return to bury his father's body in the soft earth of the hut where they lived.

Addressing himself to his responsibilities, Anu stepped out into the sunlight, scanned the cluster of huts that housed his tribe's people, crossed the small circle that separated them, and walked toward the broad grassy plane toward the sacred cave nearby.

The first part of Anu's trek was easy. The land was smooth and covered with wild grass, and except for the fist-sized rocks strewn across this well-worn path, the walking was relaxed.

As he neared the cave, Anu had to mount a narrow ledge that hugged the rocky cliff and circled around it to his destination. The sacred cave had been a part of his tribe's spiritual ceremonies for many years, chosen in part because it was not likely to attract idle wanderers, and in part because it was lit by the glow of the last sun of the day, much as the people who died were lit by the last light of their lives as their spirits passed into the other world.

He climbed over a large boulder just beside the entrance to the cave, a last impediment before he could slip inside. The interior of the cave was as dark as night, since it faced away from the rising sun on the other side of Fansu. Anu pulled a leather bag from his shoulder, crouched down, and spread the implements of his art on the floor of the cave.

The first thing he reached for was a clay pot filled with a tar-like grease and small, cold chunks of wood partially darkened from the previous evening's fire. He laid down a pile of brush and dried leaves that he had collected along his walk, then pulled two sticks of wood from his bag. He spread all these implements at his feet.

Crouching down and sitting cross-legged on the earth, Anu placed one stick of wood – the flat one with tiny holes on the side – on the earth. He moved the pile of grass and leaves close to his leg, then pulled the smudge pot alongside them. Spitting on the palms of his hands, Anu grasped the other stick and rotated it back and forth between his palms. As his spit coated the wood, it made the stick glide more easily across his skin. When he thought it was moving quickly enough, and with as little painful friction as possible on his dry hands, Anu applied the end of this stick to one of the holes in the wood on the ground.

Spitting once more into his hands, Anu began to rotate the vertical stick rapidly, creating friction and heat in the joint with the other stick. More spitting and brisk rotation of the stick, he continued with this action for nearly two minutes. Slowly, the lower end of the stick began to warm up and wisps of smoke rose from the wood on the ground next to Anu's leg.

A bit more spitting and rapid rotation of the stick produced even more heat and smoke. Pausing only briefly, Anu moved the grass and leaves closer to the stick and resumed spinning. The glow of the heat caught the tinder and a small flame erupted. Anu added more fuel, and then placed the smoldering pile of leaves into the smudge pot. The cool embers and tarry substance quickly caught the heat and the small flame grew larger.

From this, Anu was able to produce a long-lasting light source which he would use to survey the walls of the cave and conduct his ritual carving.

Once he was satisfied that his smudge lamp was self-sustaining, Anu stood up and stared at the carvings that already occupied the cave walls. He didn't recognize many. It was the custom among his tribe that the carvings would be rendered by the family of the lost person, alone, without the help of others. Anu had lost his mother whom he had memorialized on the cave wall as a woman with an abundant belly, proof of the brothers and sisters that Anu had enjoyed; some lost, some still among his kin. The other carvings were put there by his fellows back at the village, but such art is too primitive to attribute to a particular creator.

Except for one. The father of Lotya, Anu's friend, was famous in their tribe. He had fought and brought down a mammoth, twice the size of a human being. After the man's later death, Lotya celebrated him by carving the scene on the wall here, and the size of the animal – easily dwarfing the man whose spear was aimed at its heart – made it clear that this was his father.

Anu found a part of the wall that was relatively untouched and set the smudge pot down in front of it and just to his side. He wanted the dim light to be cast on the wall he planned to carve, and not have his own body shield the flame. Reaching into his bag, he retrieved two stones. One was elongated and had a tapered end. The other was a large, rounded stone that Anu grasped in one hand as if to smash its bulk against the other.

He examined the wall once again, this time to imagine the art that he would carve. Anu had spent the evening before deciding what image would represent his father. Anutu, the older man, was a hunter but so were most men in the tribe. Anu wasn't trying to decide what set Anutu apart from the rest; these were simple people, they were mostly alike and all contributed equally to the survival of the tribe. But he remembered Anutu also as a keeper of animals. His father tended the sheep that the tribe kept fenced in with a stick-and-vine corral.

Raising his left arm with the elongated stone to the wall, Anu brought the hammer stone in his right hand down with a smack. This produced a small hole in the wall as a chip fell at his feet. He repeated this motion several more time until a smooth line of pits appeared curving from left to right. Reaching for another tool, a stone sharpened at one end more than the last, Anu repeated the action along the line of holes already created. This secondary work deepened the small pits already made and strung them together in a closer line so that, when he stepped back, Anu could appreciate his work as a curved line that would form the start of his carving.

Anu worked a long time on this project, switching from the first stone implement to its sharper successor, carving curves and arches in the stone to depict a sheep. The art was mostly composed of straight and curves lines that, although apparently representing an animal, had no depth or detail. It was all monochromatic, with no suggestion of color, and so depth was impossible to achieve. But once he had completely this stick figure of the sheep, Anu proceeded to etch what was obviously a man alongside it - his father, Anutu.

At one point, Anu rested, his right arm tired from striking the large bulbous stone in his palm against the carving implements applied to the wall. He tended to the smudge pot by gently stirring the embers and grease adding more leaves to create a flame. After a moment's respite, Anu returned to the silent chore of adding his father's image to this sacred cave.

Finishing the carving gave him great satisfaction. He knew that Anutu would not arrive in the afterworld until this work was completed, but now Anu nodded his head in a confident feeling that he had completed the task. He gathered up his implements and put them back in the bag, slinging it over his shoulder. He lifted the smudge pot and treated it with care. A fire once started could never be deliberately put out; it was a simple rule of life in his tribe. Even though they now knew how to create fire on their own, it was still a gift from the gods and no one in his tribe would extinguish the flame once started.

———

Anu stepped out into the midday sun, blinked twice to adjust his eyes from the dark of the cave, and began the long trek back to his village.

Anu trudged the distance back to the village, through small stands of cypress trees that grew at the edge of the cliff encircling the small island of Fansu, past meadows of short grasses making their annual appearance in the wild. The tough hides that he used for his footwrapping absorbed the sharp stones that were encrusted in this cliff, and his strong legs easily navigated the small crevices and minor slopes that crossed his path.

He recognized a type of ruddy tree on his path, so he tapped its branches, which stirred a fresh scent that he inhaled with pleasure. The tree, with its twisted trunk and silver green leaves, was a distant ancestor of olive trees. Anu was already familiar with its primitive fruit and aroma and he had harvested the tiny berries in the past which he and Baia crushed to turn into an oily substance to tenderize and flavor the meat they grilled over an open fire.

The cool morning air had been replaced by moderate midday temperatures so he loosened the sinew strings that bound the leather hide around his shoulders, letting the animal skin fall loose around his arms. A hint of a breeze blew steadily across the plain as Anu crested the slight hill and saw the clump of huts in the distance. The slope of the earth was now downward and he began to smell the village fire and the scent of baking bread, so he quickened his pace.

Upon arriving at the village, Anu went straight toward his own hut. By this time of day, the people were out of their shelters and moving about. Lotya, a man of the same age as Anu, approached him and they exchanged greetings. It wasn't necessary to shake hands or embrace or engage in any other physical communication. Life in the tribe was very communal and most considered the people around them to be kin as, in fact, many of them were.

At the hut, Anu's son was at the doorway, looking up at the man as he approached. Baia kept close watch over the boy but knew that the others in the village would also keep an eye on him, just as she would for the other children of the tribe. She looked up when Anu entered and smiled. He had completed his task and, today, would set about the business of burying his father, Anutu.

"This day," Anu told her, "I take his name, Anutu," he said, indicating his deceased father at the back of their hut. "And he," pointing to their son, "takes mine."

Like most things in the simple life of these people, names were not used in abundance. It was common for one's name to change as life's circumstances were altered, as when a man took on the name of his father at the older man's passing. Anu, now Anutu, was honoring not only that tradition but also his father. And, at last, his son would have a name.

The baby girl didn't need a name yet, so none was chosen. It would be in due time and, if her mother perished for some reason before that event, the little girl might just as well use Baia's name, rather than waste it. Creating things that didn't need to be created, like new names for every birth, seemed unwise and unnecessary.

And like names, their language itself had its own inherent conservation, just as with other resources for this people. The villagers spoke in the present tense, rarely using the past and never the future, because time, for them, was the moment they were living in. It wasn't hard to conceive of something that had come and gone, and the people understood that an animal or person had lived before but didn't now, but they were unable to imagine the future and so they didn't think in terms of it.

Therefore, Anu didn't say that his son "will take" his name. So Anu took on the name that his deceased father no longer needed, just as his son would take on his name. The laws of linguistic conservation acted like boundaries on their speech, so the phrase instead was "he takes mine." These same boundaries affected their nonverbal communication and the primitive art forms that they practiced. Cave drawings had little imagination, because imagination required conceptual thinking about something they hadn't witnessed, just as thinking about the future required imagining about what they hadn't observed.

The words and vocabulary common to these people grew out of the necessity of survival, so verbal exchanges between men – the hunters – involved more hand gestures than vocalized sounds, so as not to attract the attention of the animal they sought to bring down. The gathering activities of the women allowed more vocalization, but not remarkably so, as the villagers were still developing their own list of words that would be necessary to achieve their purpose of communicating. The focus was more on nouns, since a person might want to refer to a thing that they knew but which was not present, while they would use their hands and arms to suggest the action of a verb. Swinging one's arms in a steady motion, spinning an index finger in circles, or pushing upward with exposed palms all had their own meaning, and indicated actions better than words could have.

Each tribe might have created its own word for essential resources like water, because it was the foremost noun that the people would label. In fact, it was precisely the words for nouns – things that they could hold and show to other tribes – that served as the codex for translation of tribal languages whenever they encountered new people on the plains. Beginning with things like water, fire, tree, pig, and so on sowed the seeds of understanding between people who encountered new tribes for the first time.

And words for concepts like "where" or "when" were hardly ever spoken; rather they were indicated with the body and facial expressions like raised eyebrows, shrugged shoulders, or a glance cast left and right.

————

Death was never welcome, but it was a common part of life in the primitive world. Anutu's father had seemed to just pass on out of life. There was no indication before his last day that anything very important was wrong. He moaned about a belly that ached more than normal the evening before, while eating his food and after completing the repast. But he lay down on his mat without mentioning anything else, so his son and Baia were surprised the next morning when he didn't wake.

At first, while Anu – now Anutu – stood over his father wondering what had happened, Baia let out a single whimper. She was very attached to the man who had brought his son into her life, and she didn't expect him to leave so soon. Baia became sad that morning while she helped her man arrange the older man's body, crossing his legs and folding his arms in a fetal position, the common position used in preparation for burial. They knew that his limbs would become wooden and not easy to fold, and that a body left to harden without folding would be hard to bury. So, it was common for the villagers to arrange it this way.

While little Anu looked on, Anutu picked up a tool fashioned from a short wooden handle with a wedge-shaped stone tied to one end with twine made of braided reeds. First, he stabbed at the earth with a sturdy stick to loosen the soil, then picked up his tool to scrape and carve out a small indentation in the floor of the hut, near one end away from their sleeping mat. He dug with care, trying not to tear the bark or let it break in half. He removed layer upon layer of soil, piling it by the side of the excavated hole, while the grave went deeper.

At first, little Anu tried to imitate his father's actions, using a small piece of wood to scratch at the dirt. But soon, he lost interest in the activity and moved outside to find his mother.

Anutu continued digging, leaning farther into the hole as it approached the depth necessary to hold his father's body. When the grave was dug sufficiently, Anutu stood up, stretched his back, and laid the bark down at his side. He would need help moving the body and wanted a break from the work before completing the final task.

———

All together the tribe consisted of about fifty people. Childhood wasn't recognized except for the very young like Anutu's son, barely walking about on his feet. It was assumed that as soon as a young person could use their hands for useful endeavor, they would be taught to help out in the activities of the village.

There were eleven huts to shelter the tribe. The family was the nuclear unit, but some huts provided for more than a man, woman, and their children. Anutu's father and mother had remained with their sole surviving son and Baia until their own deaths. Separate huts would usually be built only when the dimensions of the domicile could no longer accommodate those within.

The eleven structures were loosely arranged in a tight compound, with each clump of four to five huts existing in a separate cluster with a fire pit in the center of the area between them. The men and women of each cluster would prepare their own fires, large enough for the people sheltered there, but not so big that the flames wasted the fuel that was carefully collected and stored.

When the early morning cooking chores were completed, the embers were packed closer together and more large stones added to the perimeter, to contain the heat and keep the fire burning with less wood. It was in this way that the village fires would burn throughout the day, tended carefully to avoid having to restart each one, but conserving the fuel needed to cook the meat later in the day and keep the people warm on cool evenings.

Lotya followed Anutu back to his hut. Stooping down to pass through the portal of the hut, they entered the shaded confines of the shelter. The roof was raised to a peak in the center, but it was still not very high. The two men were able to stand, but with little space between their heads and the thatched roof of the hut.

Anutu waved his hand to tell Lotya to follow him, and the two men moved to the back of the structure where the lifeless man lay curled up next to the gaping hole that Anutu had dug. They moved silently into position, Anutu taking the upper body and head – the correct role for the son of the man to be buried – as Lotya reached for the lower body, with legs folded together. Without words, they lifted the old man's remains into the pit and carefully arranged him, laying on his left side, arms and legs still folded and the body fitting comfortably into the grave Anutu had dug for this purpose.

Anutu reached for two stone implements, a broad, rounded hammer stone and a large, sharp-edged flake, and put them into the hole beside the body. He added a thin cloak of leather, some sprigs of olive branch, and a small clay cup. Then, standing to see his father one last time, Anutu decided that the burial was complete as prescribed by village culture, and nodded his head.

Lotya and Anutu pushed dirt from what was piled up beside the hole and covered the body beneath the soft earth. As the grave filled and the dirt pile disappeared, Anutu slowed his work, as if he was now at last thinking about his father and the life that the man had given him. He paused briefly, causing Lotya to stop pushing dirt. Kneeling next the grave, Anutu rested his hands on his thighs, breathed a sigh, then resumed the burial process.

Lotya, too, spent a moment in reflection, to honor his friend's father and one of the elders of the clan, then resumed work as Anutu did.

———

Tano carried in his right hand a sharpened stone tool, rounded at one end that fit into his palm, and sharpened to a fine edge on the other. He had shaped this tool earlier that day, following the instructions of the older men of the village, so that he could use it to bring down the green, pliable saplings that were now stacked up in the clearing.

It was a tool that had been used by the villagers on Fansu for as long as anyone could remember, and a technique that continued to improve over the lifetimes of the men there. They taught him two ways to make the tool, using the sharp-edged black rock called *sida*, or a bulkier, gray stone that could be rounded at one end and sharpened by flaking at the other. *Sida* – or obsidian - was found in small quantities, dug from riverbeds that had once been scorched by lava flows or washed ashore by waters that brought it from another volcanic island. Tano knew the material could be very sharp, but it was harder to round off the other end for holding. The edge of the obsidian that would cut through the wood could also cut through his hand.

He chose the other stone, carefully searching the gravel beds for a rock called chert. Tano found several that were just the size of his fist, so he collected them and returned to the campfire to shape them. Sitting down on a fallen log, he spread a leather hide on his left upper leg and pulled another, smaller leather patch onto his left palm. He cradled the first of his stones in his left hand and examined it, drawing his right index finger along the white lines on its surface, outlining the place to strike.

He held a bigger, heavier stone in his right hand – a hammerstone – which he brought down with force on the white line he had just targeted. Nothing happened at first, so he paused, raised the hammerstone again, and brought it down as closely as he could to the line on the chert. This time, a thin grayish-white chip flew from the targeted stone, leaving a smooth, inner surface. Tano rotated the target a bit, visualized the spot to aim for, and struck again, once more cleaving a fracture from the chert.

He proceeded in this manner, switching the chert from side to side, until he had removed several chips and produced a cutting stone that had been fractured in a precise pattern, a pattern that created a long, sharp edge on the side opposite of the smooth, rounded end that he now palmed.

Tano took this new tool with him into the forest and set upon a clutch of saplings that were growing tall in the spring air. Some were twice his height; some just came to his shoulder. He knelt down and, raising the sharpened tool to his side, he hacked at the base of saplings, cutting each one down and piling them up as cordwood.

Collecting enough of the sticks and saplings to build a hut took Tano an entire day. By the time the light was fading, he only had time to carry a few piles back to the village. He would return the following morning for more of the chopped wood. With a child on the way, he had to provide a shelter for his new family.

Back at the fire pit, Nanda and Baia had prepared the evening meal along with the three other women and children who lived in that cluster. Nanda was able to share three loaves of acorn bread that she baked that afternoon. Baia heated a clay pot in the middle of the fire, occasionally throwing handfuls of water into it to create steam, and then tossed in handfuls of shellfish collected from their nets that morning.

The other women, led by Neeri, leaned over a shallow pit next to this surface fire. Into the pit they carefully rolled red-hot stones that had been heated in the center of the fire and lined the pit with these stones to create a sunken oven.

A boy sitting with the women hefted the shoulder of the slaughtered pig which Neeri propped on a still-cold stone next to the pit. She rolled the shoulder over and, using a razor-sharp blade of obsidian, scraped the hair from the hide, then cut several slender slits into the leathery hide. Inspecting the hunk of meat and pounding it with a round stone to gauge its tenderness, Neeri rubbed the meat with the same oily mash that Baia used on her vegetable wrap. Then she tucked sprigs of sweet rosemary and the white bulbs of small spring onions into the slits. After once more checking her work, Neeri carefully slid the meat into the pit, resting it on the large heated stone in the bottom of oven.

The boy reached out to Neeri and handed her green saplings about the length of his arm, which Neeri used to cover the opening of the pit. The boy then handed her large leaves that had been rubbed with the olive oil, which were placed on top of the saplings. Over that, Neeri placed the bark of a tree so that the pit was completely covered, except for the few vents that emitted the smoke from the meat cooking within.

Anutu, Lotya, and Tano found comfortable spots around the fire. Tano was joined by Folu, the woman carrying his baby. Baia withdrew a few bundles of the root vegetables that she had prepared and handed them around to those at the fire. Next, she shared handfuls of the shellfish that had burst open in the heat of the fire to reveal the pink-orange flesh within. Two children approached the circle with baskets of berries that had been collected and passed the fruit around. Nanda removed the loaves of bread and tore off a hunk before handing it to the next person to her right.

They ate while sitting around the fire, occasionally speaking to express themselves, but their contentment was evident from the food, and consumption of it was more important than conversation. The aromas of roasting meat filled the air and they anticipated that next course. When the bread, fruit, shellfish, and vegetables had been consumed, but while still waiting for the pig shoulder to feed them, Anutu looked up to the sky. The sun had disappeared behind the hill in the distance and the faint glow that trailed it was being chased by the darkness that closed around the tribe.

A few stars blinked on in the deep blue bowl of the sky. Anutu pointed to the brightest cluster, a brilliant burst of light that stood out easily even with the mild glow from the fire pit. Lotya, then Baia, followed his finger and looked up.

Before Anutu could add words to his gesture, they felt a low rumble under their feet. It persisted for several minutes, and a red glow appeared on the horizon opposite the setting sun. The people sat quietly until it passed, then exchanged worried glances. Little Anu huddled close to Baia and her baby whimpered. Adults around the fire sat motionless, and some tended to the younger ones whose eyes were wide with fear.

Looking once again at the sky, but this time with a change in his attitude, Anutu spoke.

"Gods awake."

The people knew he was talking about the glittering stars that appeared whenever the sky went dark, but they also wondered whether the shaking of the ground was another god that they feared.

They were quiet for a long time, and nothing was heard except the hissing of the steam and burning fat in the hunk of meat in their oven.

Finally, Neeri pushed aside the bark and leaves, then poked the fire, realizing that the meal would be wasted if they sat in stunned silence any longer. She tested the toughness of the meat to indicate its doneness and, satisfied with what she found, picked up another stick to remove the meat from the hot stones.

She used the same piece of obsidian to slice the pig's shoulder into manageable portions and passed them around to the others gathered there. They ate in silence, pausing occasionally when the earth quivered again. Baia's baby wailed and a small girl crept into the arms of her mother for protection.

Anutu looked over at Lotya, who returned his glance but didn't speak.

"We go," Anutu said.

The brief comment was understood by Lotya but didn't carry the full meaning of conversations that the men had already had. In the flickering light, Anutu saw that Baia had bowed her head, and she nodded her agreement with his solemn suggestion.

"We go," Lotya replied.

The two men had talked for some time about whether the gods were angry at this place, or at them. Their understanding of the relationship between people and gods was primitive, and they hadn't conceived of concepts like guilt or sin, since their lives were led too simply to have rules that could be broken. They didn't fear the gods' punishment since there was not guilt. But they still worried that the gods seemed to be fighting each other, and the humans didn't want to be caught in the middle of such a battle.

Anutu had expressed these things to Baia and told her that this might be the place where the gods would fight. He didn't want to be there when they did. He and Lotya had talked about leaving, going to the big island toward the rising sun, a land they called Ganta. Maybe they would be safe there, and not interfere in the battles between the gods.

Like Anutu, Baia was concerned about the shaking of the ground, and the red fire that shot up from the earth, and she agreed that they should go to Ganta.

"Others, too?" she had asked.

Anutu only shrugged his shoulders at her question.

Folu sat working on a new cloak for Tano. He had brought her a deer hide, one that he managed to scrape from the downed animal two days earlier. The deer meat had already been consumed, but it was time to scrape and prepare the leather before it became stiff and brittle.

Folu left the outside coat of fur on the pelt but turned it over on her lap to inspect the underside. It was mostly finished – the villagers didn't like to leave edible muscle fibers stuck to the hide – but she had to pull some fibers and scrape the surface gently to make it as smooth as possible. It was important for her to make this covering comfortable to wear against Tano's bare skin, so any imperfection in the hide should be removed.

When the task of cleaning the underside was done, Folu reached for a slender, finger-sized bone fragment taken from the same animal. This bit of antler came from the very tip, the narrowest diameter, and had been rubbed, scraped, and polished until it could serve as a type of needle. In one end of the antler bone, Folu had created a hole using a very hard stone sharpened at the end, digging in a circular motion until a depression was created on both sides. Persisting in this circular motion, then turning the bone over to repeat on the other side, she slowly bored a hole that sinew could be passed through.

She put the pelt back on her lap and, using the pointed stone tool, pressed and pushed on one end of the hide until a hole was made. She repeated the action at a point of the hide opposite the first hole until she was satisfied with the result. Then, retrieving her antler-bone needle, she passed a long strand of animal sinew – taken from the same animal that yielded the hide and antler – through each hole. With these in hand, Folu rose to her feet, turned toward the tree branch behind her, and strung the pelt up on the branch by these threads. There, the deer that had brought the villagers meat, leather, sinew, and needles, would hang until the prepared hide was dried out and ready for use.

Meals took hours to prepare. Flour would be ground for bread which then needed to be baked, root vegetables and other tough edibles needed long hours at the edge of the fire pit to cook through, and meat – whether it was going to be grilled over the fire or roasted in a pit – took considerable time to clean and prepare. And meat was not always available. The hunters were out most days, so the catch may be consumed before two sunsets, but any surplus was cut into slivers and hung to dry, so the moisture in the meat would not be a breeding ground for maggots or bugs.

Fish was a staple of their diet, since the island of Fansu was small and had a long shoreline. And this night, some small octopus and squid were part of the meal. Each was sliced into mouth-sized pieces and tossed into a heated clay pot greased with animal fat. The pieces sizzled and popped in the heat, and delicious aromas rose into the air, making stomachs growl and faces smile.

When the food was consumed, they people relaxed around the fire. There were no earth tremors to frighten them on this night, but the memory was still fresh. There was more talk this evening about the gods spitting red fire into the air.

"What do they want?" asked Nanda.

"Huh," grunted Tano. It sounded like a muttering of disgust, and Lotya quickly corrected him.

"The gods are here," waving his arms to indicate all of nature that surrounded them, "It is not for us to ask what."

"What do we do?" asked Nanda.

Baia shrugged her shoulders and tried to formulate an answer. Anutu looked at her and waited for what his woman would say.

"They argue and fight," Baia said, and then laughed, "sometimes like you and me," she said, looking at Anutu.

He only smiled.

"They fight," he then added, "they fight here," pointing to the ground, but spreading his pointed finger to indicate the entire island.

"We go," Lotya concluded.

Those around the fire agreed, some nodding their heads or sitting in silent acknowledgement. Their little island, Fansu, seemed to be a battleground for the gods. It sat very near another island, Ganta, so big that it hid the rising sun each morning. To these people, the gods were not supernatural beings that watched from afar; they were natural and they inhabited the concrete world around them.

But these powerful beings, so great they could whirl through the air or creep along under the ground without being seen, were known to the people only by their actions. To the tribe of Anutu and Baia and the others, angry gods acted in heat, wind, and tremors.

––––––

In the early morning air, Tano stepped out of the portal of his new hut, turning once to peer back at Folu. She was awake, rubbing her belly to dispel the pains she felt, but otherwise showing no signs of distress.

He planned to go to the place where the stream met the big sea and cast his net into the water for fish. He reached down to the folded net that was kept just beside the hut and hoisted it over his left shoulder. It was soft to the touch, the braided fibers from the tree bark having been moistened and made pliable by daily immersion in water. Shifting the net to balance its weight, Tano walked between the shelters in his cluster and down toward the water's edge.

The village was built far enough from the sea to avoid the water that rose and fell twice edge day, but close enough that fishing on the edge was still within sight of the people tending morning fires. When Tano arrived at his chosen spot on the shore, he greeted an older man who was already there. Farutu was seated on a large rock that straddled the lapping waves and he held onto two ropes, one in each hand. He kept his arms spread so that these tielines would keep the mouth of his own net open for the schools of fish that played about in the water.

Farutu sat in Tano's favorite spot, but the villagers didn't feel like they possessed the land and so fishing spots were claimed by those who arrived first. Tano nodded to Farutu, who returned the greeting with "Seeio," this village's way of saying hello.

Tano moved to a place where there was an elevated dropoff into the water and set down the wooden bucket he had used to bring water to construct his hut. He then pulled the net down from his shoulder and spread it wide on the ground to his right. Standing with his left shoulder pointed to the water, tielines in his hands, he reached up with this left hand first and, in synchrony, tossed the net into the shallow water below his feet.

Waving his hands a bit caused the net to wave in the water, an action that would attract the attention of the small fish by the shore. After about twenty seconds, Tano drew his hands in toward his body and grasped the tielines together, swiftly yanking the net out of the water. A few fish flopped on the ground next to him, tangled in the net and gasping for the air their gills sought from the water.

Tano picked through the net to grab hold of the fish, tossing them one by one into the bucket. Their silvery scales were slick and he had to have a sure hold on the thing, or else it would slither back into the water. Having thus freed all those in his catch, he picked up the net and prepared to repeat the process.

He continued in this way, listening as the sound of the little fish flapping in the bucket died down with each layer of catch he threw in. Within an hour, Tano had collected more fish than they could consume that day, but it wouldn't be wasted. Folu knew how to dry some and others could be traded with the villagers in exchange for tools or other foodstuffs.

When Tano picked up his net and bucket, he saw that Farutu was still sitting on the large rock by the shore. The old man had caught some fish but didn't seem too concerned about sitting longer and collecting less. Tano raised his bucket in Farutu's direction.

"Some?" Tano asked, suggesting that he could share with his fellow fisherman.

Farutu smiled and nodded his head. He was a master at crafting arrows by stripping the green skins of the bamboo shoots that crowded the forest near the village. He also knew which trees yielded the best wood for the bows that would launch his arrows. So Farutu could barter for fish; catching them was more of a pastime.

Tano turned and walked back into the village. When he presented the bucket of catch to Folu, he could see that she was even more uneasy. She rubbed her belly more, and occasionally reached her fingers down between her legs with a look of concern on her face. Rather than ask her to deal with the fish, Tano went in search of women who could help her, since no man could understand what to make of a woman who delivered a baby.

In a moment, he returned with both Baia and Nanda, and the women immediately knelt beside the pregnant woman.

"Hurt," Folu said, grimacing and touching the area between her legs.

Baia reached her hand into the same spot and, retrieving it, saw that her fingers were wet. She showed them to Nanda, and both women knew the time had come. They spread some straw on the ground next to Folu, bunching it up to form a cushion against the rocky ground. Baia then stretched a large leather pelt over the straw, and she and Nanda helped Folu slide across from her mat to the pelt.

"Stand, yes?" asked Nanda.

Folu looked surprised by the suggestion. She had never given birth before and wasn't prepared for this part.

"Yes, stand," Baia repeated. They helped the woman to her feet, groaning, who now wondered why they had made a bed so soft if she had to stand.

"Now, down," said Nanda, pressing her right hand gently on Folu's shoulder, guiding the younger one into a crouching position. Baia was behind Folu, helping her rest her body against her and remain slightly elevated above the ground, while Nanda moved around to the front the deliver the baby.

Tano remained on the periphery of this event, fear etched in his expression. He had never been this close to childbirth before, but he was well aware of the dangers and knew that many of the village women had not survived the experience.

At first, Folu cried a bit and grunted, but then she fell very silent. Tano saw that she was still conscious and still working to push the baby out, but a calm came over her just as the baby was approaching delivery. A sudden action by Nanda caught his attention and he peeked over the midwife's shoulder to see a wet, pink baby cradled in her cupped hands. A cough, and a sputter, and the baby's toothless mouth opened wide in a tiny cry.

Baia couldn't see from her spot but read the events correctly. As soon as the baby was out, she lowered her support so that Folu could sit down on the hide, then lay back in repose. Nanda placed the still wet baby on

Folu's chest, then examined the white and blue-veined cord that connected the newborn to the mother's innards.

"You push now," she told Folu. The young mother had been told about the life that trailed the baby, and knew there would be one more, easier delivery to take care of. But she seemed startled when she saw that there was a thing that connected the baby to it. A brief fear furrowed her brow, but then Baia spoke.

"It is the life that brought baby. But not a real life."

Encouraged to push by Nanda, Folu worked the afterbirth out of the delivery canal, and the sack sagged on the ground between her legs. Nanda had come prepared and she reached into the folds of her wrap to produce two twisted threads. Attaching one to the cord close the baby's belly and the other a hand's width down the cord, she reached her open hand back to Tano.

The man's eyes went wide, confused at why Nanda was gesturing to him. Baia was facing his direction and took in the scene with a light chuckle.

"Cut," she said, cupping her hand upward and flipping it toward her, telling him to bring a knife. "Cut," she repeated.

Nanda's hand was still held open in his direction, so Tano turned quickly, grasped the sharp cutting stone he had used on the saplings two days earlier, and gave it to Nanda.

The midwife quickly sliced through the cord between the two knots and lifted the afterbirth to remove it from the hut. In the meantime, Baia was sprinkling water on the baby and gentling removing the birth fluids from the skin. Then she stood and followed Nanda out of the shelter.

———

Tano sat next to the fire with the women of the village. They were preparing the meals for the day; he was using his scraper to sharpen the tips of arrows that he got from Farutu and one lone spear he himself had crafted from a birch branch.

The fire was low at this point in the day, packed tight with heated rocks and kept small, just enough to bake the day's bread and soften the fibers of the vegetables that would be too tough to chew. Nanda arrived with an armload of harvest from the village's common plot. She brought a dark green, leafy plant, a twisted and dusty bundle of small tubers the size of a child's fist, pale-leafy lettuce that seemed to be a bit sunburned, and long stalks of field grass with bulbs on the end of each branch that sported tiny white-yellow kernels and wisps of feathery hair. She lowered the bundle onto the ground next to the fire and prepared to distribute the largesse among the women seated there.

Tano knew little about food; preparation was not left solely to the women in the village but the men contributed in only certain ways. They built the fires, brought in felled game, and helped prepare some of the harvested food. But the women knew how to use their heightened olfactory sense and their experience at the fire pit to deliver the food that would nourish the tribe.

Nanda and Baia made daily trips to the water's edge, stepping lithely through the soft mud and reeds to pick up the small sea creatures that populated the sea grass. There were small shells that they would throw into the fire to cook and pry open. There were larger, black-shelled elongated bivalves with a creature of soft orange flesh inside, and a broad, white-shelled animal with pink and white flesh.

When they had enough for the day's meals, they would walk, slowly, back to the village, their eyes on the green sprouts that hugged the trunks of trees and grew in lonely clumps along the path. The aromatic leaves of these plants – early forms of thyme, sage, and rosemary – would be used to flavor the meat and root vegetables to be eaten that day. Some of these were so fragrant that Nanda tied bunches together and hung them from the roof of her hut.

The leaves and scented herbs could be picked in bunches, but they did not harvest more of the sea creatures than they needed in the day. Fish, once caught, could be dried, but there was no way to keep the dead shelled animals, and the people could return anytime and there would be more to get.

These treasures they brought to the campfire where Tano was sitting, working the end of the shaft of an arrow that he had bartered from Farutu. While the women prepared the foodstuffs for cooking, Tano rubbed his sharpened stone over and over across the tip of the arrow, sometimes shaving splinters away, and sometimes simply using the stone to smooth and compress the fibrous wood grains of the bamboo-like shaft. Every so often, he inspected the results, holding the tip up close to his face, then putting this end of the arrow into the embers of the fire to harden the point.

Tano finished sharpening and hardening the tip of the arrows he got from Farutu that day and returned to his shelter to check on Folu. She was lying on her mat, with the newborn suckling her. Folu looked up at Tano and smiled, more relaxed now than in the morning. She lightly tossed her head to the side to draw Tano's attention to something. Hanging from the long, wooden ribs of the ceiling was a string of fish. In the excitement of the morning, he had forgotten his catch but one of the women had come along and cleaned and strung the fish up to dry.

"Neeri," was all Folu said, and Tano smiled in appreciation.

While he was in the hut, the earth shook and Folu cried out in fear. Tano quickly ran outside and stood stock still at the sound of a roaring wind rumbling through the village. Other people were out of their shelters, and Folu called out to Tano.

"Here, here!" she said urgently, and waved for him to come back inside.

He put his hand up to reassure her but stayed in the middle of the cluster as more people arrived. There was fevered talk among some, as children clutched at their mothers' sides, as the elders gathered together.

The ground tremors continued, accompanied by an eerie wind, and suddenly a brilliant red glow rose in the southern sky. The source was too distant to spot, but the fiery light continued to grow until it lit up much of the sky in that direction.

"Manta," one man said, pointing toward the unseen island in watery sea beyond their own island.

The eruption continued to shake the ground for a long time that day, even until the sun fell into the water and the southern sky was ablaze with orange and bright yellow fulminations. Initial fears subsided with the earth tremors, but concern was still present on the faces gathered around the fire pit.

"Gods awake," said Anutu, and Lotya nodded.

By this time, Folu had come out of the shelter with her baby and huddled close to Tano. Neeri, Baia, and Nanda were there too, with their children and another few adults. They ate their meal in silence, but after finishing, conversation resumed.

"We go," was Anutu's advice.

"Gods fight here," said Lotya pointing to the ground at his feet. "They fight on Fansu. We go to big island, where sun rises," he added, pointing to the east, to the land they called Ganta.

"Safer there?" asked Neeri. "Why safer there?"

Anutu shrugged.

"Not safe here," he replied, shaking his head and looking down at his feet.

Farutu had joined the group to offer his elderly advice.

"Ganta never shake," he said. He had no way to know this, but the people trusted those who had lived so long.

"We go," repeated Anutu.

Tano was silent. He feared for himself, Folu, and the baby. He didn't want them to perish in the great fight between the gods. But he had raised the subject with Folu and she was terrified of the sea. "I won't go," she had said then, clutching her baby to her breast. Tano tried to persuade her, reminding her that the elders knew better, better than Anutu. Even Farutu said they should go.

But Folu shuddered at the talk, and looked at Tano, shaking her head. Around the fire that night, she repeated her position.

"No, we not go," she said, rocking her baby and looking at her man with fear and uncertainty.

Tano sighed, and others watched as this young couple debated their future.

Not much more was said that night, and people in the other clusters in the village had begun to talk of it. Anutu and Lotya were leading the talk, but only professed their opinion and didn't try to convince the others.

———

In the village, survival depended on cooperative work. There weren't very many people – even procreation had its unique traditions since most of the villagers had some blood relation with the others – any actions that split the group were dangerous. Past experience dictated that they stay together, an internal defense system that protected them from the unfamiliar ways of other tribes, ensured cooperative food gathering and preparation, and perhaps most of all proved to all members that they were part of a community that would respect and protect them.

But a consensus was developing among this cluster and some members of other clusters. Anutu, Baia, Lotya, and Nanda had decided that abandoning Fansu and moving to Ganta was better, and Neeri who had lost her man intended to follow. They all knew, though, that in the end the tribe had to move as one for safety. There would be more talk, and more disagreement among the villagers, and out of the debate each side hoped their view would win the day.

———

Anutu and Lotya stood talking to people from another cluster in the village. Among the fifty people in the tribe, about half wanted to move to Ganta and the others wanted to remain.

Tribal life was lived near the edge of existence. The risks that were inherent in hunting wild animals was still a present concern, though it was reduced somewhat by the growth of agriculture, so fewer men were lost in violent endings. Childbirth was still the greatest threat to the women, but the social support structure – not to mention the generations of midwifery – was slowing easing the deadly consequences there.

Still, a critical mass was required to maintain the variety of primitive technologies that sustained the society, not to mention at least a limited heterogeneity in the gene pool. This matter of biology was beyond the understanding of the people on Fansu, but the improved prospects of survival of large groups over small groups was a lesson not lost on the ancients.

Lotya cast a glance at the campfire in his cluster, smiling at Nanda and their children, then returned his attention to the small clique gathered around him.

"Fansu trembles," he said. "The gods are fighting. The fight is now bigger."

Anutu stood silently by, staring at the ground and slowly nodding his head.

Farutu, the oldest among them, listened carefully, studying the faces of those in a circle that included both men and women. The only children to hear the conversation would be the littlest toddlers, those standing in the shadow of their mothers.

"Folu," began Tano haltingly. "She won't go. She says the baby is too small, this is our land, and she is not strong enough." He paused, then added, "I think she fears the sea more than she fears the gods."

"The gods are not fighting us," Farutu offered. "We do not have to fear them."

"But we are too small for them. We are like the leaves on the trees," Anutu said. "When they fight, the trees shake and the leaves fall. When they fight, we fall."

Neeri said she would go. She had no man; he was killed in a hunt long ago and she had no child.

"I will go with you," she said.

Baia walked over, holding Anu by the hand and cradling the baby in her cloak. She entered the circle of people and stood beside Anutu.

"We will go," she said, and looked around the circle to see the faces of those around them.

The same discussion was being held around the many clusters' campfires each evening. More so, now, as the gods made the earth tremble more often and the sky turn a bright orange-red. Anutu and Baia knew the people who would go and counted that it was about half of the tribe. They knew that moving half away and leaving half behind would put each group in danger. There were other tribes on the island who kept mostly to themselves but taking their people across Fansu to the side where the sun appeared in the morning they would meet these other tribes.

There is a danger in that, too, thought Anutu. The other tribes didn't fight with them, but that was because there were equal numbers. If only half of the people made this journey, would another tribe attack them? Would they take their weapons and food? Would they take their women and their children?

In the end, the villagers who decided to go feared the violence of the gods more than they feared the other people they would meet. And more than they feared the sea they would have to cross to get to Ganta.

It was a huge land, much bigger than Fansu, so large and so close it was easy to see from their land. The water that separated them was not angry; the waves were small and the sea didn't seem very deep. Ancient stories told them there was land under the water, that a person could walk to Ganta without sinking. These stories emboldened those who wanted to move, but they were old stories and maybe couldn't be trusted.

The next day, after fishing for the day's meals, Anutu and Lotya returned to the village. Baia and Nanda had collected the vegetables they needed for cooking and were at the campfire already. Neeri was grinding some acorns to prepare the bread for baking, and Folu had brought down some of the dried fish that had been hung in her shelter.

They gathered at the center of their cluster and conversation returned to the move. The groups were each becoming more certain of their decision; only a few people were still wavering. But each time the people gathered for food, the subject arose again. Moving to another land, something their ancestors did often before, was a tremendous moment and couldn't be pursued without understanding the dangers that awaited them.

Lotya and Anutu sat on the edge of the circle, with Lotya showing Anutu how to bend saplings into a curved shape. With his hand, he indicated a bucket-shaped shell, then a covering over sides and bottom.

"The sticks can be wet, then bent, and held in place like this," he said, twisting one branch and tying its ends together to hold the bent shape. "After it dries, it stays," he added, picking up a curved branch that had been molded in this way. He held the bow-shaped branch, and showed duplicates of it arranged in a row, using his hands to show one after the other, demonstrating for Anutu how a long shell could be made of these bent sticks.

Lotya then picked up a fragment of the leather mat at his side. He wrapped it around the bow, showing how a surface could cover the series of bent branches, again in an open-topped bucket shape. Anutu nodded his head but looked worried.

"How can it stay out of water?"

Lotya was ready for the question. He twisted around, looking for something. When he spotted the leather bucket that Nanda used to carry water from the stream, he directed Anutu's attention to it.

"Bucket keeps water in," he said, and Anutu agreed.

"Bucket can keep water out, too." At that he rose quickly and waved for Anutu to follow him. He picked up Nanda's bucket and the two men went down to the stream. Standing on the rocky platform that Tano had used to cast his net, Lotya took hold of the braided rope that was tied to the bucket and lowered it into the stream. Instead of plunging it in to gather water, he lowered the bucket slowly so that it bobbed on the surface.

A grin spread across Lotya's face, but Anutu wasn't convinced. He picked up a rock, held it in front of Lotya and said, "People," and dropped the rock into the bucket. Both the rock and bucket sank into the sandy bottom of the stream.

———

Later that day, as the people gathered around the fire to eat the evening meal, Anutu and Lotya once again sat on the fringes. This time it was Anutu who had prepared something. He took some branches that had been soaked in the stream, just as Lotya had soaked his to build a floating bucket, but Anutu wove them into a flat, square shape, many sticks going one way and many going the other way, looping them over and under each other and then pulling the arrangement into a tight, flat bundle.

"This way," he said confidently, "like twigs and sticks floating down the stream. But this will float toward Ganta."

Lotya stood and hooked his hand toward Anutu, directing both men to return to the stream. Anutu knew what his friend intended, and he wondered too whether his idea would work.

At the water's edge, Anutu tied a short length of braided rope onto his woven platform of branches and lowered it into the water. Altogether, the raft was no more than the length of an arm on each side, certainly too small for a man to stand on, but Lotya couldn't resist taunting his friend. With a leg stretched out in the direction of the water, he acted as though he was going to step onto the raft, and Anutu howled.

"No!" he said quickly, then realized his friend's tease. Lotya withdrew his foot but crouched down and picked up a rock. It was larger than the one Anutu had used to defeat Lotya's design, but still he leaned forward over the water and lowered the rock onto the raft. Both stayed afloat, although the added weight allowed some water to lap over the edges of the little wooden platform.

Lotya stood and smiled at Anutu, who decided to celebrate the event by letting go of the rope. The men stood on the shore and watched as the raft floated down the stream.

The two men walked back to the village, eagerly talking about Anutu's invention. The smoke from the firepits and the smell of roasting meat reached them and they quickened their pace. Still, Lotya couldn't resist proposing his plan.

"We go that way," he said, pointing away from the sun that now was settling into the sea. "And we build your rafts."

"We have trees and branches here," Anutu noted. "We can build now."

"But then we have to carry the rafts across our land, to the place where the waves come from Ganta."

Anutu considered his friend's comment seriously while they walked in silence for a few minutes. Just as they arrived at the circle of their cluster's campfire, he said "If there are no trees there. Do you know?"

Neither man had been that far from their village, so Lotya couldn't answer the question. But Anutu was right. What if they walked across their land and found there were no trees.

"We cut trees here," Lotya said, pointing to the earth to emphasize his point, "but not make rafts. We carry branches with us and make rafts at water's edge."

It sounded good to Anutu, but still involved a lot of carrying. And they would have to bring their food and clothing too.

"Sheep help," added Lotya. This hadn't occurred to Anutu; in fact, it was only a sudden realization from Lotya. Anutu's father had kept his sheep for wool and meat, but he also showed the people how strong they were.

"We need sheep for food," Anutu picked up the theme. He knew that they couldn't bring sheep onto the rafts, but they could be slaughtered before they launched their rafts, to provide food for the travelers.

"We could tie the sticks and branches to them while we herd them to the water," he suggested.

Lotya agreed, smiling and nodding his head.

With this, each man slumped down into a sitting position at the firepit with their families, knowing they would continue their planning at a later time.

The meal was as delicious as the aromas that drew Anutu and Lotya to the hearth. The roasted mutton was drawn from the pit oven, and the fleshy vegetables were enriched by the savory notes of animal fat and fresh cut herbs. Fresh water washed down the meal, and spiny blackberries were passed around to flavor the meat.

As the sun disappeared at the horizon and the sky slowly darkened, the people gathered closer to the firepit and enjoyed the warmth it gave off. Women suckled their babies and engaged the other women in talk of vegetable gardens and the weight of the chickens and sheep penned together near the cluster of their shelters. The men were mostly quiet, staring at the flames and listening to their women talk. Except for Anutu and Lotya, who were busy planning the voyage to Ganta.

Using his hands to indicate the size of the raft he planned, Anutu was also telling his friend how long the branches and tree trunks must be. Big enough to float and carry at least three people, and enough pieces to weave a tight platform to remain buoyant and resist sinking. But small enough to carry the pieces with them to the other side of Fansu.

Counting practices were primitive, in this case it was centered on the construction of a single raft. When the two men talked through the process, they had a good idea of how many tree trunks would be required for one platform. Knowing that a man, woman, and a child would be on it, they then considered how many of the people would go, and how many times they would have to make this raft.

Anutu spread the fingers of both his hands, pressing his outspread palms into the dirt. It created a simple diagram of ten lines, and he pointed to one after another to indicate how many rafts they would have to make. Then, he took his index finger, pointing upward to get Lotya's attention, and pointed to one of the lines in the dirt.

"Anutu, Baia, Anu, baby," he said.

Pointing to another line in the dirt, Lotya added, "Lotya, Nanda, baby."

Both men nodded, and proceeded to silently name the men, women, and children who would occupy each of the rafts indicated by the lines in the dirt. When they were satisfied with their estimates and how the people were dispersed, both men sat back on their haunches and nodded agreement.

"When?" Lotya asked. And as if the gods were listening to his question, the earth shuddered, then shook more violently, as a bright orange plume of light appeared on the distant horizon.

"Big fires are set by gods," Anutu said. "When we push onto the sea, we set a big fire. The gods will leave us alone then, until we get to Ganta."

Over the next few days, the people who decided to leave Fansu busied themselves for the trip. The men hunted less, killing only enough deer and wild pigs to feed them while still in the village. They couldn't bring large animals on the rafts, but they continued to hunt for small animals, mice, shrews, hedgehogs, and birds that could be carried aboard the floating platforms without sinking.

The women tended their garden and helped their men fish the shores. They bundled the harvest grain and tubers in large skins given by the sheep they raised and hung the fish by strings in the sun to dry. Within a few days, they had acquired more food than they usually harvested, a cache needed to sustain the people over the trip they envisioned and for the first few days on Ganta, since they didn't know what they would find there.

Some of the men were assigned to felling trees and cutting branches to the specified lengths. The piles grew large as the days passed, and the people who had decided to stay on Fansu talked often of their decision. Doubts grew, but so did the arguments. The anger never challenged the peace of the village, but the indecision spread stress and confusion.

By the time the wood piles had grown enough to account for the rafts necessary for the voyage, the "leavers" were ready. At night, the conversations at each cluster roamed over the actions to take, and the people who would go. At times, "stayers" joined the "leavers" discussion to test their ideas and ponder their decisions. Some "leavers" grew more worried and evidenced second thoughts.

Tano had talked to Folu many times about this; he clearly wanted them to go with the "leavers." She resisted forcefully at first, but each time the earth shook with the tremors of more earthquakes and volcanic eruptions, she rushed to his side, clutching their baby to her breast. Over the few days that they watched the "leavers" gather the wood and food, Folu slowly changed her mind. So, they joined them.

On the evening before they planned to go, the people abandoned their singular clusters and met together at the biggest firepit in the village. There were many families there, too many for Anutu to count with his fingers, but he knew all of them and recognized friends among those who decided to leave and those who decided to stay.

As he had promised to Baia, they built a huge fire in the midst of their clusters, one that could be seen by the gods, a fire intended to protect them that night and to strike fear into those who would harm them on their journey.

And around the circle of this fire the people of the village stood, sat, and talked. The children played, thinking this was a special occasion when they were all together. The men talked in hushed voices, making plans as much as they were replying to the "stayers" questions about leaving. The women held similar conversations, but also shared stories that by repetition they hoped would imprint the history of their people on those who would no longer live among them.

A very old woman entered the circle that included Baia, Nanda, and Neeri. This woman, Seeta, had outlived two men and produced seven children, losing three to the ravages of life in primitive times. Seeta approached the three women and knelt before them.

"This for you," she said to Baia, and she handed her a string of shells that had been pierced and hung together as a necklace. Turning to Nanda, she offered her another band, one that had antler tips dangling from it.

"And this for you," she said to Neeri, finally allowing a small tear to drop from her eye. Neeri was older than Baia and Nanda, and closer to Seeta's age. For Neeri, the old woman offered a special gift. It was a stick that was thin at one end and thickened to a bulb at the other. The thin end was wrapped with many windings of thin leather strips, as in a grip. The bulb opposite it was festooned with eagles' feathers which danced in the light breeze of the evening.

Seeta was thought to have special powers, a special strength often attributed to anyone who lived so long among the people. And this stick was one she used to tap someone who was sick, a totem that was intended to transfer Seeta's energy to the person in need. At her advanced age, she couldn't travel but she knew that anyone who dared to cross Fansu and challenge the sea would need special power.

And she knew that Neeri possessed it. Now, all she needed was the totem.

Seeta knelt before Neeri and presented the wand. Neeri initially held back, not anxious to assume that role, but with Baia and Nanda looking on, she took the totem from Seeta and pressed it to her breast. Seeta gave her a serious look at first, shedding more tears, but then smiled at the knowledge that her friends would be safe.

———

The next morning, the village awoke early. The women had already brought the hot embers of the night fires back to flame, and they were preparing food for the journey. The men who tended the sheep carried armloads of tree trunks and branches toward the corral that held the animals. Anutu and Lotya made sure they planned to take no more than half the sheep, leaving the others for their friends who would stay on Fansu.

They used the cordage and braided rope from fiber plants and bundled the wood together. One bundle was tied to each side of a sheep so that an animal could carry two bundles at a time. The men knew they still had more wood to carry, but they had already hatched a plan for that.

Tano hunted deer and had brought down several in the days leading up to their departure. He shared some of the meat with his family cluster but gave the rest to the "stayers" who could dry it and eat it long after their friends had gone. But Tano kept the hides for a special use.

In the evenings after hunting deer, Tano chipped more of the hammer stones he had used for chopping wood. Flakes flew from the core as he shaped the edge of the bulbous rock he cradled in his left hand. One such flake tumbled across the ground and landed at Folu's feet. The flake itself was thinner than the hammerstone that Tano was shaping, but its edge was also sharper. Folu turned it over in her hand and considered how this sharp-edged tool might be used later.

Tano used his sharpened hammerstone to scrape the deer hides clean and he converted them to broadcloth that he spread on the ground. Onto these hides he heaped the remaining wood so that he could drag the cloth as they walked, pulling along their stockpile of timber.

The time had come to leave. The people who had decided to go to Ganta gathered in the middle of their village, surrounded by those who stay. The earth was still that day, and some "leavers" became doubtful, but Anutu, Baia, and even Tano spoke to remind the assembly of their reasons for leaving, and to remind them of the dangers of staying amongst the gods while they were fighting. "Stayers" listened to the words of these three people, and they wondered too about their decision to remain on Fansu. Several men were seen looking at their women, asking for confirmation that their decision to remain in the village was right.

After some brief embraces and unspoken farewells, the "leavers" assembled their children, food, and what meager clothing they had and turned toward the small herd of sheep they would use as pack animals. As the departing group emerged from the circle of the village, they looked back at those who remained. It was the only society they had ever known, the only environment they had ever inhabited. Some of the hunters and a handful of the women had ventured to the other side of the island where another tribe lived but leaving Fansu altogether was a dangerous undertaking.

"It is good," Anutu said, as if to convince not only his friend but himself.

Lotya merely nodded.

The sheep bayed a bit when they started out and the two boys tending the animals had to check and shift the bundles of sticks bound to them, to keep them balanced.

The people walked up a slight incline to a minor ridge that separated their island into two parts. They left behind the sea that swallowed the sun at night and crossed over to the side where the sun struggled back out of the water in the morning.

After cresting the ridge, they could see that other coast. It would have been a two-hour trek if walking alone, but the animals moved more slowly than the people, so reaching the other shore took longer, and they did not arrive until the sun sank below the rocky ridge that the people had walked over.

They came to a halt near the water but safely up from the soft waves that lapped on the beach. They would be sleeping in the open air that night before challenging the seas in the morning, but they also needed to eat.

The four sheep the people used to get that far were now unburdened of their loads of wood. One would give milk the following morning, and so was spared while the others were slaughtered. Sheep wouldn't fit on a raft, but the people could use their wool and hides, and cook their meat, taking some of it on their rafts.

As the sky darkened, another fire could be seen farther away on the same shore. Anutu and Baia and some of the others had met with these people before, usually in the middle of their island, on the rare excursions away from their own village. The people stared at the little fire that lit the edge of a stand of trees and considered whether to engage those nearby.

"We leave them," said Lotya. "No need to go there."

"What if they come here?" asked Tano.

In fact, as the men considered their options, several people emerged from the darkness and approached them. They were carrying heavy sticks but did not appear to be menacing. These new arrivals spoke some words to the villagers, but Anutu, Baia, and Tano couldn't understand them. Baia and Nanda joined their men while Folu hid in the shadow of the people.

Attempts at conversation were futile. The people of the village and those they were meeting had few common words, and direct communication was difficult. One of the intruders pointed his stick at the large bundles of cut wood; another one approached Neeri, the only woman not attended by a man.

Folu, who had stayed hidden, stepped into the circle. She was quick to analyze what was happening and what needed to be done to resolve it.

"They want wood," she said. Then, nodding in Neeri's direction, "and they want her."

Without waiting for consent or words from the other people, Folu handed her baby to Neeri and walked over to the sheep that had been preserved for her milk. Taking the sheep by a rope, Folu walked it over to the intruders, lifting the leash up to the man who stood in front. Then, she took a leather band that she wore around her neck, from which dangled a special carved wooden object, and handed it to the man.

Stepping back, Folu didn't bow, but quickly nodded her head. She interpreted well that nodding was a gesture of assent and bowing would be seen as subservience. Some signals communicate best without words.

The man raised the leash up and inspected the sheep. Then he looked at the necklace and at the other men around him.

"As the sun comes, we go there," said Anutu, pointing toward the sea. He put his hand up on his forehead as squinting at a bright light and stared off toward the water.

The leader of the intruders didn't understand his words, but he gathered that these villagers were continuing on and would not stay near their own hunting grounds. The idea of venturing out onto the sea didn't seem to take him by surprise, and Lotya wished for a moment that they could communicate better to find out what these strangers knew about the waters. But with Folu's gifts and some assurance that the villagers would not be a problem, the leader of the intruders swung around and guided his men back to their own encampment.

When they were gone, the villagers shared relieved smiles and looked at Folu.

"But why did you give him the sheep?" Tano asked her.

"He would take it anyway, and maybe our wood. We can't bring the sheep, but we can't cross the sea without the wood."

———

When the people were certain the other men had returned to their own camp, they resumed their preparations for the meal. Some of them began arranging the wood and reeds for raft-making and began assembling their crafts.

Just as the aromas of cooked meat were lifting up and starting the stomachs to growl, they took a finished raft down to the water to test its ability to float. Rocking gently in the surf, the raft reminded them of the flotsam that crowded their stream after a storm. But their device was too square and too tight to be mistaken for an accident of nature.

Lotya pushed the raft out a bit further into waist-deep water to test its flotation, holding the rope that was tied to it so the craft didn't slip away. Seeing that it remained aloft the waves, he hailed Anutu standing on the shore and smiled broadly at their creation. Then, he leaned over at the waist and tried to wrestle himself onto the raft, but it kept slipping out from under him. Seafaring was not in their experience and boarding a floating craft was an untested skill.

Watching this, Anutu roared with laughter and Tano joined in on the fun.

"Yes," Lotya said, laughing along with them. "But we can't use this unless we can get on."

Tano was carefully observing what was happening. Whenever Lotya would pull himself up on one side, the other would tip into the air and throw the man off. So Tano stepped down into the water and offered a suggestion. He took the reins from Lotya and waded around to the other side. Holding down his end of the raft, he invited Lotya to try again from his own side, and this time they were successful. The real test would be if the craft would float.

Anutu came down to the water and edged up onto the raft with Tano on the opposite side. It stayed afloat, so he and Lotya reached down and jerked Tano up onto the platform with them. The three men stood in a tight circle in the middle of the platform, giggling at their success, an event that was observed by the people who had gathered at the shore and now cheered them on.

After successfully testing their invention, they retired for the evening, knowing they would resume in the morning and build other rafts sufficient to take their small tribe across the waters to Ganta.

Around the campfire, the men decided to stand watch through the night. The intruders appeared to have been satisfied with Folu's gifts, but Anutu and Lotya didn't want to take any chances. Each sat up for a while at a time, joined by Tano and another two men, tending the fire. They had to sacrifice some of the wood they brought for the rafts, but a bright fire would serve as protection too.

The morning came early since the cool weather of a night without shelter kept most of the people awake. In the light, they could see a small land mass offshore, with the shape of Ganta looming over it in the distance. The villagers gathered their belongings, finished building the remaining rafts, and gathered at the shore.

Boarding their sea vessels entertained all who tried, and the laughter tamped down the fear that some felt embarking on this journey. Each raft was held in place by a man holding onto it with a rope, and when all the people were ready, these guides pulled the rafts out to sea. They expected to sink deeper into the water and then would have to board the rafts themselves, but they were surprised that the depth of the water on the short voyage to the nearby strip of land was easy to manage while still standing immersed in the water. It never got above the men's heads, so they stayed in the water until they reached the other shore, before the sun had even risen to the highest point in the sky.

"Up," said Lotya when they made landfall.

"Off," said Tano, meaning the same thing, and the people disembarked from their craft.

What they were standing on was a thin strip of sandy beach no wider than the village they once lived in. They could walk across it quickly, and go back into the sea, but Baia said no.

"We can wait," she said. "When the sun just begins its journey through the sky again, when there is a longer day, we go then."

The people had brought along dried fish and some already cooked meat, so they didn't need a fire. It was fortunate, since this barren island had no wood and a fire would require giving up some of a raft. They settled in a comfortable circle, shared the food and told stories about their village and the friends they had left behind.

"They are gone," Neeri said. It was an interesting way to phrase it, since she and the "*leavers*" were the ones to depart the village. But it was true, since they never expected to see those people again – they were gone. With saddened faces, the people around the circle nodded or stared down at the sand.

"Farutu didn't fish," Lotya said, smiling at the thought that came out of the blue.

"What do you mean?" asked Tano. "I see him fishing."

Lotya chuckled a bit.

"No, Farutu only sit and stare at the water," Lotya added. "Did you see him pull up his net?"

Nanda joined the little joke.

"He did," she offered, "but he would only have one fish. Sometimes two."

"Why not more?" Tano asked.

Nanda held one hand up and, with the other, poked between her fingers to show that the net had holes.

"He couldn't keep them," she said, laughing then. "So, he made bows and traded them for your fish. He only sat there to have quiet."

The people in the circle traded other stories and laughter about their old friends, to remember them.

"They are our people," Neeri said, "but they are gone."

The people huddled closer together, putting their children between their bodies for warmth, and drifted off to sleep.

The next morning, they rose quickly, gathered their things and once again launched their rafts into the sea toward Ganta. The men assumed they would encounter shallow waters again but the sea got deeper quickly and the water was over their heads before they were very far. Hoisting themselves onto the rafts, the men knelt down on the platforms and resorted to using tree bark for paddles. They could not get much speed but made steady progress to the shores of the big island of Ganta.

Before the sun fell and the sky darkened, they reached the sandy beach and pulled their rafts onto dry land. They were too tired to turn to hunting or even gathering for the food, so they relied on the remaining stores of meat and vegetables they had with them. But a fire was necessary.

"Tano," said Baia, "would you build us a fire?"

He nodded and went in search of some fallen wood. They had landed on Ganta and could probably have sacrificed a raft, but that seemed too brazen a decision so soon. Tano brought two of the children along so he could load their arms with branches for the fire they would build.

The three returned with enough wood to get the fire going; more could be gathered later. So Tano sat down in the middle of their circle and reached for his bow starter. The invention was still new so everyone watched, as Anutu did with admiration. In very little time, a flame licked up in the straw and Tano piled more grass and tinder on it. Supplying more wood, a handful at a time, caused the fire to grow high enough to reach the waists of the people around it. That night, they would have warmth.

Once Tano was certain that the fire was going and could be tended by others, he went back into the brush for more wood. His helpers came along and they worked together gathering kindling and thicker branches for their camp.

A grunt was heard from near a stand of trees, followed by another one. Honking and grunting grew louder and with occasional shrieks that almost sounded human. Tano thought he recognized the sound of wild pigs, so he picked up a sturdy stick while the little children raced back to the campfire.

Tano waded through the tall grass and reached a small clearing where two wild pigs were grunting and leaping at each other. There was some kind of fallen animal near them, and it seemed to him that the pigs were fighting over it.

"This is a good meal," he thought to himself, then he crept closer to get in position to stab one of the animals. Looking at the rough stick in his hands, he longed for his sharpened spear, but he didn't have time to retreat to the campsite. When he was closer than his own height, one pig turned his attention on Tano, and the man plunged with his makeshift weapon. The point dug into the pig's shoulder; the animal squealed but quickly shook the weapon loose.

In the meantime, the other animal sensed an advantage and tore at the wounded swine. In a grunting, shrieking pile, the two animals tumbled together toward Tano, who was then caught in the rolling heft of these creatures as they fell upon his legs and pinned him to the ground. Stabbing again with his weapon, Tano was more concerned with freeing himself than with bringing down an animal. The two pigs continued to bite and claw, unmindful of the human trapped beneath them.

Just then, Anutu and Lotya ran up, each brandishing sharpened spears, which they used to impale the animals. With a second thrust, the men finished off the pigs, then pulled them apart to roll them off their friend.

Tano was covered with blood, both from the pigs and from his own body, and he looked very weak. Neeri had arrived with one of the hides Tano had stripped for carrying wood. Now, they carefully loaded him onto the hide so they could take him back to the camp. Other men arrived to try to preserve the animals; no food should be left to scavengers.

With Tano moaning and twisting about in pain, they dragged the stretcher back to their makeshift camp, where Neeri tended to the fallen man.

They washed Tano with the waters from the sea, and Folu sat with him through the night. Neeri was self-conscious about trying to impart magic, as Seeta had told her to do, but she mimicked the actions of the seer left behind, tapping Tano's forehead with the wand and speaking in hushed tones above him. She focused her energy on the stricken man but lacked the confidence that such actions would require.

The fire kept everyone warm, but the people would have stayed awake anyway, waiting for Neeri's magic to work. They wanted to know they would be safe on Ganta, safe in this new land.

In the early morning light, Folu placed her hand gently on her man's chest. Whipping it away in fright, she cried out. His chest wasn't moving, and Folu's eyes opened wide in terror.

Anutu rushed over and examined the man, as did Neeri who approached with what could only be seen as a look of inadequacy and guilt. Tano was no longer alive, that was certain, and even an elder woman's magic couldn't bring a person back into life.

Folu sat by his side, rocking and sobbing, clutching their baby close to her. She cried mostly in silence, though she sometimes let out a stream of whimpering that tore through the camp with her grief. Anutu and Baia talked about burying Tano and wanted to do it in a shelter, as their people had always done, but they had just arrived and there were no shelters yet. Yet they were reluctant to just bury him out in the open.

"Not good," said Baia, to the background sounds of Folu weeping.

"Where?" asked Lotya.

"He will be buried in a shelter. Should we build one here?" asked Anutu, pointing the ground that was their temporary camp.

"No, takes too long," said Baia. "Tano should not be here that long," referring to their tradition of burying a body before it started to decay.

Lotya looked at Anutu, who looked up on the cliffs above their beach. He squinted because the sun was just coming over the mountainous rise of Ganta, shielding his eyes to look at the contours of the cliff above. He could make out a shadowy black spot on the face of the rock, not too far up. Anutu looked at Lotya, then turned to walk toward the cliff. Lotya didn't need any instructions, so he followed his friend toward the mountainous rise.

After about an hour of climbing they reached the mouth of a cave, which they entered and inspected as a place for shelter.

"We will shelter here?" Lotya asked.

"We may stay, we may not," answered Anutu, "but this will be Tano's shelter."

The two returned to the camp where Anutu gathered his tools for cave carving. They wrapped Tano in one of the hides to transport him to the cave, and started out, leaving Folu crying with Baia and Nanda. Neeri stood nearby, shaken by what she thought was her failure.

Just before leaving the camp though, Anutu went back to Tano's pile of tools and hides. He searched among them until he found the bow drill used by Tano to make a fire and carried it with him up the hill.

The two men were the strongest of this little band, but their unwelcome task still required great endurance to climb up the face of this cliff with a dead body in tow. This return trip took three times longer than the first trip, and they arrived only when the sun was already falling into the sea. When they dragged Tano's limp body into the cave, they immediately set about digging a place to bury it. Folding his arms and legs so that he would fit in a sitting position, they put into the grave some of Tano's cutting tools and the broken branch that had not served him well in the fight with the pigs. But they didn't cover the pit yet.

Anutu set his tools down on the dirt and proceeded to apply Tano's bow drill as he had watched the man do. Sparks quickly grew, and he fed them with tinder and grass to produce a small fire to light his way while carving. Once it was well underway, Anutu turned toward the pit with Tano's body in it and laid the bow drill beside the man, then he and Lotya began to cover the hole with dirt.

Anutu turned his attention to carving, but Lotya only sat nearby and watched. He was not skilled in cave drawing and let his friend tend to it.

Finding the right surface on the cave wall was important, and Anutu took his time doing so. Wiping his palm against the rock until he thought he had found a flat surface of sufficient size to handle his art, he set about the task. Anutu would carve Tano's body lying flat, and he would add many etched scratches across the fallen body, with its arms akimbo.

Lastly, Anutu would carve a large wild pig next to Tano, slain on the ground, with similar etchings to display the wounds that the dead man had inflicted before he succumbed. It was a fitting tribute to a man Anutu had loved and treated like a brother. And it would remind everyone who every saw these carvings of what a brave man Tano had been.

TIME BEFORE HUMANS

GONDWANA AND LAURASIA

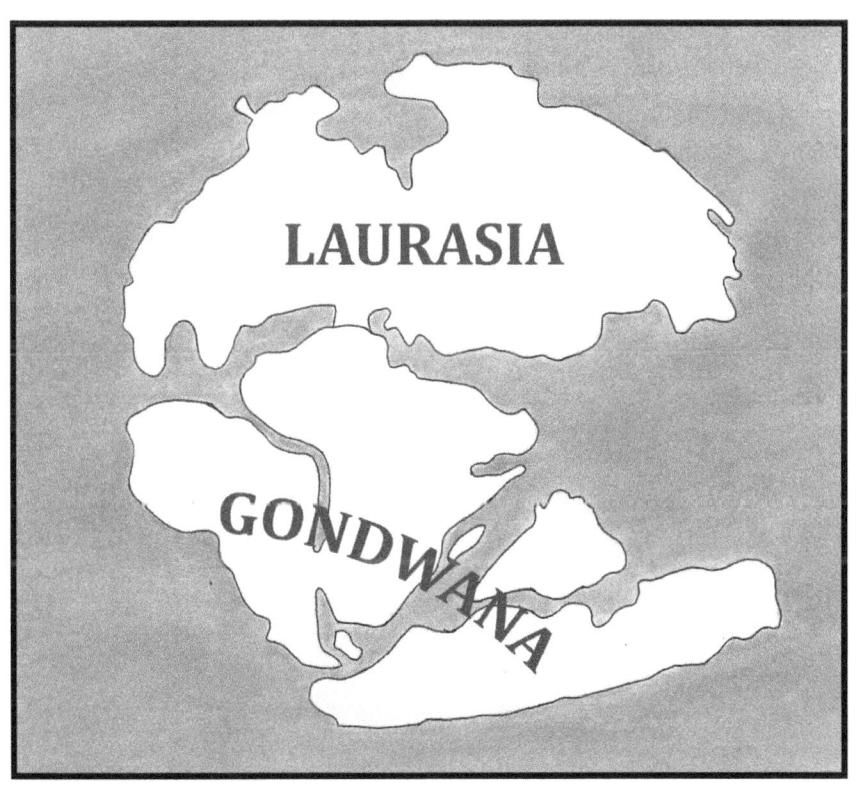

5.3 MILLION YEARS AGO

5.3 MILLION YEARS AGO

In far distant times, the Mediterranean was merely a yawning extension on the eastern edge of today's Atlantic Ocean, west of the primordial Tethys Sea and without clear boundaries. It was a broad watery world wedged between Laurasia and Gondwana, which themselves were drifting continental remnants of an even older, more massive super-continent – Pangea.

One hundred million years ago, the aquatic gap that separated these two land masses was already teeming with the beginnings of life on Earth. The waxing and waning temperatures in the region allowed the growth of wild ferns, primeval grasses, and forests of tall trees while the planet's oceans hosted a rich brew of diverse sea creatures. Tetrapods emerged from these waters and evolved limbs from their fins for terrestrial mobility, then they evolved into a diverse population of land animals ranging from small shrews and reptiles to birds, hedgehogs, and dinosaurs.

The tectonic plate that held Gondwana – including the modern continent of Africa – continued to slip northward and clockwise while the plate supporting Laurasia – including all of modern Europe – slid southward and counter-clockwise. The two continents were closing their jaws around the wide ancient sea and were heading toward a collision on their western tips.

The movement continued until this massive marine habitat had become a land-locked sea, an elongated aquatic world tethered on its western edge by a narrow passageway to the Atlantic Ocean and spreading laterally to the east, enveloping volcanic islands and peninsulas, its waves crashing upon ancient coastlines.

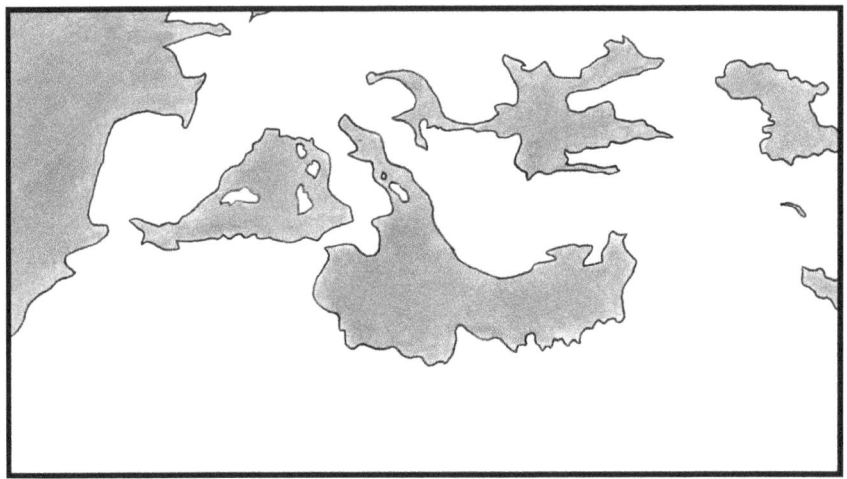

The Primordial Mediterranean Sea

About six million years ago, the vital strait which served as the link between the Mediterranean habitat and the Atlantic Ocean was slowly closing. The African plate was still moving clockwise toward a promontory jutting out from the southwestern tip of the Eurasian plate. The separation had grown narrow enough that a primitive species of bird could lift off from one continent and alight on the other within minutes. The shrinking passageway, what we now call the Strait of Gibraltar, was finally sealed by the continental movement, completely shutting off the "middle sea" from the Atlantic Ocean and sentencing it to a slow death by evaporation.

This event – what modern scientists refer to as the Messinian salinity crisis – completely isolated the primitive Mediterranean, depriving it of its source of restorative water from the vast ocean to its west and relegating its feedwater to a scattered assortment of rivers running from land masses north and south. Closed off from the boundless reservoirs of the global sea, the trickle from these landbound sources of water could not keep up with the evaporative effects that tens of thousands of years had on the sea. The Messinian salinity crisis lasted millions of years and turned a lush landlocked sea into a dead valley devoid of life.

As the waters of the sea dried up and rose to the heavens, the contours of the basin were revealed, complete with soaring volcanoes that were once sub-marine but now jutted up from the exposed floor like mountains belching the devilish brew of the planet's core. The relentless evaporation continued to lower the sea level until it had turned the Mediterranean region into a massive, dry gouge in the earth, a desiccated scar, a coarse barren dessert where no life could survive.

About five million years ago, the wreckage that was the fusion of the African and Eurasian plates at the Strait of Gibraltar began to give way. A meteor strike just east of the strait has been credited with blasting open the passageway. But the erosive effects of years of unrelenting Atlantic tides also played a role, perhaps even the slow falling-apart of the boulders that had toppled onto one another and merged in that great cataclysm in the Cretaceous period to close the strait. There may also have been a reversal of the continental drift, a counter-clockwise movement of the African plate. But, in time, there appeared a sliver of an opening where the continents had once collided at Gibraltar.

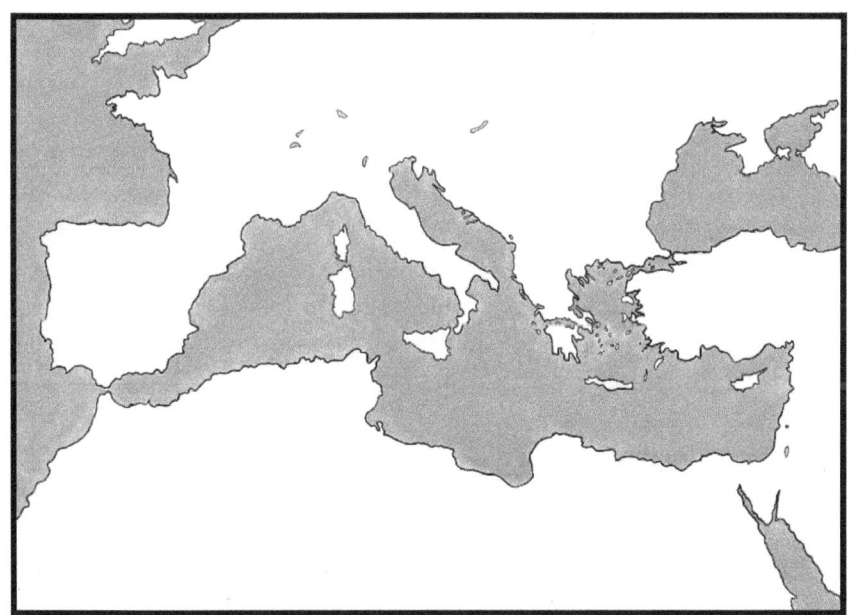

| The Zanclean Flood

That sliver succumbed to the weight of pressure from the ocean to its west and slowly opened. A trickle became a flow; the flow became a thundering tide. The history books refer to it as the Zanclean Flood, or the Pliocene revolution. By whatever name, one of earth's greatest waterfalls sprang to life at that moment, pouring Atlantic Ocean water into the dry Mediterranean cavity, raising the sea level in the basin as much as ten meters per day, and taking two years to complete its task of leveling the Sea with the Atlantic Ocean.

By then, the climate was warmer and glaciation was receding. With the return of the vital waters, the forests and grasslands returned and thrived. Tall weedy grasses grew down slopes and right to the water's edge, stabilizing the soil and throwing oxygen into the atmosphere that stimulated even more growth. Brilliant green leafy canopies of the forests could be seen by ancient birds that plied the blue skies over the region.

Mammals also thrived in this rich environment. There were elephants with stubby tusks that presaged the enormous protuberances of later mastodons. Alligators and crocodiles ruled the shoreline, able to race across the sand as well as they could swim through the waves. Stubby-legged little horses appeared, ancestors to the great thoroughbreds of modern day.

The volcanic mountains of that once-dried basin were formed as far back as the Triassic-Jurassic period. They survived the Zanclean Flood but now, instead of the towering peaks that dominated a dry valley, they were nearly submerged by the onrushing sea, their tops appearing only as solitary islands with protruding peaks above the lapping waters of the Mediterranean. These islands of fire became terrestrial outposts strewn across the inland sea, including some small clusters of islands as well as larger landmasses west of the great boot-shaped peninsula that penetrated the middle of the sea. Among the largest of landmasses was a lush Garden of Eden that would become the favorite way station for travelers from all over the then-world of Europe – the island of Sicily.

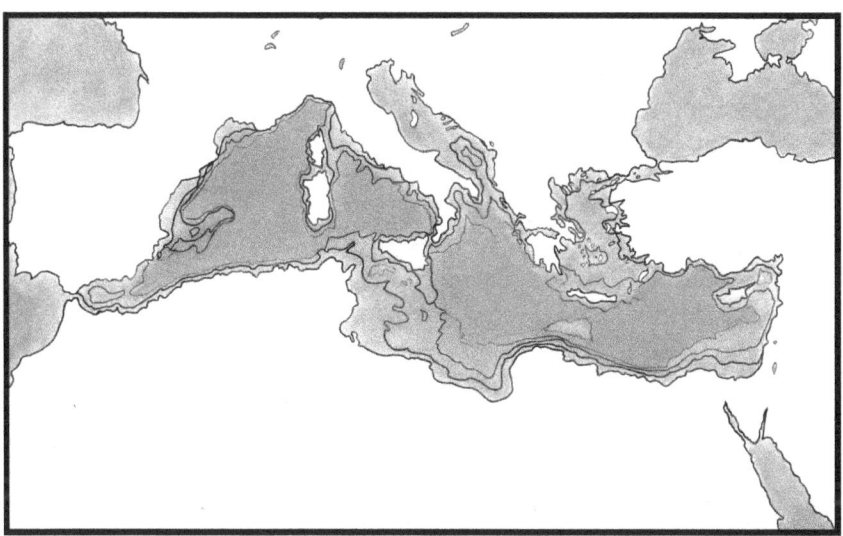

Land Bridges throughout Mediterranean Sea

Over the millennia since the flood, the landscape of the region was transformed from a stark, barren gouge on the face of the earth to a region of wild grass, sprouting flora, and small fish plying the lush waters. The animal kingdom of the Mediterranean area did not yet include human beings, although their ancestors were already organized in tribal clusters on the continent to the south. It would still be many years before migration patterns emerged and brought this biped east around the Middle Sea, then north through the Levant, and west across the ice fields of Europe.

Meanwhile, myriad life forms thrived in the region, developing in complexity and diversity, creating a habitat that teemed with life, on land and beneath the seas. A series of cooling and warming patterns brought uncertainty to a climate that had hosted so many flora and fauna. With the return of each cooling trend, ice fields once again covered the land, challenging plant and animal forms to compete for diminishing resources.

Even before humans inhabited this Mediterranean region, the theatre for human civilization was being built for their arrival. Convulsions of weather and climate, ice ages yielding to warming trends, emergence of new animals matched by extinctions of life forms that failed the survival test – all combined to enrich the Mediterranean and make it the perfect incubator for human habitation and development.

Another form of life flowed through arteries deep in the earth. A volcanic pipeline below the planet's crust stretched from western Italy near modern-day Vesuvius and traveled due south to Etna on Sicily's east coast. This highway of magma was created by the crushing forces of the earth's plates, as the rocky edges of each plate melted in fiery encounters under the force of the tectonic shift.

At times, this subterranean furnace bled off along the route to produce fantastic spasms of gas and lava that gushed out of the sea, giving birth to a string of islands between the two great volcanic monsters. The explosive eruptions at Vesuvius and Etna continued to release the trapped energy of the volcanic highway, but not without smaller and less frequent eruptions that pushed lava out of vents in the chain, each successive burst of molten energy creating new layers of volcanic deposits on these signal flares in the sea.

The rising domes of cooled lava crested the waves of the Mediterranean Sea, hissing and steaming as the heat spewed from the water and rose in smoky clouds into the air. The layers of lava cooled off to create a cluster of rocky outposts off the northeastern shore of Sicily, now called the Aeolian Islands. The magma that oozed from these volcanic vents cooled quickly in contact with water, and this rapid temperature change created a black glass – obsidian – a rock that would be a critical resource to early humans who reached this region and who discovered the many uses for the sharp edges that could be achieved when the rock was flaked.

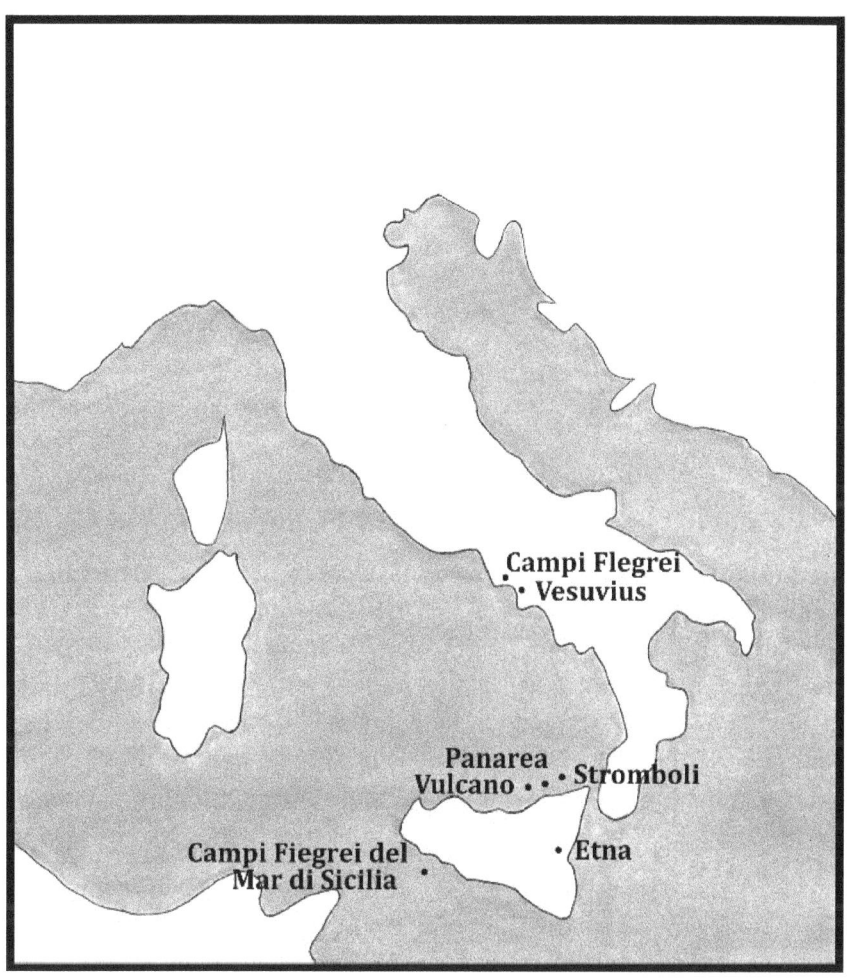

Ancient Volcanoes

The first archaic humans reached Europe around 800,000 years ago, but their arrival on the island in the Middle Sea rested on another geologic event. Through the millennia of ice ages, glaciation had sucked water from the earth's surface, holding it frozen in large fields of ice around the poles. Seabeds that had been inundated by wild seas were then exposed to the air in regions around the hemisphere. In the Mediterranean basin, the growth of the icy sheets that covered the European and African continents lowered the sea levels and produced land bridges that connected spits of land previously separated by deep water. One such land bridge linked the African continent to islands in the Middle Sea, making it possible for animals to migrate from that vast continent to the islands without having to swim or maneuver across the waves.

Plant life creeped across these land-bridges, spreading forest and undergrowth into the new area. Animals roamed across these spits of land to graze on the fertile soil and pastures of budding green growth before them. The animals ingested plants and dropped the seeds from their intestinal waste or clinging to their fur to release them to germinate in the new environment.

Flora and fauna spread from continent to continent, enriching the ecosystems and creating diversity in indigenous life forms. These primeval life forms made the trek from the African continent to the islands and the new land with their genetic material.

In time, more modern humans were already afoot in the southern continent, having emerged from their African origins to migrate through and around the Mediterranean region. Some tribes followed the northern shoreline of the African continent, traveling westward to the point where they discovered the same open fields and a broad bridge of land that had already been explored by the animals ahead of them. Following this peninsula of land, this bridge between Africa and Sicily, the tribes set foot on a new land without having to dare the dangers of the seas in their crossing.

They came in pursuit of the animal prey that were headed in that direction or in search of greener pastures to explore. They brought a simple stone age culture, using hammer stones as tools or tying them to cut branches to create a lethal weapon that could be swung down upon the head of their prey.

They had already mastered fire, using flint to create sparks and set a pile of twigs and brush ablaze. When flint wasn't available, early humans knew how to use friction by rapidly rotating a fire stick on another piece of wood, allowing the smoldering tinder to set dried leaves and grass to flame.

By 12,000 years ago, the people who lived on the island of Sicily were shifting from nomadic hunting and gathering to a more settled agricultural society, with an increased knowledge of plant management and animal husbandry. Farming techniques improved, sometimes with lessons learned accidentally from centuries of trial and error, and these techniques gave humans more control over food production. It also allowed the production of bounty, a crucial turning point in human evolution because a society forced to roam in search of its ration of food did so on a daily basis, with no reserves to allow them to rest for long. With improved farming, they could grow and preserve more food, eliminating the daily necessity of collection, and allow the tribes to develop social organizations and stability.

The civilization of the large island in the Middle Sea was in full flower by the 10th Millennium B.C.E. But as with the heavenly fire that they carefully preserved in smudge pots and tinder, there was another source of fire brewing beneath the land they inhabited. At the furious sound of rumbling below their feet, the people knew that the land would once again belch fire, scorching flows of viscous liquid, and scalding rocks. This fire they couldn't harness like the flames from the tree branches they collected. This fire they avoided but worshipped as evidence of a great power that must command all of nature.

Over the centuries to come, the culture that settled in Sicily would be shaken time and again by threats from volcanoes below the ground, and invaders above.

2018

JULY 2018

CAFÉ AMADEO, MAZARA DEL VALLO

Near the end of the semester, I was telling my sociology students about the lessons to be learned from immersion. Just as it worked for language, immersing oneself in another culture was the best – maybe the only – way to actually learn about a people.

Over the years, I had heard our own family stories of Sicily and how my grandparents had come from there. So, it was natural for me to be curious about the Sicilians, and I had long considered immersing myself for a month or two to see what the culture was truly like.

I booked my flights before the semester ended and was at the airport soon after submitting final grades. The traveling took its toll on me, and with jet lag to contend with, I woke early in Hotel Grecu on a quiet street in Mazara del Vallo on the first morning. I spent the day in the library, hoping some local books would set a baseline for what I intended to study while I was here in the southern coastline city in Sicily.

The next morning, I felt like I could assume a more vigorous schedule and wanted a hot cup of coffee to begin.

It was still early morning but the warmth of the rising sun was already beating on my neck. I wore a short-sleeve shirt and baggy khakis to allow my skin to breathe in what promised to be another hot day in Sicily. I chose to wear leather-strapped sandals so that my feet could breathe a bit, even though I knew that no Sicilian would be caught dead wearing those shoes.

But I'm American. Well, actually, I'm Sicilian but only in the way Americans would use the term. As a descendant of Sicilians, I can claim that heritage, but to all the eyes who appraised me as I walked into Café Amadeo that morning, I was only, and truly, an American.

The focus of my study would be on the life of Sicilians over the last hundred years, piecing together how the island fared during World War II when the Allied forces marched across the land. They were fresh off the victory over the Nazi army in North Africa and were chasing the Germans back toward the Fatherland. Sailing from the African coast, they made landfall in Sicily but found little resistance as the Axis armies were already fleeing the island in their retreat across the Straits of Messina and back up mainland Italy.

What I read in the local library made me curious about places all over Sicily, like Licata, Gela, and Cassibile, all coastal areas on the southeastern part of Sicily that were landing places for the Allied Army. I planned to rent a car and drive to these other towns, but first I would begin with Mazara del Vallo, a small seaside city at the mouth of the Mazaro River.

I pushed open the door to Café Amadeo hoping to be greeted by the air-conditioned comfort within, momentarily forgetting that I was in Sicily, and forgetting that the locals considered AC to be bad for their health.

In any case, I was pleased to be out of the sun. I approached the cashier and paid for my espresso and hard roll, a routine breakfast for me, and took the ticket to the barista for him to prepare the drink. Then I took my roll and coffee to a table in the corner so I could sit, review my journal entries, and watch the people at the tables around me.

As I nibbled on the roll, a man who somehow managed to look even older than his gray hair and wrinkled skin would suggest leaned toward me.

"*Bon giornu,*" he said softly. His eyes twinkled as if they were decades younger than he appeared, and a relaxed, friendly smile spread across his face.

"You are Luca," he said. It wasn't a question, but I wondered how he knew who I was.

"Yes, I am Luca. Luca Siragusa," I replied, a bit confused. "And you, sir?"

"I am Vito. Vito Trovato," he said, and we shook hands. The rolls of loose, age-spotted flesh on the back of his hand belied a strong grip. His light smile remained as he looked down at my journal.

"I see you are taking notes. Many notes," Vito observed.

"Yes, yes. My grandparents grew up in Sicily and I'm here to learn more about the island. Have you lived here all your life?"

"*Si, si,*" he assured me with a studied nod of his head.

"While I was reading about this place," I began, "I couldn't escape the volumes of recorded history dealing with the invasion of the Germans and the later invasion of American and British forces. It seemed like Sicily had been used as a staging ground for one of the greatest conflicts of the Twentieth Century."

"*Si,* staging ground." He repeated the phrase as if it was a reminder of some terrible moment in history, richer in meaning to him than to me.

"How far back do you go?" he asked me.

"Well, I thought I'd go back to the *Fasci Siciliani,* maybe the first true uprising against the power structure in Sicily." I was proud of my mastery of early Sicilian history, but garnered only a wan smile from Vito. So, I continued.

"The *Fasci Siciliani* really arose..."

"In 1889. *Si,* I know," he said, not in criticism; more like amused appreciation. "But the *first* uprising, you say. First. Hmm, I would have to think. You talked about the Germans and the Americans as an invasion. But what of the others who have invaded my island?"

Not waiting for my reply, he offered, "There were the Spanish. *Si,* they came and brought the Inquisition with them. And the French Angevins a few centuries before that. Then there were the..."

"The Greeks," I interjected. Knowing that he was going back in time, I pulled up my only knowledge of prior invasions.

"Okay, so, yes, the Greeks arrived long before, about 800 B.C., and they brought their culture, and architecture, and social institutions with them," Vito said, waving a finger in the air as a teacher might reward a student for giving the right answer.

"But you went straight to the early Greeks, and you skipped right over the Swabians in the twelfth century," he added. "You know they were the first tribes in what we call Germany, right?"

I nodded, but mostly to conceal my ignorance.

"The Normans came a century earlier, the Fatimids a century before that, and the Arabs in the eighth century. Oh, yes, the Arabs. So much of Sicilian food, art, science, and philosophy comes from them."

"You're almost back to Medieval times," I suggested.

"Oh, no, not yet," and he laughed a bit. "There was the Byzantine period," he noted, with a finger pointed to the sky, "and all those new laws. Then there were invasions by the Goths, the Visigoths, the Ostrogoths..." Now his finger beat time on the table with each name.

"One more step and you would have the island back to the birth of Christ, and..." I added hopefully, "the Greeks."

"Of course, but before we get that far back, you have to consider the invasion by the Romans, the Phoenicians, and even the Carthaginians, as they called themselves. And, then, my good friend," Vito said patting my arm, "we have your Greeks."

"British and American, the Spanish, Angevins – Swabians, did you say?" I asked. When he nodded, I continued, "Normans, uh, uh...," scribbling notes in my journal.

"Fatimids," Vito offered.

"Yeah. And the Arabs, Byzantines, ummm..."

"Goths," he said. "Lots of Goths."

"Romans, Carthaginians...how do you keep track of all them?"

"Don't forget your Greeks!" Vito added with a playful smile.

But then he nodded his head as if this walk back in time was not yet over. I paged backward in my journal for other evidence that might address his commentary.

"The tribes. There were the tribes," I added quickly, as if by serendipity I had struck a final blow to this interrogation.

Vito leaned forward, his right forearm resting on the edge of the table, his clear brown eyes peering into mine. I thought he was going to urge me onward, but instead winked, and lifted his cup of espresso to his lips. Taking a quick draught of the cup, he leaned back against his chair and I leaned back too, a bit more relaxed.

"But, who were these tribes?" asked Vito suddenly.

I had a vague memory of the names of the tribes, the earliest settlers of the island, but didn't want to trust myself without checking notes. So, while Vito looked intently at me, I paged further backward in my notebook. Flipping pages back and forth, I found what I was looking for.

"Elymi," I said at first, absentmindedly pointing my finger in the air, as Vito had done. "Then Sicani, and Siculi."

Vito stared at me with a mixture of satisfaction and inquisitiveness.

"Yes, but not in that order," he offered after a pause.

I sighed. I knew that wasn't the order, but these were primitive people, far beyond my immediate research and I didn't keep such strict notes on their origins. I doubted that much was known about them.

"The Sicani came first, probably from Spain," he said, "but not by water." He sometimes tapped his forefinger on the table as if his thoughts were ordered by metronome.

I could picture Spain and Sicily, but I didn't understand how they could get there without going over the water.

"Wait, do you mean that the Sicani came all the way down the Italian peninsula just so they could turn west to reach Sicily? Why take the long route?"

"They didn't," he added, his finger tapping on the table. "They came up from a point we now call Tunis, where Carthage once stood."

"Uh, wait, that means they came from Spain, across the Strait of Gibraltar, then around the north coast of Africa to sail up to Sicily."

"They landed at this place, Mazara del Vallo." With this, he tapped the table as if the Sicani had actually landed in the Café Amadeo itself. "Of course, the Sicani didn't call it that. And they weren't the first ones to settle there."

"You mean the Elymi or the Siculi?" I asked.

"No, no," Vito said, showing a bit of frustration for the first time. He leaned forward, this time grabbing my full attention.

"The Siculi came down the toe of Italy," he said, "and occupied the eastern end of the island. This made the Sicani withdraw a bit, to abandon the eastern part of the island to the Siculi. And the Elymi, well, they shot across from Anatolia – you do know where Anatolia is, don't you?"

"Yes," I said reflexively. "It is the area now known as Turkey."

He smiled faintly, and tapped his finger again as he continued, "Yes, they came all the way from Anatolia, made settlements along the north coast of Africa," drawing a horizontal line on the tabletop, "continued on that westward itinerary across the coastline of the Mediterranean Sea, then swung north."

I was trying to keep track of all this migration into Sicily while Vito laid it out for me.

"Then," he said, pointing his index finger in the air, "the Elymi sailed across the water from the area of Tunis to the west coast of Sicily. They took over some of the western habitat claimed by the Sicani and forced them inland. Now, those original settlers of Sicily – the Sicani – were squeezed between two newcomers, the Siculi on their east flank and the Elymi on their west flank.

"Invaders," he added for punctuation.

Vito painted a picture of three warring tribes struggling for dominion over Sicily, centuries before the periods I had even considered in my research.

"When did all this happen?" I asked him.

"Well, let's see," he said, tapping his finger again and staring up at the ceiling.

"The Sicani, no, no, the proto-Sicani...arrived around – let me see – at first between 4000 and 3500 B.C., followed by more Sicanian tribes around 2500 B.C. The Elymi landed on the island around 1200 B.C., and the Siculi, about two hundred years later."

I stared at him for a moment, then consulted my notes. Looking back at Vito, I added, "Do you think I should begin my history of Sicily with the first settlers, then?"

"Oh, yes, that would be a good idea. But to do that, you would have to go back a bit further."

"Really? There were people before these first settlers?"

Vito chuckled at that.

"'First settlers,' you keep calling them. Luca, the first people to settle Sicily came across a land bridge from the African continent about twenty-five thousand years ago!"

"Wait, wait, what land bridge?" I asked.

My teacher began patiently.

"When the glaciers covered all of northern Europe and much of the southern part of the continent, much of the water in the seas was trapped in these ice fields. So, the sea level was lower, much lower," he explained, patting his hands downward to emphasize the lowering of the sea. "The water was so low that in the shallow seas – between the point where Tunis is now on the north coast of Africa" – as he spread his left hand wide – "and our own little Mazara del Vallo" – then spread his right hand out to the side – "the sea disappeared altogether."

My mind was racing, trying to keep up with the mental images he was creating for me.

"The low level of the sea allowed a broad expanse of land from the African continent to stretch all the way to Sicily, a land bridge that brought people and animals right to our shore. Just there," he said pointing to the beach outside the café, "right in front of us.

"And these settlers – these people who arrived long, very long before the Sicani – are my ancestors!" he added triumphantly.

In the silence that he introduced with that declaration, I suddenly became aware of my surroundings. The clatter of ceramic cups against stainless steel counters was the background music of life here. Aromas of freshly roasted espresso mingled with scents of vanilla and cinnamon from the cappuccino being quaffed by the people on their way to workplaces scattered across the streets and piazzas of the town. The fragrance of fresh bread and fruit pastries mingled with the random whiff of a cigarette in a quotidian display of Italiana. Then, like a time-traveler who is whisked back to the present, I turned back toward Vito.

"Wait," I interjected, "you're saying that you're descended from those first people who came across the land bridge from Africa to Sicily, those proto-Sicanians who arrived five thousand years ago?" I asked Vito.

"Why not? I've lived here all my life," he replied with a smile. We both knew that his enigmatic response didn't answer the question, but I had to chuckle.

"Sicily has been the crossroads of the Mediterranean since humans' first appearance in the region," Vito declared. "Not only crossroads, but..." he paused, "what was the word you used? 'Staging ground' for battles?"

I simply nodded and smiled. I was quickly coming to recognize how clever he was. He had mentally tracked our entire exchange and was weaving connections among the various historical links. I was anxious to learn more from him but chose only to sit and listen as the safest approach.

Vito lifted his espresso cup but, noticing that it was empty, hoisted it high so the barista would see it. The gentleman behind the counter looked up, nodded, and turned toward the shining, multi-handled steel monster at his elbow, preparing to make another round.

Vito returned his cup gently to the saucer in front of him and turned his attention back to me.

"Actually, my friend, I don't know which tribe I'm descended from. It's one of the charming things about being Sicilian: We are the true, uh, what do you call them in America? Oh, yes, 'mongrels.'"

I knew that Americans used the term derisively, but Vito called it charming.

Pulling a strand of his thinning hair, he continued.

"This hair used to be long and dark brown. And very curly, a feature that I might have inherited from my African ancestors." Pointing to his stubbly beard, he added, "And this used to be brown too, with red streaks. Maybe from the Normans."

Following his arthritic finger jabbing the air above his head, I looked up to see the geometric pattern on the ceiling that was clearly Arabic. I then watched as the same finger indicated a small, nude statue at the end of the bar, a statue of Dionysus, the Greek god of wine, as he panned the bar counter to draw my eyes to the other end where stood the proud statue of Bacchus, the Roman god of wine.

My gaze rolled back toward Vito. His smile was still there, though faint. The global tour of Sicily that he had just taken me on was for information, not humor.

"As a friend once told me: To assume that there are any pure races, we must assume that invading armies never got off their horses," he said. "I think he was talking about Sicily."

Just then the barista came to the table with Vito's espresso and another one for me.

I wanted to rethink my research on my father's island, but it all seemed so overwhelming. Vito had introduced me to a past that I had never imagined, a Sicilian history of invasion and conquest, a history of repetitive social upheaval, eras of one empire replacing another, a way station for trading vessels and a battleground for warring armies.

"Some of the people continued to wander, going far beyond this area where they first came," he narrated. "They migrated a bit west and north and moved on to higher ground that is northwest of where we are now."

"West?" I asked. West of here was the sea.

"Sì, west," he replied. As if sensing my confusion, Vito reminded me of the land bridge.

"It's not enough to think of the spit of land from Africa to Sicily as a simple, narrow bridge. The way the seas were lowered, land appeared in an unbroken expanse between the continent and our island. It wasn't like Moses had parted the seas," he laughed. "It took place over many years, centuries, and remained for many years. What we see as Sicily and Pantelleria to the south and the Egadi Islands off the western coast of Sicily – they were all the same land mass. To primitive people, these were not separate land masses as they are today. They were a continent that included mountains connected by broad plains.

"Some of the tribes wandered as far west as the Egadis – Levanzo and Marettimo and Favignana – now islands, but back then they were large hills that stood above the broad stretch of lowlands. They settled there, and when the glaciers melted and the sea level rose once again, those hills turned into islands, surrounded by the Mediterranean Sea.

"Early peoples inhabited the coastlines and river shorelines, near the water to catch fish, corral their animals, and rely on the rich earth to grow their plants. Those who ended up on the Egadi Islands had all that, and these people didn't risk crossing the sea if they already had abundance where they were. So," he said, with a small smile of triumph, "they stayed."

My mind swam with the immensity of it all, primitive humans migrating out of Africa over land laid bare and dry by rising glaciers. Migration patterns that brought them to outposts in the Mediterranean – well, outposts now, or islands as we say – but to these early settlers their travels were overland, not seafaring adventures. Not yet, anyway.

I was intrigued. I was ready to offer myself to Vito as a student and immerse myself in ancient Sicilian history, just as he drained his cup and stood to go.

"Vito, er, excuse me, Signor Trovato..."

"No, Luca. It's Vito."

"Sì, yes. I can stay on here, in Mazara del Vallo, if you will speak with me again, and I can learn about Sici..., your island."

Vito smiled broadly and took my hand to shake. Just as he turned to go without uttering a response, the barista approached the table to collect our coffee cups.

"He's here every morning at this time. Come back," he told me.

———

I had spent a mostly sleepless night in my room in Hotel Grecu, copying down as much as I could remember from Vito's commentary on the history of Italy. I started with pen and paper, scribbling under the light of the single-bulb lamp by my side, adding bits of trivia to my notebook, but this method was too slow.

I rose from the chair and pulled the laptop from my bag. Lifting the lid, I pressed the start button with my index finger, and the blue screen lit up. Most of my files were already on the computer but I knew I would have to create new folders to capture all the notes and historical trivia that poured from Vito's memory.

The following morning, I hurried to Café Amadeo, anxious to talk to Vito again but equally anxious to secure the same table for our conversation. The barista saw me hustle through the door and nodded to welcome me. My eyes swung immediately to the corner where Vito settled every day, but the old man wasn't there. I then looked at the barista, who smiled.

"He's always here about this time, but you're too early. Sit and I'll bring you a coffee."

I did as instructed, sliding in behind the table to a chair that faced the door. By the time the barista set a cup and saucer in front of me, Vito pushed open the door and walked in my direction. It was apparent to me that Vito wasn't actually headed toward me; it was the familiar table that drew Vito like a magnet. He would enter its orbit even if I wasn't sitting there.

But when he looked up and saw me already in place, a smile slowly appeared on his face, spreading the heavy folds of wrinkled chin and lit up his eyes. It combined both surprise and recognition, swirling together the elder's feelings about following his routine and sharing it with this obviously curious young man.

"*Buon giorno*," I said spiritedly.

"*Bon giornu*," Vito said in his Sicilian dialect.

I fidgeted a bit in my chair, so full of questions and wanting to get the conversation going, but I could see that my new mentor moved at a slower, more studied pace. I decided to bide my time and let the older man get his coffee first. So, I was surprised when Vito jumped in with a question himself.

"Why do you want to know about my people?"

I had covered that the day before, about my father growing up in Sicily, the World War, and how the Sicilians had endured that conflict. Before answering, though, I also considered all the new information that Vito had given me, and how the millennia of migrations had brought myriad different cultures to the island.

"I want to study the Sicilians themselves, who they are, how they came to be that way. What influences affected their culture..."

"But just that? Just the island?" Vito asked.

I looked down at my hands, unsure of where this lesson was still to go. Just trying to embrace the whole of Sicily seemed too large a task for my modest abilities.

"Uh, yes," I almost stuttered.

Vito smiled broadly, so much so that the creases in his forehead furrowed deep, and the corners of his mouth spread cheek to cheek. He patted my hand to reassure me.

"Oh, don't worry, my friend. We won't be going beyond my beautiful island. But we can study all of Western Civilization without leaving. Western Civilization began in the Mediterranean region and all the powers that drove development of that civilization came through Sicily – well, they invaded, I guess you would say, at one time or another."

"Sì, I know. That's what we talked about yesterday."

"Of course," Vito said with a look that was almost condescending. "We talked about the Greeks, Germans, Spaniards, and so on, landing on our shores. And you saw some of the art and architecture from each."

With these words, his arthritic hand swept the room, indicating the ceiling, wall frescoes, and bar sculptures I had studied yesterday.

"It's all still here," he said matter-of-factly.

At first, I thought he meant that the artwork was still here from yesterday, but it dawned on me that Vito was saying that all of the conquests, all of the invasions, all of the history, were still here.

I knew that Europeans in general, and Italians specifically, imagined that they lived both in the past and the present at the same time. And in Sicily, an Italian region remote from the mainland, I assumed that this past-present habituation was even more a part of life. I looked down at the cup before me, processing this, but when I looked up Vito was smiling once again at me.

"Sicilians, like Italians, live in both the past and present," I said. "So, when you say 'it's all still here,' you mean that the artifacts of the past are still among us."

Bobbing his head side to side as if to weigh this comment, Vito shrugged his shoulders and replied.

"Yes, well, of course. We still have the old buildings, including Sicanian temples built three thousand years ago. And we have ancient Phoenician cisterns that saved our ancestors from thirst. And we can excavate the foundations of small Roman encampments and dig up carved bone and antler, proof that the people lived and survived here for thousands of years.

"But people from America think that time is like an arrow," he continued, "that it moves ceaselessly in one direction – from the past, through the present, into the unknowable future. But time, and its products, also stands still, a mosaic that has old art, new life, and imagined spirits occupying the same frame.

"To understand us, or any society," Vito said this with a raised finger, "we need to wrap the blanket of the past and the present around us, and recognize that neither exists without the other, and neither can be understood without contemplating the other."

I let out a sigh, and Vito took a sip from his espresso. Raising the cup in the air, he signaled the barista for another.

"Okay, I get your point although I don't fully understand all of it yet. Can you put this in perspective for me? How it relates to Sicily at least?"

Vito remained silent for a moment. As the barista placed a new cup of steaming espresso on the table, he relaxed back into his chair.

"I thought you'd never ask."

Vito's comment hung in the air. He wasn't waiting for me to comment, or lead the discussion, but he held his silence for a moment, leaving me in anticipation of his reply. I wanted to understand how Sicilians, in fact most Italians, could actually live in the past and present simultaneously, and I felt like – with Vito's tutoring – I was on the verge of a revelation. It wasn't just that the people lived among the artifacts of antiquity. It was a time-defying orientation that I had pondered but never fully grasped.

Vito appeared to know that I was mulling all these things, because he held his tongue for a bit. Then, he leaned toward me and began.

"Luca, let me ask you something. Do you remember what we talked about yesterday?"

"Yes, of course," I replied, wondering why he would ask.

"So, that is the past. Do you remember where you were the day before that?"

"In the library," I replied quickly, then added, "studying the history of Sicily."

"Sì, sì, certo," Vito said impatiently, waving off my extra commentary. "But you remember the day."

I nodded.

"What were you like when you were ten years old?"

"Uh, hmmm," I stalled. "I was, I don't know, curious might be the word. A fair student. I liked baseball. What does this have to do with anything?"

Vito ignored my question but plowed ahead.

"That's what you were like, okay. What did you do on your tenth birthday?"

"I have no idea. I can't remember those details."

"But you had a tenth birthday, right?"

Again, I nodded.

"So, the details exist, they're still there, you just don't remember them. What about tomorrow? What is in your future?"

I smiled a bit, noting that Vito didn't ask "what was going *to happen* in the future," but "what *is in my future*." His use of the present tense to ask about the future was telling.

"Tomorrow I'll be here, again, unless I'm run over by a bus."

Vito smiled and looked down at his coffee cup.

"Americans must be very afraid of buses, because they always say 'unless I'm run over by a bus.'"

I, too, smiled, realizing that this was a very American perspective, and wondered how it must sound to a person from another culture.

"No, not really afraid of..."

But Vito waved his hand to suspend my response.

"Let's return to the future," he suggested. "If you're here tomorrow, and you were here yesterday – and today – why do you think the past, present, and future are separate things?"

I paused before answering, squirming a little in my chair, but Vito was not going to give me a chance to respond.

"I'm not talking of the space-time continuum and quantum physics," he offered. I breathed a sigh of relief because I really didn't want to venture into that.

"Let's focus on the existence of time for Sicilians," he said. I noted how he used the word "existence" rather than "passage." Emphasizing the presence of time rather than its phases steered me in the direction of his thought.

"Time exists for us like a picture album. It has photos of our lives, our histories, and present status, and even pages yet to be filled by us with memories of the future. All are knotted together as if in a single instant, to be read, observed, and relived.

"Think of it the way Sicilians do. Life – and time – are cyclical. People are born, live, and die, just as their parents and grandparents did; just as their children and their grandchildren will do. Life arrives, is enjoyed, and passes. There seems to be an unlimited supply of cyclical time. Eastern religions like to say that when God made time, he made lots of it. Your man, Albert Einstein, said that time warps – and is warped by – space, and that the lines of time wrap back around to touch their beginning again.

"Americans see time as slipping away into the unusable past. A Chinese friend of mine said that doesn't really happen. 'Time doesn't recede from us into an unreachable past,' he said. 'It comes back again in a circle, where the same opportunities, the same questions and challenges, and the same risks present themselves once again for our consideration.

"Instead of seeing time as linear, as a straight line proceeding from our own footsteps off into the horizon of the future, cyclical concepts of time teach us that seasons come and go, and we will revisit them again. In this way, time curves back on itself to return us to the times we remember and will live again."

"So, you're saying that Sicilians view time as cyclical?" I asked.

"Well, yes, maybe. At least flexible, something that flows from one phase to another, not something that jumps from one minute to the next, chronicled by the ticking of a clock," Vito replied.

"And how does this affect the narrative of history, or planning for the future?"

Vito chuckled at this.

"As you know, Italians can never forget that beautiful moment they fell in love, nor do they count on the past administration or government to be around for long, nor are they particularly good at planning for future events."

We left it at that. I think back on that conversation a lot, and maybe I discovered something, some nuance of life that I hadn't understood before. But when I reach for the thought, it suddenly – almost mischievously – disappears like a wisp of smoke on a windy day.

7810 B.C.E.

7810 B.C.E.

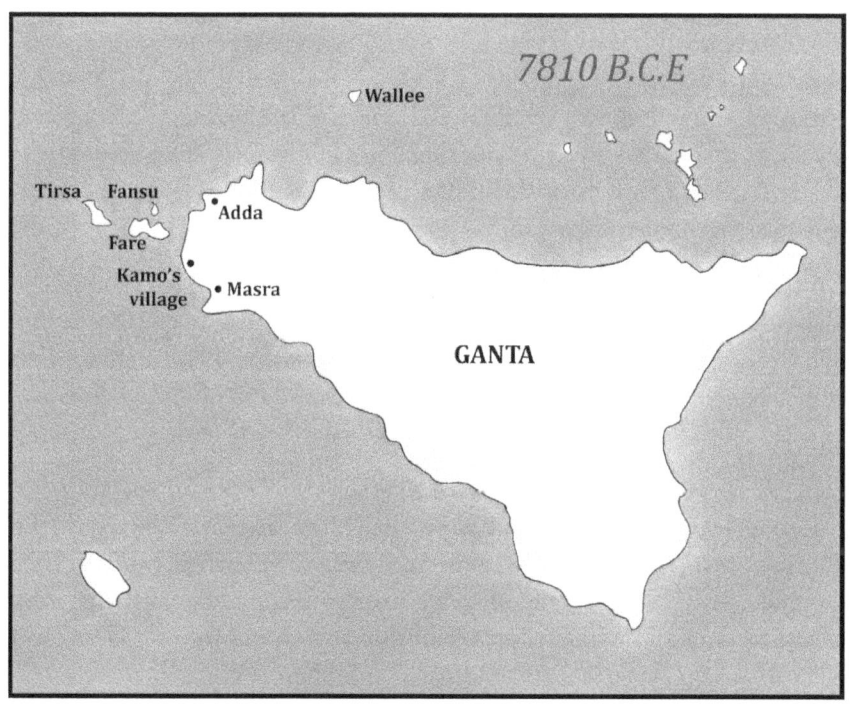

EARLY SETTLERS

Palo quickened his pace. The morning light was bright and clear and he was determined to find the sheep that had escaped his corral. He threaded his way along the trail and stepped carefully among the rocks that jutted out from the slight rise before him. The blue waters of the sea fell below him and the rising sun peered over his shoulder, spreading its light and heat on Ganta.

On the edge of the cliff, he faced the waters where the sun sank in the night to disappear from view before returning the next morning. The sea below him gleamed and glittered, and the rising light behind him emblazoned the sun-drenched coast of the tiny island off in the distance. His ancestors called that place Fansu, but it seemed little more than a mound of earth from his distance.

"No one lived there. No people could live on such a small land," he mumbled while picking his way through the brush and rock tumble. His thoughts reflected a touch of pride in the primordial land his tribe occupied, and an unspoken prayer of thanks that he was on Ganta, and not Fansu.

Palo's sheep had escaped before, especially this one that seemed to venture far from his village often. He resolved to turn that sheep into dinner when he caught it. Palo would happily give up the milk the animal gave each morning in return for not having to chase it down every few days.

He wondered why the sheep always chose this risky rise on the western shore of Ganta. "He's not a goat," Palo thought. "They climb fearlessly, but sheep are supposed to be easy to care for, and not wander away.

"Must be learning more ways to escape," he continued in thought. "As if daring the narrow ridge of this cliff would get him far away from me, and from dinner!"

Palo laughed at the thought. It was him against this stupid animal, and the sheep thought he could outsmart the man.

As he climbed the mountainous rise, Palo slid along a stony precipice and, rounding a curve, spotted an opening in the rock. He dared to look down and saw that from his new position the sea was now very far below him.

"If I fall, I'll be dinner for the fish in the sea, or the wild pigs in the woods below me." He swore an oath to the gods and promised to make the sheep be the victim instead of himself.

Palo reached out with his right hand to grasp a rock that stuck out from the face of the cliff. Getting a firm hold with one hand, he swung his body around and landed on a wider path that rose to the opening in the cliff that was now just a few feet away. This new ribbon of ledge was a bit easier to manage, so he turned to face it and sidestepped along it with ease.

Standing at the mouth of this cave, Palo looked around. Up, down, and to each side, still looking for the sheep, which was not in sight. He turned toward the yawning darkness within the cave. By now the sun had advanced somewhat in the sky and although it threw some little light toward the west-facing mouth of the cave, Palo knew that the inside would still be dim. He ventured forward carefully, watching his steps so that he didn't slip into a hole or turn his foot on a rock.

The floor inside was smooth, so he had little problem making his way. He leaned his left hand on the wall of the cave to keep his bearings. He could see the rocky wall in the dim light but hugging the perimeter of the cave like this made him feel more secure. Palo certainly didn't want to discover suddenly that he was standing in the middle of a large, dark space with no certainty as to direction.

As he slid his hand along the cool surface of the rock, he noticed the irregularity of the wall, with its curves, rolls, and dips, but then he noticed something strange. His fingers delicately brushed over scratches in the wall. He moved his fingers back again, then up and down. Surprised by the discovery, he stood to face the wall and use what little light the sun would allow in the cave to discern what the etchings meant.

As his eyes grew more accustomed to the dim light within, Palo was able to make out more detail in the scratches his fingers had discovered. He could see a primitive figure of a man, apparently lying on his side, with multiple scratch marks drawn across his body. Next to him lay what looked like an animal with a large snout, a pig perhaps, with the same multiple scratch marks across its body.

Palo was familiar with the art of his people in Adda, the village that lay on the stream near this cave. But this cave art was much more primitive. No color was used, as Palo knew the elders of his people could do. Just scratches on a cave wall. He was sure that this was left by people who were much simpler and more primitive than his tribe. The thought made Palo look around the cave, peering into the shadows for the forms of these primitive people.

He had no concept of millennia and had no way to know that the art he had discovered was laid down many years before, because his people had little knowledge of how many generations such a time would require. In his time, the people knew of the generations before them, mostly the parents and grandparents who came before; sometimes of the ancients spoken of around the campfire. But he couldn't perceive of people who existed so long before his period.

Hence, Palo assumed that the person who scratched this picture on the wall of the cave was alive in his time, more primitive perhaps, maybe no more than an animal, not like his own people.

A sound from the darkness within startled Palo and he quickly abandoned the cave for the sunlit air outside. He returned to Adda by reversing his route but with little interest anymore in recovering the missing sheep. Palo was anxious to tell Sari and the people in the village about the primitive, cave-dwelling animals who lived above them and scratched rude pictures on the walls.

He arrived at the village and trudged into the embrace of the cluster he lived in, where he found Sari and their children, Eliu and Sinsa, tending a small fire. It was nearly midday and Sari was preparing their food with the help of the others. Lefu, a man about Palo's height and age, stood to greet him, while Lefu's woman Bele only nodded, pausing briefly while she rolled a rounded stone back and forth on a flat rock, smashing and grinding the grains grown by her hand on the fringes of their settlement. Her little daughter, Tana, was drawing arcs in the dirt with her finger, too young to help Bele in any useful way, but always be her side.

"There are primitive people living above in the cave," Palo told them, pointing with his hand toward the rise in the land and to the cliff that surrounded it.

For a moment, Sari, Lefu, and Bele stopped their activity and sat back to listen to Palo's description.

"They have cut a picture of a man and a pig in the wall of their cave. But it is not like what our elders do, with the red and green colors. It was just scratches in the rock. And I heard a grunt."

"So you ran?" chided Lefu.

"No," Palo huffed, emphasizing the word to prove he wasn't afraid.

"Why are they primitive?" asked Rota, an old woman who had no man but who lived in their cluster.

Palo considered her question but responded again with his description of the simple cave art, reminding his listeners that they only scratched lines in the rock, and had no sense of using the paint they made from the dirt and rocks of the earth.

"Did you see them in the cave?" asked Opra.

"No, but I heard a grunt, so I left. They are animals, not suited for us."

"Well, if they're animals," said Femo, Opra's man, "we should hunt them."

The people around the campfire give Femo an odd look. They knew that there were animals that they hunted for food, but any animal that could carve pictures in the wall of a cave might not be animal enough for them to eat.

In the moment of reflection, Palo looked up and saw the sheep that he had hunted had returned to the corral.

"Where has that animal been?" he asked with irritation evident in his voice.

"It wandered off," his young son Eliu replied, "then came back."

Palo stomped off in the direction of the corral, intent on carrying out his earlier oath to turn the sheep into dinner that night.

———

True to his promise, Palo slaughtered the sheep and the cluster ate well that night. Wild animals were the most common source of meat in the tribe – a feral deer wasn't much use to farming – but sheep and goats were kept for the milk and they, along with the pigs, were only killed for eating when they could be replaced by other animals.

So, herds of deer, horse, and elk were left to roam the countryside, keeping mostly away from the seashore but often huddled near the streambeds and river's edge. They traveled in packs and generally did not fear the humans who occupied the same untamed space between villages; still, the animals kept their distance.

When trying to catch these larger animals, the people learned to find a clearing in the trees first. The underbrush between the trees gave the hunters some cover while the deer or elk grazed in the open field and killing the beast with a well-thrown spear or series of arrows would be easier. Over time, the people decided to create these spots for grazing to draw the animals to their lair. They learned that clearings burned out by a lightning strike were perfect for their purposes, so they cut down small saplings, piled them up, and started their own fires a short distance from their settlements to clear the area and create a space to attract these large animals. The distance was enough to avoid entanglement with their village, but close enough to make the new grazing field a natural corral for hunting.

Still, bringing down a large animal and slaughtering it for meat posed other challenges. Cooking such a large beast required a very large earthen oven and digging a hole for the enterprise would take several people two long days with still-primitive spades. But deer, elk and bison-like cows made tasty eating, so they appeared on the menu for special occasions, usually when the size of the guest list was large enough – beyond the count of a single family and even a single cluster – to consume the meat and innards without leaving any to waste.

Meat from smaller animals, including rabbit, hedgehog, field mice, and the corralled pigs and sheep was the sustenance cooked for families and clusters. Small creatures could be roasted in smaller, dugout ovens and were consumed when caught, but many meals went by without meat, as the people subsisted mainly on the vegetables that they now farmed, the berries and wild grain they harvested from the surrounding area, and the fish pulled from the sea in nets or at the end of a spear-point.

And then there were the wolves. These scavengers already populated the hills and wooded areas of the island, and they helped themselves to any carrion not dispatched by the people. Their own broods increased slowly, their population rising with the leftovers and offal left by the people but held in check by the limits on the same. So wolves developed an intimate relationship with the people, a symbiotic association that, initially, resembled more a parasitic connection than one of mutual dependence.

Over time, wolves became so tamed to human presence that they would approach the village and occasionally be rewarded by people who tossed unused meat their way. Centuries passed, but this budding relationship evolved from a parasitic one to a mutually accepted association. The hunters in the tribe sometimes turned the tables on a local pack of wolves. When the pack brought down another wild animal for food, the hunters would drive the wolves away with spears and clubs, then poach their fallen prey.

The wolves expected to be rewarded for the theft of their dinner, so the hunters left enough meat for the first predators to be sated. In that way, the humans reduced the possibility of being attacked by the ravenous creatures. Over time, the relationship developed and the wolves would return again to the village looking for handouts and building their connection with the people.

This kill, feed, and steal routine created a bond between the two types of animals, and each discovered that they could bring down an animal that might feed both. The humans tossed unwanted waste to the wolves – sometimes even desirable meat to attract them – and the wolves knew that their catch would occasionally end up in the humans' fire pit.

More time went by and the wolves that were best adapted to human interaction remained closer to the village. The human hunters no longer chased them away, and so the wolves became a common sight in the cluster. Some wolves didn't adapt to this association, still programmed internally to resist the scent of human beings and in fear of the people's height and power. But the wolves who were genetically less fearful, and perhaps those that had been less punished and more rewarded by the relationship with the people, began a millennia-old relationship with humans.

Over time, the wolves and what became more like modern-day dogs evolved into different types of animals, although their outward appearance remained largely the same. The humans – and their furry companions – were well aware of the difference between wolves and dogs, but from that time onward, they lived, hunted, and slept together.

"We fish today," Lefu told Bele, but the words were meant for all to hear. Palo and Lefu fished together so they could handle the net they had woven when its belly was filled with the catch. Femo, from the next cluster, was too old to pull the net in but he would be there to gut and clean the fish when they brought the harvest back to the village. His woman, Opra, had already gathered herbs from the tree stand nearby, and pulled up little bulbs of allu – what we now know as garlic – they would use to enhance the flavors of the fish while it cooked.

Palo liked to fish because the sea teamed with food and he wanted to keep his people happy. And perhaps the catch that day would be enough to dry some for later eating and reduce the need to hunt until another day.

Rota sat at the edge of the circle. Her cloak was dyed the color of dusty rose from soaking in water and red ochre, and she wore an impressive string of periwinkle shells around her neck. She listened to the people talk but offered few comments, a habit she had developed in her many years in this tribe and, in recent times, as their shaman. Her right hand wielded a tree branch that bent like an inverted "L" and she tapped the protruding head lightly on the ground in front her. It was a rhythmic drumming and, when Palo noticed that Rota's eyes were closed, he concluded that the elder was talking to the gods.

"We stay here and..." but Sari's words were cut short by some movement she saw at the edge of the camp. At this early hour, no one would be about, so the activity outside their close circle didn't seem right.

A tall man appeared from behind a tree, his twisted and curly beard covering most of his face and his dense head of hair drooping below his eyebrows. Beside him appeared two other men, and behind them two shorter women. As the group unfolded before the villagers, many young children came into view. In all, there appeared from the trees a small tribe that, in number, exceeded the villagers' own cluster, and maybe equaled the size of the entire village population itself.

Palo and Lefu stood and Femo slipped into his hut to retrieve hunting spears. Joining the other men and the adult women who had now stood in opposition to the new arrivals, Femo, Palo, and Lefu brandished these weapons in defense of what, they did not know.

There were small villages that inhabited this western coastline of Sicily and, if they had traveled farther, the people assumed they would discover more and more. But the camps were settled and, despite occasional interactions during hunting forays or on the shoals of the sea – sometimes to trade goods and food – the people of each village seldom approached the other settlements. So, the sudden appearance of an entire tribe was unusual, and threatening.

The tall man in the center of the visiting tribe spoke, but his words were not understood by Palo and his people. Interactions between the various villages allowed some familiarity with the words of each, especially on essential matters like food, animals, and action. But the more distant the words sounded the more distant seemed their origins. Palo, Sari, and their assembled friends were quick to assume that these new people were from far away, and brought a language – and, more importantly, rules and behavior – that were foreign to their own.

The leader of the arriving pack, pointed his right index finger at his chest and, in a soft voice, said "Kamo." Then, he immediately sat down cross-legged and with his outstretched arm waving downward, instructed his other people to do the same.

The new people had stayed a short distance from the encampment, and this decision plus the action for all of them to sit, dispelled the element of tension and fear in the encounter. Kamo was showing that he wanted to meet the villagers and communicate with them, but they weren't trying to force themselves on the people.

Palo, Lefu, and Sari approached the new people but stopped short of the seated tribe. Kamo first bowed his head and then rose, leaving all of his fellows seated on the ground. Without words, he was clearly intending a non-aggressive intent.

Nodding once more, he stepped forward and spoke. Some of the words were understandable, but his hand gestures and facial expressions added much to the communication. He paused and waited for Palo, Lefu, or Sari to speak, but they did not do so initially; rather, they bent toward each other and expressed themselves in private conservation. When they stepped back from their huddle, they saw that a young girl had risen and taken a position at Kamo's side. Pointing toward her own chest, she said, "Lilia."

The young girl then spoke in a language that Palo and his friends could understand, using all of their words and translating back to Kamo. She explained, with excited hand gestures, that they had come from Masra, their village, which had been burned out by a great fire, one that destroyed their homes and killed their animals. Kamo watched Lilia as she spoke, with a subtle glow of pride etched across his face. Sari took note of this, a subtlety that the men with her might not have picked up on, and she concluded that Lilia was Kamo's daughter.

Kamo then spoke up, using words only distantly recognizable by the villagers, but he was accenting Lilia's speech with hand movements to suggest a great conflagration, and the urgency with which the people had fled their village to avoid being caught up in the fire. Kamo then voiced animal cries, and covered his head with his hands as Lilia explained that the fire swept through the trees and blazed along the grasses of the pasture.

"How do you know our words?" Sari asked her, but Lilia only looked at the ground. As the color darkened her cheeks, a woman who must have been her mother came to shield her. Kamo's eyes flared for a second, but Lilia stretched out her arm to prevent him from reacting. She explained that she had become lost one summer ago and was found by another tribe. It was this tribe who spoke these words and she had learned to speak in their language.

"Kamo is angry," she said, "but the people were good to me. He said they took me, but I was lost. When the people brought me back to my tribe, Kamo ran at them with a spear, so they left before they had to fight.

"They didn't harm me, but I was lost," she continued, "and...Kamo...he worried." With that Lilia took Kamo's hand and squeezed it.

Another woman appeared and spoke in a way that Palo and the others could understand. Pointing to herself, she said "Tira," adding that she spent much time with Lilia and learned these words too.

Through their translators, Kamo told the villagers about their experiences. Lilia and Tira explained slowly that they lived far away, pointing to the south and along the coastline, and Kamo swept his arm in a wide arc to suggest a great distance. He said they had lived close to the sea for a while but continued walking until they had reached this place.

Kamo then lifted an arrow from a pack at his side, an action that caused Palo and Lefu to assume a stance ready for combat, but Lilia intervened. Lifting one hand in supplication to them and putting her other hand on her father's wrist, she said, "No, no fight. He tells story."

When Palo and Lefu relaxed, Kamo slowly drew the arrow the rest of the way out of its scabbard and gave little thrusting motions toward the ground. Tira explained that after the fire, there were few animals left, and they didn't know how to fish. So Kamo was saying that they had to rely on little mice, groundhogs, and shrews for food. He drew his shoulders up and stood firmly to show that he was responsible and was the leader of this tribe, but the shadow of sadness that fell over his eyes left little doubt that he was ashamed of what had happened.

For a few moments, all was silent. Then, without waiting for the men to speak, Sari stepped toward Lilia and waved her arm toward her, and to the seated visitors around Kamo and Lilia. They all rose, many men and women and their little children, and walked toward Sari's signal.

"They come to our village," Sari said to Kamo, and offered her hand palm up as an invitation. Lilia and Tira smiled in recognition of the invitation and the salvation it might represent for their people, and the entire crowd trudged back to Adda and to the people's village.

Food for people of all tribes had a social context. Beyond survival and near-starvation, they respected the natural resources and each other, knowing that co-existence was essential to life in their times. Meals were served and shared with both pride and regard for their circumstances and each other, not just superficially as a "breaking of bread" but as a celebration of shared experience. Such occasions were a more powerful reconciliation than sharing a peace pipe or offering a broken sword, because sharing food was not only giving to the needy but sacrificing at the expense of one's own.

The event, fair to call it a celebration, included both ceremonial actions and reverence for the gods that brought them air, water, and animals. Through so many generations, the people of the island believed that the gods fought over their heads, and that the humans were only accidental witnesses – and sometimes victims – to conflicts that dominated the earth and heavens. But in time, a feeling of being apart from the celestial clashes evolved and the people came to believe that the gods paid attention to them too. And maybe, just maybe, all the volcanic eruptions, lightning strikes, fearful storms and floods were the gods communicating not among themselves, but to the people who dotted the coastline of this great land.

This realization was not totally comforting since it suggested that their own behavior could bring on the wrath of the gods of nature. Prayers of supplication were primitive and usually involved bowed heads and raised hands, as if in surrender. Food became the best way the people imagined they could communicate with the gods, so they adopted practices of sacrificing the flesh of some animals at the start of each meal.

It was an extension of the communal meal, but instead of including just the people in the village, it invited the gods to witness and approve.

This was especially required when the meal was a true celebration, as this day when the people of Adda were visited by those fleeing Masra and in search of safety.

As the glare of the sun sank toward the sea and the air cooled, the villagers sat in large circles with the people who had come from so far away. Lilia and Tira continued to translate but because the languages were not very different, it wasn't long before many of the villagers and the visitors could understand small bits of the conversation without the translators' assistance.

Those from Masra told of the long trek they had made along this coastline of the island, and how they had sensed the people of Adda before approaching them.

"How long?" Palo asked.

Kamo held up three fingers and, with Lilia's explanation of the sunrise and sunset, translated that into days.

"But you had no food?" Lefu asked.

Kamo licked his lips, and Tira nodded.

The pits had been dug for the feast, faster than usual with the help of the visitors. A larger pit was needed since a cow would be required to feed all including the newcomers. The fires were burning before the sunset and the women of Adda were bringing leafy greens, knotty loaves of unbaked dough, and small legumes to the circle, while the men gathered stones to fill the excavated pit that would roast the animal.

Such roasting normally would take all day, but these people were hungry so the animal was butchered into smaller hunks of meat, allowing them to cook through in less time. This required the work of a sharpened stone axe since the cutting edges they used for knifes would not cut through the sinew and bone to separate the parts of the cow. For that, Femu produced a tool he had made from a sharpened rock that he tied with long stretches of vine to the end of a hardy tree branch. Femu was proud of his tool, but it was too heavy for him to master in such a job, so he turned it over to Lefu to swing at the carcass of the cow.

Sari and Bele brought out a leather sack and, from it, produced handfuls of dried and barely hardened fat from animals slaughtered for earlier meals. They kept the fat that had been rendered by the fire and stored it in the skin of the animal for later use in softening the tough textures of raw vegetables. They applied the fat to small bowls and turned raw beans, lentils, and another primitive legume called yero, or bitter vetch, into it. Turning the ingredients with their bare hands, the women produced an oily batch of these vegetables to prepare them for baking over the fire in an earthen pot.

Opra molded the bread dough with her hands and flattened and shaped it into rough circles in preparation for the hot stones it would be laid upon. She extended her hand over a rock positioned near the center of the fire, sensed that it was hot enough, and patted her dough balls onto it. Tira helped, and another woman of the visitors joined in, to make the work go faster.

Sinsa, Palo and Sari's daughter, used a crude cutting edge flaked from chert to saw some raw tubers into manageable hunks while water was set to boil on the little fire at her feet. Using a leather sack filled with water, she dropped in some of the red-hot rocks from the edges of the fire and brought the water to a boil. Then she threw the tuber bits into the water and waited till they were soft enough to eat.

With the women busy at their tasks, the men from Adda and Masra worked together to render the cow into chunks of meat that could be roasted quickly in the large pit fire that was now hot enough to use. First, they rolled the large rocks that had been gathered around the perimeter of the fire pit into the depths of this oven, listening with pleasure as the moisture in the rocks hissed when they made contact with the bright red embers down below. Over the rocks, they put more wood so that it would lick up the flames and grow the fire underneath, heating the rocks on all sides to prepare the pit to serve as a proper oven.

While they waited for the oven stones to burn bright red, the men collected more branches and broad leaves of the bushes around the village. These they piled up at the edges of the pit for now, then returned to tending the fire and encouraging it to glow brightly. When they were satisfied that the rocks were ready to cook the meat, the men returned to the butchering site and carried the parts of the cow toward the pit, lowering each along the burning branches and glowing rocks in a long line from one end of the earthen oven to the other. When all the meat had been placed in the pit, they covered it the branches collected by the side, laid the leaves of the bushes on top, and spread more dirt and wet sand over it all to seal in the heat.

The sunlight was dying about the time that Rota appeared. Once again, she wore the periwinkle necklace and the rose-colored cloak, but she had turned her face the same color by smearing wetted red ochre on her cheeks, forehead, and bridge of her nose. She wore a wolf skin over her shoulders, the eyeless head of the creature straddling Rota's own head, and the sight of her made the dogs in the camp whimper.

Rota walked with exaggerated arm movements, swinging the wooden talisman that she carried as her scepter, and then she struck it in the middle of the fire.Bright red and orange sparks sprang into the air and Rota accompanied the fireworks with mumbled words too subtle for anyone to understand.

Kamo and his tribe watched in silence but seemed to understand the basics of this ritual. His woman, Lotu, even bobbed her head in time with Rota's cadence, perhaps in recognition of the actions she witnessed, but she didn't dare to interrupt the old woman of the village. When she was satisfied that the feast had been properly consecrated, Rota look heavenward, raised her scepter in one last salute, and plopped down next to Bele near the fire. Bele and Sari looked at each other and smiled. Something about the necessity of the ritual amused them, but they didn't dare laugh out loud, fearing the unpredictable anger of the gods.

The tubers boiled while the vegetables simmered in another crock on the fire. When the bread had risen and turned a blackish-brown, it was removed from the rocks and served with the other food, a short opening to the meal while the meat continued to sizzle and pop on the rocks below the earthen oven top.

———

The people of Adda and Masra sat together enjoying the meal, and Kamo made sure that his people, although ravenous with near starvation, ate quietly and with patience. It would have been an insult to the people of this village if the newcomers tore into the meal without respect.

Kamo continued to tell the stories of his people, the fire, and how they had fled Masra, pointing his hand toward the south as if to indicate their origins. Since they said they were not skilled at fishing, Palo and the others assumed that Masra was not near the great sea. The visitors must have lived on a waterway since rivers, streams, and ocean shores were the only places where people had enough access to water and garden of weeds and thrush to survive. Plus, animals for hunting also gathered where there was water, so Masra must have been on a river.

"You have a new home," Bele told them. She knew that she was extending an offer that would have an impact on the entire village, but she also knew that the visitors couldn't continue to migrate.

"We are settled here," added old Femo, who had seen may summers and winters pass in this village. "It is good, and there are fish and animals to hunt."

Kamo surveyed the village enclosure, taking in the corral of animals and the large patch of earth devoted to growing grain and simple vegetables. He was impressed with the settlement but worried that his people would strain the resources and become unwelcome.

"We thank you," he said with little assistance from Lilia's translating. "But it is a full village," he added, sweeping his arm to indicate all the shelters and small fires burning in the clusters.

"And you make a bigger village," Lefu assured him. "We will work together."

And so an agreement was struck. Kamo's tribe would join the people of Adda.

Lotu, Kamo's woman, stood and stepped back from the circle and retrieved something from her pack. She handed it to Kamo and then sat back down by the fire.

Kamo held the object in the palm of his hand and looked toward Rota, the shaman. His message was too complicated for his little skill in the villagers' language, so he turned to Lilia.

"This is our god," Lilia said, as Kamo lifted his arm and showed the carved wooden object to those at the circle. "She is Earth, our home, and our maker. She wanted the people, so she made them, and she protects us against the fire in the sky."

Kamo swept his arm toward Rota and, gripping the carving in his hand, he turned it over, opening his fingers to let the object fall into Rota's outstretched hand. The old woman took the thing and examined it. It was clearly carved to look like a woman, with bulging breasts and belly, but the features of the face were undistinguished, as if the god's expression was less important than the features of fertility.

Rota then smiled and swept her arm to show everyone. The people of Adda also worshipped gods, one very like this but also another god that was the sea. Earth and sea were the dominant forces in their existence and the people from both Adda and Masra wished to have their gods provide the best of each, including animals, plants, and fish; but also to protect them from each, including the "fire in the sky" and the trembling earth below.

The people from Masra slept well that night under a clear sky and the twinkling light of the stars. It was the first night in some time that their bellies were full, so sleep came quickly. They spread their hides on the ground in small clusters, ten in all to handle the whole population of their tribe and located just outside the village that had welcomed them. The perimeter of their encampment bordered on the large earthen oven that had held the meat that sated their palates earlier, and the residual heat of the oven – though not needed for warmth on this night – was welcome as a sign of comfort and security.

Palo and Kamo had talked of the work that faced them in the morning, of the need to build new shelters and arrange new clusters for the people from Masra. Palo refrained from calling them visitors anymore since the Masrians had become a part of Adda. The planned work was talked about and arranged and would start when the sun shown on the low sky. And with that, Kamo smiled for the first time since their meeting. Nodding to his host, Kamo showed his thanks for helping him save his tribe from isolation and possible death.

Papia, Tira's man, was the first to awaken in the morning. He sat up and looked around his tribesmen bunched together in the early mist, still asleep. He breathed a long sigh of contentment, rotating his head to see the entire circle of people, and nodded his head in silent approval of their newfound situation. Stretching his arms toward the sky, Papia tried to shake off the haze of sleep, then he stood and walked toward Kamo.

The other man was already awake, eyes open, when Papia approached. Kamo smiled back at his friend as they both enjoyed the pleasure of finding shelter and another tribe to live with. Altogether now, the people of Adda and Masra were twice the size of either village alone, and there would be many families and many clusters, and the new Adda would become a bigger village than either tribe had ever seen. Maybe this would provide more security and, hopefully, fend off some natural instincts for competition and conflict.

Palo and Lefu appeared at the fringes of this encampment and waved to Papia who was still standing over a seated Kamo. Kamo turned toward the men and waved to greet them, and then stood so he and Papia could go in their direction. It was morning and the work planned the night before would consume much of their day, and it needed to begin.

Tira woke to see the men talking together, so she rose quickly to join them. Language difficulties had been somewhat ironed out the evening before, but she wanted to help if help was required. When she joined the foursome, Palo and Lefu nodded to her, a gesture common to both tribes as a nonverbal sign of greeting.

Tira, now joined by Lotu, her mother, and Lilia led the men through the village and talked about how they would manage to incorporate the new tribe into Adda.

At each stop along the route, whether it was the vegetable farm, the animal pen, or the open warehouse of chopped wood and other natural resources, the men and women from each tribe discussed the methods they used to get the most of these materials. In some cases, the people of Adda were more advanced; in other cases the technologies from Masra sounded more productive. In this fusing of cultures and practices, the people were able to quickly incorporate new ideas and innovative ways of maximizing their results.

The survey of Adda's primitive infrastructure took all day, and with the continued conversation, the language gaps were overcome and by evening the two tribes could easily communicate. The result was not one language over the other, but an amalgamation of the two, with words chosen from each vocabulary that best fit the noun or verb intended. In a short day's time, a linguistic legacy that the people thought stretched back to the beginning of time was reshaped by the appearance of the migrating tribe, and those from Adda and Masra noticed the compromise and appreciated it.

————

When morning came, the women gathered to tour the farm plots around the village.

Between the groves of birch and willow trees, there were copious outcroppings of herbs, fennel, and onion grass. Bele showed Lotu and Tira which herbs they used the most, some with tangy flavors that reminded her of the sea water, some with the fragrance of mint and lemon.

Opra pulled at a tall green weed and ripped a round white bulb from the ground. Lilia, who had come along, immediately recognized it.

"*Cheeka*," she said, then realizing that she had used the Masrian word, switched to the language of Adda. "*Gira*," she added, and the women nodded and formed a common understanding of the two words for this ancient bulb that had the hardiness of a spring onion but the fragrance of a modern garlic clove.

They worked their way through the trees and between the plots of planted vegetables and herbs, pointing things out along the way and trading words for their meaning. Some of the words were the same and the women were surprised. They had no settled concept for the cultural effects of migration and couldn't piece together the possibility that earlier tribes had inhabited these lands and might have already moved past and among each other, trading goods and ideas as well as vocabulary. To these women, it seemed more likely that words came before them, possibly from the gods who ruled the entire world, and so some words would proceed uncorrupted by tribal banter through the ages.

Bele guided them out of this farmland and into another stand of trees, juniper and aspen in this case. At the base of the trees, a particular mossy plant was clustered and gave off an earthy, savory aroma. Tira pulled some and held it close to her nose, but the scent went away. The Addian women laughed a bit at this and pointed to the ground.

"The smell is from these," said Sari, indicating the mushrooms at the roots of the tree. She pulled one and offered it to Tira, who immediately realized what Sari meant. Tira could tell that the aromas that had drawn her attention were from the plants, not the soil that she sniffed.

"But these are best," continued Sari, as she used a stick to scrape at the surface of the ground. After a few seconds, she unearthed an ugly, gnarled hunk of what looked like dirt. It was the size of her thumb, and when she put it below Tira's nose, the woman pulled back at first, then sniffed again. It was pungent smell that combined thoughts of earth, pig dung, and tree bark, but it had a beautiful fragrance that Tira had never encountered. Surprised by the strong smell, Tira offered the globule to the others and they, too, remarked at its rich odor.

They proceeded to another plot of farmed land, this one with cultivated emmer wheat and barley, and small bushes that held seed pods of lentils and peas. Growing nearby were wavy branches of *yero*, a legume, common to their meals because it could be boiled down to provide nourishment.

When they emerged from these plots of farmland, Opra guided the women toward one of her favorite spots. They reached a tall tree at the outskirts of a small woods, and Opra pointed toward a cavity in the trunk that was just about her height above the ground. Moving closer, the women could hear a buzzing sound that grew in intensity as they approached. Once within arms' length, Tira and Lotu saw little bees flying in and out of the cavity and jumped back. They were familiar with this insect and knew it offered nothing but painful stings and, sometimes, burning postules on the skin that could develop into serious problems for the person affected.

The women watched as Opra took a long stick, about as long as she was tall, and stuck the point of it into the cavity. The length of the probe allowed her to remain at a distance from the hive while she explored its depths. At first, the intrusion didn't attract much attention from the bees until Opra struck the other end with a rock. The action drove the spear into the hole with a thud and dozens of bees flew out. Because the women were standing more than two armlengths away, the bees buzzed around their tree but never got close to the women.

Opra repositioned the stick and struck again, with the same result. She then peered more carefully into the cavity, and moved the stick again, striking the spear once more and dislodging a chunk of glistening, waxy substance that fell from the tree and onto the ground. Opra then walked a few feet away to pick up a leather bucket that was filled with water and poured it over the chunk of bees' wax lying at their feet. The water drove most of the bees away and drowned the rest. Now, with little conflict and a much-reduced chance of being stung, Opra picked up the chunk, brushed off the dazed bees that crawled across its surface, and dumped it into the bucket that she had just emptied.

With a look of proud conquest, Opra turned toward the village where she would reward her people with a catch of honey to be used in their cooking that day.

Sari, Bele, Tira, and Lotu watched in amusement as the old shaman walked away. The Addian women were pleased at their friend's keen abilities; the Masrian women were still a bit surprised but impressed.

———

When the women had completed their tour of the farmland and returned to harvest some grain and foodstuffs from the plants they had tended. On their way, the Addian women walked through the pig corral and pushed piles of dung onto the broad leaves they carried with them. The dung was then spread on the ground around their plants, a practice that the villagers had used from before memory, and which they knew made the plants grow tall and strong.

Lotu and Tira were very familiar with this and they, too, had used pig droppings to grow their plants. As a tribe that had less contact with the sea, the Masrians were mostly dependent on the cultivation of the soil, so their agricultural habits had been developed for a long time.

They returned to the cluster and laid out all the food and ingredients they had gathered. It included wild herbs as well as some from the patches they grew themselves; peas and other legumes, stalks of barley, shiny white bulbs of fennel and *gira*, and buckets of berries picked from the trees and bushes around the village. There were nuts that had been harvested the day before, spread on a long shelf of granite that protruded from the ground and left there in the sun to dry, and of course Opra's prized honey catch.

She had returned to the village before the other women and started right into the preparation. She suffered a few stings while she proceeded to finish off the bees by crushing them between her fingers. Then she used a stiff reed to dig into the cells of the comb and spoon out the honey in precious little portions. Instead of using a hardened clay pot which would impart a sandy flavor to the fragile flavors of the honey, Opra poured each little globe of honey into a small weathered leather pouch. Over a period of an hour she had harvested all of the treasure, an amount about equal to a drinking cup, but this special product could be spread sparingly and would be treasured by all.

The other women were preparing the things they gathered, including spreading some of the grain to dry and shucking the stalks from other vegetables to make them ready for cooking. While that was going on, a woman from another cluster appeared lugging a heavy earthen bucket which she delivered to Bele and Sari. The two women knew what it was, thanked their visitor, and put their fingers into the bucket to taste it.

The liquid within smelled of dough and grain, and its distinctive aromas were easy for them to recognize. It was a brewed concoction that was started from old bread and grain and allowed to stew over two nights in the back of the shelter they had built for the gods. The result was a lightly alcoholic drink that tasted good and, if enough was consumed, lightened their spirits. There would not be enough in this bucket for anyone to become intoxicated, unless he refused to share it, but there would be enough to pass around among the Addians and the Masrians to celebrate their new village that night.

Sinsa, the young daughter of Palo and Sari, was assigned the task of salt farming. The Addians had been on the coast of the great sea for time before memory and they had learned not only how to salt farm but also learned how to use it to its potential. The product could be used to flavor the foods but also to preserve them, especially the meat and fish that would spoil faster than the vegetables. Through many generations of people, they had come to know that a dried and salted fish could be kept through the cold months until fishing was viable again, and that salted beef or pork would enhance its ability to cook and, if dried, could be hung from the roofs of shelters and be consumed as needed.

Salt's affect on preserving fish came about naturally, and unexpectedly. The Addians had long fished the seas so they were accustomed to sewing nets for the little sea creatures that squirmed through the shallows. They knew how to whittle a deer's antlers into harpoon-shaped spears, and how to bait a hook made of carved bone or stone to catch larger fish. They built underwater corrals by stacking rocks and branches under the water to herd schools of fish that they could then scoop out of the trap.

They also discovered that when fish were left on the rocks outside the water, they dried out and were left covered in a thin layer of salt. Wasting food was not a good survival strategy, so these fish were retrieved and taken back to the village. Soon, they discovered that the dried fish could be kept for weeks or months, and that it had a tangier taste than the fresh caught fish that they cooked over the evening fire.

They also discovered that the rocks near the water were also covered with the same thin layer of salt. It was only certain ones – those high enough above the water level that they would remain dry for hours without assault when the waves receded, rocks that would only be made wet by the rising tide. So there were times of the day that the salt could be harvested by scraping it from these rocks, and that is what Sinsa set out to do that day.

The Addians and Masrians worked through the day, some digging foundations for the new shelters while others collected and shaped a new batch of bricks, some gathering foodstuffs to prepare the nightly meal, and others performing the routine tasks of village life. When most of the labor had been accomplished and the people gathered in their clusters for the evening meal, all contributed something. And Opra returned once again to bless the food and the health of the people.

She approached as she did the night before, with exaggerated arm movements and swinging the bent stick that was her staff. When she entered the circle of people around the fire, she raised the scepter above her head then plunged it into the embers, producing an eruption of flame and glowing ash that reminded the people of the volcanic fires they witnessed from time to time. Since the Addians had long believed the volcanoes were gods and that they spewed fire when the gods were communicating, Opra was producing the Addians' eruption as a signal to the gods.

She then took the uncooked leg of a rabbit slain for the night's repast and tossed it into the fire. It was a gift to the gods, not an addition to their own meal, and she hoped this offering would keep the gods' eruptions silenced for another day.

But when Opra sat down, she added another thing to the ritual. She reached for the bucket of beer that the people had produced that morning and dipped her fingers into it. Licking her fingers, Opra pronounced it good, but before passing the bucket around the circle, she took a small earthen cup and filled it for herself. Other buckets of the brew were brought into the circle and passed around, so that everyone could have a cup of the elixir.

Kamo and the Masrians had never had beer and wondered where this odorous thing came from.

"Bread," said Bele, pointing to the loaf of bread in her lap.

"But..." Kamo began, the confusion written on his face.

"We soak old bread in water and leave it," Bele explained. "After..." and to describe the days, she held up one, then a second, then a third, and finally a fourth finger, "...this many suns we drink it."

Kamo tasted the beer and smiled broadly, then passed it around to Lotu, who then shared it with the other Masrians sitting with them.

The food filled their stomachs and the beer sated their thirst, but Kamo had not even noticed the effect the liquor had on him until Opra stood near the end of the meal and raised her staff to call upon the gods. Kamo raised his head to watch her and he felt dizzy with the movement.

"Yes," Palo said, laughing at Kamo's reaction. "Beer is good, but too much is bad."

———

One morning, Palo awoke to the sound of rocks smacking together. He could see through the slight opening in his shelter that it was still dark outside, and he wondered who was up and what they were doing. His instincts turned toward a threat, although he had no reason to suspect that these slight sounds would demonstrate a true danger to his people. Still, he couldn't sleep and he wanted to know what was going on.

Palo cast off the light leather hide that covered him and emerged from his shelter, stretching and yawning to complete the process of waking up. He heard the chipping sounds again and looked in their direction. There was only a sliver of a moon, and in the faint light it was hard for him to see more than the area of his own cluster. Judging by the sounds, though, he concluded that they were coming from the edge of his circle of huts, toward where the Masrians slept who had not yet taken residence in the clutch of new stone shelters they were building.

He knew that Kamo let the others sleep inside the new buildings first, insisting that he remain out in the open at night until his people were settled and comfortable, and Palo thought he could see the hulking figure of his new friend squatting down just a few feet away. He walked in that direction and recognized Kamo sitting back on his haunches, striking a sharp thin rock on another, large flat rock.

"It's still dark," Palo said.

"Yes, it is, but I want to finish this before the sun is here," replied Kamo.

"What are you making?"

"A way to know when the seasons come, and when the sun goes overhead."

The Addians already had such a tool, thought Palo as he studied Kamo's design.

"We have it," he said simply, pointing in the direction of the rocky outcropping near the village.

Kamo was reluctant to cease working on his project, but understood that he should respect Palo's suggestion, so he put down the hammer rock and thin blade and rose to his feet.

Palo guided Kamo to the foot of the rocky rise. They stopped at a ledge that sloped upward at a slight angle, and Kamo could see that there was a straight, bare sapling planted purposely in the front of the rock. He looked back over his shoulder and realized that this device faced the rising sun and the sapling would cast a shadow on the inclined rock in front of him. He could see that the shadow would track the phases of the day. But he also knew that this shadow would be different with every season, and it would not track the seasons in the way that the Masrian device could.

"I see," he said with deference to Palo. He studied the device with a great degree of seriousness, stepping around the stick and raising his arm to indicate the angle of the sun. Palo was pleased with Kamo's interest in their creation, and he didn't notice that his friend's interest was a respectful act born in friendship.

After an appropriate time, Kamo asked Palo to return to his project so that he could further describe it to him.

"This makes the shadow," Kamo began, putting his index finger on a slender rock, a tall tapered pointer that stood vertically in the middle of the large flat rock that lay on the ground. He swept his hand left and right to simulate the movement of the shadow that the sun's arc would create.

"This day, the sun is very high and the air is warm. Today, I will put marks in this stone," Kamo continued, pointing to the rock. "Beginning with the sun," he added, pointing in the direction that the sun would first appear, "and continuing until the sun is there," he concluded by pointing to the opposite side of the island.

"Our time is the same," Palo said, a bit confused, but still listening. The Addian clock had no marks to indicate moments in the sun's path except a single scratch on the inclined surface to show the halfway mark. The Addians counted on the shadow as being in one quadrant or the other to suggest a general period of the day.

"When the sun is low in the sky," Kamo continued, "and when the air is very cold, "I will come back and put more marks in this stone." With that, he pointed once again to the flat rock. Palo knew the arc of the sun varied with the warm and cold weather but didn't have an accurate way of understanding it.

While they were talking, the sun was rising and it cast a steady light in their direction. Kamo looked toward it, then studied the shadow that the sun laid on his device. The tall pointer in the middle remained in place, but a long dark streak grew across the surface of the rock. Kamo moved into position, and put a smudge of red ochre on the stone. It wasn't until then that Palo noticed, in the light, that Kamo had an entire tool kit assembled around him, so he sat down on the ground to watch his friend work.

Kamo rubbed the ochre smudge in a little circle, then picked up a thin rock and his hammer stone. He struck the rock and scratched the surface in the middle of the red circle, then struck again to deepen the scratch. When he was satisfied with his effort, he leaned to the side and drew a little pebble from a pile by his feet. He nestled the pebble in the middle of this scratch while the shadow moved slowly beyond that point.

Then Kamo sat and had the time to explain more of his motives to Palo.

"The red paint and scratch keep the mark, but the pebble makes it easier to see. If the pebble falls off, we put another one there.

"This is the new sun on this day, just as it comes up to greet us," Kamo said, pointing to the pebble that represented the sunrise. "Later, we will make other marks and put pebbles in those marks also. But these will not be the same later," he indicated, flipping his hand away from him to indicate some days later.

"The sun changes, but we keep track of it. And when the air is very cold," he said, using his finger to indicate an entirely different arc on the flat rock, "these marks will be over here."

Palo's eyes grew large as he considered what Kamo had done. This was a timepiece that told the people much more than their own had done. He also knew that Kamo's invention would take many months to complete, and he was anxious to see the results.

"I can help," Palo said to Kamo, and his friend smiled and nodded. They were both members of the same village now and their skills would be shared.

———

Several months went by and the tribes grew accustomed to each others' ways. Survival was always on the people's minds, but as the settlements grew and year-round habitation became common, the tribes staked out regions to fit their way of life and hunting and gathering needs. Formed-brick structures and stone habitats took the place of wattle-and-daub huts, farming developed as an agricultural lifeline and promoted skills that were shared among the people. Wildlife hunting was being replaced more and more by domesticated livestock, and social organization created strata in the society that enhanced security, peace, and stability.

Kamo had brought his people north from the devastation of Masra. Along the way, they had considered settling in a variety of places along the shoreline, but ultimately, they moved far enough north to encounter the Addians and their culture.

Palo and his tribe had occupied Adda longer than memory. By welcoming the Masrians, they yielded to some changes in their tribal customs at the same time as they acknowledged the Masrians continued hold on their own customs. The original Addians were lighter-skinned than their visitors from the south, but among primitive peoples, skin tone often varied, so this did not represent a separation. Nor did the two tribes' different beliefs about the gods. The Addians feared the gods less because they had lived in relative peace for many generations, while the Masrians had a recent catastrophe that they blamed on the gods and which convinced them that the divine powers were fickle, or at the very least not easily pleased.

One morning, Palo and Kamo were talking together and discussing matters of tribal convenience and stability. They were the uncrowned heads of their peoples, and they conferred often to maintain the security of the village. Kamo steered his friend in the direction of the calendar he had been constructing patiently ever since his arrival in Adda.

"This tells my people that the sun, the moon, and the weather changes with the days," he explained, "but it always returns to the same place when the weather comes back again. This means we are safe, and we can count on this to be the same always, and this makes us feel secure."

Knowing that the Masrians probably built a calendar in their former home, the one that was destroyed by fire, Palo wondered how that memory affected Kamo's thoughts on the matter. But he didn't want to disturb his good friend's meaning and hope for the future.

They arrived at Kamo's stone when the sun was still rising, and the shadow cast by the spindly pointed rock in the center did not align with the pebbles already positioned on the flat surface. Kamo withdrew a finger-sized sharp stone from his pack and looked around his feet until he spied a hammer stone. With these two tools, he dropped to his knees and began the work of etching more crevices in a new arc to hold yet another round of pebbles.

The weather had started to turn a bit cooler, and Kamo explained to Palo that he would put the pebbles in four arcs around the flat rock. Each pebble represented a different part of the day, and each arc represented a different season: hot weather, cool weather, cold weather, and cool-rainy weather. Palo understood most of his friend's actions, but not all. He expected to learn from Kamo and be able to show it to his people.

Bele and Sari returned from the river's edge with sacks of wet mud and clay, but when they approached and saw the sunlight reflecting off the edges of Lotu's green glass, they stopped short.

"What is that?" asked Bele.

"*Sida*," said Lotu, then she picked up one of the knives and handed it to Bele to examine. The Addian women had seen one or two things like this in their many years, but never so sharp, and never in the quantity that Lotu possessed. The light shown off the polished edge and drew the dark green color out of the glass, streaked as it was with veins of blue and gray.

"*Sida?*" said Sari with a questioning tone.

"Yes," answered Lotu. "It comes from the sea," and with this comment she swept her arm toward the south but indicated that it came from farther than the village of Masra, swaying her arm over her head to indicate a very great distance.

"We have found this in the small waves off the coast. It comes up from the water and lays on the sand for us to find. We go there from our river sometimes to retrieve this gift from gods." Then she lowered her head as if recalling a difficult experience.

"But the fire ran us away." Again, she looked toward the south, over the waters, toward a land of fire and smoke. "So we returned to our village up on the hill."

"You cut with it?" asked Sari. "With *sida*?" she added, drawing her finger across the razor's edge of the thin knife of obsidian that she held in her hand.

"Yes," and with that Lotu picked up the scraps of leather and showed how she could cut them into more regular shapes, some rectangular for the back and front of a garment, some tapered toward one end for the pieces that would be sown in under the arms. The Addians watched with appreciation and wonder as this green knife sliced cleanly through the tough leather, and Sari shook her head.

"We learn much from you," she said addressing Lotu.

"We all learn," said Lotu without lifting her eyes from her work.

Masrians were unfamiliar with ocean fishing, having spent much of their lives by the river, so their methods of fishing usually involved standing stationary on a rock and either casting a line baited with animal chum or tossing a net into the running water and gathering the fish within its fibers.

But the Addians had long fished in the sea as well as the river. And where the running water of the river provided its own trawling power, fishing on the ocean waters required that they develop a method of movement to create the trawling effect that would net their catch.

Rafts and dugout canoes were the most common conveyance. The first provided a strong and wide platform that they made by interweaving tree branches and tying them together with vines and rope they twisted by hand. The raft was big enough for three people and had to be strong enough to carry them while dragging a net of fish behind. One man would use a pole to push the raft through the water while the two others on the raft would have their hands on the net that dragged behind. Whenever they sensed the weight of the catch, they would haul the net onboard.

But the raft, strong as it was, couldn't continue to hold more than one catch; besides, the men had nowhere to put the landed fish if they were to turn them out and cast the net back in. So with each haul, the raft would ply the waters back to shore where other fishermen were waiting to relieve the craft of its catch, then let it go back into the waters again.

Other men had carved out canoes from fallen trees. They scraped at the bark to expose the flesh of the tree, then continued scraped as they withdrew fiber after fiber, pulling hard at the crude stone edges they used, their backs glistening with the sweat of work that would take an entire day to complete.

These canoes floated in the water and although most were made for one man, and certainly no more than two, they had an advantage over the rafts because a man could cast a smaller net over the side, draw it onboard and spill the catch at his feet in the bottom of the canoe. Then he could cast again without having to return to the shore.

The Addians had mastered both the raft and the canoe in their many years of fishing, making each bigger and stronger than before, and they showed the Masrians who had joined their village how to make them, and then how to use them.

At the end of a long day on the water, the fishermen returned to the village with a considerable haul of white fish, spiny bivalves that they knew would split open when heated, and odd-looking sea creatures with tentacles and bulging eyes. Each would find its way into a pot or over an open fire, and the village would eat well that night.

———

While the food was being prepared and cooked, Kamo sat by himself and worked something small in his hands. He used a sharpened edge of flint which was good enough for his purposes; he knew that *sida* would be too thin for such work and might snap in two. His hands worked back and forth but because of the fading sunlight and the small project in his hands, Palo looked but could not quite make out what his friend was doing.

Kamo lifted the little thing toward the light to inspect it, and Palo could then see that it was shaped like a bit of a deer antler, but he wondered what Kamo was planning for the thing. Just then, Kamo pulled the piece closer to his mouth, first blowing on the surface of the antler to shake off the dust caused by scraping with the flint, and then putting one end into his mouth.

A soft breath blown into the end of the antler brought out a little sound, part whistle and long, gentle honk, and the people at the fire stared in disbelief. Kamo breathed in again and exhaled into the antler and another soft whistle was emitted, but this one was stronger than the first and had a fuller sound.

He pulled the antler out of his mouth and smiled at those who sat with him.

"In Masra, we call the gods with these," he began, holding the bone flute up for all to see.

"Can I try it?" asked Lefu, but Kamo demurred.

"No, I am sorry, it can only be used by the shaman."

"But you are the chief," Lefu protested, "not a shaman."

"Yes, it is true, but our shaman was killed in the fire in Masra. We lost everything, even our god songs. As the chief, I am responsible for my people even though I am not a shaman. But I thought your shaman would not be able to use this," he said and, turning toward Opra, he handed her the flute.

Opra's eyes widened. It was a tremendous gift, something she could never have made, but she also knew that the sound it made was very much like the chant she mumbled to herself when her eyes were closed and she was calling on the gods. She lifted the flute to her mouth and blew into it tentatively.

Very little sound came out at first but as Opra emptied her lungs, the tone improved and strengthened. Winded by the effort, she paused, then breathed in deeply and blew very hard into the instrument. A sound that seemed like "blatt" to the people blurted out of the end of the antler and there was some nervous laughter. It seemed funny but everyone knew not to laugh at an act that called the gods.

Opra tried once more, this time with a lighter breath and the bone flute sang a pure note even cleaner than the one Kamo had produced. There was an audible sigh around the fire and Opra looked at the flute in her hands with amazement.

———

It had been a year since the Masrians came to Adda. The two tribes had bonded well and learned skills from each other that made it easier to manage routine chores, and to shore up their culture and society.

Palo and Kamo were the acknowledged heads of the union, and they seldom fell upon any important decision on which they would disagree. The Masrians knew and had obeyed Kamo's rule for many years, and Palo had risen to a great stature among the Addians and didn't need an assembled vote to convey the powers that he used so wisely.

But as the months turned to cold weather, the earth trembled and the sky was often painted in broad strokes of orange and red. The tremors struck randomly, with no way to predict or anticipate them. They could come at night, during the morning meal, or shake a fire pit on an evening during the village meals. There would be days without the shaking, but the repeat occasions were coming more often and the tribe knew that the gods were awake.

The morning sky toward the south, far past the place the Masrians had come from and far beyond the waters that crashed upon the southern shore, was alight each morning with a pulsating, throbbing glow of fire. At times, the brush strokes of red, yellow, and orange would stretch far to the west, and it seemed on those days that the entire sea was ablaze.

Opra used her chants and her bone flute to placate the gods, and the tribal leaders sacrificed more animal flesh at the nightly meals. But the trembling of the earth and the fire in the sky continued. One morning the brilliant glow in the southern sky dimmed a bit, then slowly faded over another day. There was still trembling in the earth, but it too slowed and the village relaxed for a few mornings.

But the villagers were suddenly awakened by a great shaking of the ground one morning. Rushing from their shelters, the people felt the ground move beneath their feet and the fire in the southern sky return more brilliant than before. It was not yet dawn and the sun remained hidden below the eastern horizon, but the blazing sky in the south lit up their clusters as if it was fully daytime. Over the hours, the sky grew more somber and a great black cloud gathered. It was very far away from them and could be seen only as a vast, sinister black umbra that obscured the southern world. They could see spikes of fire shoot up into the cloud and flashes of light that crackled and sent the sharp piercing sounds all the way to Adda.

This went on for a few more days. When the earthquakes and volcanic eruptions to the sound failed to slow down, the village elders gathered to talk about what they could do. It included the Masrians, Kamo, Lotu, Papia, and Tira, and the Addians, Palo, Sari, Lefu, Bele, Femo, and Opra. They all knew that their shaman had been beseeching the gods to end their terrible fighting, and that she would continue to do so. But they also realized that, for whatever reason, this wasn't working.

Palo proposed going to the sacred cave on the cliffside where they left paintings of their dead, and where they went to seek the gods' help and advice.

"I will paint a great prayer to the gods, and we can hope they will end their fire and shaking of the earth."

Just then, a gigantic spike of lightning forked up from the sea in the south, in the area that they had called Manta, and the earth shook with greater intensity than before.

Kamo looked at Palo, nodded his head, and they returned to their huts to gather the tools necessary for the cave painting. Palo was in charge of this task, and he knew exactly what to bring. Unlike the cave carvings that had been rendered by the primitive people, the Addians used color and painted their wall carvings to make them appear more real. Palo had chunks of soft stone that were tinted with red, yellow, and brown colors. He put these, his carving tools, and three small clay pots into his sack.

Kamo retrieved climbing tools, such as his twisted rope and stone axe, because he would be leaving the art to his friend, but he knew the path up to the cave would be hard to manage.

When the two men met again in the center of the cluster, the ground still shook and the sky still shone with the angry fire of the gods. They started right off toward the cliffside cave where Palo had climbed in search of his escaped sheep a year earlier.

Both men expected the climb to the cave to be arduous, made more dangerous by the uncertain shaking of the earth. They reached the mouth of the grotto quickly, moving along the ledge rapidly to avoid risking any slip along the way.

Kamo sat down on the cool stone floor of the cave as Palo scanned the rocky surface of the wall to find the right place for his art. Once he had selected a spot, he quietly withdrew the small pots, arranged them at his feet, and began to wet the ochre to produce the colors he was looking for. Once he was ready, he returned to the wall and, using his hammer stone and sharp etching rock, he quickly scratched the outline of his chosen picture.

Palo had been imagining the proper homage to the gods while the two men climbed in silence up the cliff, so when it was time to begin, Palo was prepared and moved quickly. The image that emerged from his pounding and scratching was one of a broad sky, an undulating line to indicate the terrain, and many little images of stick people gathered on the earth. When he was satisfied with this etched outline, he turned his attention to the paints he had created from the ochre.

For a brush, he had a stick around which were tied the stiff bristles of a pig's hide. Palo dipped it first into the smudge of wetted red ochre and smeared this brilliant color across the sky that he had carved on the wall. Below the red fire in the sky, he dotted the horizon with dabs of yellow ochre, then smeared a thin layer of brown paint on the earth below. His rendering was completed when he combined the yellow and brown paint together to brush the outlines of his people on the ground below the volcanic fires above.

Palo stepped back to see what he had down, then closed his eyes and prayed. He held his hands out from his side, palms up, in the gesture of a supplicant and he hoped that his offering would be accepted by the gods and they would cease the terror that they rained down on the village of Adda, over the entire island of Ganta, and across the seas to the south.

In a moment, though, he opened his eyes and turned toward the seated Kamo.

"We go," Palo commanded, neither man waiting to see whether Palo's rendering would placate the gods. They swept up the tools that Palo had been using, Kamo collecting the pots of ochre while Palo grabbed the etching tools.

They emerged from the cave and began the treacherous trip along the edge back toward the settlement. They disregarded the continued trembling of the ground below their feet. They knew that, regardless of the moods of the gods, the men's first obligation was to pay attention to their footsteps and not take any unnecessary chances.

Halfway down the slope but still clinging to the narrow ledge that was their only escape, the ground surged and rocks tumbled down from the slope above their heads. Palo and Kamo each put up one hand to protect their heads, while the other hand swept across the rock face that they leaned toward to avoid the edge of the cliff.

As rocks tumbled and the ground shook, they took shorter steps and kept their eyes glued to the path ahead. There was a sharp crack and a tremendous shaking, and when Kamo looked back over his shoulder at Palo, he watched as time seemed to slow and his friend slipped over the edge of the broken ledge between them.

Springing into action with an agility that he didn't know he possessed, Kamo swung his body around and reached toward the man who was quickly dropping over the edge. He gripped Palo's hand and they held tight, even as the ground beneath Palo fell away. There was nothing holding him to the earth at that point, except Kamo's hand and the uncertain pathway that both men's lives now depended upon.

"I have you," Kamo said, "pull!"

Both men struggled to hold their grip as Palo pushed his feet against the face of the rock. He made some progress and was able to reach with his other hand and get a piece of the ledge in his grip. Kamo could only hold onto him with one hand because his other tried to keep his balance by grasping the rock that jutted out from the wall behind him.

So it was Kamo's one hand to help Palo's, and Palo's other hand that was trying desperately to pull the weight of his body up so that he could chest the edge and roll onto the path.

All of a sudden, the earth and clay that was in Palo's hand fell away and his hand slipped away into the nothingness that he dangled in. It happened with such suddenness that both men felt their grip slipping.

"I have you," Kamo said again.

"My people," Palo said, and Kamo immediately winced at his friend's words. For Palo to talk about others when his own life was in danger was an ominous change.

"Your people are okay. Hold on."

But just as Kamo said that, Palo's hand began to slide from his own. Hanging now only by their fingers, Palo dangled above the abyss. He looked up at Kamo with a stillness and peace that Kamo had not seen before.

"I am gone," said Palo. "My people," he repeated once more.

"Hold on," Kamo said again, but as he did so, Palo's hand eased away from his. Kamo looked over the cliff and saw his friend descend rapidly, still looking back at Kamo. Then his body tumbled past the rocks in the cliff and finally flew quickly down the mountain's edge and into the sea below.

Kamo stood back against the cliff, trying to steady himself and not follow Palo to certain death. His eyelids lowered and mouth grew taut. There was no time for tears; he must still save himself. But just then he realized that the ground had stopped shaking.

Kamo returned to the village alone, and the people could tell that something terrible had happened. Those in the cluster had begun to show relief because the quaking had ebbed, but Sari knew that her man would not be coming back, and her grief swept the tribe.

Kamo didn't stop, even to console Sari, but he went directly to the calendar that he had been creating for the year that his Masrians had lived with the Addians. Standing next to the stone slab, Kamo finally let the tears flow, tears and sadness for the man whom he admired and had come to love. After a moment of pain, his anger returned, and with a swipe of his hand, he sent the pebbles on his calendar flying onto the dust of the earth around it.

Then Kamo knelt down, knowing that destroying this important tool would not bring his friend back. He pulled the sack that hung around his neck and shoulder and began to reassemble the pebbles. After a moment, he paused, and reaching back to the sack he withdrew the pot that held the red ochre of Palo's painting. Using his finger, Kamo smeared a large red circle around the indentation on his calendar where the shadow fell, the indentation that marked the time of his friend's death. The red circle stood out on the calendar as a singular moment, unlike the other nicks and pebbles that made up the course of the sun.

Once he had marked the calendar with the red ochre that the Addians had referred to as the color of life, Kamo put the remaining pebbles back in their place.

JULY 2018

CAFÉ AMADEO

"The people who landed on Sicily's shores from the tiny islands to the west weren't the first to come, although their arrival can be dated with the artifacts and cave carvings we have found," Vito told me. "The human experiment had advanced very far by that time, and they knew how to farm, herd animals, and turn emmer wheat and other grains into bread.

"Tool-making, like a blunt-headed maul, creating spear points and early harpoons made of deer antler, and building wattle-and-daub shelters were within the talents of an average person, but making cutting edges from flaking chert, or honing the point of a microlith from flint to be used as an arrowhead or needle was still not very common. Especially for a small island population isolated in the middle of a great sea, largely although not completely shut off from other lands.

"The people who had crossed the landbridge from North Africa brought seeds and the beginnings of husbandry and simple art forms that celebrated their ideas of god, and those who sailed from the west brought early methods of pottery-making. All these would have evolved – indeed, they did evolve – over the centuries, but the technological and social advances on the island were given occasional shock treatment by new tribes who sailed from distant shores, each bringing their own unique ideas about tools, nourishment, and social organization.

"Most importantly," Vito continued, "bonds of dependence and friendship developed as the people honed their new skills whenever specialization and long-term attention was required. Where once each family or cluster would produce all its own food, clothing, and shelter – living in larger settlements or clusters only for security – the growth of specialized skills and advanced knowledge of technique encouraged people in each tribe to concentrate their efforts on specific talents and products that could be exchanged for other products from craftsmen in the village. To specialize."

"Did these bartered things include ornamental objects or luxuries?" I asked.

"Both, but sometimes," Vito clarified, with a bony finger pointing to the ceiling. "They were just the necessities of life. So, the people became more reliant on each other and on the growth of complex social ties to ensure that these artisans could continue to be counted on to supply these needs.

"As an economy of sorts grew, systems of exchange emerged, social organization grew, and so did the relationships among people, between families, and within the tribe. Social rules that in primitive times were based simply on survival needs became more complicated as leadership and command structures became more commonplace."

Vito slipped the last bite of almond biscotti into his mouth and drew the last sip of espresso from his cup, then leaned back and eyed me intently.

"What's the difference between a migration and an invasion?" he asked.

"The first sounds nonviolent, while the latter does not," I replied.

Vito leaned forward in his seat to get my full attention.

"Two hundred years ago, when bison in your country roamed across the plains, were they migrating or invading?"

I had no idea but told him it sounded like migration.

"Five hundred years ago, when Europeans came to the New World, were they migrating or invading? And one hundred years ago, when my people were coming to America at the turn of the 20th Century, were they migrating or invading?"

I didn't know whether to answer.

"But years later, the result is the same, no?" he concluded before standing to leave.

———

"Patterns of behavior are learned as we grow up and mature," Vito began the next morning.

"They can be adaptive or maladaptive. That's the beauty of evolution: It rewards those who can adapt – and choose to – and punishes those who cannot or refuse to! Invaders will often force their traditions and beliefs on the people they've conquered. Sometimes, the victors will enslave the people they now dominate. There are many stories of this in the course of world history, but the most effective conquerors were those who left the local traditions, social structure, and belief systems in place. Take, for example, the Romans."

"We're not up to Roman times, are we?" I asked.

"Oh, no, not for a long time, but the example the Roman conquerors' mindset didn't come to them as a sudden insight. Instead, the tradition of respect for local lore was a product of adaptation and evolution.

"A Roman army would take a village or region – not a difficult task since their armies were so advanced and they tended in the beginning to only attack the less formidable regions moving outward from Rome. When they won the battle, the commanding officer would invite the local tribal leaders in for a conversation. He would explain to them that Rome did not want them as slaves, well, not all of them anyway, but the emperor would expect to reap some income and resources from the new area. If the tribal leaders would agree to this rather peaceful approach, all would go perfectly. And if they didn't agree, they would be 'dispatched' and a new set of tribal leaders would be made a similar offer."

"Roman legions weren't known to be generous lords, though," I pointed out, knowing that Vito didn't have to be reminded of this.

"Of course not, they did enslave many people but they cobbled together a set of rules that were roughly well understood and, if you stayed on the right side of that line, all was well. The point I'm trying to make though, is that while the Romans invaded many countries, their patterns of behavior and their traditions were only lightly overlaid on the ones from the conquered region. In fact, that is one of the most adaptive behaviors of conquest."

"In other words," I carried his thought forward, "suppression breeds violence."

"*Esattamente*! And the freedom to go about one's life, business, and religion, breeds compliance."

"And, so, what we talked about earlier, migration versus invasion, shows which of the social approaches was most adaptive..."

"And which was maladaptive," he said to finish my sentence.

"Okay," I began slowly. The point was too obvious, so I knew I was missing the punchline.

"Most people think that the mindset of invaders and migrators are different, that one means harm while the other is focused solely on finding a new home. But whatever their reasons, the success of their endeavor – and the behaviors they exhibit while carrying out their invasion or migration – will depend on whether they choose adaptive strategies or maladaptive strategies."

"The Roman Empire lasted for, what, a thousand years?" I pondered.

"Sì, in different forms, but that's about right," Vito responded.

"And other empires or monarchies that pushed subjugation rather than incorporation didn't, or couldn't, last that long."

Vito simply shrugged, but he gave me a lot to think about.

———

I was already at the table, alone, early again as I anxiously awaited Vito's arrival the following morning. Instead, the barista came over and sat down across from me.

"Your questions are very interesting," he began, and I realized that he had been paying close attention to my conversations with Vito since our first meeting.

"What will you do with this information?"

I shrugged my shoulders, not sure of how to answer yet.

"I don't know," I began, "but I came to study Sicily and Sicilians, and Vito's tales spread the panorama of knowledge to an entirely different degree."

"Vito is the oldest man I know," the barista continued, "and it seems sometimes like he has lived the thousands of years that he talks about."

I smiled gently at the suggestion, because it did truly seem like Vito had walked with the people he was telling me about, had struggled through their challenges, and had grown old with their societies.

"So, what will you do with this information?" he asked again

I suddenly realized why I was there. It wasn't to learn about Sicily; it was to become Sicily.

4870 B.C.E.

THE FIRST INVADERS

4870 B.C.E.

ARRIVAL OF THE SICANI

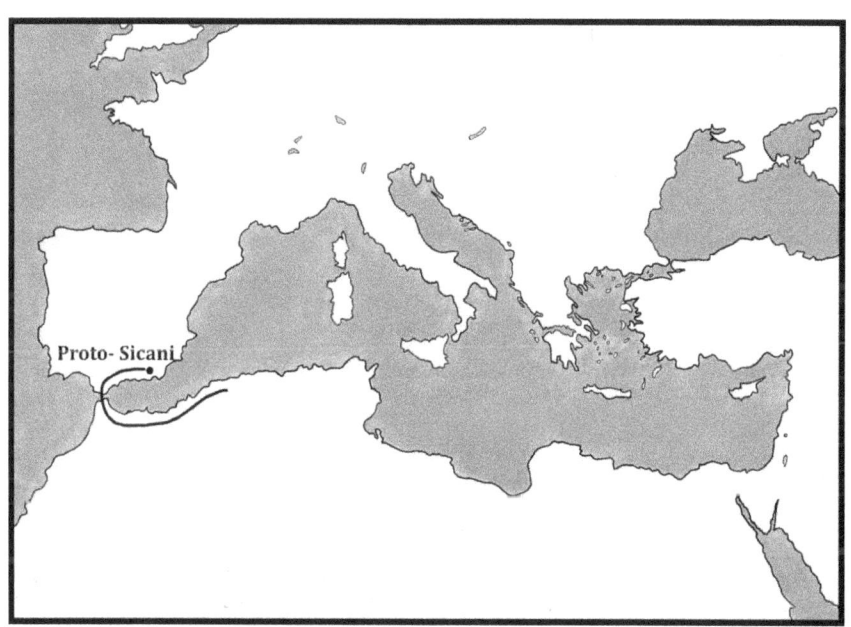

4870 B.C.E.
CROSSING THE GAP

THE BLOOD RAN DOWN THE PALM OF HIS RIGHT HAND AS HE examined the gash. Wiping away some of the flow with the fingertips of his left hand, he pulled the skin apart, examined the wound and grunted. Below the skin, he caught a glimpse of the muscle fibers before the blood returned to obscure the opening. There appeared to be no damage to the muscles themselves, which Tomas tested by making a fist and squeezing his fingers into a ball.

There was pain, but the strength and function remained, so he grunted again, this time with a bit more confidence in his utterance. He wrapped the wound with a strip of hide taken from his pack, and got assistance from Villa, his woman, to secure it around his wrist.

Then Tomas pulled a length of rope across his palm, grasped it tight and tested his hand. With only a slight grimace, he could still lift the pack tied to the other end, so he hoisted the strap over his shoulder and nodded that they should proceed.

They had climbed down the rocky face of the cliff below their cave, which is where Tomas had hurt his hand. The surface of the shale was smooth in some places, worn to a sheen from a century of hands climbing up and down to the plains below. But other places on the jutting rock was sharp, a fact that Tomas now begrudged. On this day, though, he swore at the rock itself, not a common gesture because such behavior could insult the gods who presided over the massive rock.

After spending the preceding weeks considering the land to the south, Tomas and his tribe were abandoning this cave and this peninsula, certain to find another home on the tip of land just across the water to the south. Maybe he just felt safe that he was going to put distance between him and the cliffs they were abandoning, so he hurled a defiant insult at the mountain in parting.

Villa preceded him on the climb down to the beach, alongside the others from the series of caves above. Tomas was the last to reach the bottom, setting his feet firmly on the last boulder and jumping down the few feet to the sand. The watercraft they had created in their weeks of planning awaited them on the beach. The tribe had felled three large trees, cut the branches off to smooth the sides, and turned the three trunks into dugout canoes. Using the major branches that were severed from the trunks, they created four large rafts by lashing them together in a crosswise pattern, using hemp and the vines that had been entwined around the trees while still standing.

The people then dragged these seven floating craft down to the beach two days before and returned to them on this morning of embarkation. First, the canoes and rafts were pulled into the low surf. It was still early morning and a cool breeze blew off the water, whipping up a spray of salty water every few moments. The women climbed into the canoes and accepted the little children who were lifted into the vessels by the men. The animals were put on the rafts, pulled by the rope harnesses because they stubbornly avoided wading into the water. Last of all, the bundles of food, coverings, and tools were spread about the crafts to avoid putting too much weight in only one or two.

Once settled, and people, animals, and belongings were balanced, the seven men who remained on the shore pushed the canoes and rafts into the water, one by one leaping onto the tail of each craft as it began to buck and crest the small waves that washed upon the shore behind the little flotilla.

As they sailed out into the watery gap the separated them from their homeland, the tribe looked back. The towering rock and caves that now grew small in the distance had been home for their people for many generations. They were in search of new lands and new promise, but only the seamen and other wanderers could tell them what was in store on the other side of the strait. A vast ocean spanned a great distance to their right, and the Middle Sea stretched out to their left. Tomas and Villa dared to lead their people away from the pastures and forests they had known for many years, to the enormous continent to the south where fertile fields abounded with flora and the broad expanse of land was filled with animals.

The sun swept across the heavens and had begun its downward curve toward the horizon before the people landed on the southern shore. The primitive oars they had fashioned were very effective on the river, but the men and women had to battle the strong currents that swept through the strait while trying to keep a clear heading toward the promontory that awaited them on the other side.

The low waves that complicated their journey turned into a frothy slop by the time they pushed onto the shore beyond. They landed on a sea slope blanketed in pebbles and small stones. It was harsh landing and an unwelcome sign, but the visitors chose to accept it as just a part of their new home.

The men and women slipped off their crafts into the shallow water to push the canoes and rafts through the foamy sea wash at the shore. They pulled the vessels up past the lapping seas and stood to survey their new surroundings. The rough, rocky hills sloped upward into low mountains just as did their homeland on the Gibraltar side. It was the high peaks on this side of the narrow strait that they had spied from their embarkation point, and which guided them to the foreign shore.

Too tired to move much beyond their landing spot for the day, the tribe set about bringing an overnight camp to life. The men dragged the boats and rafts farther from the surf while the women and children collected tree limbs and dead branches from which to make a fire. Time would not be wasted on building shelters; Tomas and Villa had decided before the day began that this first stop would only hold them until they could move on and find a permanent location.

Simpo helped Tomaso with the boats while his woman Vastra and her children joined Villa.

"Suraisa," Vastra called out. "Here," she added, pointing to the ground at the edge of the newly dug pit, to show the little girl where to drop the armful of twigs and brambles she was carrying. Suraisa's older brother, Anxio, had wandered off in search of the sounds he heard in the bushes by the foothills, and Keto, the middle child, scampered about pulling larger branches together in her arms to feed the fire.

Lila was bent low next to the pit and was working the flint starter she carried on the trip, striking it soundly against her fire brick and sending sparks toward the tiny mound of broken twigs and dried leaves. She had her back to the slight breeze that came off the water and shielded the kindling while she worked to get a flame to rise.

Suddenly, there was a screech that came from the low trees far from the camp. Another screeching sound and Anxio emerged carrying a baby boar in his arms, while the animal squirmed and fought against the boy. At first the sight of meat for the evening made the people smile, until Simpo and Tomas, trailed by Lila's man, Chandra, came running past the women and the small fire, heading in the direction of Anxio and the little pig that he was wrestling with. They knew that little piglets seldom wandered off alone and where there was a baby, there would most likely be a very angry mother bearing down on them with weight that surpassed two men's bodies.

The entire tribe sprang into action. The women snatched up the smallest toddlers while waving their arms to warn the older children to stand behind them. The men raced from the water's edge, running past the crowded women and children and grabbed their spears, hefting them above their shoulders in preparation for battle.

Simpo ran straight to Anxio who was still wrestling with the pig, while Tomas and Chandra ran past into the woods where they expected to confront a raging sow. Upon reaching his son, Simpo raised his spear and plunged it into the side of the baby pig, drawing a gasp from the boy's mother. Simpo knew that strike would endanger his son, but he had to silence the little pig before joining the hunters to wage a bigger battle at the forest's edge.

The piglet went slack and Anxio, with a startled look still on his face, dropped it at his feet. Vastra ran to her stunned child and pushed him back toward the tribe and away from the trees.

They waited in silence, eyes fixed on the edge of the woods, but heard nothing from their men. The hunters would not talk or make unnecessary noises until the battle was engaged, and the tribe wondered why there was no sign of trouble yet.

After another few minutes, the three men came out from the trees dragging a large boar behind them. When they approached the people, Villa first, and then Vastra, could see that the mother pig was already dead, but not by their men's hands. Its side was split open and organs hung from the gaping wound.

"Another hunter," Chandra said, "a good hunter." He pointed his spear at the death wound, and swung it across the length of the gash.

"Something killed her, and she's been dead for hours," he added.

Villa looked more closely and could see some insects flying about the bloody opening in its hide.

"An animal with a powerful jaw did this," suggested Tomas, a comment which drew aahs from the children.

"But why didn't the animal eat it?" asked Vastra.

Tomas shrugged his shoulders.

"Can't tell. Maybe frightened off when Anxio approached. And he threw a soft laugh toward his son. Tomas knew that a large animal wouldn't be frightened off by a young boy, but he had no other explanation.

Knowing they shouldn't discard an easy find, two men and their women dragged the boar to the water and washed it off. After rinsing the blood, pus, and flies off the animal, they returned to the campfire which was now ablaze, and began to properly gut and dress the animal. The young piglet would be similarly gutted and dressed but would be hung to dry for another day.

"The animal blood," Simpo said, "even our own blood," as he pointed to the scratches on Anxio's arms, "will bring the bigger animal back tonight." Everyone knew he was referring to the big-jawed predator.

With that, they resorted to methods that had served them well on the other shore. When there was a new catch and drying meat, it would have to be hung from a tall branch, and a pit would be dug beneath it. The pit would be lined with sharpened branches and filled with a dense mess of vines. In this way, the piglet's carcass would either be saved from an attack, or the attacking animal would fall into the pit and become ensnared by the vines while struggling to escape. If the animal struggled in the pit, the action would toss it backwards and forwards toward the sharpened sticks impaling it multiple times until the predator succumbed to the wounds or was exhausted by the fight.

"Here," Tomas suggested, pointing to a spot that was far enough from their camp so that the smell of the dead piglet would draw the attacker away from the camp. The men collected the green shards of obsidian that they carried always with them, and some stones sharpened before their journey, and set upon the trees at the edge of the forest. Working through the time it took for their dinner to be prepared, they felled three trees and dragged them to the spot chosen by Tomas.

They lashed the tops of the trees into a teepee shape and stood it up above the pit that the children had already dug. Tossing a rope over the tripod, they secured the end of it to the hind legs of the piglet and hoisted him up, to the height of a man. They knew an attacking animal could not reach that high so they hoped to both entrap the predator and preserve their own prey.

Now the children and men worked together to bury the sharpened sticks in the pit, then shrouded it all in a tangled mass of vines. Satisfied that they had completed the task, they retreated to the campfire and joined the others to feast on the mother pig that had been rendered into their arrival meal.

———

The women and men took turns staying awake all night, letting the children sleep. They maintained a vigil to be alerted in case any animal strong enough and cunning enough to bring down the mother pig might come into camp. Nothing happened, and the night passed without any threats of that kind.

Before drifting off to sleep, they whispered among themselves and looked up at the midnight blue of the heavens over them. The sky was familiar to the tribe, with the same brilliant points of light made by the sparkling stars illuminating the deep darkness above them.

Tomas and Vastra took the first watch; they decided it was important to have one parent from each family sleep while the other remained awake, so the watch couple was mixed in that way. Other couples in the wayfaring tribe did the same thing.

Tomas leaned back on his pack and stared at the night sky, pointing out familiar groupings of stars and telling stories about them. Vastra had heard the same stories before and laughed when Tomas made fun of the constellation that looked like a short, fat animal chasing a human.

"That's Anxio," he said.

"No, Anxio didn't run away," she replied. "Maybe he should have, though," and they shared a laugh.

"You think this world is for us?" she asked.

Tomas nodded slowly, though in the darkness Vastra couldn't see the movement of his head. It was as if he was considering the question. Or he was considering something broader – not the question, but the decision. In their old habitat, many challenges had been conquered, like nighttime safety since they lived in the caves. They hadn't considered whether there were caves on this side of the gap, and assumed that their life, thus far, was a guide to what was to come. But, here, there were no caves, no sudden rocky incline to shield them from feral animals. Tomas sighed when he thought about the threat they faced, and how their caves would have kept them safer than sleeping out in the open as they were.

But here they were, so he shook the thought from his head and returned to staring at the stars. He rocked his head from left to right, from one horizon to the other. Absent any ambient light from campfires, there was nothing to obscure the infinity of twinkling bulbs in the heavens above. The people believed in the Earth Mother as the greatest god, but they also believed in minor gods who supervised the affairs of the world, from the gods who caused the fiery eruptions from the tall mountains, to the gods who steered wild animals toward their village for slaughter, to the gods who turned tiny seeds into towering trees and edible plants.

The heavens were the most beautiful thing to the tribe, in part because the sky was always there and was always the same, and they knew that the Earth Mother ruled that part of the world. Even the passing storms with lightning and flashing rain – just outward symptoms of some minor god's displeasure – could not spoil the people's appreciation for the sky that the great Earth Mother gave to them.

After a few hours, when Vastra was growing tired from the long day of travel, Tomas woke Villa and Chandra to take their spot. The changing of the guard was silent and moved without disturbing the sleeping children, and the new pair took up their posts, sitting with their backs to the water and their eyes pointed toward the darkness of the dense trees in the foothills.

In time, a glow dawned over the sea and grew brighter as the sun appeared above the waterline. By that time, Simpo and Lila were on watch, and they shuffled to their feet as the other people sat up from their makeshift beds and stretched their arms into wakefulness. Fires were not assembled for most meals; instead, dried meat and fruit was consumed in the morning. There would also be bread left over from the evening before, and some *gira*, the white bulbous root vegetable the people had enjoyed for thousands of years.

They knew there was no point in beginning to walk without first exploring where they were and what the locale offered. So, Tomas and Simpo pulled warm leather hides over their shoulders for cover and headed for the low mountain that stretched out behind the forest. Chandra and the other men stayed behind, still wary of the appearance of some wild animals, and left the reconnoitering to Tomas and Simpo.

The two men strode quickly up into the trees, carrying their spears at the ready for some unexpected confrontation, then approached the rocky steps of the low mountain the sloped gently ahead of them. Hours were spent climbing the boulders at its base, and they took notice that these giant rocks encircled the granite face of the highland.

"Too many here," Simpo said, pointing to the craggy broken face of one of the boulders. "Many have fallen."

Tomas agreed that this collection of rockfall indicated an unsettled earth, one that shook and rained huge rocks down from above. The towering megalith they left behind on the other side of the strait was a steady mountain, one that didn't shake and rumble much, but both men had seen this before in their wandering around the region and heard tales from the elders about these things.

"Many rocks piled here," Tomas said, in concurrence, and point upward, "not many there."

The two explorers made it to the summit and were able to escape the shroud of trees closer to the base of the rise; from there, they could get an unobscured view all around the area. In front of them, looking back at their camp and the watery gap they had sailed across, and scanning toward their right hand where the sun had risen, they could see mostly green land, and they assumed that the region would be hospitable to them. Turning around so that the rising sun would be on their left, they saw that the land in front of them was dry and brown, and seemed to have no vegetation for as far as their eyes could see.

Turning fully back around again and facing the sea, they surveyed the coastline that ran from the strait they had crossed, to the right along the shoreline for a great distance. There were small streams that ran down the mountain to this plain and into the waters of the great sea, and the men were satisfied.

"We can walk that direction," Tomas said, pointing to his right, in the direction that had been abandoned by the rising sun since the morning of their hike. "We can see what is there and settle by the sea."

With that, the men worked their way down the mountain to rejoin the tribe. By the time they arrived at the campsite, it was far past the time of the high sun, and too late in the day to begin a search for a new home. So, they spent the night again much as they had spent the night before, including the shifts of night watch to protect the people from danger.

The following morning, they arose with more purpose. After eating enough to satisfy them until the midday meal, they began to pack up.

They disassembled their rafts by pulling the vines apart that bound the thin tree trunks, then laid the wood in parallel bundles and tied them altogether with the same vines. A pair of long saplings was assigned to each bundle as rails and lashed together so that one man could drag a single bale of wood as the tribe proceeded on its march. These sturdy branches would become the foundation for the mudbrick huts they would build when they chose their new settlement. The canoes were abandoned as too heavy and without useful purpose for the overland travel that they contemplated.

The tribe gathered its belongings, the women strapping the babies to their backs and huddling the older children around them to strike off in a new direction. They headed toward the rising sun, just as Tomas and Simpo had decided, and remained close to the shoreline on their left that bordered the great sea.

4350 B.C.E.

SICANI ESTABLISH ANKARA

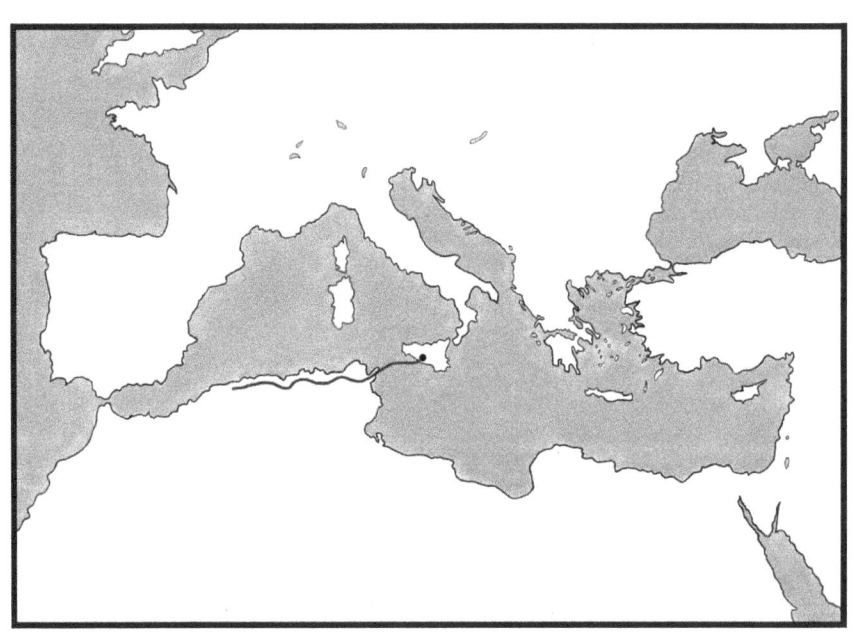

4350 B.C.E.

ANKARA

THE SICANIAN TRIBES WHO MADE THE CROSSING FROM NORTH Africa to the island of Sicily were very different from their forebears who crossed the gap at Gibraltar five centuries before. During their settlement and habitation along the southern shores of the Mediterranean, their tool-making, culture, and social structures changed and evolved. Tool-making and agriculture took on more specialization, just as non-survival skills like pottery decoration, personal ornamentation – including beads, shells, and body painting – changed.

Belief systems also changed with a dawning awareness of the nature around them. The Earth Mother who had served as their primary divinity since before memory was now accompanied by other gods who supervised the world. Appeals to these gods took on more ritual practices, with dutiful ceremonies assigned to each stage of life from birth to death. What was once a single shaman in each tribe became a hierarchy of multiple disciples believed to have some ability to communicate with the spirits around them.

Permanent structures were now required for the gods and the worship practices that they deserved. Small shrines adorned with carved idols were common and existed in nearly every domicile in the city, but larger communal edifices were erected. They were not of special construction; often simply massive obelisks that stood as sentries at spots determined by the people as appropriate for one particular god or another. But the struggle to create these large megaliths served as proof of the people's devotion.

Routine matters of life also evolved. Construction techniques had improved remarkably, a far cry from villages made up of scattered wattle-and-daub huts and seasonal habitations used by roaming bands of hunters. Now, the villages took on the appearance of cities, with permanent stone and mud-brick buildings rising up to house a settled community. The "cluster" concept of early humans still survived, however, and their domiciles were pressed together around communal spaces, a design that promoted intra-tribal unity as well as protection from outsiders.

Agriculture had advanced and it provided the majority of the nutritional needs of the people, including both plants and animals bred and kept in corrals, while hunted animals supplied additional meat without having to herd the wild beasts. Land that was designated for crop farming encircled these villages beyond the circle of living compounds, allowing people to live close together and requiring the farmers to go out to the fields beyond the fringes of the city each day to till and manage their plots. Corrals for domesticated animals were kept closer in, however, so that a lone adventurous beast wouldn't be able to spring an escape and draw other members of the herd along.

With no plough yet invented to cut the land, no horses yet trained to draw such an invention, and no wheel yet discovered to roll the plough across the land, the people continued farming with the ancient methods. They used a digging stick to poke holes deep in the surface of the ground, then dropped seeds gathered from the earlier harvest, brushing soil back over the seed with a bare foot to cover it.

They had realized the benefit of farm irrigation by this time, probably a serendipitous discovery that came from the large ditch that had been dug around the perimeter of their village, a communal practice that had been repeated for generations for the purpose of both defense and drainage. The ditch showed the farmers that they could direct rainfall to the farmed plots. This development ensured more successful crops and harvests, putting more control in the hands of the specialists.

Such changes resulted in greater social and cultural complexity, leading to a more vertical, power-based organization of the tribes. This increased the likelihood that control of authority would be jealously guarded and only shared with others in exchange for obeisance or a show of loyalty. Concentration of power was lightly held in the beginning, but it embodied the potential for an escalation of conflict, and the abuse of authority.

Concepts of time had been understood for millennia, but smaller increments of the day were now required to manage the rituals of farming, leadership, and homage to the spirits. The primitive sundial which could only manage the seasons and – in some far-flung societies – the movement of the stars, was now improved enough to measure the segments of the day, separating the time between dawn and dusk to allow for scheduling of activities as deemed necessary by the tribal leaders and shamans. The time between dusk and dawn was not easily subject to measurement, but in primitive societies that time was devoted to sleep.

Improvements in agriculture and city construction ushered in another important feature of advancing civilization. As nomadic and gathering societies built more durable buildings and drew nourishment from seeded plots of land, they came to understand the importance of crop management, rotation, and annual harvests, and they were more reluctant to leave it all behind and move on to other places. The migratory impulse slowed, but did not disappear altogether.

———

Telia leaned his left shoulder into the cold face of the rock wall, twisting to his left and peering around the edge toward the brambles and brush beyond his perch. Two men from his village crouched in the shadow of the boulder behind him, waiting for the signal.

Telia's eyes remained focused on the wild boar grunting and nosing through the brush near the men. There were two other piglets nearby, so the adult was most likely their mother, and the men knew that a female could become more aggressive than her mate if she thought her babies were threatened. Telia knew that if he could bring down the mother first, the piglets would flee. If he dared to spear a piglet first, he would have to fight a raging mare. But the tender meat of the baby was worth the risk, and then they might have both.

His spear had a fire-hardened wooden tip. They carried stone-mounted axes for hand combat, but Telia liked the balance of a spear with only a tapered point. He raised it above his shoulder, but kept his body hidden for now. He was waiting for two things: The mother should turn her attention away, and one of her babies should wander closer to the men.

Beads of sweat appeared on Telia's forearm and face; his wrist and shoulder became stiff from holding the pose for so long. Finally, after grunting and tearing up some roots from the ground, the adult pig turned slightly away just as one of her babies wandered aimlessly into the vicinity of the hunters. Telia remained still, wanting to release the pent-up energy in his arm muscles but knowing that an ill-timed strike would not only miss the target but give the mother a charging advantage. He had to make sure that his first thrust hit the baby, then he would quickly retreat while the two men with him launched a coordinated attack at the bigger pig.

The piglet took three steps closer just as the mother snorted and gulped on a tuber she had ripped from the earth. Quickly, Telia sprang from his position to within two men's length from the baby pig, and drove his spear into the flanks of the animal. The squeal got an immediate reaction from the mother and, as Telia fled back behind the rock, the two other men appeared with their spears and ran straight at the mother. They knew from practice that if they merely stood their ground, she would become braver and attack with more abandon. Their strategy was to charge side by side and, thus, to inspire fear in the adult pig.

By that point, the other baby had run away, escaping the men's assault, and the mother slowed to consider her options. The hunters were only a few steps away and continued to shout and charge at her. The mother pig would not surrender or flee, still unsure whether her stricken baby could survive, so she continued to close the gap between her and the men, more cautiously though. When the hunters were within striking distance, the men leaped into the air, an action which stunned the huge pig and brought her to a halt. The men came down upon her, both spears striking the fleshy side of the animal, driving their points deep into the rib cage and organs of the pig. She squirmed and squealed, fanning her muzzle and teeth left and right, chopping with the small protruding tusks of a female hog and inflicting minor injuries on the men.

While the hunters stood over her and pinned the dying animal to the ground with their weapons, Telia retrieved his spear from the dead baby and went in search of the one that got away. When he discovered the piglet in the brush under a spreading tree, the kill was easy. The little animal had no defenses and no knowledge of how to fight the man, and so he died quickly with a muscular jab of the spear which caught the animal in the flank just behind the shoulder bone.

"Set the points," Telia told his men. That was his instruction to turn the spears into a stretcher, so the men arranged their weapons in a parallel fashion, about an arms' length apart, with Telia's in the middle. They retrieved vines from their packs and, with looping ties that left a space between each spear, lashed it all together to create a sling for the animal carcasses. Then they loaded their catch onto the device and began the trek back to the village at Ankara.

————

Women and young children bent toward the ground between the long rows of bright green leaves that peeked out of the soft dirt. Under their feet, the soil was compacted from the trips they made each day to visit their nascent plants, but the darker soil that had erupted to display the blossom of new leaves was loose and could easily be poked and spread with their fingers.

Sapira led the people in their farming, having learned the best practices from many years of the tribe's customs. In her right hand, she wielded a stick as long as her forearm, sharpened to a point at the end, which she set lightly in soil at her feet. Reaching behind her into the pack hanging by a leather strap from her shoulder, with her left hand she withdrew a handful of dried, light brown seeds from the emmer wheat harvest that she had saved through the winter. The cold night air and dry days had turned what were little green pods into brittle tan pockets, but she knew that inside each of the seeds she held in her hand was a life that would grow with her help and feed her family.

Leaning into the stick once again, she pushed its pointed tip into the ground about the depth of her finger. Deeper and the seed might not get enough moisture to grow; shallower and it might rot from too much moisture. They knew how to bring surface water from the shallow ditches drawn in parallel lines from the village ditch to this farmland but were still learning how to control its volume.

A little more than an arm's length from her, Nessie and Barla, the women who lived with Telia's hunters, Fante and Kropia, mimicked her actions. Their children walked along behind them, each, in a practiced rhythm, brushing his or her foot across the little hole to cover the seed. The young workers also were kept there to support the women's work, bringing more seed or digging harder up ahead where the soil was known to require extra effort.

The women had to stoop to perform their work, but the children walked along upright. Together they would plant many seeds that day, and they would farm the plot till the breeze that came before the cooler weather told them that the plants could be pulled up and the grain ground into flour.

This plot of land radiated outward from the village and was beyond the deep ditch that surrounded their settlement, a construction that provided security, drainage, and a means of distributing water to the growing number of people who occupied Ankara. Alongside the wheat field, other women were tilling the ground for *gira, pomolo,* and *yero.*

Another patch of farmland was dedicated to green leafy herbs that the people had picked wild for many generations but which they now knew how to grow from shoots taken from the plants that grew promiscuously in the trees beyond Ankara. These plants were showing signs of life before the emmer wheat plantings, since the shoots had a head start over seeds, and their lustrous bright green color turned the pale brown soil into a colorful display.

Sapira and the others completed their work and returned to their village after the sun had passed the high point in the sky. They would spend their afternoon in the broad, roughly circular common area defined by a string of stone houses that had become the new form of settlement for these people.

The common area would be shared with the animals which would be kept penned by stout tree branches interwoven into a makeshift fence. One side of the beasts' corral would be formed by the wall of a house facing the courtyard; the other sides would be made of this post-and-beam railing. In this way, the pigs, sheep, and cows could be kept for milk or slaughter, and would not be at risk of fleeing or attack that might happen if the animals were kept outside the ditched village where the farms were.

Lano was tending the pigsty with Cheechia, their job to fulfill for the cluster's diet. She, Lano, was steering one rambunctious pig back toward the pile of greens and chicken waste that was the animals' food, as Cheechia laughed at the tussle between human and creature.

"Why does he not want to eat?" Cheechia said with laughter.

"He wants to run, and he thinks that he'll find more food out there," Lano responded, flicking the end of her stick over her head, vaguely pointing to somewhere outside Ankara.

"But the food's right here!" Cheechia added, still laughing.

"Si," she replied, and cast a cold glance at the disorderly swine. "And our food might be right here, too," she concluded, prodding the side of the pig with her stick, with a smiling emphasis on the words "our food."

"Just be sure not to argue with the *boviu* that way," Cheechia warned her. "That big head would knock you to the ground and then you'd be her food!"

Lano shot a hard glance in her direction but ended it with a smile.

Lano and Cheechia were born the same year and had remained close while growing past childhood into their mature years. The Ankarans usually paired in man-woman unions, but these two women chose to be together, never choosing a man to live with. They did everything together and seemed very happy with the arrangement, and their fellow Ankarans saw no reason to object.

Sapira and her two children huddled near the low fire that was kept at the center of the courtyard. She had taken down a bundle of the dried fish and salted pork that had wintered over in their home and was preparing the correct portion of each to feed her family with enough left over to share with others in her cluster.

Across from them, an older woman, Alia, leaned into a stone trough about the length of her lower leg, slight curved from one end to the other, but otherwise flat on top. She knelt at one end and leaned forward, with her hands on a long cylinder of stone that she rolled back and forth on the thin layer of ground seeds in the trough. She rocked her hips forward and then backward, rolling the stone back and forth, an action that broke through the hull of the seeds and scattered the wisps of covering from the nut within.

Over many such repetitions, when the wheat and chaff were separated, Alia would bend even closer to the stone and blow lightly across its surface. By this method, the soft, hollowed coverings would drift out of the trough, leaving the crushed grain within. She would then use her hand to sweep the flour into a clay pot beside the operation and reach behind her to the sack of harvested wheat awaiting the grinding stone.

"Keeta," said Sapira to the child beside her, "get the *sida*," she said pointing to the small assortment of tools beside the door to their home. "The sharpest one," again pointing, to indicate the obsidian edge that she needed to cut the salted pork.

Keeta sprang to her feet and padded across the short distance to their home. It was made of stone, with a low opening for a door and no windows, and it squatted shoulder to shoulder with the homes of their neighbors. The Ankarans had learned to build their shelters side by side, even constructing some above the others in a ladder-step design, thereby creating a phalanx of robust stone buildings that encircled their city. The interior was broken up into neighborhoods, with additional homes built in strings that cut across the original wide space, creating a labyrinth of interior spaces, all with homes that opened onto separate courtyards, defining a rich assembly of clusters in the village design that had survived the centuries.

Keeta squatted down next to the nest of tools by the door to her house and selected the green-black shard of *sida* that glistened in the afternoon sun. Lifting it carefully to avoid a cut, she delivered it to her mother, who nodded and set to work on the salt covering of the pig's carcass that was stretched out between her legs.

Meanwhile, Alia sat back on her haunches, throwing her shoulders back and rotating her head to loosen her stiff muscles from the work on the grinding stone. Making bread had long been one of her assignments, something that she had developed into an art over her lifetime, but the physical labor that preceded the making and shaping of the dough was becoming more difficult in her later years.

Seeing this, Pali, a young boy who had apprenticed himself to Alia, approached her and tapped her on the shoulder.

"Let me do this," he offered, pointing to the grinding stone. "The bread we put in the fire needs your attention."

Breadbaking was a continuous process, from harvesting the wheat, to drying it over the winter months, to grinding it into flour, to shaping the bread and baking it. Pali had followed each of the steps and would become one of the tribe's bakers, but for now he needed to allow Alia up from her knees and let her finish the loaves that were turning a blackened brown in the banked stone oven.

Earth ovens were the people's original means of baking bread, and as stone cutting and brick production was developed for construction of homes, people realized that the same products could be used for smaller structures like ovens. These were built close to the stone walls of the homes but facing the courtyard so that all members of the cluster could use them. In this case, only Alia and Pali made bread, which they shared with the others in their neighborhood of Ankara.

Alia stood slowly, leaning on Pali's arm as she did so, and walked stiffly to the oven outside of her home. It was fortunate to have the oven there for reasons that they hadn't originally considered. Baking of bread or other foodstuffs would be a year-round requirement, so these ovens were fired up nearly every day. They generated considerable heat, even after the original fire was banked and the stones were scattered after the meal was prepared. The radiated heat would not easily be controlled, so it warmed all that was in its vicinity. With the closeness of her doorway to the oven, Alia enjoyed the additional warmth in the cold months and, with her advancing age and brittle bones, could even tolerate it in the warm months, so the oven's placement in the courtyard was perfect.

Drawing the loaves from the intense heat of the oven with a thick paddle, Alia examined the color and crust. Proclaiming the bread to be ready, she nodded back at Pali who was now bent over the grain as he rolled the stony cylinder across the curved surface of the trough.

The sun was directly overhead by the time Telia's hunting party returned to their settlement. Dragging their catch, the men circled toward the south to maneuver around the long, c-shaped trench that enclosed nearly the entire village of Ankara. The ditch had been dug many years before any of them were born, but was still used for all the same purposes.

The original farmers of the village had long ago learned that the soft brown earth on the surface was best for growing crops, so they scraped it up from untilled areas and carried it to their gardening plots. As they did so, the elders considered the possibilities of soil removal, and directed the efforts to focus on an arcing design, one that wrapped around their settlement and created the c-shaped channel around Ankara, each of them with specific goals in mind.

The men of the village saw the creation of this ditch as a way to delay the approach of outsiders, including attackers, if they made the channel deep enough. The herdsmen in the tribe saw the ditch as a way to corral their animals and make it harder for them to wander off. Other Ankarans saw that the ditch served to direct the rainfall away from the common buildings that made up their city.

The shaman saw the ditch as a good place to bury their dead, while other people in the cluster saw the ditch as a waste fill where they could throw their shards of broken pottery and other discarded utensils.

A narrow opening in the c-shaped curve was kept at ground level, as a bridge connecting the areas inside of and outside of the trench. Today, Telia and his men approached from a position opposite the opening and had to walk all the way around to deliver their kill.

Sapira, Telia's woman, welcomed them and smiled at what her man brought back.

"We will eat a great feast tonight," she said, pointing to the adult female carcass, "and salt the remainder for later," she added, pointing to the piglets.

With that, she organized the help of the children, one of the returned hunters, and other women to put together a large fire in a section of the ditch. The oven in their cluster could be used to cook smaller animals, but they still relied on the depth and width of the ditch around their village for roasting large game. There, the trench was deep enough that large cooking pits could be made of a part of it, so rocks were gathered and placed in a circle at the bottom of the section under Sapira's supervision. Small branches of tinder were gathered, then covered with thicker branches of similar, slow-burning wood. Then all was lit afire. When the conflagration became self-sustaining, more branches were added, and more stones and rocks were added to heat them.

While the main meal was thus being prepared, Telia and his hunters prepared the two piglets. Dressing an animal needed to be done outside the city, so the smell of offal would not pervade their dwellings nor attract animals of prey.

Normally, small animals might be slaughtered, dressed, and cooked right away to feed small groups, one family or two, and their tender meat was enjoyed sooner rather than later. But that day's catch had secured an animal big enough to feed their entire cluster, so the meat of the baby pigs would be prepared for salting to avoid losing them to decay. The hunters cut the belly of the pigs in a long slash from throat to anus and removed the innards. Some of the organs could be preserved, like the heart and liver, and served as delicacies that preceded the evening meal of the mother pig. Fante and Kropia, Telia's fellow hunters, removed these organs, taking care not to rupture the soft tissue. These would be added to the oven in the cluster as the meal time approached and distributed throughout the group. Nourishment from organ meat would not be wasted.

They then placed the intestines, lungs, and stomach into a large waiting ceramic bowl, to be washed, cleaned, and preserved later by the women trained in this. When the small pigs were completely dressed and cleaned, the men brought them into the village proper to hang the eviscerated carcasses from a tripod built between two of the buildings for that purpose. The placement between the stone structures was important because the narrow corridor pointed to the dominant wind, and the steady breeze that was funneled through that opening enhanced the drying process for the hanging meat.

It would take a few days for the piglet carcasses to fully dry, and then they would be taken down from the tripod, dismembered into usable portions, and preparing for salting. The men would use a large ceramic bowl, half the length of a man's height, placed on the ground. It was wide enough for the pork pieces to fit in side by side and deep enough to nestle them together. A layer of salt was spread on the bottom of the bowl first, then the pork was placed skin-side down. Another layer of salt was poured over the top of this assembly and rubbed gently into the meat to press it into place. When all the pieces were assembled and salted in this way, another ceramic bowl was tipped upside down and laid upon the pile of meat.

According to tradition, each day the pork pieces would be turned over and salted again. After a week the meat would be taken from the salting bowl and hung from the rafters in a hut built in the middle of the compound for smoking. A fire would be built of green wood and leaves and tended for two days, smoldering slowly and smoking the meat to preserve it.

Most activities of the early Sicani – like most prehistoric peoples – centered on survival. Food, shelter, and defense were primary concerns. In a long-settled community such as Ankara, there were already many family homes; new ones being added only when the families of new couples grew too large to remain in their parents' home. But there would always be some level of construction activity for communal structures, salting huts, and other things. Some of the buildings were dedicated to religious or ritual ends. The Sicani had long since been assembling huge, flat boulders called dolmens out in the fields beyond the city boundary for these purposes. These megalithic structures were simple assemblies of rock slabs, usually two vertical pieces topped by one horizontal piece, backed into the slope of a hillock or free standing in a field.

Effort expended in defense was always necessary, even if there was not a perpetual danger of attack from other people on the island. By this time, there were dozens of settlements spread across Gania, with most of them maintaining peaceful relationships through trade and arranged marriages, so most defensive measures concerned the wild animals in the region, although the possibility of assaults by other humans was never forgotten.

That left the Sicanis' attention to be devoted to food production, gathering, and preparation – and crafts and social entertainment.

When she was done preparing the fish and salted pork for that evening's meal, Sapira led her children and two other women into the grove of trees beyond the edge of their village. They went to a clustered arbor of ancient trees whose twisted, gnarled trunks yielded little orbs of succulent fruit, firm globes of fleshy meat that dripped a whitish yellow oil when squeezed between thumb and fingers. They called the trees *keyla*, and the fruit *tomae*, the earliest harvest of olives known to the world.

The Ankarans had already learned how to get the oil from the *tomae*. They gathered the fallen fruit and scattered them in one layer on a large flat rock. Initially, using a tree branch that had been smoothed by stripping its bark and removing knobby protuberances, they rolled this tool back and forth on the *tomae* to make the fragile skin crack and the meaty insides break down into pulp and oil. They would then stir the contents, and roll the tree branch over it again, until most of the oil could be gathered and poured into a clay pitcher.

The pulp had its purposes too. While the oil was too precious to use in slathering meat before cooking, the grainy pulp of the *tomae* could serve that purpose, or it could be spread on slabs of bread torn from a recently baked loaf, sometimes with a bit of salt added from the salting bowl. The *tomae* oil would be set aside for other uses, perhaps applied directly to bowls of food or drizzled on the legumes and vegetables the people brought from their farms and cooked in open clay pots over the village fire.

Which is exactly what Sapira intended for that evening's meal.

———

Telia and Sapira completed their chores in preparation for the evening meal and joined the others just as the sun was dipping behind the mountains to the west of Ankara. It was the warm months, so they didn't expect the night to be cool, but gathering around the cluster fire was still a welcome tradition and a fine way to enjoy the end of the day.

Every neighborhood in Ankara practiced similar events on similar schedules. With a population that included now forty different families and about one hundred forty people, even a common event like the evening meal must be broken up into many separate congregations, a tradition that developed generations before when Ankara's population was even smaller. In this case, Telia and Sapira's cluster included four families and eighteen people, and everyone had their assignment in delivering the food.

The roasted pig would be retrieved from the earth oven and cut into manageable pieces, carted back inside the village walls and to their courtyard, then handed around. Small onions and other root vegetables that had been cooked in the courtyard oven near Alia's home would be chopped and stirred into the clay bowl filled with the pulp of the *tomae*, then salted, and snacked upon by the people. The pig's organs that had been carefully removed and warmed by the heat of the red-hot rocks in the oven would be sliced with a sharpened obsidian blade, then shared among them all.

A frothing liquid produced by the shaman was served for everyone to drink. The creation of this beverage had passed from the bread bakers of the society to the religious leaders, who were charged with caring for the "spirits" in the drink. Like those who had made this intoxicating beverage over the centuries, the shaman made it by pouring water over leftover loaves of bread and leaving it to ferment and bubble for a few days. The resulting liquid was cloudy and went down easily. It had a fizzy texture and an odiferous smell, but it also produced an effect of relaxation and pleasure among the people as they settled in for storytelling after the meal.

Once the food had been consumed, the people remained at the campfire until all the stars were lit, sometimes deep into the night. Pottery making took place in the light of day, but some pots were still not yet painted or fired. The smoldering rocks in the earth oven and even the smaller fire in the courtyard oven could be used to serve as a small kiln once the food had been cooked, so pots that had been shaped were brought out to paint now and then would be placed in the circle of rocks in the oven.

Other clay molds had been created that morning, including big-breasted, big-bellied figures that were considered talisman for the women expecting babies. These would also be fired in the pit, and then hung in a birthing area and left there as a good luck charm. And they would be preserved and used again and again, unless the pregnancy went poorly; if so, the clay charm would be smashed and its pieces carefully scattered hither and yon in the ditch that surrounded the city.

Some other figures were block shaped with oversize arms and legs, depicting the strong features of the hunters. And there were other clay shapes, simple round stamps, adorned with a simple marking or a dot surrounded by a circle. These were religious ornaments and were placed in the dolmens or in the ritual building at the center of Ankara, or the small shrines to the gods of nature that each cluster claimed as their own. Some featured a small cross with four equal-length arms, and a thumbprint impressed in the intersection.

Inspired by the fizzing intoxicant – what they called *brit* – Alia launched into stories about the people from when she was young.

JULY 2018
CAFÉ AMADEO

Vito seemed to have melted into his seat at the corner table when I walked through the door. He was slumped down and leaning over his coffee and, at first, I worried that something was wrong. I looked up and saw the barista wearing his usual broad smile.

"He's studying," was all the young man said.

I slipped easily into the seat beside Vito, and my movement distracted him from the espresso cup on the table. He must have been in that position for a while because the crema – the light brown froth on the surface of the coffee – had dissipated and the black surface was clearly to be seen.

Vito turned suddenly toward me as if my appearance jolted him out of his reverie.

"I was just watching for the wrinkles," he said, pointing his gnarled arthritic finger at the cup. "I had to wait for the cream on the surface to evaporate so the coffee could be seen."

He returned his gaze to the tiny cup. The black surface of the espresso was perfectly still, at least from my observation. But Vito's sly smile made me focus again. Suddenly, he sat back against the chair with a thud.

"Nothing today," Vito sighed.

My brow furrowed and my mouth twisted in a confused smile.

"Earthquakes and volcanic eruptions are a part of this island's history. They don't happen all the time," he added without needing to, "but as the earth shifts below the seas and the fire erupts from the vents..." with this, his smile spread with the broad sweep of his arms, "...all hell breaks loose!"

I couldn't help but laugh. I had misunderstood his positioning – he hadn't been slumped over in his chair. He was watching for the telltale "wrinkles" in the coffee that would indicate tremors in the ground below us.

"The ancients would watch the waters of the sea just like that," Vito explained, jabbing his finger at the coffee cup. "They could sense changes in the waves, even changes in the subtlety of tides, usually before they could pick up the tremors at their feet.

"Oh, and the animals!" he continued. "The birds would start to squawk, and the deer, dogs, and horses would feel the shaking in the ground. Back then, our ancestors were more attuned to their environment than we are today." With a chuckle, he added, "Probably because they didn't walk on concrete and asphalt all the time."

He explained how, centuries ago – "millennia" he said, to stress the immensity of time his island has been inhabited – earthquakes and volcanoes were more common and they had shaped the contours of the land, even the seabed around Sicily. I knew this already, through my research and many of the colorful discussions I had had right here, sitting next to my mentor, but this time Vito seemed particularly interested in impressing the thought on me.

"Upheaval and renewal," he said, as if the three words constituted an entire sentence.

"Upheaval and renewal," he echoed, then took a sip of his now tepid espresso.

He described the geologic history of Sicily in broad strokes of living color – raising, sweeping, then lowering his arms to emphasize certain points. I was swept along by his nearly operatic prose, his hands moving in the arcs of an orchestra conductor, and I could see the blue of the sea, the green of the forests, and the dark brown of the animals' hides as they chewed on the primeval grass. From his narration, I could hear bird songs and the soft whistling of the breeze that stirred off the sea and swept up the hillsides.

And I could feel the rumbling beneath my feet. Was it the power of suggestion, or had Vito chosen this precise moment when there actually were tremors to convince me of the unsteady state of the earth below us?

Was this truly an earthquake in its incipient waves? I quickly looked back at Vito's espresso cup; it was now empty, but he had a broad smile that pulled his wrinkled cheeks apart.

"Many things were taking place in Sicily," Vito said, in a voice that mixed wonder and pain. "Time and progress moved slowly in ancient days. But changes...oh, yes, there were changes."

Vito studied his hands, turning them over as if discovering them for the first time. He stretched his fingers then rolled them into a curve, rubbing the pads of his thumbs against his forefingers. The expression on his face didn't change, and I couldn't tell if that was because he was lost in thought or because he wasn't really thinking at all.

"These days," he returned, "change comes quickly. We have so many changes all the time. In just one hundred years, we went from lifting off the ground in a biplane to soaring to the moon and back. And now we have flown millions of miles into space. In the same time, we have gone from typeset printing presses to computers, and from computers to voice-activated composition. We no longer even write, although those who produce books are still called writers. We dial friends on our phones, but we have no dials on the phones themselves. We still grill our meat on an open fire – sometimes..." he added with a grin, "but we can't tell what part of the animal the frozen packs of meat in the grocery store came from.

"Such change," he said, and paused. "A long time ago, there was very little change over thousands of years, and now things change from one day to the next."

It seemed like a complaint, but his voice didn't show agitation or disagreement.

Vito sighed, and continued.

"Change may come quickly, but we learn slowly. And we progress slowly."

I couldn't tell from his phrasing whether Vito was still talking about the past or the present, but his comment that we still learn and progress slowly was like a finger wagging in the face of modern people to slow down and not race ahead so fast.

He turned and looked at me.

"All the world changed slowly, long ago, but especially in Sicily. The people were influenced by all the cultures that came here, but the change was slower than with most other societies. In its position in the middle of the Mediterranean Sea – the cradle of Western Civilization, in its exact center," he said, tapping on the tabletop to emphasize the location "– Sicily enjoyed a special privilege: the privilege of witnessing – and embracing – the cultural developments and idiosyncrasies of all the nations and all the peoples from this entire region of the world. Those from North Africa, the Middle East, Anatolia, Egypt, Greece, southern Europe and northern Europe, all the way to Scandinavia.

"But one of the ironies of Sicilian history is that its position in the middle of the sea separated it from the other areas that could be reached by overland travel, which meant that Sicily would be introduced to most of the technological, social, and cultural changes in a delayed fashion. The sea insulated us from other peoples, but it also distanced us from them.

"The result was that, through the ages, Sicily always seemed backward to the outside world, discovering the modern ideas and innovations always after the other tribes and nations had already taken them for granted.

"Over the centuries, this changed. Oh, yes, we have computers and wireless...we even have refrigerators and radios," he added with an impish grin. "But the impression that Sicily is living in the past, with more primitive ideas and systems, has never gone away."

Vito lowered his head and rocked it side to side, a gesture of disappointment and almost confused acknowledgment.

We remained quiet for a few moments. It wasn't hard for me to absorb what he had said; I had heard all the time growing up that Sicily is the hard scrabble, old-fashioned region of Italy. Vito sipped his espresso and stared off for a moment, a sheen to his eyes that belied his emotions.

I drained my espresso and raised the cup to the barista who responded with a wave of the towel that he used to wipe the counter. He turned to the machine, pressed a couple buttons, and I listened as the old monster heated up and hissed the fresh broth into the cup.

Returning to our earlier conversation, I asked Vito about the volcanoes.

"What about all those eruptions?" I asked, paging through my notebook looking for notes I had taken already of volcanic activity in that time.

"Did it wipe out the population?" I continued. "You said the eruptions were mostly happening in Italy, around the Vesuvius-Aeolian corridor, and in Pantelleria."

"Manta," Vito corrected, but it didn't slow my stream of questions. I knew he was using the ancient name for Pantelleria.

"Volcanic eruptions like that can change the contours of the earth, of the Mediterranean basin. Did it?" I asked.

Vito shrugged, and sipped his espresso.

"They called it Gania," he said.

"What is Gania? The volcano?"

"No," Vito said softly. "By then, the people knew that there were different islands, different worlds they sometimes called them; some they had sailed to, some they could only see but never reach. So, they called their island Gania. What we now call Sicily."

"Was that the first name for your country?" I had learned to attribute this patch of land in the middle of the Mediterranean as Vito's "country." And I noticed the positive effect of my acknowledgment when Vito smiled back at me.

"Yes, it was what they called Sicily at that time. But you will have a very hard time finding that name anywhere in your books. Researchers and writers need to stick a flag in places to communicate what and where they are talking about. Gania appears in the ancient literature, and seems to be the earliest reference to Sicily. Without any other alternative, we have come to accept it as the 'flag' that denotes this place."

I knew that much of Vito's knowledge had come from generations – perhaps millennia – of folklore. So, I knew when he referred to "your books" that Vito was making the point that stories passed down through the centuries might have greater weight than the books inscribed by historians who thought they knew it all.

"Will I find it at all?" I asked.

"What? The island of Gania, or just the name?" He said the first pointing at his feet. I knew better than to answer that question, so he just smiled.

Vito thought for a long time, finishing off his espresso and signaling to the barista for another. I knew that these moments of reflection were important to him – and usually yielded deep insights – so I was willing to wait. The barista brought Vito's espresso and set another down in front of me, plus a small plate with two thin blue borders around the edge. It had a few slices of orange and some *cantucci*, little almond cookies resembling the *biscotti* known to Americans. I didn't know the Sicilian word for them yet, but made a mental note to find out.

"Societies and their organization also didn't change much, or at least very slowly," he began after his moment of reflection. "Between 6000 B.C. and, oh, probably, 3500 B.C., southern Italy and Sicily were completely unremarkable. Tools and weapons, such as they were, were still made from stone; there was no real metalworking yet...the Bronze Age was still one thousand years yet to come and, as I told you, its arrival on the shores of Sicily would be delayed still longer.

"As for social organization, understanding of these things comes from burial grounds. Symbols of power or a person's particular skill would be interred with the body, for example a staff for a ruler or a necklace or amulet for a shaman. We look in burial pits for implements of prestige or power, or weapons of war, or some other indelible artifact that separates certain people from the rest. But we have found none from this period. So, we assume that there was little social hierarchy. Probably, the tribes were very horizontally organized, all members with equal or near-equal status, with little to indicate a vertical arrangement of power or authority.

"A horizontally organized society also tells us that there was little in the way of specialization yet. Like the ruler buried with his staff or the shaman with her amulets, an artisan might be buried with the tools of his trade. When trades and skills become specialized, a barter system arises, allowing the craftsmen or those in possession of the goods – like pierced seashell ornaments, carved antlers, or sharpened tools – to trade in exchange for other implements not produced by them. But specialization also introduces the need for organization and delegation of authority. Leadership roles emerge from both, and command structures emerge within a society.

"In the earliest days, when everyone was considered equal, all were expected to learn the necessary skills to survive, from acquiring food and cooking it, to dealing with injury and sickness. For large projects like building shelters and hunting game, members of the villages usually helped each other, but producing food through collecting and farming was managed by each family unit.

"Production came through enterprise, some through specialization, and the growth of specialized trades was best expressed in the relationships between villages and settlements. And one form of production," Vito suggested with a wink, "population growth" – and another wink – "was speeding along without pause."

"I read somewhere that people were beginning to arrive from mainland Italy," I said. "Did it happen during this period?"

"Yes, most likely, but probably not from the mainland at first. The earliest tribes to arrive were the Sicani."

"But the Sicani came from Spain, right?"

"There was no Spain yet, but these – what ethnologists called 'proto-Sicanians' – came from that area, from the Iberian Peninsula."

I consulted my maps and wondered once again how that could have happened. Iberia is much farther away than Sicily is from than the toe of Italy, even farther away than from the protruding peninsulas of North Africa. It was hard to comprehend that people six or seven thousand years ago could manage the high seas and navigate toward an island that was too far away to be seen – or even imagined – from their embarkation point.

"These people came across the Strait of Gibraltar," Vito offered. "People had lived on that peninsula for thousands of years, dating as far back as the days of the Neanderthal."

"But the Neanderthals died off...what...twenty-five thousand years ago?" I asked.

"Yes, about then, but a big part of the demise of that line of hominids was intrusions by others. Invasions, if you will, of other people better adapted to the environment, with bigger brains and, no doubt better weapons.

"As I was saying, these newer people, the ones who replaced the Neanderthals on the Iberian Peninsula and, specifically, the promontory that we call Gibraltar, lived in the caves of the sheer rock face. Thousands of years ago, much of the earth's water was still held in the sheets of ice at the poles, so the water level in the Atlantic and the Mediterranean was lower than it is today."

"Yes, I know. We talked about that. But what does that have to do with these people, the proto-Sicanians?"

"Well, the lower sea level gave them two advantages. First, it meant that there would be fertile plains at the foot of Gibraltar, plains stretching into the sea, land that they could farm and live off of. There are still caves in the rock, you've probably heard of Gorham's Cave..."

I hadn't but didn't want to admit it to my mentor.

"Scientists have found evidence of habitation there as recently as four thousand years ago, right there where the towering Gibraltar juts out into the sea.

"The lower sea level meant that the gap between the Iberian Peninsula and the tip of Africa would be smaller. The narrow gap made it easy for wanderers to peer across the sea and know that there was land over there, and then made it easier for them to navigate the waters in small craft that were common in that time.

"They got across the gap and explored the land on the other side, what is now Morocco. They discovered that the coastal areas were lush so they knew they could survive there. At the same time, they saw that more barren lands existed farther south, farther from the seacoast, so this encouraged them to make their settlements on the African edge of the Mediterranean Sea. Over time, and with growing tribes and resettlement of peoples, they continued to migrate east along the seacoast, remaining close to the contours of the shore, across North Africa, creating new settlements and setting down new roots.

"The tribes occasionally partitioned as tribes have always done, and the fragments of the society that split continued the same pattern, moving east across the coastline. Over hundreds, perhaps thousands of years, this trek brought them to the area we now call Tunis. Some continued to the peninsula farther east, called, now, Kelibia."

I paged through my notes but I didn't have any good maps, including my own scribbles, of North Africa. And I knew that I didn't have anything on a place called Kelibia.

"Remember, thousands of years ago when the waters of the Mediterranean were low, the island of Sicily was still connected to the North African coast. It wasn't an island at all; it couldn't even have been considered a peninsula, since the land mass that is now below the seas connected Sicily to the African continent. As recently as 5000 B.C., when the waters were returning, they remained shallow and easily navigated. The tribes who settled in modern-day Kelibia, especially the fishermen who plied the waters, could see the little island of Pantelleria, or Manta, ahead of them.

"The shallow seas allowed them to go on foot farther north toward that land mass, close enough that they could see it from their position. So, it didn't take much to sail there and establish new settlements. Many years later, as they continued their exploration to the north, they were drawn to another island, a much bigger land, Gania. There were already primitive peoples scattered about the land, had been for tens of thousands of years, but these new people from Iberia brought with them a culture that had gestated on the European continent for some time already. It was the first European invasion of Sicily that we can certify from the archeological record."

Vito paused for a moment, lowered his eyes and chuckled.

"I like to think they came to Mazara del Vallo first, which would mean that the earliest European settlers came from Iberia and established the region we have here," he said, sweeping his arms to include a vast territory more than just this little café. "But we have more evidence of their villages in Ankara, the area that is now called Agrigento."

"But I thought the Greeks settled Agrigento?"

"Yes, well, they came there and called it, at first, Akragas. The Greeks came to Sicily in the time of 800 B.C. to 600 B.C., but the early Sicanians were already there." Then he turned his head and stared directly into my eyes.

"Why do you think the Greeks chose that spot? There were already people there!"

Vito looked back away, toward his espresso, and took a sip.

"There were already people there," he repeated. "So, there were tribes to invade and suppress, and tools to take, and women to make babies with. But we're getting too far ahead talking about the Greeks. Let's return to the people from Iberia."

―――――

I arrived before Vito the next morning. The time of his appearance was usually predictable, but I had noticed over the week of meeting with him that his old age and creaky bones could occasionally cause a delay in his arrival at our morning rendezvous.

But here he was again, strolling through the door and waving a hand at the barista to begin the day's proceeding. He slipped into the booth with me and pointed his sparkling eyes and smile in my direction. I knew he was going to spring something on me.

"Ankara."

"Yes, you told me," I responded. "But tell me more about the Sicanians who settled there. I did some research last night."

"Sì," he nodded impatiently, but waved his hand palm down as if to shush me. "And so, we begin with Ankara. There's much debate about the origins of the name for the people – the Sicani. Some people think it suggests they came from the region around the Sicanus River in Iberia, hence the name Sicani. They were driven out of their region by the invasion of another prehistoric tribe, the Ligurians who swept across the northern edge of the Mediterranean from the peninsula of Italy, west, into Iberia. The Ligurians' arrival pushed the Sicani farther westward, until they got to the opening between the sea and the Atlantic Ocean, the gap we now call Gibraltar. They crossed it to reach the northwestern tip of the continent to the south and escape the invasion of the Ligurians."

"Yes," I interjected, "but we talked about that yesterday. Well, except for them being driven west."

"Si, but I want to talk about their name. They weren't known as Sicani or Sicanians until they reached the southern shore of Sicily, where they took up the name to remind the tribesmen of their origins. In any case, most historians agree that the terms 'Sicani' and 'Sicanians' were the first recorded name for the people of Sicily."

"But there were people there already, right? In Sicily, I mean."

"Si, but we have no record of their name."

"You say 'first recorded name,' but written language didn't come around for a while, I thought."

"Si, si," he persisted with a slight hint of inpatience. "Nowadays, scientists use the invention of recordkeeping – symbols, words, whatever – as the boundary between pre-history and history, right?"

I nodded.

"Writing," I said. "That's what you mean."

Vito mused for a moment, rubbing his chin with his withered right hand, then nodding quickly, he resumed.

"The earliest form of symbolic writing was around 3000 B.C., right?"

I had to agree but didn't really know.

"The first symbols suggested nouns. Things that mattered in their lives mattered most in their communication," he continued. "Actions, or verbs – they could be simulated with gestures, no?" Vito said, waving his arms and cupping his hands to make the point. "But objects couldn't."

I was trying to keep up with him. Seeing my confusion, Vito pointed at the little caffé spoon that rested next to my espresso.

"Spoon," was all he said, but he curled his finger back and pointed to himself.

I handed him the spoon, then realized what had happened. He used a word for a noun – the spoon – but conveyed the action with a gesture. If he had only said spoon without the finger motion, I wouldn't have known what he wanted; and if he had just crooked his finger without telling which object he was referring to, I wouldn't have been able to understand him.

"A bit later, these symbols were broken down into sounds," he continued, "things we call syllables that could be infinitely rearranged to create new words. And this led to a further breaking down of the syllables into individual letters, again with infinite possible reconstructions.

"This deconstruction and reassembly of the sounds they made with their vocal cords allowed the evolution of a more detailed spoken language, but it was critical to the advance of written language."

"Thanks for the tour of the invention of writing," I teased him. "But what does that have to do with the Sicanians' name?"

"Nothing," he laughed in reply, gleefully throwing his hands up. "That's just written language." I knew that Vito often took pleasure in such random tangents from our subject.

"But you asked if it was recorded," he continued, getting back on subject. "The names of people and things were recorded in their memories and persisted for centuries through spoken language, especially in their folklore and poetry, long before symbols for the words were scratched into rock. The Sicani probably held that name for a thousand years before anyone wrote it down. Now, to Ankara..."

"Okay, okay, but before you begin: Isn't Ankara the capital of Turkey?" I asked. "Doesn't that suggest a connection to that region?"

"*Certumente*," Vito said, as his chin bobbed to acknowledge the point. The ever-so slight Sicilian variation in pronunciation of the Italian word for "certainly" – *certamente* – distracted me at first, and I had to catch back up with what Vito was saying.

"...why some people get confused. They say these first invaders to Sicily must have come from the eastern edge of the Mediterranean and they brought the name Ankara from their homeland and assigned it to their new settlement. But the invaders from Anatolia – the Elymi – hadn't arrived in Sicily yet. They wouldn't come for another three thousand years. And, besides, Ankara, the capital of Turkey, wasn't founded until about 2000 B.C., long after the early Sicani arrived here."

"So, the similarity of the people's name to the Iberian river basin is more convincing evidence of origins than the similarity of their city's name to Turkey," I suggested.

"*Esattumente!*" Vito proclaimed, revealing a bit of glowing pride in his student. Again, that vague twist of the Sicilian dialect. Vito had been careful to speak English with me, and otherwise to stick to mainland Italian which he assumed – generously – that I understood. But, every once in a while, he slipped back into vernacular.

"Alright," I continued, "let's get back to the people. What were they like? I know they came across the Strait of Gibraltar, down the Mediterranean coast of modern Morocco, and across the northern part of Africa until they saw Sicily in the distance."

"No, not Sicily right away. At first, they saw the island of Pantelleria, settled there for a while, then jumped across the shallow waters to southern Sicily."

"Okay, yes, I remember that now. But let's talk about the people, the Sicani," I pressed.

"*Sì*, but first of all, let's begin with their world."

Vito seemed not to be able to resist these tangents.

"You see, a warmer climate had been settling in as the European glaciers receded. This allowed the growth of forests and, with more trees, came more animals. The seeds that had traveled in the bellies of birds and animals from North Africa had established the basis, but the lengthening of the warm seasons allowed the plants and trees to multiply and cover the landscape. The islands of Sicily, Pantelleria, the

Aeolians – all forced up from the earth's crust by volcanic eruptions – became lush green hills and fields.

"And even before the arrival of the Sicani, the aboriginal tribes had grown and spread across the land.

"When the invaders from Iberia came around 4300 B.C., they brought their culture and introduced it to these original people. These Sicani were more advanced, had more tools at their disposal, so their technologies, however primitive compared to ours, dominated the practices of the aborigines. A very special tool that the Sicani brought with them was obsidian, a tough yet brittle glass formed from cooled volcanic lava. They adapted it to use not only to cut things and make tools, but to serve as the edge of the tool itself.

"Woven fabrics made from goat hair, wool, and plant fibers were already on the island, but the Sicani brought more skill to the enterprise. They imported an early version of the loom that allowed them to spin the fibers more quickly and weave them into stretches of cloth.

"They brought their own style of pottery. Making clay bowls and urns was common in Neolithic Sicily, even before these early Sicanians arrived, but they added art and artistry to the purely functional items crafted on the island prior to their arrival. Decorations added to early pottery was limited to some parallel scratchings, impressions of seashells or fingertips, and no more than the red coloring offered by the ochre to be found on the island. But the proto-Sicanians had learned how to coax other colors from the earth – colors found in different compounds that, when hydrated, became a paste. They had for many years inscribed their clay vessels with parallel lines running in zig-zag fashion, and they had already discovered how to make white, brown, black, and red paint to apply to the shell of the pot."

"They sound like a much more developed civilization," I commented.

"Yes, and this is the reason that they mastered the land with little trouble. They used items of trade at first but, where trade didn't accomplish cooperation between tribes, they would use force to claim lands and take over coveted spots on the banks of rivers and shoreline. There was one amazing development that made all this possible."

Vito paused without finishing that thought – pausing for effect, I was sure – but I could also tell that he was waiting for me to ask.

"And...what...is...that?"

"Horses!" he said with glee.

I knew that horses already existed on the mainland and I assumed that the early Sicanians would have them as well.

"Why is that an 'amazing development?'" I asked. "Horses were already a part of European life."

"They were only used as pack animals, sometimes for meat," he offered. "It wasn't until about this time that the people began riding horses and enlisting them as draft animals for plowing. It's likely that the proto-Sicanians invaded this island and then proceeded to – what shall we say – 'conquer' the locals, to use their position atop the horse to intimidate the original settlers of the island."

"Like the Spanish did to the Aztecs in South America?"

"Just so. But this was happening on Sicily six thousand years earlier. And when the invaders got down from the animals, they contributed to the gene population with great vigor," he said with a broad smile.

3950 B.C.E.

3950 B.C.E.

SETTLEMENTS AT ANKARA AND CASELLO

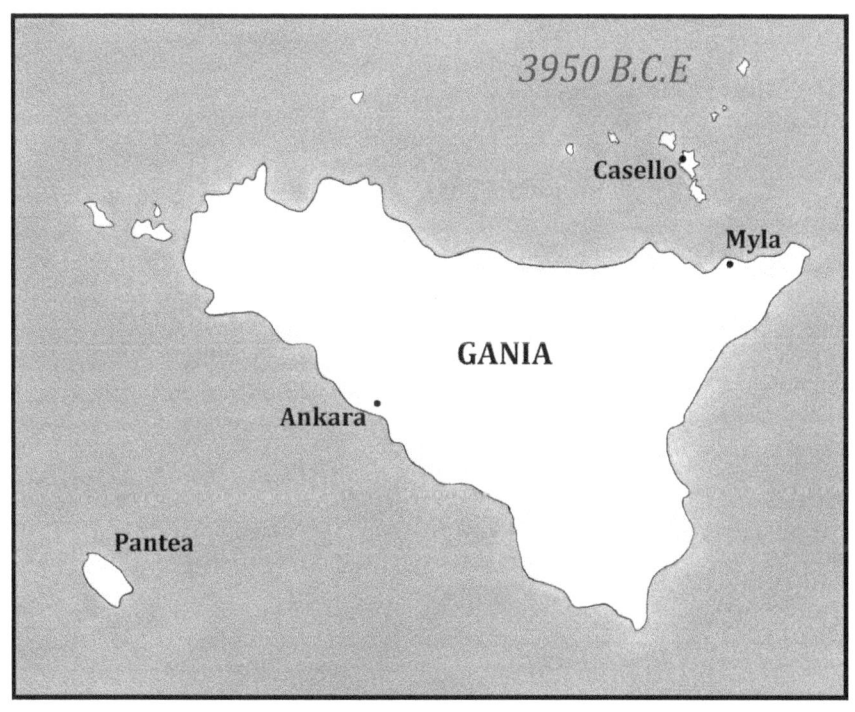

AEOLIAN ISLANDS

3950 B.C.E.

MYLA

Fina was struggling with the cargo, down on her knees and leaning into the dugout canoe that rocked gently in the soft waves at the very edge of the sea. Her man, Xappo, always seemed to make these things harder than they should be, like starting out so early on this cold morning that had come after another long, chilly night. He said they needed to make a deal with the people who had the *sidia*, and the trip would take them all day.

"There is no fire in the sky," he had told her, pointing to the island in northern distance on the evening before going to bed. "It will be safe now, but not later."

Fina could see that there was no glow from Lipari, no red in the darkening sky beyond the sea, but she didn't believe Xappo could predict when it would come. He had been right many times before, and he would jut out his chin, put his fists on his hips, and declare that he had the wisdom to know. But she also knew that he had been wrong, at times proudly sitting up on the low hills outside of their settlement in Myla and waiting for the volcanic eruption that he knew was coming – that didn't.

On this particular morning, they had agreed to go to Lipari and trade for *sidia*, and Fina knew the trip would require two full days and a night spent on the cold beach on the southern tip of Lipari. But Xappo wanted to take more goods to trade this time, and he was not helping much in loading the boat.

Braided rope and soft furs went into the bottom of the canoe. Antlers carved into human shapes, plus more imaginative carvings intended to suggest divinities, went into a bag sewn together from a sheep's hide – another item that, once the contents were traded – would be used as barter. The seashells Fina had collected and pierced for stringing went into the bottom of a pouch, and flint rock that Xappo prized for starting fires was added too.

"Xappo, come here and hold the boat steady. It's drifting out with the waves."

"Pull it in farther," he replied.

"Come here!" she shouted with unconcealed anger.

Xappo moved quickly to her side, dropped the roll of rope that he had been coiling, and grabbed the dry end of the boat with a heave. The craft bobbed once more in the white foam of another wave, then broke free onto the sand.

"We can't leave it here," he said, pointing to the dry dock where the canoe landed. "If it's loaded with our things, we won't be able to push it back into the water."

"You're strong," she argued, contriving to appeal to his ego to get him to cooperate, but Xappo still looked dissatisfied.

Once the boat was loaded, Xappo stepped into the cold water and attached the rope he was carrying to the end of the canoe that pointed toward the water. At the same time, Fina grabbed a flat board shaped like a paddle that they had made from broad tree branch and began to dig a trench from the same end of the boat toward the water. As she shoveled deeper into the sand, water began to fill up the channel, and at that moment Xappo gave the rope a heavy tug. The rounded bottom of the dugout canoe slipped into this temporary channel and was buoyed by the water that seeped in alongside of it. Another tug from Xappo and the boat lifted free of the sand and into the foamy wash at the edge of the sea.

They pulled themselves shoulders first, and then hips, into their boat and Fina sat in front and dipped her paddle into the water as an oar. Xappo reached into the belly of the craft and retrieved another paddle and joined his woman in stroking the water beside them and pushing the dugout into the sea.

———

Xappo and Fina left the shore near Myla before the sun broke out of the water to their right. Once the giant fireball had crested the waves, though, it threw light and warmth their way. Their leggings had been wetted by the launch, and the sun helped to dry them while the daylight helped them see the craggy peaks of the mountain in the island in the distance.

"What are you stopping for?" Xappo asked Fina. She had pulled her oar from the water and sat back to rest for a moment, and he was quickly displaying his disappointment.

Without turning around to look at him seated behind her, Fina sent a convincing rebuttal with the harsh shrug of her shoulders, but she returned her paddle to the water and resumed the effort.

They reached the far shore past midday, both of them hopping out of the canoe and working together to drag it above the waves onto the dry sand. The dugout was heavier now than when they began their journey. The cargo was unchanged but the crude wooden boat absorbed some water in crossing and carried that weight with it.

Xappo and Fina worked quickly to set up a camp, start a fire before the air temperature dropped again, and empty the cargo from the boat. It was important to make themselves ready for the night, but if they wanted to return to Myla the next day, it was also imperative to be able to turn the boat upside down to help the hull of the craft dry out and leave its extra water weight behind before they embarked on another crossing.

Once the necessary steps were accomplished, they arranged their barter items, collecting them in one pile around which they would sleep that night. Xappo had been here before, at times with Fina, and he hadn't encountered any wild animals to fear. But he didn't want to have his cargo – the whole reason for this trip – exposed too far from them to perhaps be pilfered by the small band of traders from Casello who spent long months of every year on the southern tip of the island. They waited for trade, and would already know that the Mylans had landed, and could steal the goods under cover of darkness instead of paying for them in the daylight.

Xappo and Fina then prepared to eat a brief meal of leathery beef strips, milk from the pouch that Fina had brought along, and a day-old loaf of bread that was baked in their village oven the afternoon before they departed.

"There's no one here," Xappo said between bites of food. "No one on the beach, and no one in the hills."

"How do you know there's no one in the hills?" Fina asked. She was skeptical of some things Xappo professed to know, but she agreed that he was a good hunter, and hunters have strong eyes and keen hearing.

"I don't know. I just don't think there's anyone there."

For a moment, he stopped chewing and just listened. The sky had grown darker as they prepared their campsite, and the stars had emerged as bright sparkling lights above them. Xappo and Fina sat with their backs to the hills and faced the water; the slope of the sand made this the most comfortable position. But Xappo also turned to look over his shoulder to examine the hills behind them. Then he turned completely around in order to direct his attention to the mountain and the little island world they had landed on. He sat there for a moment, his back to the water, chewing on the beef and washing it down with sheep's milk.

Then he stopped.

He looked back over his shoulder at the sea or, more precisely, at the sky above the sea. The myriad little lights above shone down on him, an unbroken carpet of shiny dots that twinkled in the night sky. Turning back toward the hills, Xappo figured out what had alarmed him. It wasn't animals or the more-feared bipedal threats.

Craning his neck to survey the sky once more, his view swept from the south, in the direction of Myla where the stars shined brightly, to above, where the vast collection of stars became more scattered, to the north and the hills in front of him over the island mountain, where there were no stars to be seen. He knew the stars above the island's hills were not being obscured by the treeline. There could be clouds which had come in as they were setting up their camp, clouds that would gather from the other side of the mountain and crowd the sky above them.

But clouds and the portent of rain would make the air cooler. Xappo knew that. So, he concentrated on the air temperature. It was warmer than he would have expected. Then he sensed an odd smell of burnt ash.

The hair stood up on his forearms and Xappo knew that it wasn't from the cold air. It was the fear that settled in over him as he realized that the clouded sky was probably from smoke, and the warm air was probably from the volcano that loomed over Lipari.

"What is it?" Fina asked.

Xappo was afraid to say anything until he was certain. Besides, what could they do? If he was right this time and the volcano was already erupting, they were stuck on the beach, on the southern side of the island, the side that the Liparians had abandoned to live in the north, in Casello, because of the destruction caused by each eruption.

Just at that moment, a red arrow of light shot into the sky. In the darkness it appeared to emerge from nowhere, but they knew it came from the peak of the fiery mountain on whose foothills they rested.

It was quiet then, but Xappo looked over at Fina, no longer able to hide his discovery from her. Fina's face was lighted by the fire between them, and there was a look of undisguised panic on her face as another red arrow of light pulsed from the mountain.

Xappo and Fina knew what was coming, but they were stuck. They couldn't go back into the water in the darkness and, even if they could, would they leave all of their barter goods here on the beach? And they couldn't outrun the volcano if the gods decided to throw up molten fire and cover the beach they occupied with its hissing, scalding lava.

Without waiting to discuss the matter, Xappo jumped to his feet, flipped the boat back over and dragged it to the sea. Fina sat, motionless in terror, while her man prepared to take them back into the water.

Finally, quickly, she burst from her stupor.

"We can't go back," she screamed, her voice now mingled with sudden pops and roaring sounds from the mountain. "We can't make it!"

"Come. Come quickly," said Xappo. "We won't sail back to Myla, but we can't be on the beach either. We must get in the water!"

Wherever that idea came from, Fina trusted Xappo, so she quickly joined him in preparing to launch their boat. They left all their goods on the shore, and the campfire still burned in the sand. But they had little choice other than to escape to the cool waters and hope to survive the gods' anger.

"Get in!" he shouted, and Fina did as she was told. The boat was still sodden with sea water and still heavy, and Fina's weight added to it. But with a mighty shove, Xappo pushed the boat out into the waves and deep enough for their oars to work. They paddled furiously, taking the boat far into the water before pausing to see what was happening on the island.

The red and orange light that shot from the top of the mountain illuminated the hillside. They saw brilliant liquid waves of lava pouring relentlessly down the slopes, engulfing their campsite and obliterating their trade goods. The red-hot carpet of destruction poured forth into the sea, hissing as it breached the waves, filling cavities in the shoreline and seething with a terrifying yellow-white brilliance.

Xappo and Fina returned to paddling their boat out to sea, realizing that they had not gone far enough yet to escape the lava that now blanketed the beach and low waves. Boulders and steaming rocks were hurled into the sky, landing with great terrifying thuds along the mountainside and what was once the beach. They heard a screaming sound above them and looked up to see a pointed rock pierce the sky and fly over, and beyond them, crashing into the sea that they were paddling into.

The mountain convulsed and more rocks and boulders were thrown up from the volcano, some now landing in the water near Xappo and Fina. Only once did he look at her, seeing the fear mixed with sweat that poured down from her face.

A craggy rock, trailing smoke and burnt with flaming orange edges, splashed right next to their boat and threw a wave of warm water in their faces. The water filled their canoe and made it harder to control, but Xappo and Fina returned to their task of rowing out to sea.

Just then another rock, half the size of their canoe, flew into the sky and headed straight for them. It was only a few seconds, but Xappo and Fina looked at each other just before the boulder struck their craft.

The impact snapped the boat in two and tossed the passengers into the water. Stunned and bloodied, Xappo waved his right arm to get control of his situation and find Fina. She floated by him, face down in the water, but he could see by the light of the volcano that her head had been crushed by the rock that capsized their canoe. He took hold of her arm and pulled her close to him, then he realized that his other arm only dangled by his side in the water. Trying to lift his left arm above the waves, he saw that he had no control over it.

Xappo looked at his shoulder, saw that the fur covering it was gone and the bones protruded through the skin, and he wept for the first time. With one last look at the seething fiery mass of the mountain that towered over them, he gathered Fina's lifeless body in the cradle of his right arm and slowly slipped below the waves.

*****.

In Casello, the darkened sky lit up suddenly with terrifying roaring daggers of bright yellow-orange light. The people on the island could smell the smoke that drifted down the mountain toward their village, and the sulphurous fumes of brimstone burned their noses.

Soluri was just a little boy, easily frightened by spirits in the night, and his older sister, Chinsi, usually comforted the boy when he woke in the darkness from a frightening dream. But this dark night they both sat up, clinging to one another, startled awake by the sound and fury of the eruption on their mountain. They were north of the volcano, and it usually spread its deadly lava down the southward slope, but the brilliance of the fiery arrows of light and the booming sounds of explosions left them huddled in each other's arms.

Their village in this northern part of Lipari, called Casello then, was home to about seventy people with their meager flocks of sheep and small farm plots. It was tough existence, never far from starvation and closer still to any manner of seasonal setbacks, including crop failure, famine among the feed animals, or a pestilence of insects from the proximity to the sea. Riverlets of tinny water wandered down from the heights of their mountain, but never with enough flow to provide an abundance of clean drinking water.

So why did they stay? Why did Roaro and Mina, the children's parents, decide that the island of Lipari could support them. And why choose Casello, on the northern tip of the island?

The adults were out of their hut at the moment, checking on the other rude constructions around Casello, making sure that their community was intact and surviving this newest eruption of the volcano. That left Chinsi to comfort Soluri, and for these two children to rock the baby Donota to quiet his cries in the night.

Fiery spasms from the volcano were not a new experience. They might be years apart, and they varied in intensity, but the events were frequent enough that every living person on Lipari had seen one firsthand. And each had their own stories to tell of the thunder and lightning that accompanied these angry outbursts from the god of the mountain.

The community survived – and remained there – mostly for the trade in *sidia*, the ancient word for obsidian. It was easy to recognize its value; people came from islands around Lipari to trade valuable items for even a few shards of the sharp black glass.

But the Casellans endured great hardship in exchange for that item. The children couldn't understand, and even the adults questioned the wisdom of the choice of settlements, but there they stayed.

On this particular night, when the sights and sounds from the mountain were particularly awe-inspiring, each and every member of the village wondered aloud about their choice once again.

"We must leave here," said Mina. "We cannot live and will not survive here."

In the sudden transformation of their world from one of relative calm to one of outright panic, Roaro had to agree. In his survey of the damage to the village, and in his conversations with other members of their tribe, he raised the subject again.

"This is worse than before," he told the men gathered by the night campfire. A few of his companions nodded in agreement.

"But where? And what would we do?" asked the man by his side.

No one had a quick answer and, just then, another more titanic boom split the air and a geyser of ash and sparks lifted into the air.

When the sounds had passed and only the low rumbling of the mountain was heard, the people returned to their discussion.

"This island and its *sidia* have always supported us. We came here with nothing, from the land where the sun comes up, where our animals were dying…"

"And the other tribes were killing us," interjected one of the women.

The various tribes in the central part of Italy had fought for many generations, and Liparians had finally given up on their villages and sailed to this island. For many years, the volcano was quiet and they were satisfied with a paltry existence as long as the *sidia* held out. There was a large deposit, and they understood from the elders' stories that the glass came from the volcano, but they didn't want or need any more cooled lava to trade. They didn't want any more eruptions to cast down new fields of *sidia*.

Now the mountain had reawakened, and some thought it was the gods growing angry at them trading the *sidia* for other things. Roaro and Mina disagreed.

"Why would the god of the mountain care?" she asked. There's so much here we could never sell it all."

"Maybe the god of the mountain thinks it belongs to him," was the quick retort.

Another boom and fiery eruption disturbed the brief peace.

As the sequence of volcanic events slowed and, eventually, subsided deep into the night, each of the villagers returned to their huts to consider their situation. The morning would be another chance to talk, if the mountain didn't bury them under burning ash.

3950 B.C.E.

ANKARA

THE FOUR MEN HAD GONE TO EXPLORE THE FIELDS AND HILLS FAR beyond Ankara. They brought sacks made of sheepskin slung over their shoulders, and short spears tipped with sharp blades of chert. The weapons they carried on this trip were shorter than the hefty spears that were specifically for hunting animals.

On this day, they were hunting for flint and other useful raw materials to use for trading or for toolmaking back at their village in Ankara. A long spear would have been unnecessary, but the men never ventured far from the security of their civilization without carrying some sort of protection in the case of unwanted attacks by humans or wild animals.

Their toolmaking had advanced, and they had moved from chipped stone to the more angular shape of points, often with sharper edges produced when the river stone was fractured on natural seams. When mounted on a wooden shaft and tied in place with a short thread of soft bark stripped from a tree, the assembled weapon was lighter and better balanced than weapons that had been used for so many years in the past.

Nefa especially prized his short spear. The chert-tip was prized by all in his cluster in Ankara because embedded in its crystalline sections was half the skull of a little bird. Nefa assumed that his god had killed the little aviator and placed its head in the stone for Nefa, a talisman to guarantee his ventures in hunting.

As the little squad of men made their foray into the hinterlands north of Ankara, the others teased Nefa about the unusual gift that formed the point of his spear.

"It is already dead," Papu said. "What can you catch with a dead animal?"

"It looks like your little 'catch' already lost the battle!" chimed Insta.

Chaka laughed along with them, but Nefa only smiled. In a culture where so many things were not yet understood – from the weather to the seasons, even to the frightening days when the sun disappeared or the mountain spewed fire and ash – any such little sign, especially ones that didn't suggest a threat, were welcome knowledge that the god or gods were paying attention to the people.

They had been gone for a full day and continued to roam farther and farther from Ankara. Ankarans, especially the men, had explored the areas to the north and east of Ankara over the years and had a mental map of the terrain, the rivers, and the mountains in between. They knew what wildlife populated the plains and what rocky challenges might present themselves as the hunters moved about the countryside.

They settled on a small clearing in the trees alongside a streambed. There, they could have water and use their weapons to land spear fish to be cooked that night over the fire. The four of them set about their separate tasks without too much deliberation. In an advanced civilization such as theirs, it was already common to recognize the special skills of each person, and each man in this party already knew who would perform what task. In addition to that, this small group of men had hunted together many times and knew what each would do as soon as they laid down their packs.

Chaka set the stones for the campfire while Papu wandered between the trees collecting small twigs. He knew to gather the sticks that were brown and brittle first, and he delivered them to Chaka who had completed his design of the fire pit. Then Papu returned to the treeline and began filling his arms with thicker branches, even some that were a bit green and recently fallen, because he knew that Chaka would have quickly set the kindling ablaze with his flintstone, so the branches that were not so brittle would still succumb to the heat of the flame.

Nefa waded out into the shallow waters of the stream, looking for the faint ripples in the water's surface that indicated the path of fish below. He knew how to separate the regular ripples that the moving water produced when it flowed over stationary objects like river rocks from the undulating, twisting splashes made by moving creatures under the water. Watching closely, he stepped farther into the channel and spied the long twisting rivulets that convinced him that a school of small fish were swimming between his legs.

Meanwhile, Insta had also come to the edge of the river but only stepped ankle deep into the water. He planned to harvest *ponchu*, the flowing shoots of green weeds that grew in tight clusters just below the surface. Insta could grasp a handful and pull the plant up by its roots, but he knew to do that downstream of Nefa, or else the turbulence would divert the small fish that his friend was trying to catch.

After harvesting the *ponchu* and catching enough fish, the two men returned to the campsite. Chaka's dog had accompanied the men on this foray into the hinterlands of Gania. He was one of the many canines in Ankara, the domesticated descendants of the feral wolves that plied the hills around every settlement on the island. Only certain dogs adapted to accept a human in place of the alpha dog. But they made excellent companions and, after several generations, were visibly different in structure and temperament from their wild ancestors.

Chaka's dog was always by his side. The earliest domesticated breeds of dogs could only do what the people taught them to do. They were not considered part of the family unit and they weren't trained in retrieval of felled birds since the humans hadn't even mastered the talent for bringing down the aviary prey with arrows yet. The dogs had mostly accommodated to the humans, thanks to bones and small morsels of meat thrown their way. For the humans to accommodate to the dogs would wait for the people to discover the utility of these domesticated animals in their midst.

Chaka's dog was innately smarter than some other feral canines to settle in with the humans. His dog did a bit of hunting with his master and assisted in the killing of small animals when the contest involved close-order combat. But otherwise, the dog merely stayed by the man's side and lived off the discarded food of the group. A parasite by any name, but with a growing, and exalted status.

The men enjoyed their meal and passed an hour or so afterward telling stories of their lives and adventures so far. The stories had taken on a familiarity known and liked by each of them; they had spent so much time together that little of each man's life was not already known to the others.

"No," Papu laughed, "he'll learn."

"It is not too hard," said Insta, laughing with him. "Your boy will be a strong man, but he can't fight with chickens. It's not right," and all the men roared with laughter.

Papu's little son had taken to chasing the chickens around the pen where they were kept in Ankara. The boy would emit peels of laughter, at times doubling over in fun, while chasing the chickens back and forth across the pen.

"It's not right," said Chaka, trying to suppress his smile and pretend that this was a serious topic.

"No...yes," attempted Papu, "it's not right." But he was not bothered by it. The boy had energy and found the semi-wild chickens to be a source of glee. Papu and the boy's mother, Sincia, would not deprive him of his fun. Only the child's older sister, Lalana, was bothered by it.

"She says the boy is *pazzu*," – crazy – said Papu.

"Maybe we are all a little crazy," reasoned Nefa, nodding his head slightly, but halving the smile that had spread across his face.

They passed a little more time that way before forming their rolls and bedding down for the night. Nefa took the first watch, and was followed by the other men, one at a time. There was no schedule for this. It was a moonless night and although they understood the movement of the stars, the only clear way to tell when it was time to change the watch was when the man who sat up began to lean forward in near slumber.

*****.

Chaka was the last to serve the night watch, and he was still alert as the bright rays of the sun broke through the stand of trees to the east and illuminated his world. His dog had curled up astride his lap, helping to keep both man and dog warm, and its eyes were still closed when the light dawned on the camp.

Chaka didn't wake the other men. There was no schedule to this expedition, and they would have plenty of time to proceed with their project as the day warmed and they were ready. But within a few minutes of the sun's rise, the light spread across the sleeping eyes of his friends, and the other men began to stretch and rise from their positions.

The dog's eyes sprang open also, but without any movement of its head. It seemed that dogs were able to move from sleep to full wakefulness in an instant, a feature the men liked because it also served as an alarm in case some threat lurked nearby. The dog's eyes rolled upward and it saw that Chaka was awake and alert, and this caused the animal to lift its head and look about the camp.

All seemed to rise at about the same time, men and dog, and Chaka stirred the embers of the campfire to get the small flames that still licked the blackened sticks to come back to life. He had reserved some kindling for just this purpose, and as soon as a spike of orange light sprang from the grey ash, he spread these little twigs over it to catch a flame.

Papu stood and stretched, and Insta waved his arms to free them from the stiffness of sleeping on the ground. The men prepared a short meal made of the leftover blackened fish and some greens from the river, then prepared to close their camp and move on.

They spent the morning hours moving farther north and into the hills in the interior of the island. They began to fill their pouches with flint, some chert, and small clumps of sandstone found in the cave openings that they passed throughout the day. There would be the occasional clump of amber found among a cluster of trees, and the men prized these greatly because of their luminous yellow-orange color and the possibility of finding some small item within the dried tree resin. All amber globules were kept; if a small stone or leaf was present within one, it was wrapped carefully in cloth and protected from the other rocks that filled the men's sacks. Such things were treated with reverence, as if they were messages from the gods.

After several hours, when the sun had passed over the high point in the sky, the men spread out to survey as much as they could of a particular clearing near the stream. They had already decided to camp there for the night but, before settling down, wanted to harvest what they could from the area in the fading light of day.

The sound of a struggle and a muted scream reached Nefa first. He spun on his heel and searched for the source and direction of the sound. He called out to his fellows and heard Papu reply. No other sound came at first, until Insta's voice could be heard calling to them. Another scream came, and a vicious snarling sound, and the three men were able to direct their attention to the place where it came from.

Nefa, Papu, and Insta ran toward the sound of the struggle, and had already concluded that Chaka was the one involved with it. They knew their friend would not be fighting the dog but assumed that the snarling sound was coming from the canine.

They ran across an open field and back into a stand of trees, where they found Chaka and his dog in the final moments of combat with a large, tusked wild boar. The animal was thrashing about and ripping bloody gashes in man and dog, as the pair tried first to subdue their prey, then to flee it. The boar, spotting the arrival of more men, fled the scene, and Chaka fell to his knees over the whimpering sound of his dog.

Blood poured from Chaka's left side, mid-section, and leg. The dog seemed to have fared no better, and Nefa could see the animal's chest heave in failing attempts to breathe. Then, in an instant, Chaka lurched forward and fell to the side of the animal. As the dog moved his head close to his master's, the man let out a long whistle of air, and his chest collapsed in an unnatural state.

By that point, the men had arrived by Chaka's side. The boar was gone and, although Insta stood watch to make sure it didn't return, Nefa and Papu tended to the fallen. It was soon apparent that Chaka was dead, and that his dog was in the final throws of life. Nefa looked at Papu, and they both looked back down at their stricken friend.

Nefa reached his arm below the head of the dog, gently lifting it to allow his arm to encircle the skull. With a sudden twist, he snapped the dog's neck to end the struggle, and then laid the animal's head back down beside Chaka.

Nefa and Papu slouched back on their heels, and Insta came to kneel beside them. The men knew their friend was gone and that his dog had fought to save his master from the pig, both lost in an allied struggle against the wild.

The survivors abandoned their quest for treasures that afternoon and decided to abandon their hunt altogether and return to Ankara the following morning. Instead of a hunt, they buried their friend with the dog at his side, and placed the man's spear and two amber globes from his sack in the ditch where they put his body. After covering the hole with soft dirt, they piled stones upon it to make sure some wild beast wandering the field couldn't exhume the remains and foul the memory of Chaka and his dog.

———

Nefa, Papu, and Insta trudged back to Ankara later that day. They had sacks only partly filled with amber, chert, and flint; and they had some of the hard knobs of tubers the dog had unearthed the day before the attack occurred. These *tartrae* as they were called were sought after by those who cooked the meat in the village, because their aromas made the sometimes-foul smells of the old animal flesh more inviting.

But their hearts were empty.

They emerged from the woods as they approached their city but were not noticed until they had rounded the ditch and approached the main entrance to Ankara. The suddenness of their appearance – without Chaka – set off waves of crying.

The men would never have returned home without their partner, and the people – particularly Fintala – knew the meaning of this right away. She rushed up to the men and pleaded for an explanation, which Nefa provided in a halting way. Mina hid behind her mother; the little girl only peered around Fintala carefully hoping to find the dog, her playmate. It was then that the loss fully sank in and Fintala collapsed in crying with Mina wrapping her arms around her mother's neck.

Nefa and Papu dropped to a knee and tried to comfort Fintala, knowing that such tragedies were known to their people, but also knowing that the first moments of the realization were always the hardest. Fintala and Mina would need support from those in the village, and Fintala might one day look for a new man, but for now they had to mourn the loss of Chaka.

News of Chaka's death spread through the city, and Ankarans from other clusters came to Fintala's courtyard. Some came to comfort her; others came just to stare. One feature of the human condition that has survived millennia is the desire to be witness to tragedy as if somehow this closeness to it is a shield against the same fate befalling ourselves. Ancient people were no different, and for every sympathetic mourner who huddled close to Fintala and Mina, there were several others who merely stood in silence or talked in whispers about the terrible thing that had happened.

But the pace of life resumed quickly. The death of one member of the society wouldn't stand in the way of food gathering and preparation, child tending, construction, and other demands of Ankaran life.

Two young men who were just growing into their maturity left the scene in the courtyard to resume their work in a narrow alley between two of the buildings. They had dug a shallow hole in the ground and had a stack of curved sharpened sticks bundled nearby. Once the curve of the depression suited them, they took each of the sticks in turn, and pushed the pointed end into the ground at the circumference of the rim of the pit. The sticks curved inward as if to cast a wooden net over the hole. Although they didn't touch at the center, the branches arched over the hole and formed a covering.

When that task was completed, one of the boys went back to his home and returned bearing a turtle about the length of the boy's forearm and lowered the animal into the pit. Standing back, the two youngsters considered the pen they had designed for the turtle.

As the animal's head emerged from the shell, and his legs explored the dirt of the depression in the earth, it tried to climb forward up the slope. But the encounter with the arcing sticks turned its movement into a more vertical vector. Threatening to be overturned, the turtle backed off and explored another part of the pit, finding the same obstacle the other way. The boys watched in some humor as the turtle tried repeatedly to escape, without success.

Turtle meat and the shell that would be left after the cooking process were highly valued in Ankaran society. The captured animals were kept in the people's homes until a pit could be dug. But with proper planning, such a device could be prepared to hold more than a single animal, which was the goal of these young boys who had produced a holding pen large enough for several of the animals.

The father of one of them looked on with pride. The man sat on a leather-covered rock, resting against the cold hard surface but hunched over to perform his task. He held a fist-sized rock in his right hand and rested his left hand on another rock that was encircled by his legs.

Hefting the smaller rock in his right hand, he rocked it and twisted it, inspecting the surface, as if looking for something in the grain. Then, gripping it tightly in his hand, he looked down at the stone at his feet and brought his right hand down hard, smacking the hammer stone in his right hand against the bigger rock. A fragment of the hammer stone flew off, two large chunks flipped to the ground and several splinters sprayed about his chest and face.

He examined the fracture marks on the rock in his right hand, then put it down and searched at his feet for the large chunks that had splintered from it. Picking one up he ran his finger along the edge, gave an approving nod, and compared it to the other large chunk that had settled at his right foot.

His woman sat next to him and grunted her approval of the man's point making. She was busy with the production of another pot for their family, working with the young child at her elbow to shape the clay and round it for use as a large cooking vessel.

The child brought clay from a nearby pit astride the stream outside Ankara. The material came from a natural deposit of dense, pliable mud that the families in this cluster had been mining for a long time. The child piled the clumps on a board and delivered the harvest to her mother, who used her fingers to drip some water on the substance and loosen it a bit.

The woman had a flat wooden board between her legs that rested on the rounded top of a small rock. The board was balanced on the broad level crest of the rock, and she could spin it as she worked the clay into the shape she desired. The rock below wouldn't move, but the smooth surface would allow the movement of the flattened board on top, so the woman could rotate the entire project rather than having to pry up the clay bowl that she was forming and turn it each time she wanted to shape the opposite side.

She didn't trust the little girl at her side with this new pot, since it was still fragile, but she allowed her daughter to deliver the finished project – still standing on the board – to the communal kiln nearby. At the oven, another woman gently slid the new pot off the board and into the oven, using a long-handled paddle, and returned the board to the woman by her home to repeat the process.

Meanwhile, the woman tending the kiln continued to manage the flames within, ensuring a steady temperature, and occasionally rotating the pottery to achieve consistent firing. She used dried animal dung with the tree branches in the oven, learning over time that the organic substances worked in tandem to keep the fire burning at a steady temperature.

Like the many other tribes spread across the plains in Gania, the Ankarans had organized their lives according to simple, yet productive patterns. Farming of plants took place outside the city walls, except for some small plots of herbs in the cluster courtyards, while animal management took place inside the walls. Pottery production techniques had improved as had tool and weapon manufacture. Meals were produced at the family level and at the social level, depending on whether the event was simple for daily sustenance, or whether some large animal had been slaughtered and could be shared, or if the shaman decided the day called for a ceremonial practice.

Social organization and specialization continued to develop. Each cluster had its leaders, normally chosen by natural selection but sometimes by conflict and competition. And these cluster leaders represented the community when the city elders wanted to meet.

Below the highest level of leadership there were experts in each field, including agricultural experts. Even though each family still tended their own crops, some seasonal farming and harvest fell to the experts in the area. Wheat was an essential crop and could be most easily grown in large plots of land, so it made more sense to have one or no more than a few of the villagers assigned the task for all. So, too, would be animal management. Each family might contribute a wild pig wrestled from the woods, or a litter of young chicks that came from their hen, but the cluster and city shared many of these resources for the good of all, so the tasks of managing the resources was also often shared.

Some people became adept at flaking and would make and share points fractured from the chert or flint that others brought them. Animal hides were made into clothing, carrying pouches, and other useful items since before memory, but the people of Gania had discovered that they could remove the rank odors of the animal flesh if they treated the hide before assembling it into wraps or other things.

Some women had learned to scrape the hair off the hide, using the sharp edges of the flakes created by the men, and to soak the leather in the running water of the nearby stream for two days. Once wrung out and hung to dry, the hide could be scraped again and rubbed with salt. This process made the material more pliable and less odiferous and could be worked into more shapes with the lacing techniques the women had developed over time.

Creation of religious implements and items of personal decoration also advanced from raw seashells and flattened stones to impressed clay stamps, carved and colored antler forks, and strings of dangling shells that were assembled to portray a rainbow of colors.

Another consequence of the specialization of trades was that some tribes and villages advanced beyond others in the production of certain items. This enhanced the inter-tribal trade system, encouraging the Ankarans and fellow Ganians far and wide to travel along the coast or inward toward the hinterland of the island, to seek out other people and arrange to barter their goods. This advancing of communication and contact distributed regionally produced goods over a broader area and linked language systems so that some commonality of vocabulary resulted.

It also resulted in a blending of the various gene pools of the tribes as mates were chosen from among distant civilizations and women moved to live with the men that they paired with.

JULY 2018

CAFÉ AMADEO

"We don't know much about Liparus," Vito resumed, "but mythology tells us that he led a large tribe of people from the mainland to the Aeolian Islands."

"Whoa," I quickly objected. "I thought we were talking about Ankara."

"Oh, *certumentu,*" Vito assured me, raising a hand and gently waving it at me as a sign of agreement.

"But other things were happening at the same time, other villages, other growing settlements, even cities on Sicily. We'll get back to Ankara, but I just remembered Lipari and – well, at my advanced age – you have to let me continue or I will forget it."

Vito smiled in my direction, but I doubted that his sharp memory required any coaxing. However, I had to let him continue. But first...

"You said Liparus, then Lipari. Which is it?

"Liparus was a tribal leader whose people, according to legend, came from Campania, the region where Vesuvius is. Lipari is the island where they settled. It's in the Aeolian chain of volcanic islands."

"So..." I was stalling, trying to get my thoughts in order, time to scribble some notes. "So, the Aeolis..."

"No," Vito said with his finger pointed to the ceiling. "Not 'Aeolis.' That's in Asia Minor. We're talking about the Aeolians."

"Okay, the Aeolians. These are the islands just north of Sicily, sorta north-east, right?"

Vito nodded.

"And they were formed by volcanoes," I hedged, half stating and half asking.

"Sì," he agreed. "Deep within the earth, there is a channel, a pipeline of volcanic magma. It stretches from Vesuvius to Etna – in other words, from Campania on mainland Italy south, all the way to our Mt. Etna and beyond. The molten lava that is squeezed between the tectonic forces occasionally spurts out, like a tea kettle blowing off steam. Along that pipeline, the lava has burst from its confinement at several places, gushing out from the seafloor and creating vast subsurface mountains that grew and grew. The tallest vents formed caps that rose above the sea. These volcanic peaks became what we call the Aeolian Islands.

"Stromboli is still very active," he continued. "Vulcano is not yet dormant either. Then, there's Lipari. It seems to have been quiet now for many centuries."

"And all this matters to us, because..." I left the sentence for Vito to finish.

"Lipari was probably first inhabited, according to the archeologists, about 5000 B.C., although a vibrant civilization didn't really grow there for many years. But a small tribe was already there on the island from ancient days, and they had already discovered the value of obsidian, something they could harvest from the shores of the volcanic island, turn into tools or weapons, and even trade with others who visited the island."

"I'm a little lost here," I admitted. "Was there already trade between the Sicanians on Sicily and the people on the Aeolians?"

"Some. Not much," he explained.

"Where did the Liparians settle?"

"They arrived on the eastern shore but the earliest evidence of a settlement is from the northern tip of Lipari, a place they called Casello, what we now call Castellaro Vecchio. The obsidian came from the southern shores though."

"Why didn't they settle there?" I asked. "They came from the east and found obsidian in the south. It would have been easier to stay where they were."

"Easier, except I think they moved toward the north because the eruptions of the volcano on the island poured lava and destroyed their habitation on the eastern and southern end. They could survive on the northern tip, but not if they stayed where the obsidian was being produced by the flowing lava."

"They lived in the north, but they went to the south for the obsidian?" I followed.

"To harvest the glass, and to trade with the tribesmen coming from the other islands. That place in the south is called Contrada Diana now, but it's not on the maps. It only appears in the literature as an ancient place."

"So, to return to my question, this matters to us, why?"

"I told you there were now many tribes on the island of Sicily, many different peoples with different cultures. There was a place called Myla, now known as Milazzo, on the northern edge of Sicily, just south of the Aeolians. The people there must have gone to Lipari at times, collecting the obsidian and exploring, because we have found Liparian obsidian in the excavated villages of Myla. So once they secured their obsidian, which they called *sidia*, they returned to the main island with their treasures. The Liparians would have traded with them, which explains how some artifacts from northern Sicily began appearing in the Aeolian Islands around this time...and vice versa.

"These people from Sicily and the surrounding islands – scattered tribes who had already come from Iberia, Northern Africa, mainland Italy and, perhaps, even farther east – these people mingled and learned each other's languages. They traded goods and, sometimes, they traded partners," and Vito chortled at this, as if he was a bit embarrassed.

"They learned each other's ways but remained as separate tribes. Because of the growth of population, they needed space between them, so the primitive tribes – the Sicanians who had been on the island for thousands of years – moved inland away from the seashore and away from the people who kept coming to Sicily from other places. The Sicanians must have moved along the riverbeds to ensure a constant source of water and fish, and, in the process, they established villages farther from the sea.

"In this way, the many separate tribes that inhabited Sicily spread across the landscape, making travel to other islands more likely, and necessitating trade with these other tribes – even other islands – more important to barter for goods...and exchange mates."

———

"3950 B.C. – yes, it was a very good year," Vito said, as if he had just sipped a fine wine from that era.

"What does that mean," I asked, with a chuckle in my voice. "Sounds like a very difficult time. Volcanoes erupting, wild animals attacking unprepared villagers, people barely subsisting..."

"But," he interrupted, "you've missed the point. Think about what was happening between 4000 BCE and, oh, maybe 3000 BCE?"

I knew a bit of pre-history, but I had no clue where he was going. Still, I imagined that Vito didn't need any prompting, much less any assist from scribbled notes in an archeology treatise.

"Farming techniques became widespread," he said, "the horse was not only domesticated, but began to help with that farming. The digging stick for seeding had already developed into a pick-axe design and, later, during this period, the ard plough became common."

My furrowed brow begged for more detail.

"The ard plough is a longer version of the pick-axe design. They would lace together several sticks. A sharp pointed one would be attached to the end of a long handle. At the opposite end of the long handle would be another crosswise stick that the farmer could grab onto. To plough the ground, the sharpened end would be driven into the earth and the farmer would grab the crosswise stick at the other end and drag it across the surface, scratching a rough, shallow trench. A helper could walk along behind him dropping seeds, while a third person would walk behind the operation to kick the dirt back over the plow row. Much quicker, and with less bending.

"So, instead of jabbing a stick into the ground to create a hole for the seed, the farmer could drag this plough through the earth and create a long trench in a fraction of the time.

"People also learned to preserve the animal milk and even to make cheese, rather than just butchering their herd for meat. So they had a reason to develop corrals and pens, to lure adult animals into captivity and to protect their young so that they could become part of a more complex diet, involving milk, cheese, and meat.

"Primitive forms of writing emerged during the same time, first as symbols," he said, his arthritic fingers tracing imaginary shapes on the tabletop. "Symbols were composites, multiple strokes meant to reveal complete thoughts. But like the history of language, over time these symbols were broken down into their component parts and rearranged. *Voilà*, the alphabet!"

It sounded funny to hear Vito utter a word in French, but he was on a roll.

"There was no reason to develop a surface on which to inscribe a written language until there was one, right? So, people transitioned from etching on stone tablets and invented the papyrus and other surfaces – including tanned animal hide – to write down their symbols. Have you been to Palermo yet?"

"Yes, but years ago," I admitted.

"Did you see *la Pietra di Palermo*?"

"No." I didn't even know what that was.

"*La Pietra di Palermo* – the Stone of Palermo – is covered with hieroglyphs and is thought to date back to about 2800 B.C."

Not convinced that I was sufficiently impressed, Vito plowed ahead.

"The Rosetta Stone," he repeated. "You know what that is, right?"

"Of course, it's the tablet that carries the same message in Egyptian and Greek. A kind of cypher for translating from one language to the other, the first ever language-to-language dictionary if you will."

"*Esattumente!*" he replied. "That's the Rosetta Stone, but the Stone of Palermo is nothing like that." Vito chortled at having lured me into this trap.

"*La Pietra di Palermo* is an etched stone that describes in hieroglyphs the lineage of the pharaohs of Egypt stretching over many dynasties. So, the fact that you want to remember is that it is not about Sicily, but Egypt."

"Why is it important to remember, then?" I wondered aloud.

"Because it was found in Palermo," Vito said, finger raised. "How did it get there?"

I had no idea but assumed that I would soon find out. But Vito stalled, raised his cup to get the barista's attention, and then sat staring off into space. Growing impatient with his ploy, I jumped in.

"Okay, I give up. How did it get there?"

"I have no idea," he said with a mischievous smile.

When the fresh espresso was delivered, along with a little plate of orange slices and *cantucci*, Vito continued.

"How important is the wheel?" he asked.

"Oh, my god, the greatest invention of all time," I replied. "Without the wheel, we wouldn't have cars, wagons, the potter's wheel..."

Impatient with my recitation of benefits, Vito jumped in with a rapid-fire list.

"Gears, wrenches, pulleys, tractors, olive presses, spindles, screws, optical devices, augurs, the grape press, the refractor telescope's focusing mechanism, airplanes, engines, computers..." He paused only to take a breath. "And where did it begin?"

Guessing, I offered, "With the ancient Roman and Egyptian log-roller?"

"*Si*, but there's a big jump from a series of logs to the flat disk-shaped device, connected to an axle, that we think of when we picture the wheel."

I had to consider this for a while but couldn't quickly put together the steps to get from the ancient machine to the other, modern design.

"Archeologists have found a peculiar object, a stone, that dates back to about 4000 BCE. It's roughly rectangular and flat, about two meters in length and one meter in width. It has a long semi-circular groove that dissects the stone. Picture it as a carved trough that cuts across the middle of the stone, the waistline of the rectangular block.

"For a long time it seemed that this thing was a sliver of a greater design, maybe an early form of irrigation or water movement, using the trough to guide the flow. And they found a long, cylindrical stone near it. The scientists didn't understand the reason for this other thing; maybe thought it might be a stopper of sorts, something to lay into the groove to stop the flow of water across the block of stone. But that didn't sound right. If they wanted to dam the trough, they would have simply cut a round disk to put into the depression. This cylinder was as long as the width of the great stone.

"One day, they were examining it and they noticed two things that got their interest. First, the outer edges of the stone slab were smooth, not broken and chipped, as it would be if the massive rock had split off from something larger. So they decided that this slab was not part of a bigger design; it must have stood alone.

"They already knew that the surface of the trough was smooth, as was the surface of the cylindrical stone roller. They nestled the stone roller into the trough and it fit, but...nothing else. After more thought, one of the scientists suggested that they heft the large stone, invert it, and lay it across the stone cylinder wedged into the groove on the underside. It looked just like an axle inside a guide on the underside of the slab of stone.

"But it would hardly budge. It fit, almost like an elongated wheel, but the device wouldn't work. That is, until someone on the team said, 'Grease.'

"Over the next few days, they gathered animal fat from butchers in the nearby village, enough to coat the cylinder, and then they reassembled the device. They lined up along one end of the large block and leaned into it with their shoulders. It took some effort, but after they got it rolling, the entire contraption rolled across the ground like it was on wheels."

Vito smiled at this with the satisfaction of someone who might have invented it.

"Where was this found?" I asked.

"On Malta, where the Sicanians spread their culture about 4000 B.C."

2575 B.C.E.

2575 B.C.E.

SETTLEMENTS ACROSS DIAN

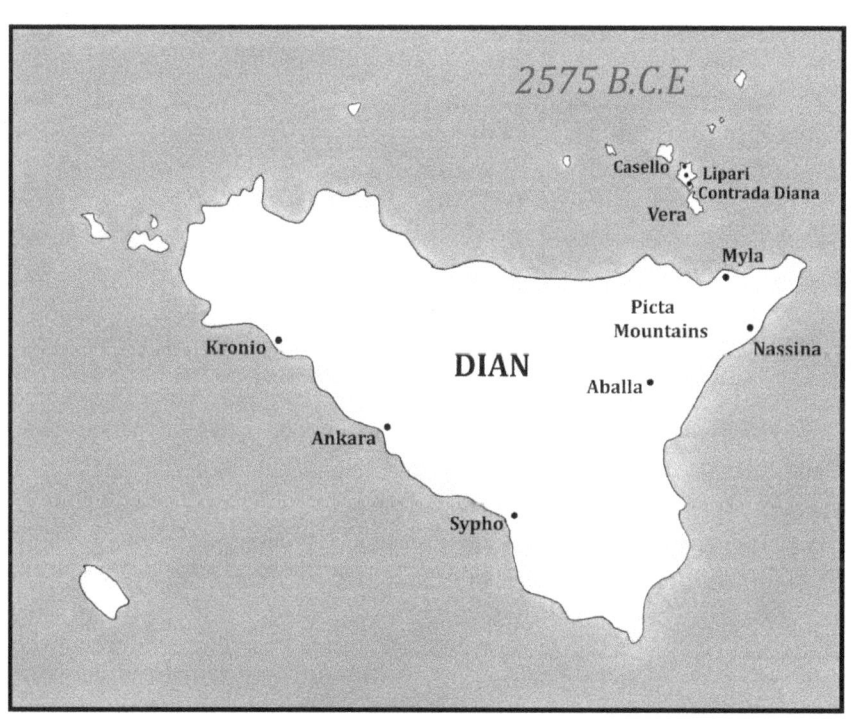

2575 B.C.E.

NASSINA

Dɪ̯ᴀᴠᴏ ʜᴀᴅ ʙᴇᴇɴ ᴍᴀᴋɪɴɢ ᴀʀʀᴀɴɢᴇᴍᴇɴᴛꜱ ꜰᴏʀ ᴛʜɪꜱ ᴊᴏᴜʀɴᴇʏ since the days began growing longer again. These seasonal journeys had become routine for him and his woman, Enna, and this time other people from Nassina would make the trip too.

They would have to cross the mountains on their island, Dian, and it would take more than two days to reach Myla. Enna came from a family in that small fishing village, and she would like to see her brother and sister again. Her mother was not well when she left Myla to live with Dravo, but her father would be there too, she hoped.

After crossing the mountains, they would stay in Myla for a few days. Delallo and Linate would come with them, and Wanto and Fippa. Their children would remain back in Nassina, some old enough to look after the young ones while the adults were away. Zinia would stay behind, but her man, Berari would go with the others to Myla.

So, the journey was arranged. Dravo, Enna, Delallo, Linate, Wanto, Fippa, and Berari would be enough to support each other and get back quickly. The entire expedition would take several days, but the Nassinians would make the entire round trip for the season and be set until the cold weather returned, and passed, and until the next warm season approached.

Dravo and Delallo were most interested in getting obsidian for their knife blades and cutting tools, while Berari thought of the exchange going the other way. He had learned from people in Sypho, farther south, how to make a strong metal by melting two others together. The new substance could be molded to shape or hammered to a fine edge; when it was allowed to cool it was stronger and sharper than the stone tools and would last longer.

Berari knew the sharp blades he cast in this way were worth much. He wanted obsidian too, and whatever else the people on Lipari had to barter, but he felt that his craft gave him the power to argue for more goods. His friends, Dravo and Delallo had traded with him at home, in Nassina, and would agree that Berari's blades were very good.

Enna, Linate, and Fippa brought tanned hides and woolen shirts, made by their hands and sewn together tightly using animal sinew and soft fibers to close the seams and make them into warm garments. The Casellans on Lipari would like these new clothes, because they lived on the north side of their volcanic island, where the wind blew across the water, keeping the village of Casello colder than any other part of the island.

Enna was particularly skilled at weaving patterns into the wool-made cloth. She made threads woven together on a spindle then dyed them in a shallow bowl filled with red ink she had made from minerals and sap, and the bluish-purple ink from the octopus they caught in the sea. She used tree sap to serve as a fixing agent so the color would hold firm and not run.

They brought small pottery too, mostly small pieces painted with colorful designs wrapped around the neck of the cups and pots. Bigger jars were too heavy to carry over the mountain, and the boats that they would borrow from Enna's villagers in Myla would not bear too much weight, so pottery formed only a little bit of their goods to sell.

They brought along one horse that would carry most of their goods to Myla and could be left with the people there in exchange for the boats the people borrowed for the crossing to Lipari. When the boats were returned, they would get the horse back, and it would be loaded with the new items they had traded for. Then they would continue their journey home to Nassina.

In the early morning, the trading party set off. The horse was loaded with sacks of goods, carefully balanced so that he didn't have to shift his own weight and wear down the animal before they crossed the mountains. The people lifted the remaining goods in sacks that they carried on their backs. Stretchers and other types of litter-bearers wouldn't be of any use. They would have to be abandoned at the foothills of the mountain and, so, the people didn't even bother making them for the trip.

Before the sun was up, they were gone. Due to their early departure, their children were still sleeping. The little ones had been put to bed the night before in one home, that of Zinia, to be watched. Berari and Zinia's daughter, Chala, would help with supervising the brood of kids, but they would be well taken care of until Berari and the other parents returned in ten days' time.

As the party headed away from Nassina toward Myla, they had the great mountain volcano, Aballa, at their backs. They didn't fear eruptions from it now that they were moving away, and they knew from its history that Aballa – even at its most effusive – didn't harm their city of Nassina which stood on an elevated plain.

They looked past the chain of mountains before them into the deep distance at the sky over Lipari where they were headed. It was too far to see, and the slope of the low chain of mountains in front of them obscured their vision, but they were more concerned about eruptions on Lipari where they were headed then from Aballa which they were leaving behind.

"Let's stay for a while," said Dravo, lowering his pack to the ground at the foot of the next mountain. "We should eat and rest, then begin the climb."

It was a directive that his fellows were quick to obey.

"How long?" asked Enna, as she was settling down on a log and passing around some of the vital supplies that they had brought with them.

"Quickly, just to rest our legs," said Dravo to the group. He knew that Enna wasn't stalling; she was aware of the uphill climb they had to manage before bedding down for the night. This mountain stood exactly halfway between Nassina and Myla and if it was to be a two-day trip, the party understood that either they did a little the first day and overnighted on the southern foothills, or they pushed all the way over the mountain and settled on the northern foothills, leaving a long but leisurely march on the following day.

Dravo had decided on a compromise. Considering the season, he knew that the sun would be bright and warm in the morning, and on an earlier trip he had discovered a low shelf on the northern wall of this mountain they called Picta, so that he and his party could camp there for the night. It would be more than halfway along on their journey, not down to the plains on the other side of Picta but past the crest and down a bit on the slope. It had worked before and, barring bad weather, Dravo hoped that it would work again.

There was one other reason for choosing that site over the mountain for the night: Dravo recalled looking toward the lower plains, and he could see the waters in the distance, and the giant mountain on Vera, the volcano that towered over the strait beyond Myla. It was a beautiful site and he wanted to witness it again in the bright light of the sunrise.

For now, they would rest their legs and shoulders and pass around the dried fish and meat to prepare for the climb. They drank the goat's milk they carried in their pouches, sure to finish it off completely so that they could refill the sacks with snow from the mountain, to let it melt into water for the next day's sustenance.

————

The sun set and the chill came in early that night in Nassina. The children in the cluster were gathered in one hut under the supervision of Zinia and the oldest sibling among them, Chala. When the evening meal was finished – a much lighter affair on this night because so many of the adults in the cluster were off on their journey – the swiftly darkening hours turned into playtime for little kids tussling together in a single household.

Zinia kept a safe distance from the youthful melee, as Chala enjoyed her newfound role as the mature one in the family. She would certainly work her best to prove to her mother, Zinia, that she could handle the responsibilities. Chala was nearing womanhood and thought that the time to choose a man would come soon.

"They're like little dogs," Zinia said with a laugh. "Tumbling about and nuzzling each other."

"Yes," Chala responded, enjoying the moment of comradery with her mother. "I wonder if they learned it from the animals."

Zinia smiled, and then looked at her daughter. The girl had grown straight and tall, with a thick mane of dark hair and willowy arms. The animal hide cloak hung about Chala's shoulders, but her mother could see the budding breasts through the folds.

The girl sensed that she was being inspected and looked over at Zinia. Words weren't necessary; both women knew the unspoken subject, and both of them smiled.

———

Dravo and his band made it up the low hills of Picta Mountain and crossed through a divide that he had surveyed the previous year. It was a pass through the mountain that was created by a tectonic rupture, not eroded into its present state by running water. Dravo knew this, and therefore knew that they wouldn't find a burbling spring on the other side. And, so, he reminded his fellow travelers to fill their pouches with snow for drinking the next day.

The light was growing dim as they surmounted the highest peak and worked their way gingerly down the slope. After another two hours picking their way carefully through the rocks and crevices, they alighted on the rocky shelf that Dravo knew from before. It hugged the slope of the mountain at that point, a broad, flat apron of rock wide enough that two men couldn't reach across it. The valley lay below a gentle slope, and the mountainous side behind them had a hollowed-out portion that was not quite a cave, but would provide a break from the wind.

Altogether, Dravo's campsite provided safety from roaming animals, enough room for all to sleep comfortably, and a barrier to the chill breeze that came frequently to Picta Mountain.

The party dropped their packs with relish, stretching their arms and rotating their shoulders to get the muscle kinks out. They had picked up kindling and short sticks on the downhill trek, as planned, so they had the material for a fire without having to bring it with them all the way from Nassina. Delallo reached for the flint that he carried, built a small teepee of kindling, and struck the stone to produce the desired spark. He timed it between two gusts of wind so that the air wouldn't extinguish the small fire, then added more wood as Dravo and Berari built a low wall of rocks to stall and redirect the breeze away from the campfire.

Over the next hour, as they produced more dried food and some crusty bread from their packs, they built the fire into a larger blaze, adding another smaller one about a man's height away. Two fires would be necessary for everyone in the party to sleep close to the flame. They drank the water that had melted from the snow in their pouches, and Dravo reminded them to refill the bags in the morning before they broke camp. The leather bags could hold liquid, but without running water or any kind of stream, they had no way to collect water in their bags except to harvest the snowbanks that clung to the side of the mountain where they were camped.

After a good meal and some stories told about their village in Nassina, they all settled in for what they expected to be a chilly night. There were seven of them, so three would bed down in a tight circle around one fire and the other four would repeat the arrangement around the other fire. Last words were exchanged and jokes told about how Zinia and Chala were faring with a houseful of youngsters, as each of the travelers dropped out of the conversation and off into sleep.

Dravo was awake when the first rays of the sun probed the dark sky on his right. He enjoyed this part of the day. The only sounds were from birds and small animals, with the occasional whistle of a breeze, and the quiescence gave him time to think. He knew that this day would be easier for them since they had already surmounted Picta, but it would not be short. The descent down the mountain and then the walk across the plain to Myla would take most of the day, and he expected to arrive at his woman's ancestral village only in time to bed down again. The Mylans wouldn't know the Nassinians were coming, although they were expecting a visit sometime during the season.

Rustling noises came from his fellow campers as the sun pushed the night sky away, spreading its brilliant rays across the face of the mountain, their campsite, and the valley below. The azure canopy above them became lighter with the sunrise, and the star-studded blackness was replaced by a soft blue shroud.

Enna yawned and stretched next to Dravo, but smiled at him as she pulled the sheepskin cloak back up to her chin. She knew it was time to rise, but what she liked most about the morning and its brisk fresh air was being able to cuddle under the blanket and stay curved in the sleeping position a bit longer.

Fippa did the same, then shoved a bare foot out of her cloak to waken Wanto. He, not as anxious as Dravo to get up, snorted and rebuffed Fippa with a swing of his hand. But she only smiled. She knew this motion; her man would get up but wanted to argue against it for a moment.

In a matter of moments, the entire clan had arisen and were eating a little food to get them started. As agreed, they drained the pouches of the last water, then refilled the bags with snow from the hillside behind them. They had let the fires extinguish through the night, so they set out on the downward slope toward the green fields below.

As Dravo had predicted, descending the mountain and crossing the plains took the party nearly an entire day, but after a long trek, they saw the fires of Myla and the walled structures that defined their settlement.

———

Enna was the first to approach the settlement and dash into the cluster that she once knew as home. Her mother was sitting by the fire, an old woman for those times, and Enna's brother, Strano, was sitting with her. She did not see her father but knew that he tended to the sheep in the late hours before going to bed.

The Mylans in Enna's old cluster greeted the Nassinian party of seven and then settled back into their positions around the firepit. Their late meal had been finished, but women from the cluster busied themselves with bringing more food to the group, knowing the travelers would not have eaten. At this point, long after the cooked meal had been planned, prepared, and eaten, the Mylans could only offer dried meat and fish, leftover bread, and some extra green vegetables and tubers that were still piled on the clay platters among them.

"You look strong, Strano!" Enna said, pushing her younger brother in the arm to test his strength. He smiled back at her and wondered what his sister had become since leaving their village. Enna's mother was still, with her arms looped through the folds of the soft leather cloak she wore. She smiled wanly but didn't talk much. When she did speak, Enna noticed how she had changed.

"He's not here," the old woman said. Her words were muffled a bit, and Enna noticed that her mother had lost more of the teeth that often rot or fall out with older people.

"Who?" she replied.

Strano and his mother looked back at Enna for a moment with an intensity she hadn't expected. And then she realized that they were talking about her father. Strano began to tell her what had happened.

"He was fine, strong as always, but he tripped on a small stone in the field while he was watching the sheep. When he fell, an animal stumbled over him and he cried out."

Strano gripped his upper leg with both hands and continued.

"He said his leg hurt badly, and he couldn't walk. Since he couldn't walk, he couldn't work. We put him in the house to rest, but he cried out all night. In the morning, when I pulled the legging back from his skin, I saw that the small hole in his skin was bigger now, and it was a dark color."

Strano paused.

"All that day he hurt and cried out whenever he moved even a bit. By night, his leg was big," he said, using his hands to indicate a thickness that would be unnatural for the man's leg.

"The next morning, he breathed heavily, but didn't cry out. We thought maybe he would be feeling better. Later in the day, his breathing became soft, and his eyes drooped and never opened. The next morning, he did not wake up."

With the telling, Enna's mother lowered her head and wept softly. Strano continued.

"We put him in the ground along with the others from Myla," he said, pointing to the outside of the village, in a direction that Enna knew was the graveyard for many Mylans from the years. The dead, old and young, were interred there, outside the village walls, and arranged together for the gods to know what had happened to them.

The group was quiet for a while, and all that could be heard was the crackling of the fire in the pit. Death was inevitable, and all had experienced family and friends dying, but the people had to reconcile themselves to such things, and wonder whether the gods required it, or whether that was simply the fate of humans.

After sharing this moment of mourning, the group broke up the circle, the Mylans returning to their homes, with Enna and Dravo going in with her mother and brother, and the other Nassinians spread out among the other family's shelters for the night.

The next morning, Enna visited the burial place for Mylans. Some burials were reserved for important people, and cloistered in a certain segment of the cemetery; after a time, their bodies were often disinterred, and the bones dismembered and re-buried, with ground red or blue powder from ochre and other elements in nature sprinkled into the hole before refilling.

The less important Mylans deserved a proper burial, and a paste of ground red ochre would be spread across their forehead before being interred, and sometimes a tool or weapon would be buried with the body. But their resting place would not be decorated as ornately as those of the leaders and shamans of the village.

Enna wanted to see where her father was, and she stood over the unmarked plot for a short time before bowing her head and turning to leave. There was much to do on this day to prepare for their trip to Lipari.

———

The Nassinians spent another day and night in Myla, but they came this way for a purpose. They would set out for Lipari on the following morning, trading their horse for three boats and be accompanied by two Mylans in another boat for the expedition.

Strano was one of the Mylans to go, but he left his woman, Lilia, behind with their children. Tifo joined him, leaving Ridolfa and son Genio back in the village. Two men in a boat would leave room for their trading goods and the bartered items they expected to return with.

Berari showed the hammered blades that he had made with melted tin and copper, then struck repeatedly with a hammer stone to produce a thin, sharp edge. The Mylans had seen such use of metal, but mostly for blunt objects that held up better than the stone tools they had been using. They had never seen it shaped into a tool such as this though.

The people loaded the four boats, the Nassinians porting the trade items they had brought from their home and the Mylans choosing carefully from their supply of products. They knew the Casellans on Lipari lived more on seafood than animals, since the pastureland on the island was limited. Without sheep and only a few goats, the Casellans would value woolen clothes and the leather wraps and pouches that would be made from the sheepskin.

The village of Myla lay at the very end of a long spit of land jutting out into the sea toward Vulcano and Lipari beyond it. This location, wrapped on three sides by water, made the Mylans into experienced seafaring people, although the land side of the peninsula ensured that they would always have access to farming, pastureland, and other villages to be reached on land.

They pushed off the shore of Myla just after dawn, when the morning breeze was just stirring. Those from Myla had learned how to use these winds to sail across the water, rather than paddling the entire way with their wooden oars. And Strano knew that the morning breeze was the most constant and would steer their boats in the direction of Lipari.

Boat construction in Myla had improved from the time of the ancients. Instead of heavy dugout canoes, they preferred to create a tight weave of reeds, using sap and tar from the sands just a few hours walk from Myla, and from these things produced a sailing vessel that was mostly waterproof and light enough for the breeze to push across the surface of the water. Heavier craft would be completely waterproof but sink in the water; the reed boats were lighter and, even though they might let some water seep between the reeds, they would stay afloat and glide smoothly.

All four boats had been built this way and outfitted with a thin sapling of a tree standing tall in the middle of the craft. From this sapling the Mylans had strapped a cross piece of the same wood, then hung a patchwork of very thin leather from it. They had learned that sheepskin and cowhide were too tough and heavy and would pull their mast down, especially if the winds blew sea spray over them. But the sailors had also learned that stitching together the skin of smaller animals with thinner hides would work. So, their sails looked like a quilt of colors and threads but performed the intended task perfectly.

The women and men lifted the boats past the small waves at the shore and then hoisted their bodies up onto the reed platform. Strano and Tifo split up so they could maneuver one boat each and show the Nassinians how it was done. Dravo had been on a similar excursion and used the Mylan boat design the previous season, so he could manage one boat himself. Enna was a Mylan and had sailed with her people before, so she could commandeer the fourth boat.

Once past the foamy waves at the shore, the expedition set off into the sea. Normally, the voyage would take half of the day, but they had spied some smoke at the peak of Vulcano and decided to sail farther around that island to reach Lipari without encountering any eruptions from the volcano. That would add some time to the trip, but they still expected to arrive before the sun settled into the water to their left.

Calling out between the boats, Strano gave instructions and used his paddle on the side of the reed boat to steer the direction he chose.

"It is no problem," he shouted across the water. "The smoke is always there. It shouldn't be bad on Lipari."

Enna looked back at her brother doubtfully, but Tifo and Dravo looked straight ahead with determination.

"Yes, you say," she retorted, feeling a need to express an opinion even if it would be ignored by her brother and the others.

The winds grew in strength and helped to move the boats faster than the Mylans had originally thought. They steered around Vulcano and smelled the acrid odors of the fire that burned in the mountain, but once on the other side the smells weakened and they set their sights for Lipari.

By late afternoon, as the sun had passed the high point of its arc across the sky, the boats landed softly on the rocky shores on the southern tip of Lipari. The sailors quickly jumped from the boats and grabbed the craft to drag them safely onto shore. There was no volcanic activity on the mountain that formed the center of this island, and the Mylans and Nassinians felt safe enough to set up camp.

The following morning, they awoke to a bright blue sky and cool temperatures. There were no Liparians there yet, but the travelers knew that their arrival would not go unnoticed. Soon, a small tribe of Casellans appeared walking along the shoreline toward them. They had come around the slope of the mountain and walked along the surf toward the new camp, dragging makeshift litters behind them filled with goods. Dravo, Enna, and their people could not make out what things were being brought by the Casellans, but they hoped that sidia was among the bundles.

Throughout that day, the Mylans and Nassinians talked, bartered, and shared their meals with the Casellans, exchanging goods that were common in each culture to satisfy the needs of the others. Each group remained mindful of the other, not wary or untrusting, but keeping watch over the movements and intentions of these strangers. The Casellans worried that the expeditionary force would steal their goods and sail off with them; the arriving party was concerned that the Casellans would raid their camp in the night and take back what they had traded for.

When the business of the day was completed, the Casellans retreated in the direction they had come, and Dravo, Enna, and Strano settled their people for another night on the shore. There was no smell yet of fire from the mountain, but they knew they would have to strike out early in the morning to return to Myla. The winds would now be not so kind, blowing toward this place as they had the previous day and away from Myla, so the party knew they would have to paddle more and sail less.

Dravo and Enna took the first watch that night. When camping with entire families, the parents normally split up, one sleeping and one awake with the parent from another family. But this time there were no children present so each couple could remain together, either awake or asleep.

"We have much *sidia* now," Enna said, nodding her head in silent thanks for the quality of the trade. "We have plenty to bring back to Nassina for our people."

That was the main point of the trip to Lipari. The Casellans who remained on the island did so primarily because of the value of the green glass, obsidian, that would be found there. They knew that visiting people could just collect their own, so the Casellans harvested as much as they could from the fractures in the rock, saving the sailors who landed on their shores the time that such an effort would require. It was the time savings that made the bartering work.

By the middle of the night, Dravo woke Strano and Tifo to take over the watch, and he and Enna curled up by the fire to pass the remaining hours of darkness in sleep.

2575 B.C.E.

SYPHO

THE EXPLORERS FROM SYPHO WERE PREPARING THEIR TRADING voyage to Kronio and settling matters before starting out on the seas. The coastline of Dian was hospitable to venturing people, but the Syphans had recently had some conflicts with the village of Ankara, so plotting a path through or near that settlement might not be wise.

Santo and Xinta had been on an earlier venture to Ankara and knew the people well. A season before, these men had walked there, a two-day trip, on their way to Kronio which was another two or three days beyond. They wanted to trade with the Kronians for *sidia* from Pantea, the little island to the south, and metal tools that the Kronians had become expert at making. But when they had ventured this way before, then returned home via Ankara, they were set upon by a band of raiders outside that settlement. The robbers confronted Santo and Xinta with stone-cut weapons and, after a brief and weak ploy to trade with them, attacked the travelers and tried to steal the bronze-head axes and metal swords by force.

Fortunately, the Syphans had already learned from their trading partners in Kronio how to use these new weapons, and they fended off the attack and made their escape. But when they planned the trip again, Santo and Xinta decided that it would be better to sail the coast on the water and avoiding the land.

From their closeness to the sea, the Syphan culture had long known how to build boats. The great flocks of sheep, goats, and deer that abounded in the fields and hills around Sypho provided an unending supply of leather, so the Syphans had adopted a boat-building scheme to incorporate this resource. Rather than carve out a wooden canoe or lace together reeds and twine, they made their boats by tying bent wood into a skeleton of a hull then covering it with woven animal hides. Once the leather had been properly treated and tanned, it was waterproof, and this boat shell proved to be lighter and more flexible in handling the sea swells and waves.

And the lightness of the craft allowed it to be maneuvered by a single person, which meant that Santo and Xinta could take two boats along and still stock plenty of trading items.

The westward journey would not make much use of sails; still the men stashed the poles and deerskin leather that they used for sails in the bottom of each boat in case fair winds favored them on the return.

They set out on the trip on a fine, sunny morning, knowing that they would be upon the water overnight, as they skirted the shores around Ankara. After many hours of paddling and working the low waves just outside the surf, Santo and Xinta lashed the boats together and took turns sleeping in the well of one craft. This was so that the watchman could make sure the boats didn't drift too far from the land while the other man slept and readied himself for his shift.

"It is there," said Santo on the second morning, pointing to a promontory on the big island. He recognized the curve of the land where Ankara stood, a better sign of their location since the low buildings of the settlement would be hard to detect from their vantage point on the sea. Knowing the land from the sea was a key survival skill. If they wanted to avoid Ankara, the Syphans needed to be able to know it without seeing it directly.

The men piloted their boats past the land mass and past the curve in the shore, then rowed their craft into the low, foaming waves that broke on the shore beyond Ankara. Two days on the water was enough, and they only brought water and food for that stretch of time. They could land on the beach past Ankara and find water and game to refill their stock for the next two days' travel to Kronio.

"How many times have we done this, Santo?" asked Xinta.

Santo held up four fingers.

"And we were fine until that time two seasons ago."

"Yes," replied Santo, "we were okay. But I don't trust the Ankarans now."

"We escaped. More importantly, we won. Our weapons could have struck them down, if you had let me use them."

"But we were only two, and there were more of them," Santo reminded him. "If we struck down one or two or three, the others would have swarmed over us. We might have lost our precious weapons, and even more..."

Santo let the sentence hang.

Once on the shore, the men dragged their boats away from the low wash of the sea and addressed themselves to camping for a night.

―――――

Santo and Xinta awoke early the next day. The sleep they got on the rocking surface of the sea was better than the one night they had on land, worried constantly about a wild animal or human wandering into their site.

"We can get *sidia* from the Nassinians, yes?" Xinta asked while they packed up their gear and prepared to set off. The Syphans traded both north – with Nassina – and west with other shoreline villages like Kronio – although the sources of *sidia* were different. Nassinians bartered for the dark green-black glass of Lipari while the Kronians got their supplies of shiny black glass from Pantea.

"It doesn't matter to me," replied Santo. We can get *sidia* from either, but the Kronians have other things, including pots, seashells, and carved antlers that we can't get from the barren shores of Lipari."

"What do I want with pots, seashells, and carved antlers?" Xinta joked while coiling the rope around his forearm.

"Well, I assume you want to drink and eat," Santo replied, "so you need pots. And I assume you want a happy woman…"

"So, I need seashells and carved antlers, right?"

Santo had to laugh at the deduction. A 'happy' woman meant lots of things to these men.

"Yes, the seashells at least. But the antler and carved bones we got last season. These were things the shaman wanted, and she said the power in an animal's bones – grown inside the animal or on its head – could not be matched."

"Even with the shaman's magic?"

"Even with the shaman's magic," Santo said. "At least according to her."

They pushed their vessels out past the breakers that had grown larger since the previous day. The wind was in their face so the sails would still not help, so the men planned to paddle all the way to Kronio. They would have to sleep another night on the water, boats lashed together as before, but this was common fare for these men.

Another day on the water and they finally alighted on the sands near Kronio. Santo pulled his boat ashore first, then helped Xinta with his. The Kronians were more dependent on the sea and had built their large city just up the sloping rocky flank of the seaside. Its perch was visible from the water, and the seafaring Syphans clearly were visible to the Kronians, who welcomed Santo and Xinta kindly.

Just as predicted, the Kronians came first with a bevy of sharpened bronze weapons. They had converted some of their stone-topped tools to metal too, but they were most proud of the keen edge of the weapons they could create from melted tin and copper. When the hosts laid the goods for barter on the sand, and the Syphans followed suit, the haggling began. It was friendly and jovial; most people involved knew that they would get what they came for in exchange for what they brought. Hard bargaining was not the rule of the day.

Beside Dala, the elderly Kronian who seemed to be managing the entire enterprise, sat a small, wizened old man who worked a carved stone plate and some small pebbles on it. The plate was square and chiseled flat, and there were several parallel grooves that looked like they had been cut into it with a sharpened tool, possibly a pointed chisel. Pebbles sat at one end of each groove, several bunched together in every channel, which the old man moved back and forth quickly as the bargaining proceeded.

Dala turned to the man occasionally, checking the stone tablet and asking some questions. At intervals, each time Santo and Xinta counted out a portion of their trade items and noted their value, the old man would move the pebbles along in rhythm with what the Syphans had presented. At the end of each of these sessions, the old man would lift the plate gently so that the little stones didn't shift, and show the result to Dala. If he agreed, Dala would nod his head and begin to assemble an appropriate pile of Kronian goods to equal those offered by the Syphans.

"What is that?" asked Santo. He had watched the old man with interest and watched as a pebble in this channel or two in that channel were moved as he or Xinta had offered another cloth or tool.

"We still trade our products," replied Dala, "but one skin is worth many shells, and a string of shells might be worth only one blade of *sidia*. He," pointing to the old man sitting cross-legged on the sand, "can keep track of these and it tells me the value and how much we must offer in exchange."

"But if you know how to use that, and I don't," interjected Santo, "how can we be sure it is fair?"

Dala just looked at the man, someone he had traded with for many seasons already. Santo knew Dala was trustworthy, but he wanted to understand this new device.

"If we don't have the *bacu*," Dala began, pointing to the stone tablet, "we would have to trade one item at a time. This way, we can put together many items, know what they are worth, and then assemble our own crafts to equal the same. It's faster," he concluded with a shrug.

The day proceeded like this with only a little interlude to eat. Men and women worked together on the trade and on preparing the food out there on the beach, and then they resumed the session, concluding as the night darkened with the sunset.

"You will stay in my house," Dala said, as the Kronians carried their new purchases up in leather slings. Santo and Xinta watched as another group of Kronians bundled the Syphans' purchases together, then followed the bearers of this burden to Dala's house to secure their newly traded goods for the night.

They walked alongside Dala into the cluster that defined his neighborhood and as they passed by a particular stone and reed home, the village elder chuckled. He pointed to a painted clay pot outside the door of the home and chuckled again.

"You are known here," he said.

This was a custom that even the Syphans had adopted from the Kronians, and so Santo and Xinta knew its meaning. Their arrival had been noted not only by the local traders but also by the women in the village. Someone, probably a mother of a maturing girl, placed the pot outside the door of their home to indicate that there was an eligible young woman inside. Eligible for a night of sexual activity, true, but the basic meaning of the lure was that this young person was looking for a husband. With strangers in town, the pot was put outside the door to see if there were any takers.

Santo grinned broadly and elbowed his traveling companion. Xinta was without a woman so far, unlike his friend, so he might want to consider what lay within.

"We will meet you later," Dala said to Xinta, pulling Santo ahead with him into the leader's home and leaving the unattached man in the village courtyard staring at the clay pot.

———

The Syphans spent the night in Kronio and decided to stay on another day. These people had become friends of theirs over the seasons, and they enjoyed the time spent together.

Santo spent most of his time with Dala and the man's wife, Resta. But Xinta had accepted the offer at the home in the square, where he met Lefanu, a young girl whose physical traits were just turning to womanhood. Throughout the ensuing days, he spent more time with her than with his traveling companion.

"Alio, this is Santo," Dala said as the two men walked around the common area of the Kronio settlement. He was introducing Santo to a sturdy man working outside a fierce firepit. The man was weighing down on a stack of rocks with his left hand and wielding a heavy stone axe with his right.

"Alio is the one who makes the best metals. He can turn simple things into tools of all kinds, sharpened edges, strong middle, light to the touch..."

"Sounds like a true expert," Santo said. Alio could be seen listening, but he knew enough to hide his pride in front of the village leader. Pride below Dala's rank was not permitted, at least in Dala's presence.

A thin young woman with bare arms approached with an armload of wood. She dumped it at Alio's feet, then began loading chosen branches into the fire to keep the intense heat up. She was Kinta, Alio's wife and mother of their children. She knew just as much as Alio about the process and knew how hot the fire should be, but she was not strong enough to pound the metal and achieve the tools that her man could.

Santo watched the process for a while, impressed with the amount of force that Alio could bring down on the glowing blade of metal that he had wedged between two stones. A large stone served as his surface, and two other flat rocks sat beside it. The new cast metal was held between the two flat rocks as Alio pressed down on the sandwich to steady the blade while he brought the stone-headed hammer down upon it once, then again, and again. Each time, sparks flew from the brilliant orange-yellow metal blade, and Alio continued in this way until his arm needed a rest.

Kinta worked alongside him, keeping the fire at the right heat by adding wood or spreading the burning pile. Her skin dripped in sweat from the heat; his from the fierce combat with the weapon in his clutch.

Dala and Santo walked away after a while, discussing other matters of their villages.

"Are the Ankarans a problem for you here, in Kronio?" asked the visitor.

Dala considered the question for a moment; he knew that responding too quickly in a way that disparaged another village might be dangerous for both of them.

"No, not a problem, but I know about your experience," he responded finally.

"Was that not common?"

"I would not say common," Dala added, as they stopped by the cistern in the courtyard and accepted a carved wooden cup filled with water from the young girl there. Dala and Santo both enjoyed a long draft of the water that the Kronians brought from the nearby mountain stream. It was clear and fresh tasting, and even on this cool morning the drink was welcome after visiting Alio's firepit.

"When do you go back?" asked Dala, then he smiled and quickly revised his question.

"Let me say, when will Xinta let you go back?"

Both men shared a laugh. Xinta's encounter with Lefanu was a crucial part of all developing societies. The people had no knowledge of modern science and certainly couldn't understand such things as genetic diversity. But the farmers, animal keepers, and gatherers had fed their tribes for thousands of years by relying on a slowly accumulating knowledge of their surroundings, including the lessons learned in animal procreation and mixing of natural traits. Whatever word they used for it at the time, these people knew that finding strong mates and mixing the blood of multiple tribes produced a line of survivors necessary for continuation of their communities.

And this mixing had the added benefit of ensuring the peace between the settlements.

Dala and Santo returned to the leader's home where Resta sat with two other women and two young children. They were sitting outside in the sunshine in a small circle, shaping new pots on flat rotating boards, each perched atop a smooth rounded stone. Spinning the platform first one way and then the other allowed the women to control the contours of the pots they were making, and the children sat by their side, learning the process and being at the ready to run off to get more water if needed.

Santo was noticeably impressed, and when he stooped to get a better look at the process, Resta smiled at him and stopped her motion.

"The wood is covered in animal fat, on the bottom, before beginning. That makes it easier to spin this way and that," she said, demonstrating the process for him.

"We hold our hands around the edge to smooth the outside, then dig with our fingers to open the inside," she added, again demonstrating with her wetted fingers on the small lump of clay before her.

"This is the way our people do it," Santo remarked. "But we have not used the fat to make it easier. I will tell them."

By this time, pottery making had become industry. The women were often assigned the duties because it was an activity that could be done around the home while they tended their children. And the young ones could be employed and taught the importance of cooperation.

The Kronians had four basic shapes for their pottery: tall cylinders tapered in at the top, lower open-mouthed cups, and small and large flat platters. The tapered cylinders were used both to store and to carry liquids; the cups were principally designed for drinking small portions poured from the taller vases. The large platters were crucial to cooking and serving, often laden with the butchered meat or long tendrils of grasses, wild onion, and green-leafed vegetables. The smaller platters served each individual – like the cups – and were useful only while consuming the meal.

But all four of these shapes had a common design. Since pottery was now an industry, it reflected the people who produced it. And the people of Kronio had evolved a pattern of designs for their pottery that were almost a communal signature of authenticity.

All were made of the local red clay, but black paint from mixing natural orcs together with water was incorporated into the Kronian design, something that gave the etchings on the surface almost a three-dimensional appearance. The tall pitcher and the cup had long, straight lines drawn diagonally around the exterior of the object, in nearly perfect parallel. The design added to the three-dimensional motif by almost making these vertical cylinders appear to be in motion.

The large platter and smaller plates were adorned with the impressions of fern leaves and tiny seashells. These impressed designs were laid in at the center of the piece, although some families had adopted a further embellishment of impressing its own chosen shell at three points around the circumference. Although most families took care of their own needs and own meals, communal meals still occurred in Kronio, and so these family-specific identifiers could be used to separate the pieces afterward. Just as likely, the potmaker was showing off her pride in the piece, and these designs reminded all the others who had produced such things.

Dala invited his guest to sit and, with a wave of his hand, sent one of the children off. Their lives were simple and the gesture didn't require a lot of explanation. They had water and animal milk for drinking, but they also had the juice of fruit sometimes. Now, still in the cool season, that wouldn't be available, and Santo knew that there was only one other thing. *Brit*, the cloudy odiferous brew made from water and breadcrumbs.

What the child returned with, though, was not *brit*. It smelled like fruit, in a vague way, but reminded him of the smell of new bread, almost like *brit*. But the color was off. It was the hue of an old blossom, the color the flower turns when it is past its bloom and losing its petals.

Santo lifted the cup to his lips and tested it with his tongue. He immediately knew that the tentative action had insulted his host, so he quickly gulped a bit of the reddish liquid.

He would have complimented Dala in any case, but as the liquid slid down his throat, Santo realized that this was a new and delicious drink. It tasted nothing like *brit* but made him burp as if it was the same. That didn't require an apology among these people; it was commonly thought of as the salute to a well-liked treat.

"Do you have *tina* at Sypho?" Dala asked.

Santo looked at Dala but shook his head.

"What is it called?" he asked.

The people of each tribe knew that their vocabularies differed, sometimes greatly, but they often operated under the assumption that words came from outside of them, possibly from the gods. So, when Santo asked for the word, he was thinking that it, *tina*, might be some universal reference to this thing he was drinking.

"*Tina*," Dala said.

Santo would take the word back to Sypho, and it might change long after he was gone, but the word would be one of the decrypters or clues that allowed various settlements to coax meaning out of conversations with people from other cities.

"Come, I will show you," said Dala, moving out of the women's circle and toward the port at the entrance to Kronio.

They walked out of the village and into the low brush that grew at the base of the small stand of trees nearby. Dala squatted down next to a little bush and cupped his hands around a hard bunch of berries just emerging from their seed pods on the branches.

"These," he said, motioning to Santo to come closer. "These berries make the *tina*, the red berries, the white berries, and the green ones that all grow together."

Santo had eaten this type of berry before. They grew in abundance around Sypho, and he remembered that late in the warm season they were sweet and pungent tasting. But the Syphans had not made them to drink.

"We take these when they are bigger," Dala explained, using his fingers to indicate a larger size more familiar to Santo. "And we squeeze them like this," he said, pushing the pads of his fingers together.

"Or this," he added, putting palm to palm.

"And drink it?" asked Santo.

"No, not for some days."

"How do you know when?"

Dala sniffed strongly, and Santo laughed.

"I can only tell by the smell," Dala laughed. "But some others, they know better. So, I wait for them."

About then, both men were beginning to feel the affects of the *tina*, a lightness of their head and softness in their spirit, that Santo recognized from *brit*.

———

Two days later, Santo was arranging the wares they had traded for when Xinta approached him on the shore. Lefanu was with him, as Santo had expected. There was no discussion of the arrangement between the men; this was a common event and much expected by them and their cultures.

Xinta and Lefanu joined packaging the trade goods and loading them into the two boats they had used to sail here. Fortunately, the wind was a good one, and it was blowing in the right direction, so they expected to get beyond Ankara by the end of the second day. They would lash their boats together on the first night, as they had done on the voyage to Kronio, and sleep upon the waves. Hopefully, they would be able to beach east of Ankara on the second night.

Lefanu represented additional weight in Xinta's boat, so they loaded more trade goods into Santo's boat to balance out the craft.

Pushing their boats into, and over, the surf, Santo and Xinta hopped aboard while Lefanu steadied the craft. The men pushed the sail post into the criss-cross of wood panels in the bottom of each boat, then flung the deerskin sail over the lateral beam. Pulling hard on the ropes that were knotted to the edges of the skin, Santo and Xinta wrapped the twisted braids around the small posts wedged into the side edges of each craft.

A stiff breeze suddenly arose, drawing an 'ahh' from Lefanu, who was unused to traveling in this way. She swayed with the impulse of the boat, then laughed at the new experience, assured by the smile on Xinta's face that this was what was expected.

MIGRATION

1510 – 1120 B.C.E.

MIGRATION OF TRIBES

4870 B.C.E. – 1050 B.C.E

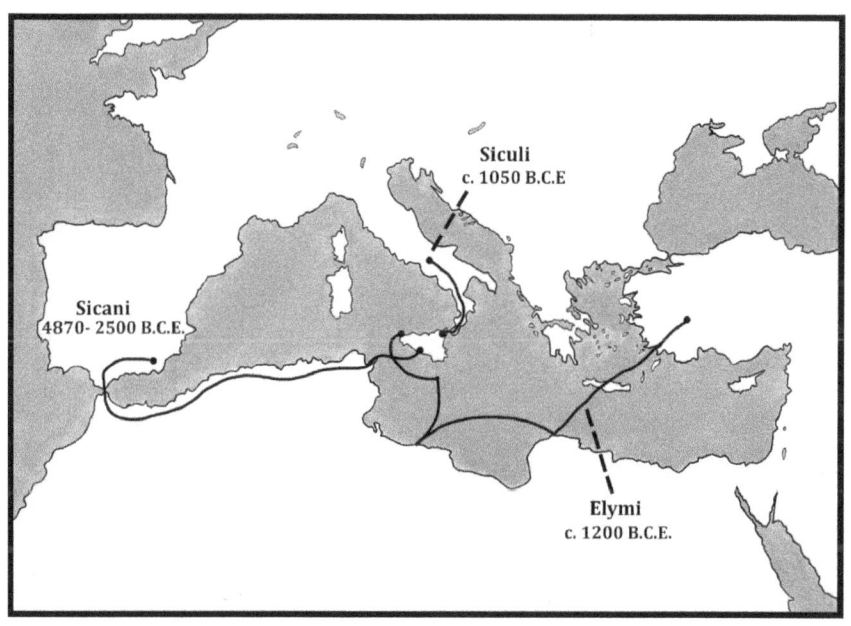

TRIBES IN SICILY

1000 B.C.E.

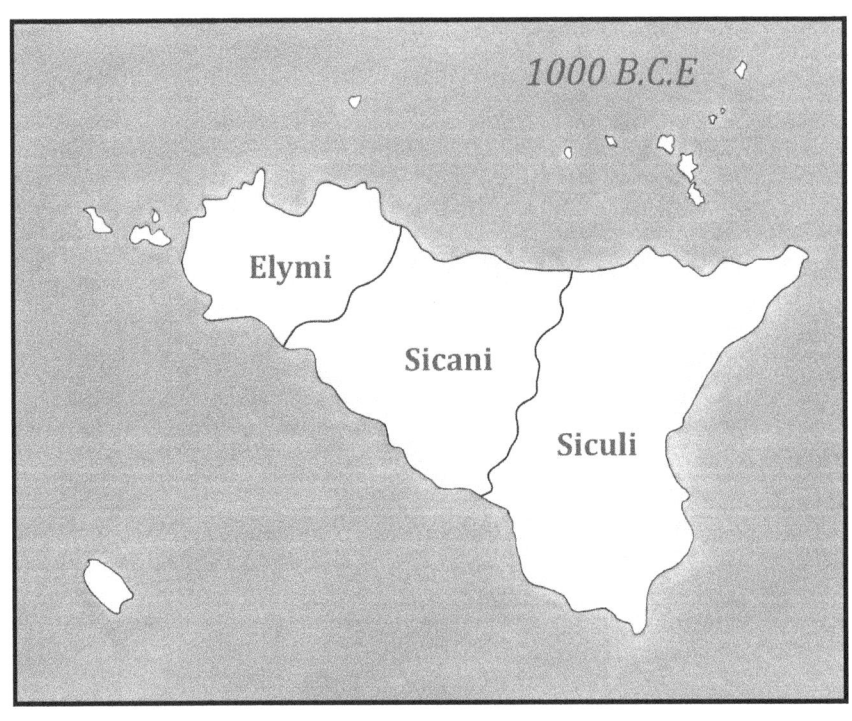

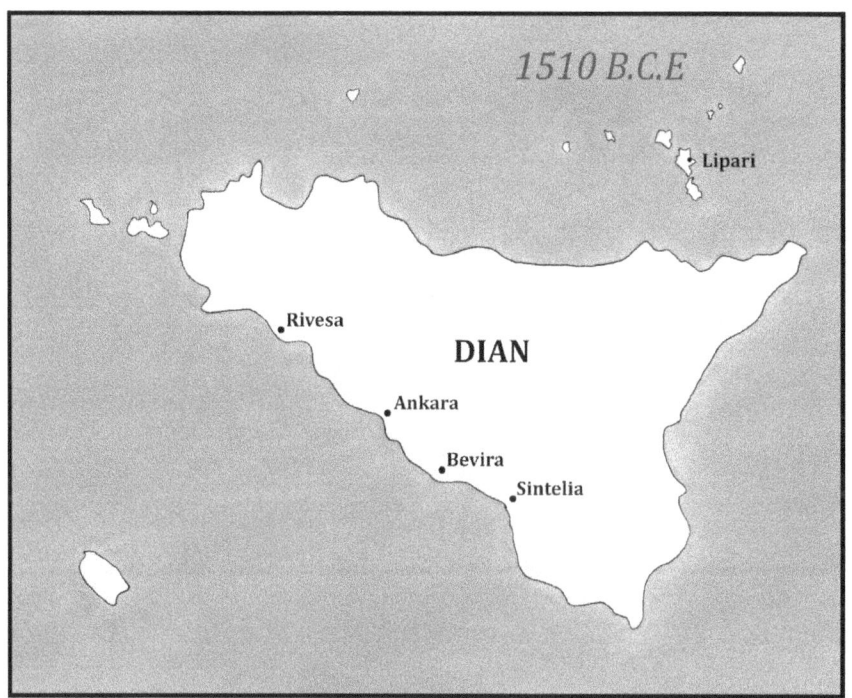

1510 B.C.E.
THE SICANI IN RIVESA

Aloxa and Rota woke early. Their young son Parapio was already up and walking around the stone-walled home, stumbling into them on his wobbly toddler's legs and emitting squeals of delight with the newfound independent mobility. It didn't seem to matter to him that his parents wanted to sleep in on this cold morning.

"Parapio, come here," said Rota, drawing her arms out of the warmth of the deerskin covering and extending them to him. The boy responded with a peel of laughter and quick-stepped on uncertain legs in her direction, falling into her arms with laughter.

Rota cuddled the boy at first, and then tried to entice him under the covering, showing him how warm it was beside her, but Parapio would not be constrained. He had just begun walking a few days before and, in the crisp morning air, he was not about to rest gently between his mother and father.

Rota was the first to give up and emerge from the deerskin, but Aloxa knew he wouldn't be allowed to linger either, so he tossed the covering aside and stood to pick up the little boy. While he did so, Rota was freed up and padded over to the dying embers of the fire they kept in the stone fireplace in their home. The tiers of block they had carved from large boulders were set close together, and the thin gaps left between the carefully squared blocks were filled with clay to keep even the slightest breeze from entering. Even while keeping the cold air out, though, the cold night air made it wise to keep a small fire burning through the night.

The Sicani people in the village of Rivesa had long ago learned to build a fireplace into the exterior wall of their homes. When the foundation was first laid, they added a semi-circular platform of flat stones as the hearth, and when the repetitive courses were added one layer of stone at a time, they built a curved alcove above this hearth that sloped gently upward toward the wall itself. The result was a curved niche big enough to build a small wood fire at the bottom, but with a sloping roof that pushed the warm air back into the home itself. The design had been refined over the lives of the Rivesan people so that a small hole at the back of the fireplace allowed the smoke to escape, pushed in that direction by the heat of the fire below, avoiding the infiltration of the noxious air into their sleeping quarters.

By morning, the fire set the evening before was struggling for life, but Rota brought it back to flame with a few quick stabs with a wooden stick, and a little more kindling added to the pile.

"He's hungry," Aloxa told her. The Rivesans milked their cows, sheep, and goats, but young children such as Parapio still went first to their own mother for nourishment. It would be soon, however, that she weaned the little boy from her breast. She would still be able to make milk for a long time, if her body was encouraged by his suckling to do so, and Rota didn't mind. But he would have to learn to drink the milk of the animals in time, and this would free his mother up for other duties.

Rota was from another settlement, Akra, to the east of Rivesa. While her complexion, hair color, and general frame resembled Aloxa's, who was from Rivesa, Rota had different habits and worshipped different deities. Most of these were slight variations; the villages were not far apart and had exchanged mates for many generations. But there were little differences, some too minor to bother about – like when Aloxa always turned sideways when he entered their home to avoid unsettling the god of the stones – but some were a bit more difficult to put aside. Rota offered her first bite of food each evening to Tlana, the god who gave her the animal meat to consume. She didn't waste the morsel; she merely raised it above her head before putting it in her mouth, thanking the god for providing the animal to feed her family. Aloxa didn't make such offerings and his woman worried that, one day, Tlana might withhold this nourishment.

They had talked about returning to Akra for a short stay. Aloxa wanted to trade some of Rota's woven clothing for the sharpened blades made by Laru, in her ancestral village. And now that Parapio was bigger and had survived the dangerous months of early life, they thought it would be time. It was still early spring, and they would like to go before the days became very hot, so they would consider the trip in the coming days.

The journey would take two days, especially with Parapio because he would have to be carried, and Aloxa considered whether another family might go with them. Untala lived in their village and worked together with Aloxa – they were both respected brick builders – and his woman, Scripa, was also an Akran before coming to Rivesa. Aloxa resolved to talk to them before making their plans. Their friends had no children yet, the first born had struggled with her breathing from the time of birth, and she soon died. But before another baby came, it would be good for Scripa to make the trip.

But today would be like most other days, and Aloxa and Untala must first think about the two structures they had been paid to build. One was a small shrine that the Rivesans had wanted in the northern sector of their village; the other was an addition to an existing home to accommodate the growing family of Poppo and Gia, whose children now numbered five, including Befalo who had returned from a trip to Akra himself the previous season with a woman of his own.

Rota and Scripa stayed behind, keeping watch over Parapio and other little children of the women who went into the village's farms for the day. They had stores of grain from the previous season that had dried but not been ground yet, and they needed to keep up with the daily call for bread. Meat from wild animals was less used in those times; the meat of the corralled animals replaced it. Milk from the various animals, vegetables tended by the farming specialists in Rivesa, and other nourishment was provided in ample supply, but the people always needed bread. It still held some mystical connotations, since the wet flour was transformed and grew in the baking process, almost as if the spirit of their god Tlana inhabited it, and Rota routinely ripped a hunk of the new loaf to offer in thanks. Unlike the meat that couldn't be wasted, she was willing to toss this morsel of bread into the fire as a gift to Tlana.

This morning was the time for the women to grind the wheat into flour, a process that their ancestors did only in small quantities and with considerable physical labor, time spent bent over a flat grinding stone with a long heavy rock to grind the grain.

The wheel had long since been discovered and applied in many ways to facilitate work. It was from the motion of the wheel that the new device for grinding was invented.

The Sicanian implements were first used in Rivesa but were passed on through social contact and trade to the people of Akra, Bevira, and Sentilia.

It began with a large, flat rocky shelf in the ground. This foundation would be chiseled and chipped until the surface was flat and even. Then, a hole was made in the center of this shelf using an iron awl and hammer, into which was placed a smooth-sided wooden pole, standing upright in the hole.

Another rounded stone would be stood up on its edge, like a wheel, with an axle protruding from its middle. This axle would be lashed to the vertical pole emerging from the rock platform so that when the axle was pushed, the wheel stone would roll and glide along the flattened surface of the rock shelf, pivoting around the entire device in a circular motion.

Over time, some improvements were made to the design. A slightly beveled edge was chipped on the wheel to allow it to more easily be rolled round and round the center post, but from the start this new machine was recognized as a great improvement for grinding wheat and other grains, for crushing nuts, and – when the flat horizontal surface top was chiseled with a circular channel – for crushing olives into oil.

There was just such a device in their part of Rivesa, and Rota and Scripa collected sacks of dried grain and went to use the grinding stone. They spread the grain in a smooth layer around the cut channel in the top of the foundation stone, using the palms of their hands to achieve an even layer about halfway around the channel. They had learned that using only one-half of the channel at first – away from the stone wheel – made the task of starting easier. They then stood side by side on the wooden axle that protruded outside the stone wheel and put their shoulders into it. The first motion was difficult, but with effort they got the wheel moving. Even the slightest action would generate some momentum so that, by the time the surface of the wheel met the edge of the layer of grain, the weight of the stone would work with them, grinding the grain beneath the wheel with a quickening motion.

They went around the center post twice and then stopped to respread the grain. By that time, the coarse husks had been broken and some turned to powder, so the entire collection could be spread more evenly – and in a thinner layer – around the entire channel of the device. When Rota and Scripa leaned into the wheel again, it started with ease, and they made two more turns around the center post before stopping. Since the grain was pulverized at this point, it had to be scooped into clay pots instead of sacks; the weave of the sacks used to bring the grain to the mill would allow most of their flour to be lost.

When they completed the task, the women returned to the sandy area outside their homes to make the dough for that evening's bread.

Meanwhile, Aloxa and Untala were anxious to return to the home they were building for Poppo and Gia. They had been experimenting with the clay forms their wives made, particularly the tall cylindrical shapes reserved for storing liquids. That afternoon, when Rota and Scripa had finished their bread baking and had resumed potting, the men slid in beside them and tried to intervene in the women's work.

The women were surprised at first, then laughed, but when the men persisted they rebuffed them and sent them away. When Aloxa and Untala tried to draft the children into their project, Rota brushed him away again. So, the men sat down with the women and explained what they wanted – long, thin tubes of clay open at either end, with neither top or bottom.

"*Pazzu*," she said – crazy! "Nothing will stay in!" She was thinking of vessels to hold liquids, but Aloxa could picture what he wanted – which was a device to channel water, not hold it – so he commandeered the potting table and tried to make it, with miserable results. So Untala tried, and failed.

"We need a round one," Untala told Scripa, rounding the fingers and palms of his hands and linking them in a circle. "And tall," he said, spreading his hands apart to show the length of the pipe they had in mind.

Suddenly, Aloxa stood up and reached for a tall pitcher that Rota had made long ago. He held it in his left hand and raised his iron-headed axe as if to strike it. Rota screamed and he stopped the motion.

"Why?" she asked. She wondered why Aloxa would want to destroy a pitcher that still served its purpose.

"I want to take the bottom off," he replied.

"But I said nothing will stay in," she argued, "unless you have some magic that the gods gave you."

After several more minutes of cajoling, the women agreed to make cylinders of clay with no top or bottom. As they finished the shaping, trying hard to make the forms as straight-sided as possible, Aloxa intervened again.

"Push this," he said, pressing his hands on one end of the pipe to narrow the opening at that end.

It didn't take long for the women who were expert potters to figure out what they were making. When they shaped the pipes and sloped one end of each to a smaller diameter, they knew what the men were planning. This energized them and, with the help of the children running for more water and river clay, Rota and Scripa produced twenty such pipes in a single afternoon. It would take another day of hardening, and then several hours in the kiln before they could test the result, but even the women grew anxious to see what would come of this.

———

Two days later, when the pipe sections had hardened and were fired, the men laid them end to end on the ground. The tapered ends fit inside the pipe next to each. When they were satisfied that this experiment had worked, Untala tapped Aloxa on the shoulder.

"To test, let's bring these to the stream. There is water there and a slope of land. We can test them."

The women were watching the project and went with the men, enlisting the help of the children so the clay pipes could be carried without risking any breakage. Once they arrived at the stream bed, Untala began smoothing a channel of earth that sloped toward the river. He scraped at the dirt and pulled twigs and roots out of the way. When his shallow ditch was smoothed, they assembled the pipes in a line, inserting each into the opening of the other. When the string of sections was assembled, they stood back to admire the result.

With a quick nod, Aloxa signaled to Untala that they should test it. He grabbed a wooden bucket from one of the children and filled it at the water's edge. Then he carried it up the slope to the top of the pipe and poured its contents into the new device. It worked perfectly. The water glided down through the pipe and emptied back into the river from whence it had come.

A child who was old enough to talk and reason, who belonged to another couple, asked Aloxa what he was doing. "But it just goes back where you collected it," he said, confused by the experiment.

The adults laughed, and Aloxa and Untala enjoyed the comment the most. They knew what they intended, and they knew how they were going to use this new way of transporting water. They could connect it to a cistern and create pipes that led to houses, then open and close the pipes whenever they needed water; they wouldn't have to go outside to collect it anymore.

1510 B.C.E.

THE SICANI IN AKRA

Over the years that the Sicanians spread out and established new settlements on the southern coast of Sicily, the Ankarans had developed a culture of conflict. The origins of this nature are not recorded, but nearby villages like Rivesa, Bevira, and Sintelia were aware that if they traveled across the coast, they must be wary of approaching Ankara.

The city known as Ankara in the 3rd Millennium B.C.E. had changed to Akra by this time, but their culture had not changed. From this place were known to come many strong men and brave fighters, who would fight with travelers over the rights to the land and the bounty of the sea. The Sicanians knew this well, and the Akrans' reputation grew.

Rota and Scripa were from this city and they defended her people. Although they had come to live with their men in Rivesa, the women were still supportive of the culture they had grown up in.

As the warm months proceeded, and the sun spent more time in the sky each day, the Akrans started to resume their farming and gathering practices that provided the fresh food they had missed throughout the cold times. Laru and Taania, Rota's parents, were still alive but too old to continue to hoe the ground and farm their plot of land on the outskirts of Akra. Instead, their daughter Chia and her man, Abele, and their two children, Sorna and Alifa, worked the land while Laru and Taania kept closer to their home.

There were olive trees to tend, trees that had long grown wild and were harvested by the Sicanians in this area. Sorna and Alifa were mostly responsible for this and, as youngsters, they especially liked to harvest the fruit of the tree by beating the branches, causing the ripened olives to fall onto the netting they had laid at the base of the tree. They would deliver this harvest to the same type of device the Rivesans used for grinding wheat and crush the olives into a paste so that they could catch the oil in hollowed wooden spoons to be used later to flavor their food.

Chia and Abele tended the farm itself, but they were also charged with bringing in fish and shellfish from the sea. Off the coast of Akra there was an abundance of surface-feeding fish like sardines, anchovies, shrimp, and crab larvae which attracted predators like mackerel, tuna, and swordfish, and a smart fisherman adept at casting a net could haul in enough each day to feed the family for a week. There were large turtles who laid their eggs throughout the warm months, and the Akrans harvested these delicacies eagerly without depleting the supply.

Rota's parents could still contribute, however, and they spent their time tending to the herbs and spices that grew in small patches near their home in Akra. Thanks to a tradition of penning their domesticated animals, like sheep and goats, they had access to plentiful milk for a growing family; even enough to share with friends whose corral of animals might have been smaller.

Cheesemaking had been mastered by this time, also, so excess milk could be turned into a foodstuff that could last longer on the shelf. Milk that had been left in goatskins had naturally turned into cheese, but this natural product resembled spoiled milk more often than the modern version of cheese. But through the gradual evolution of the process, both natural and hand-made, cheeses were being made by the Sicanians of the period with several different flavors. At first, they thought they could make it by pouring the milk straight into the clay pots, but that didn't work very well. Since the cheese they remembered came from animal skins, they returned to that process, but the result was odorous and not completely pleasing.

They didn't know that it was the naturally occurring enzyme, rennet, in the goatskin that turned the milk into cheese, but by trial and error they settled on putting the fresh milk into the skins first, then draining it out through a hole cut in the hide and into the clay pots for aging. This allowed contact with the rennet but salvaged the cream and cheese from the skin before it began to smell of old goat.

The years of practice that were required to become an expert cheesemaker made this industry perfect for the elders like Laru and Taania, and between tending their herb garden and watching over the cluster's little children, they made enough cheese to satisfy their own family and to share with neighbors.

A form of money had developed among the Sicanians by that time, a system that made their ancient practice of barter easier to manage. There was no coinage as such, but the *bacu* of old had by then turned into a modernized form of abacus, so the value of goods could be quantified and compared, an easier form of measurement than piling goods up and judging relative value. Thanks to the abacus and early forms of mathematics and writing, the quantities and values of goods developed some rigor and a bit of consistency which allowed similar products to be bought and sold in several villages at approximately the same valuation, always subject to the needs of the market.

Laru and Taania had no news of their daughter's pending visit, but they expected her during the warm months such as this. They also didn't know about the new baby, Parapio, but Taania hoped that her daughter had had a child by this time.

They knew Aloxa well and had approved of Rota's choice of him as a mate, but they also knew that he came from Rivesa, a city that didn't get along well with Akrans. The conflicts had not been over land; there was still too much room between the settlements to be concerned with such things. And there had been no tension concerning animals and agricultural products, for the same reason.

"Akrans want to be left alone," said Laru one afternoon as they knelt between the rows of *allu*, the ancient form of garlic. "We have all that we need here and it seems that other people want to take what we have."

"You mean, like our daughter?" commented Taania. She liked Aloxa and remembered that he was helpful and caring of Rota.

Laru only grunted. He knew that Taania thought well of Aloxa, and he did too, but he had trouble shaking his thought. Akra was a very successful city and it didn't need to trade with other Sicanians, so they had developed an attitude of isolation and Laru, who had spent many years in that nature, was hard pressed too change.

"We can see her," he continued, pulling one bulb of *allu* up between his fingers, "and see if she is well." He said this between pursed lips, as if he carried doubts about the welfare of his daughter. Not all children survived in those times; he and Taania had lost two and only Rota and her sister had survived. And Laru knew that the daughters went away with their men, sometimes to other cities, and he would be left with no one.

Taania remained on her hands and knees but bent her head up to look at Laru. He was growing old, she knew, and she knew that he worried about her and their children. She loved her man and tried to understand his fears and doubts. Then she smiled at him.

"You have me," she said, as if reading his thoughts.

Laru looked at his wife, smiled, and reached his weathered hand to meet hers knuckle-down in the soft earth of their garden. Nothing needed to be said.

On the same afternoon, Chia and Abele were in the field tending their crops. Back when the cool weather was just turning warm, they had sown seed with the mouldboard plough pulled behind a horse, a dramatic improvement over the digging stick and ard plough of their ancestors. The plough was roped to the neck of the horse, and Chia tended the animal while Abele strong-armed the plough to keep it moving in a relatively straight line. With all the applications of the wheel to date, they hadn't made it part of the ploughing routine yet, but the strength of the draught animal reduced the human effort considerably.

Leafy greens were grown in abundance, and rows of tiny peppers and bulbous root vegetables were lined up along the perimeter of the farm. Trees grew randomly throughout the space that was cultivated, and these could bear fruit of many types, from small juicy oranges or crisp-tasting lemons, to hazelnuts and chestnuts that were prized by the Akrans. Cherries, apples, and pears grew in small quantity in the sparse trees around the city, and since these trees grew wild, they could be harvested by anyone.

Chia and Abele focused on the broad, dark green leaves of wild kale and arugula, pinching them off at the ground but leaving untouched the core of leaves in the middle of the plant to keep the roots alive under the earth that would produce another crop in a few days.

After loading their woven baskets with these, they roamed the perimeter of the patch in search of the wild onions and *allu* that would make the food tastier. The spices and herbs that they also used were grown in smaller quantities in their garden in Akra, next to their home, and they harvested them as needed.

Chia and Abele then returned to their homestead with their harvest, collecting all the foodstuffs and preparing them for the meal. The loaves of bread had been formed and baked, and sat on a wooden shelf inside their house, and Laru and Taania brought in the herbs that would match the food. This would be a meatless meal, very common among the Sicanians of the time, but with olives and their oil, green herbs and brown spices, plus the cracked and roasted nuts and fresh vegetables, the families would eat well that night.

———

All three generations of Laru and Taania's family slept in the same room. The stone-cut house was warm and dry, but there was no reason to separate it into multiple spaces. Much like the people who had lived in Akra, and on the island of Dian for centuries, they spent most of their lives out of doors; the shelters were mostly used for sleeping, and for storing the pots, pitchers, and dried food that they kept.

On the next morning, they awoke when a glimmer of sunlight streamed in between the halves of cowhide curtains that were draped across the door. The children's eyes opened first, and Sorna pushed off the covering that kept his legs warm. He slept beside his sister Alifa and his quick motion woke her up. Their father and mother were already awake; they had stayed under the deerskin cover talking softly to one another rather than wake the little ones. When Sorna and Alifa were up, the parents knew that their day would begin, like it or not.

In a short time, the entire family was awake and getting busy about the morning's activities. Rota stirred the embers of the fire in the hearth while Aloxa arranged a couple of new branches on the pile to burn. Mornings weren't the time for big meals, and there would be no need to keep a big flame going. They just needed enough to warm the broth from the night before, broth into which Rota had poured the granulated chestnut flour, in a drink that Aloxa and she liked so much.

There would be work and play that day, much like every other day, as the children learned the chores that the adults already practiced, and as the adults persisted in managing the daily routine of the Sicanians in Akra.

———

Sicanians like Aloxa and Rota, Laru, Taania, and the others, had been coming to this island in the Middle Sea for thousands of years. They traveled great distances over long journeys, setting down roots here and there and splitting off into new excursions to travel further along the African coast, into and through Pantelleria, and onto the shores of Sicily.

They encountered tribes with older and more primitive cultures already inhabiting the island, and the Sicanians merged with them, mingling their survival traditions, cultural practices, and genetic structure with those who had come before. In time, the Sicanians came to dominant the island, pressing the earlier people into a footnote of history. In doing so, the new arrivals – spread out as their arrival had been over millennia – became the reigning people of the land.

Over the next thousand years, the Sicanian tribes grew, split, grew some more, and established their cities along the southern coast of the island. Some went inland, but only a few. Survival meant remaining near water sources, and the benevolent expanse of seashore was the most prolific and generous of water sources. So, the Sicanians established hegemony over the island in the Middle Sea by creating settlements that dotted the shore.

Their cultures evolved, their technologies progressed, and the interactions between the tribes stretching across the island produced a relatively peaceful mix of homogeneous and heterogeneous societies.

The main cities were Akra and Rivesa, although each had contact with other settlements like Bevira and Sintelia, and even people as far away as Mylia in the north and Precipio in the central part of the island. On some long trading journeys, the Sicanians from the southern part of Dian even met the people of Casegno on the tiny island where the volcano made the obsidian they had long valued.

With the growth of the population and the development of artisans with specialized skills, trading within and between cities became important to their way of life, and this trading was facilitated by a growing sense of the symbolic forms of exchange, a precursor to coins and money. Accounting systems kept track of the value of goods, and multiple commodities could be grouped together and exchanged according to the system of value that the records indicated. In addition to the producers of goods, the talent necessary in accounting for the trading system created another class of experts: the earliest form of merchants who would supervise the trade and ensure its accuracy and fairness.

And with social development and soaring populations, ritualized rules became more common, as did the people in the society who were charged with adjudicating the propriety of action and applicability of the rule to each situation. Men arose to lead the tribes and cities, and a hierarchy among them grew out of the sharing and exercise of power. Sometimes they carried stylized weapons or other implements that symbolized their power, or they adorned their bodies with shapes cut or burned into their skin, or strings of deer or wolf teeth. In most cases those who ruled over Akra or Rivesa or any of the other Sicanian cities were well known to the people there.

The leaders who ruled the land were sovereign over all – except for the gods who ruled the earth. There was one exception: the shamans and a growing hierarchy of priests. They were believed to possess a unique wisdom to correct or direct all affairs, and the priests' assumption of this power was often at odds with the chiefs and kings. Just as braided hair, sharpened spears, and necklaces showcased the importance of the civil rulers, staffs of twisted vine and headdresses of bird feathers adorned those who claimed the ability to speak with the gods. Both were feared, and both were revered.

1200 B.C.E.

ELYMIAN MIGRATION FROM ANATOLIA TO SICILY

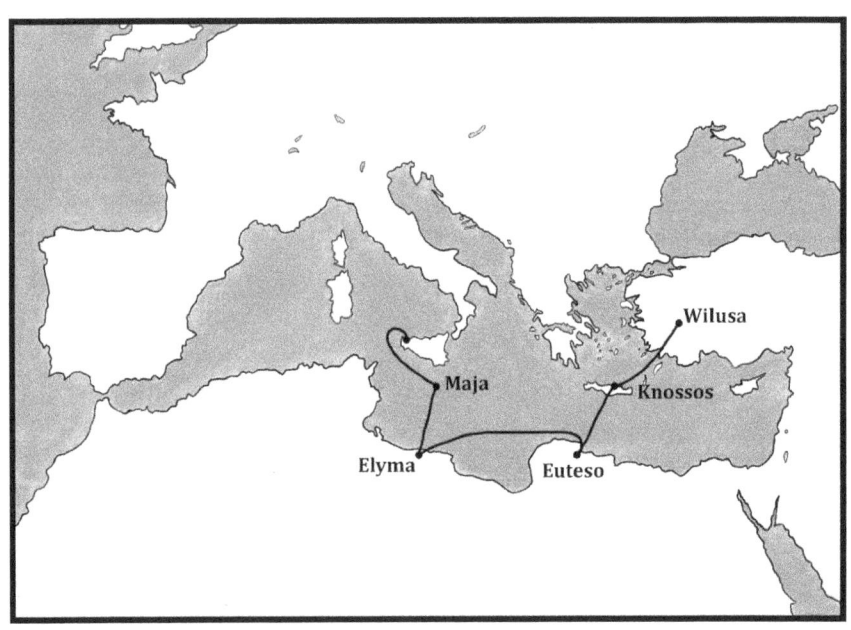

1178 B.C.E.
ELYMI MIGRATION

EPHSO STOOD ON THE BOW OF THE BOAT AS IT ROCKED GENTLY IN the waves in the harbor where they anchored. The flotilla of boats was arrayed in a rough semi-circle, positioned so that the arc of boats formed a rounded barrier against the open sea in case they were approached by unidentified craft. Ephso was the leader of this estranged tribe of Elymi, people who had left war and destruction behind in Wilusa to seek better, calmer lands.

He had led his people on this months-long journey in a hasty retreat to Knossos on the large island to

the west. That was never intended to be the last stop; it was too close to the place from which they were escaping, but the sea was vast and the voyage they planned would take long, so docking on this island was a temporary measure, one to last for a night or two.

The weather was still warm, but Ephso knew that the cold winds would be coming soon. He hoped to get his tribe as far as the coast of the great continent to the south before the tossing seas made water travel more dangerous. He assumed that settling at Euteso would be good enough; at least the Elymians could decide then whether to stay or move on.

But that didn't work either. The indigenous Eutesans that Ephso and his tribe encountered weren't at war, but they were wary of these people landing on their shores and dropping in on them. Ephso led the Elymians outside of Euteso itself, sailing their large wooden-hulled craft a bit farther to the west, hugging the coastline, reaching a point just beyond the city of Euteso to avoid confrontation. They found virgin fields, but Gorgidas, Ephso's expert in farming, nevertheless warned that the area they found would not be suitable.

"If we found a settled area and traded with the people there," Gorgidas said, "our tribe could survive the winter with the markets and farmland the Eutesans already worked. But the people here chose well; their land is bounteous. If we go farther, to a place where there is no settlement, there will be a reason why people didn't establish their communities there."

And, so, they moved on again after two days of collecting wild beans and fruit, plus some wild goats that strayed into their encampment that they would slaughter onboard.

The weather would not normally be a factor, since the northern coast of the big continent had high temperatures, but the late season winds and rain could impede their sailing. Ephso directed the flotilla to another spot on a coast which Gorgidas said was more promising.

The boats moored in a tiny bay, just big enough to hold the ten vessels, and the people used small crafts to bring their supplies to the shore. It was late in the afternoon, after the late-summer sun was dipping far toward the west, as they rowed their people and supplies to the shore. The Elymians would only bring some of their supplies, since they didn't know yet whether this place would support them for long. So, some of the sailors would remain on the boats to signal their shore-bound fellows if a suspicious craft approached from the sea.

Those who embarked to the shore dragged their rafts and wooden canoes onto the beach and surveyed their surroundings.

"There is no settlement here, but the trees grow tall and the brush beneath is thick," Gorgidas advised, surveying the land as much with the sweep of his hand as with his eyes.

"Can we live here?" asked Ephso.

"Maybe," the farmer replied. "But, at least, I don't think we'll die here."

They unloaded their supplies to set up a camp for the night, content with the notion of exploring the following day.

———

When dawn broke, Ephso and Gorgidas were already up and walking with two other men away from the beach and into the trees.

"This seems very rich," Heliocles said, nodding toward the dense forest that they had entered.

"Yes," replied Ephso. "It seems promising."

"We can call it Elyma," said Alcon, the youngest of the adventurers to come ashore, but Gorgidas and Ephso warned against such early optimism.

"We have a lot to learn about the place. Maybe it will work for us, but there is a lot to learn," said Ephso.

The Elymians spent the next three weeks building more structurally sound shelters, adding permanent firepits to serve the cooking needs of the tribe, and even building a kiln for potting. That was their first act of confidence, since pottery-making wasn't going to be necessary unless they intended to stay for a long time.

Each night, a boat would row out to the anchored flotilla, gather the sentries left watch on the ships, and replace them with the volunteers who had been ashore. There were fewer women on this excursion, but when Alcon drew the night watch aboard his boat, his wife Gala decided to go with him. The young couple drew jeers and a bit of harmless humor for being unwilling to spend the night apart. But they weathered the joshing and Gala's upturned nose made it clear that she thought she was getting the better part of the deal anyway.

Over the weeks, as the skies grew grayer, the nights grew shorter, and the winds picked up more frequently in the morning, the Elymians were discovering how to survive in this new environment. The shortest days were also the coldest, and they were thankful for having built shelters quickly. They survived on the foodstuffs that they transported with them, but Gorgidas led an effort to plant some late-season grains and peas so they could harvest something before the growing season disappeared for them.

Daytime temperatures were modest, but to a tropical-minded tribe, the air was still relatively cool so social activity through the winter months dropped off as the families spent more time in their own homes. Religious rituals still demanded observation, and the priest would tend to the ceremonies that the Elymi brought with them from Wilusa.

By the time the harshest part of winter had passed, the tribe had established firm roots in Elyma. They had explored their surroundings, built homes, communal buildings, and shrines to their gods. When the days began to lengthen, plans were made for putting seeds in the ground, seeds that they had also brought from Wilusa. Gorgidas had considered this carefully, not knowing what soil they would find, but was confident that he had packed enough different types of seeds that he would be able to get something established.

But with the warming of the days, a strong wind blew up from the arid dessert south of their settlement and sustained its power for weeks at a time. The dust and dry air brought people to coughing, and the dust particles covered the fragile green leaves of the plants just as they were emerging from the earth. Homes were infiltrated by the dust storms, and the heat made sleeping at night nearly impossible.

"Is this usual?" Ephso asked Gorgidas. He knew that his friend had not been to this coastline before, but the farmer was well-trained and learned in weather and climate.

"No, well, yes, perhaps," he replied. "I have heard about the strong winds of this land from sailors, but I didn't believe them. I had heard that the dry wind can suck the life out of a plant, and the dust can choke the people. I decided it was just sailors' exaggerations, talk of danger and excitement."

Gorgidas sighed and concluded that perhaps the sailors were right.

"I don't know if we can stay here," Ephso said with resignation.

"But we have been so long on the water," added Antemion, a man not used to sailing and ready to put down roots.

The Elymians lasted another few weeks, but the *sirocco* continued to blow. One day, as Gorgidas knelt down beside the dead and dying plants that he was trying to coax into sustained life, Ephso stood over him.

"We can't stay," the leader said with finality, and the farmer nodded his head in agreement.

They left the structures they had built for someone else to find at some later date. But within another week, the Elymian sailors and clan were back out on the water searching for another place to land.

Ephso wanted to guide them farther west rather than return to Euteso, and he feared that the harsh winds on the land would prevent them from setting the sails. The wind was more manageable out on the water, and after rowing north for nearly an entire day, the flotilla slipped beyond the edge of the *sirocco* and were able to settle into a channel in the sea that allowed more stable transit.

Still, the winds came from the west, and so the sails would do no good. Ephso, in his lead boat, and Eurytos piloting the boat behind him, drew the line of Elymian explorers out of the great continent to their south onto a northerly heading toward the land mass that they could see in the distance. After two days on the water, they made landfall on an island that seemed appealing for them, but they could also see another bigger island in the distance. After spending two days on the small island to gather supplies and some green sprigs to eat, they pushed off once again into the sea heading toward the coast of the biggest island they had ever seen.

Casting a quick look back at the small island that had sustained them on their short visit, Eurytos saluted the land mass.

"Goodbye, Maja," using an ancient Wilusan word for friend.

After casting off, Ephso calculated that it would only take two days of rowing or one long day under sail to make it to the big island. But about this time, the winds picked up in the opposite direction. Normally, a sailor would embrace winds as free power, but Ephso had no intention of sailing east once again.

He called instructions out to Eurytos and they set their sails to tack against the wind. It would mean drawing them farther west instead of going due north to the big island, but the land mass was so large that

Ephso didn't care where they made landfall. Besides, his rowers were tired and any free help from the gods would be accepted.

The string of Elymian boats cruised westerly for a day and a night. By dawn of the next morning, the air had died down a bit, and when the sun shone bright, they could see a mountainous island looming before them. Wilusa was flatter than this, Ephso thought to himself, and all aboard the Elymian ships wondered how rich and wild the island might be.

It was a warm month, early in the year, but the air was crisp and Gorgidas stood on the bow of the large ship and dreamed of reaching the island and planting their farms just in time for the hot season to begin.

They sailed in comfort the better part of the day, but in the early afternoon, the skies began to darken. Ephso looked up and about but saw no clouds in the air above them. He signaled to Eurytos in the other boat, who shrugged his shoulders in confusion. It was Calliope, Leodes's wife, who first realized what was happening. She looked up, with a cupped hand shielding her eyes, and pointed to the sun.

"What is that?" she screamed.

Her shriek was loud enough that nearly everyone in the flotilla heard her. Gorgidas looked up, as did Leodes and Ephso. Soon all the Elymians on the boats were staring at the sky as it darkened to a threatening, ominous blackness. Those who dared look into the center of the sun – the gods were thought to live there, and it was considered an insult to look directly at them – feared that it was being eaten by some huge being. The bright, shining disk was slowly disappearing, replaced by a growing blob of mysterious origin.

A breeze picked up and slowly grew into a wind, and as the sun fell victim to the beast, the air fell cool on their arms. The sea suddenly grew very still, as if the battle in the sky was pressing some massive weight upon the water. The beast continued to win the battle and the sun continued to disappear. In a matter of minutes, the entire sky went dark, stars that normally only visited at night were mysteriously dotting the sky above, and the entire earth seemed to take on a sickly, stricken state.

The Elymian priest was on one of the boats and he held his hands up above his head, then dipped his chin so that it struck his chest. All the while, he rattled the seashell rope that hung from his neck and clanged the bone anklets together on his lower legs.

While the sky was still black, and the Elymians began to mutter frightened predictions about their safety, the priest looked up again. Suddenly, he smiled and then he let his arms drop to his sides and walked casually away as if it was just another day in the village.

Ephso laughed when he saw this, and the laugh made him feel better. The beast had devoured the sun, but their priest was very powerful, and very smart. If the priest wasn't worried, Ephso decided that he would not be worried either. He sat down on the deck of the boat and waited.

The Elymi around him were not so sanguine, but the actions of the priest and Ephso gave them more confidence. No one laughed – as their leader had – and no one abandoned the deck of their boat, as the priest had done.

Suddenly, Calliope let out another cry and drew the others' attention to the sky by pointing upward. In the instant that it took for these weary travelers to look skyward, a gentle brightness returned to the earth as slim rays of the sun reappeared on the other side of the beast, as if the angry monster was letting the sun escape.

The light continued to grow, a faint breeze resumed, and the surface of the water picked up again with shallow whitecaps. Within another few minutes, everything was back to normal, and the Elymi were ecstatic. Some believed they had witnessed a great battle, others a dream, but the priest knew. He had heard before about how the moon sometimes comes before the sun, and that this was a mating ritual for the gods. He had sung to the deities above, wishing them good fortune, not pleading with them for mercy as the other Elymians thought he was doing. And when the mating ritual was completed, each of the celestial beings would go their way again.

Ephso didn't know all this, but he trusted his priest, and he was proven right to do so on this day.

The Elymian tribe led by Ephso and Gorgidas successfully navigated the seas until they reached the coastline of the big island, known by them as Sicania after the people they knew had settled there from the east. To avoid contact with the indigenous tribes, Ephso had directed their flotilla to continue along the edge of the land mass until they settled on a promontory on the western coast, on a curving spit of land that became known as Drepanon.

With the long sea voyage behind them, and a handful of deaths experienced along the way, the Elymi were anxious to make landfall and begin to build their new cities away from the long conflict in Anatolia. Each boat anchored off the shore, but they found a deep, narrow channel in the sea that led to the beach and enabled them to draw close to land and reduce the distance they would have to cross in smaller boats. Ephso instructed the travelers to rope the boats together in a single-file line pointing toward the beach, and to transfer their cargo from the backmost boat across the decks of the others, so that they only loaded their goods onto the smaller craft at the bow of the first ship closest to the beach.

MAJOR ELYMIAN CITIES

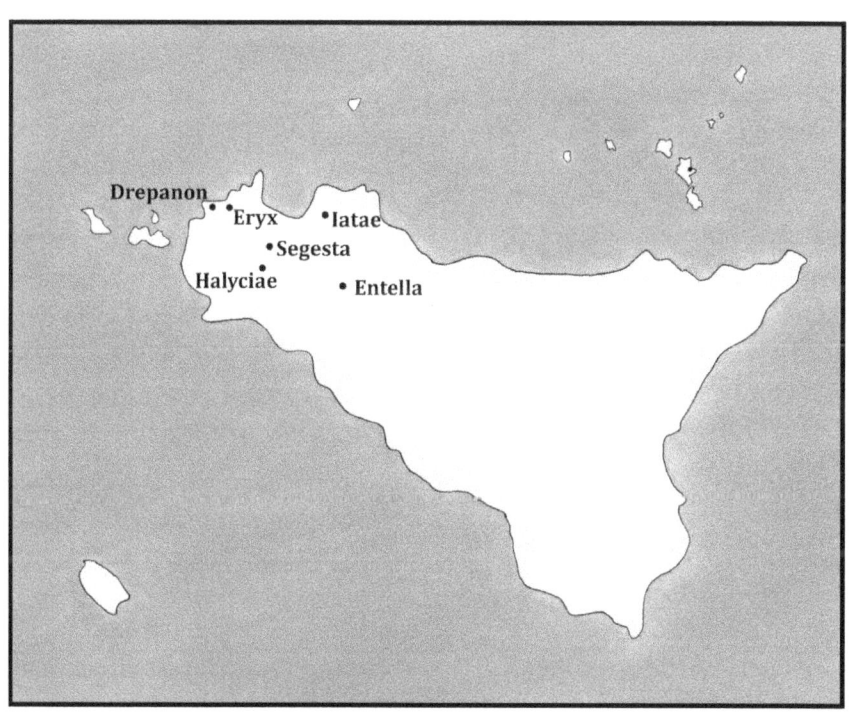

1120 B.C.E.

DREPANON

THE GENERATION OF EPHSO AND GORGIDAS AND CALLIOPE
created several small communities in western Sicily. They named the
first one Drepanon, on the shore where they had landed. Communities
grew and spread around the region and other cities were founded –
Entella, Segesta, and Halyciae. But for all these people, construction was
the first order of business. Cities grew quickly. First, there were homes to
build, then communal buildings including religious centers and shrines,
then they cleared roads and paved some of them with smooth, rounded
rocks. By the time the next generation had supplanted the explorers who
first brought the Elymi to this island, the cities hosted large populations
and an economy based on trade.

Looming over Drepanon was a mountain that sometimes hid its peak in
the clouds. They named it Eryx and believed that it was the home of the
gods. Their patron, Potnia, the goddess of love, was the one the Elymi
held most sacred, so they set about building a temple to her at the very
edge of the highest peak on Eryx. It was the logical place to pay homage
to Potnia, and they believed that she would protect them, allow their
civilization to grow, and make their cities populous. To build her temple,
a large industry was born to bring roads up the mountain and bring
construction materials to its summit.

The priest who had laid out the design of the temple fell ill just after the circle of stones had been placed that marked of the perimeter of the sanctuary where the eternal flame would burn. But by then construction on the rest of the temple and surrounding wall had begun, and his creative insights would be needed. He was slumped forward in his chair as his chest heaved mightily to bring in air. The temple guardians dropped their swords and rushed to carry the high priest to the rude circle of stones that defined the holiest part of their temple. The inner firepit was surrounded by several other flattened stones, altars already set for Potnia, and the guards believed that the goddess would save their high priest if they could lay him on one of these stones before he expired. But as they passed through the narrow opening in the encircling wall and past the footstones set for the erection of the columns of the temple, the priest sobbed once more, and his chest caved in while the men held him in their arms.

Another holy man, Phinoto, stepped in and took the place of the high priest. Some suspected that this was a hasty assumption of power, but Phinoto spoke with eloquence and convinced the men that this was a time of grave danger for the community.

"Our high priest kept us safe for these many years, he pointed to this holy spot for the temple to Potnia," he opined, "and he wanted us to build this temple to her. Potnia will secure our safety, build our cities, make our women fertile, and ensure our survival." He ended his sermon with this: "If we do not come together and accept his decision, if we do not accept Potnia in our hearts and our loins, we will fight among ourselves and perish."

Raising his arm above his head in a signal that bespoke both power and decisiveness, Phinoto declared his intention.

"I will not let this happen to my people, the good Elymians of Drepanon. We will bring the great stones up from the hillside and valley, and this Temple to Potnia will rise from the summit of this hill, and the fires we build for her honor will blaze in glory for all the years to come."

Phinoto's rallying speech and determination convinced the gathering of temple guards that he was the right choice, and concerns about his self-selection faded. After all, being the high priest of the temple for the goddess of love carried great power and great privilege.

And so, the building continued. Over the months and years, massive boulders were dragged up the hill, using huge wheeled contraptions that allowed the weight of these mountain stones to be moved up the smooth incline of the road that the Elymi had paved. Several crews of men were employed in the sole task of bringing the weight of these building blocks to the summit. Because of the difficulty of the work, and the likelihood that a man would die from exhaustion at some point in his working days, most of these "rock movers" were Sicani from the interior of the island who had been enslaved after losing in some conflict with the Elymi, and with the small bands of Punic peoples who sailed from the land to the south. They knew that they would likely work until death, since enslavement didn't come with a term of service. Other workers were taken from the criminal class, those who had committed some crime against Drepanon or the people there, and they hoped to survive long enough to serve out their sentence.

Luckier workers were assigned to the summit, most of them freemen, but some enslaved people lived and worked around the temple. It was their job to lift the cut stones into place, building the wall that surrounded the tight circle of the temple itself. One side of the temple rested on the edge of the cliff and, on that side, Potnia was exposed to the valley below and the sea beyond. From that cliffside approach, the temple was safe because no human could scale the mountain. The opposite side of the temple grounds faced the slope of the mountain that angled downward toward Drepanon below. This side required a strong barrier to encroachment, and it was this side that Kitro and Phenandia, Sicani slaves, worked alongside the freemen from the Elymian society to build the wall. From early in the day when the light first shone above the mountainside, until late in the evening when there was not enough sun left to light their way, these slaves and freemen worked together to hoist the large cut blocks into place, fitting them snugly into an overlapping pattern so that nothing could penetrate through the seams, not air, not light, and not inquiring eyes. The Temple of Potnia was required to be safe from any violation, whether physical or visual.

Crispo and Renata were Elymi builders – freemen – who managed the construction of the temple. They followed the design drawn by the high priest, one that involved three concentric circles and that single semi-circular stone barrier, more than the height of a man, that surrounded the part of the temple grounds that were opposite the cliff on which it stood. This wall Kitro and others built with slave labor.

More carefully sculpted stones were admitted into the sanctuary of Potnia itself where three fully concentric circles were made. The innermost ring was a tight circle, about eight cubits across, or the length of two men lying down head to foot. This circle was built up with four layers of stone so that the interior depth would hold large tree trunks and fire-hardened branches to keep a perpetual flame bright at night.

About four cubits beyond this pit was built another circle, alternating pairs of stones and open space, lower than the inner one, and composed of stones chiseled flat on the surface and nested together in pairs. They were spaced about so that the horizontal length of each pair was the same as a man's height, and another man's height between each pair. Placed in a series of disconnected couplets, there were eight of these joined stones arranged around the fire pit. They were called the "resting stones."

Beyond the resting stones, another circle was laid, about four cubits separation from the resting stones, and made of flattened rocks set edge to edge like pavers, buried in the ground so that only their surface was visible. These stones completely encircled the resting stones and firepit. Upon this ring of pavers stood the grand columns that were carved and polished to a smooth finish. The upright columns had rounded crowns at their peaks, like a phallus, and they stood upon the prostrate stones below as solitary obelisks pointing toward the sky above. These columns were sentries for the temple and were not tasked with supporting a roof or even a decorative cornice. Potnia's holy temple was meant to remain open to the world, spread before the inquiring eyes of the gods above.

Over many months the structure took on a finished look, the white stone gleaming in the daylight for all those below in the valley to see it. At night, the fire burned brightly in the inner pit for the villagers below, and as a beacon for sailors on the sea.

Kitro and Phenandia worked day after day in the heat and the rain, but slaves were never allowed to enter – or even peer into – the sanctuary within the walls they built. Crispo and Renata passed them almost every day, entering through the narrow portal in the continuous stone barrier to tend to their duties inside. Just inside this portal was another wall made of stone, set so that it spanned the gap and blocked any view of the activities within.

"You are not allowed to view the goddess," Crispo reminded him, walking past Kitro one evening. "No slave is worthy to cast his eyes upon her."

Beautiful maidens came too; Crispo said they were priestesses. They were there to serve their goddess. Kitro knew one of them, called Scylla. She never spoke to him but honored him with a half-hidden smile. The slave had dreams of her at night, but she was a priestess and he was nothing.

Other maidens came with Scylla, each wearing a long white robe clipped together at the breast with a single golden hook.

"Only the most beautiful for Potnia, huh?" said Phenandia, elbowing his friend in the side as the young women passed by. But Kitro didn't smile; his eyes remained fixed on the movement of Scylla's hips beneath the cloak as she swayed through the opening into the temple grounds.

The days wore on and the men wore down. Kitro and Phenandia were but two of the hundred or so slaves employed in building the temple wall. Inside the barrier, the construction began to take shape, and columns rose high from the supine stones at their base. The first stood erect along the cliffside and were hard to view from outside the wall, but as more pillars were stood up on the side facing the slope and the barrier that Kitro and his fellows were building, they could see the rounded tops of the temple columns.

Each night, when their labor ended, the slaves could see the glow of the fire within the temple and they watched as peasants from the valley below brought their offerings to Potnia. The men from Drepanon came with what they could carry. Some had wood carvings to offer, some sheep, and others had nets of fresh fish. One by one they slipped through the portal and into Potnia's sacred enclosure.

Phenandia had built a small fire for himself, Kitro, and some of the laborers kept here by the guards. They shared a meager meal and small pitchers of ruby red wine. The temple guards took turns watching over the slaves to prevent any escapes, then switched with other guards to take up their station inside the temple.

"I want to see inside of Potnia," Kitro told Phenandia between bites of crusty bread.

"You cannot," came the whispered reply. "It is forbidden. The goddess will strike you dead."

"And what if she does," Kitro said with derision. "We are slaves. We are dead already."

Just then he looked up and, in the dim firelight of their own circle he saw Scylla walking up the path. She continued on past the group of slaves, refusing to look in Kitro's direction. For her to avoid his eyes made Kitro's blood hot, and he stared after her as she entered the sanctuary of the temple.

Phenandia could sense the change in his friend's mood and turned to look over his shoulder to see what had gotten Kitro's attention. Spotting Scylla, he scoffed at Kitro, not surprised but shaking his head in disbelief.

"She is a priestess, holy of holies. Pay no attention to her," he warned Kitro.

By then, Scylla had passed from view, hidden inside the temple by the wall that Kitro had built.

He looked at the guards sitting on the fallen log on the outskirts of the circle of slaves and looked back at the portal to the temple. Kitro knew that there was another way in. It wasn't an opening in the wall, but partway around the outer wall was a pile of rough, discarded stone that had not yet been carted away. It was high enough that, if he climbed it, he could reach to the top of the wall and join the worshippers within.

When the guards had turned their attention away, Kitro rose silently and – hunched over – walked quickly toward the perimeter of the wall. He could hide in the darkness of its nighttime shadow and work his way around the stone until he reached the pile of discards that he had seen that afternoon.

Phenandia followed his friend's movements but returned his gaze to the fire that licked at his feet, afraid that if he seemed interested in something beyond the circle the guards would grow suspicious.

Kitro reached the wall and, still crouching and clinging close to the stone, he circled around the curving perimeter and stepped lightly onto the bottom slope of the crushed stone. He tested it with his toes at first, afraid that putting his weight on it suddenly would cause the pile to slip and cascade down or make so much noise in disassembling that he would be discovered. When he decided that the pile would support him, Kitro stepped quickly up to the top. It was just about three feet from the top of the wall, high enough for him to lean on the wall and see over it easily.

Once he was positioned, Kitro leaned his elbows on the topmost stone and steadied himself. Within the temple grounds he was first struck by the brightness of the light from Potnia's fire. What he had seen from the darkness in his own camp had given no hint of how large a fire this was in the temple. Once his eyes had adjusted to the brightness, he focused on the structure that filled the grounds. There was the single, deep ring that held the fire, the spaced pairs of flattened "resting stones" that encircled it, and a full circle of bedrock on which stood the columns pointed toward the open sky above.

There were people milling about the temple grounds also. The peasant men in rough clothing were delivering their tokens of respect for Potnia, while the high priest received the offerings. Kitro saw the beautiful priestesses standing beside the resting stones, their white robes glittering in the light of the crackling fire.

And he saw Scylla. She was standing beside one pair of resting stones on the far side of the firepit. Her white robe blazed in its brilliance, and her face was lit by the heat of the fire.

As each of the peasant men delivered their offerings, they went to the resting stones and stood beside one of the priestesses. As one broad-shouldered man approached Scylla, Kitro's heart began to beat faster and his breathing came in uneven strokes.

"To our goddess, Potnia, the lady of fertility and goddess of all love," said the high priest, "we offer your gifts. Potnia teaches us that love is sacred and that the act of joining in love is the holiest act we can engage in. She opens herself to you," he continued, lifting his arms toward the sky above the erect columns, "and she calls you to enter the holiest places of her temple."

With those words, the priestesses reached up and pulled the clips that bound the robes about their breasts. In a single, silent action, the white drapes fell from the women's shoulders and folded at their feet. One by one, the priestesses lifted their robes and spread them on the resting stones as if they were dressing an altar, then they lay back upon the robes, with their heels drawn up to their buttocks and their knees held open to the men before them.

Kitro's eyes grew wide and his heart beat in his chest. He was frozen in his position at the top of the wall.

The peasant men drew their cloaks off and dropped them to the floor of the temple. Then – one after another – they knelt down between they priestesses' knees and entered the holiest places in Potnia's temple.

Kitro watched and he was so consumed with the scene of sexuality being played out before him that he didn't even notice the glint of the sword that was swinging down upon his neck just at that instant.

JULY 2018
CAFÉ AMADEO

I spent some afternoons in the library and evenings in the restaurants and sidewalk cafés around Mazara del Vallo. I met a number of locals, made some friends, and became known to them as the American who wanted to become a Sicilian, or as one man said in impressive American jargon, a "wannabe Sicilian."

The thought clanged around in my head. I considered myself a Sicilian, a mindset common to people living in a country – the United States – who all felt like they had come from somewhere. The so-called "melting pot" mentality.

But people here came from here. They thought of themselves as Sicilian and me as American. My new friends didn't have a hyphen in their self-portrait like I did and like most other Americans did.

"What is it like?" Antonio asked me one evening while we sat at the bar in Trattoria Bettina.

"What do you mean?"

"Well, everyone I know here is Sicilian. But you walk around New York...well, I don't really know, because I've never been there...but I hear that you walk around New York and there are people with red hair and blond hair, blue eyes, brown eyes, white skin, brown skin. People from

Asia, Germany, Ireland, Italy...all over." His imagination seemed to expand to fill the space of his comment.

"How do you know who's who?" he asked.

"Who's who?" I repeated, and then pondered my answer. "We're, well, we're..."

I tried to put together an explanation that would be correct and, at the same time, satisfy Antonio's curiosity. Then something occurred to me.

"Sicilians are not all the same either," I offered. "The Greeks, Carthaginians, Romans, Goths...what not. These people swept across your island and made it into the real melting pot." I took some little pride in shifting the "mut" analogy to this island from America.

Antonio sipped at his tumbler of wine and grinned.

"Okay, so that's true, I guess. But we look much more the same than you Americans do."

"It's only because of the centuries that have passed, right?" I countered. "Your immigrant waves have been happening for thousands of years, America's for only about a century."

"So, the paint samples haven't mixed yet, huh?" he said with a laugh. I forgot that Antonio was an artist whose paint analogy would come quickest to mind.

"Yes, but when you mix all paints together, you just have a puddle of gray," I smiled back. "I don't think you would describe the richness of Sicilian culture to be a 'puddle of gray,' would you?

"Besides," I added with finality, "where did you get your green eyes?"

———

The next morning, I was back in my seat at Café Amadeo sipping espresso and nibbling on a hard roll, waiting for another session with Vito. I felt sometimes like I was taking advantage of him, both in terms of the time spent and the fact that the old gent was now spending every one of his mornings with this young American pestering him with questions.

But the barista came over to sit with me on that particular morning, towel slung over his shoulder and his white sleeves rolled up to his elbows. His thick head of black curly hair hung down on his forehead, and his eyes shown with a startlingly non-Sicilian blue color. The pads of his fingers showed the tell-tale brown powder of his profession, the dust of an infinite number of espressos and cappuccinos.

He told me not to worry about Vito, that the old guy was enjoying the chance to tell his young protégé about the history of his country. The barista's use of the word 'country' came to his lips without a pause, and without considering the proper use of the term. Like Vito, he and the others around me thought of Sicily as their country, even though they were fully aware that it was really a region of a far larger country. And while they accepted that geo-political fact, they still considered the island a unique part of the world and, in fact, their country.

"I have known Vito for a long time," the barista continued. "And we all know that he lived through World War II and for these long years since. He has lived a lot of the history of Sicily, but he knows even more. In my years of serving him his morning coffee and an occasional roll, I have never known Vito to talk so much as he does when you're around. It seems like he likes that."

My eyes drifted upward and beyond the barista as I saw my old friend come through the door. Vito walked straight to his usual spot and supplanted the server from our table, as the barista bid him *'bon giornu'* and returned to the bar. I had become better at the Sicilian language in my time in Mazara del Vallo, but I still smiled at the subtle difference in pronunciation from Italian.

"Bon giornu," I said also, as Vito slid into the chair beside me.

"Bon giornu," he replied with a smile, and it seemed that he was only barely hiding a certain pleasure at hearing me pronounce the greeting the way the Sicilians do.

I waited for Vito to get comfortable and for the barista to deliver the first cup of the morning, but Vito was more impatient than I was.

"Tribes," he opened with.

That didn't go very far, so I probed.

"Tribes?" I asked.

"Sì, tribes. You see, most of the people who originally inhabited Sicily really just inhabited it," he said, emphasizing the passive nature of the word *inhabited*. "They were here for thousands of years until the tribes started coming to the island."

"Like the Siculi and so on," I added.

"But the Siculi were later. Let's go back first.

"These earlier settlers, the ancient people, we know something about where they might have come from. The early Sicanians probably came from modern Spain, and some other people walked across from North Africa. Populations were scattered, villages remained far apart, at least some did."

"What do you mean 'some'?" I asked.

"Well, some villages were created by fission. And some were created by fusion," he continued.

Vito's use of terms from physics made me wonder what his educational background was.

It wasn't hard to picture what he was describing. Some settlements were the result of small societies splitting into separate villages, while others were the product of mergers that brought different people together.

"The first, those created by fission, usually were set more closely together. The people who broke off were merely setting up camp in another settlement, possibly for more room, possibly because the generations of people needed to establish their farms and hunting grounds with more interstitial space to allow for growth.

"The second, those created by fusion, were usually the result of previously unrelated tribes who found some advantage in sharing a region or agricultural habitat."

"So, let me guess," I interjected. "The settlements that were closer together were probably those created by fission, companionable villages who needed to spread out and have room for farming and whatever."

Vito nodded his head at this.

"And the others remained farther apart. But…I'm not sure I know where you're going."

"The theory is that unrelated villages would have maintained greater distance because their unrelatedness would have been a pretext for conflict. Being farther apart reduced the tension."

"What about mixing of blood?" I asked. "That seems to be a better proposition between these so-called unrelated villages."

"Yes, of course. Diversity strengthens the gene pool, although they wouldn't have thought of it in this way."

"Then why intermingle, or inter-marry as it were?"

"Because having unions of men and women from different societies gave each village a reason not to fight, to keep their conflicts to a minimum, and to respect the sovereignty of each village. But they still needed distance, and distances between one's ancestral village and one's marital village were great. Therefore, visits 'home' by the woman who married out of her village were cherished opportunities to see her family again. Not to mention to slip back into the comfortable folds of traditions, food, art, and culture that she had grown up in. But," he said, and paused, "let's get on with the tribes.

"Between 5000 B.C. and 1000 B.C., people were migrating all over Europe and, so, of course, into Sicily. The Sicanians came a long way, from the Iberian Peninsula, but the Elymi also traveled far. They came from Anatolia, through the Levant in the reverse direction that the original humans had come from Africa. These migrating tribes didn't come in one trip; they were expanding their world and setting down roots along the way. They left behind settlements of each tradition, but the explorers in their tribes continued to move: the Sicanians in a counter-clockwise rotation from Iberia into Africa and up into Sicily; the Elymians in a clockwise rotation from modern Turkey past the eastern edge of the Middle Sea, through modern-day Egypt, across the coast of Africa and into Sicily.

"It appears that the people from Iberia took over two thousand years to reach Sicily, and even then the Sicanian migration left many settlements dotting the northern African coast and their arrival in our country was a slow ebb, not a sudden landfall.

"The Sicanians settled in among the aboriginal peoples of the island, although they brought a more advanced culture than the one that existed here. As they spread out and established communities along the southern coast of Sicily, they displaced the original tribes."

"How much of Sicily did they control?" I asked.

"'Control' may be the wrong word in this case. Primitive tribes fought for survival and only engaged in cross-cultural conflict with other humans when that survival was threatened. With so much land, the villages could exist easily with great distances between them, and so they didn't battle each other for occupation of land that they didn't need and couldn't control. No, the Sicanians created their own cities and settlements, leaving the native peoples alone. But, in time, the growing population of Sicanians – not to mention the advanced technologies and social structure they brought with them – overwhelmed the original population, so the ancient tribes began to disappear."

"I assume there was some inter-marriage," I noted.

"Si, and this contributed to the gene pool as well as it contributed to the slow thinning out of the original people."

"During the latter part of the Sicanian migration, the Minoan civilization was growing in the east, from the island of Crete."

"Wait, the Minoans were Greek. I thought they never made it this far west, at least not that early" I said.

"True, or so we think. But the Minoan culture gave rise to the Mycenean culture, and it's quite clear that the Myceneans traveled farther west, even to Sicily and beyond. In fact, during the final big push of Sicanians from Iberia to Sicily – probably from 2000 to 1500 B.C. – the Myceneans were already landing in Sicily. Their impact on the culture at that time was limited; the Myceneans were mostly interested in establishing trade routes around the Mediterranean region. But they brought some cultural artifacts and some traits from their civilization and these things were embedded in the Sicilian traditions even after the trading boats returned to Mycenae."

"You said 2000 to 1500 B.C., right?" I asked.

"Si, for the Sicanians," Vito replied. "Why?"

I consulted my notes, flipping pages in my journal, looking for something that seemed on the edge of my consciousness.

"Here," I said, pointing to the hastily scribbled note in the middle of a page, but circled.

"The Elymians arrived around 1200 B.C."

"*Sì.*"

"But they came all the way from Turkey. I mean Anatolia."

"*Sì.*"

"So, if they arrived around 1200 B.C., and they traveled every bit as far as the Sicanians had to, the Elymians must have started their migration hundreds of years earlier."

"*Sì,* that's correct. We don't have a departure date, exactly. The Sicanians were driven from Iberia by tribes of Ligurians that pushed them west, and across the Gibraltar divide. So, we have some sense of timing. But we need to understand why the Elymians left Anatolia. We need to find a specific event to spur them, so that we can understand not only when they left, but why."

"Like what?" I asked.

"We'll get to that later," Vito replied.

"Okay," I agreed. "But staying with this Great Migration of Sicanians around 2000 B.C...."

"And continuing for five hundred years," Vito interjected.

"*Sì,*" I said, "for five hundred years."

"*Correttu,*" my mentor repeated. "Remember, also, that the Myceneans were sailing about the Mediterranean during this period, and so were the Phoenicians."

"Okay." I held up my hand in surrender. The information was beginning to overwhelm me. "What about the Phoenicians?"

"There's ample evidence that the Phoenician trading routes took them as far as Ustica, an island north of Sicily, around 1500 B.C., and they established trading posts around the Middle Sea. They continued to trade around the region, under sail, for nearly a thousand years, and..."

I held up my hand again. Vito had such command of the history that, when he got on a roll, he was hard to slow down.

"Okay, the Phoenicians. And now we have the Sicanians, the Myceneans, and the Phoenicians," I tried to summarize.

"And the Elymi," he added.

"Yes, of course, the Elymi. By the way, I read somewhere that the Elymians might be related to the Hittites?"

"No. Well, yes, perhaps," he wavered. "They came from Anatolia, just as the Elymians did. But the relationship between them is not important to us."

"Good," I laughed, "because I'm already having trouble keeping track of the tribes invading Sicily."

"Oh, but don't forget about the Sicels," Vito said with a smile.

"They came later, right?"

"Yes, a bit later, but in the same period. We put the Sicanian invasion of Sicily at about 2000 to 1500 B.C., although some came earlier. The Elymian invasion at around 1200 B.C., and the Sicelian invasion about 1050 B.C. And while these tribes were coming to the island, the Phoenicians and Myceneans were bouncing around the Middle Sea, trading with people here and there, of whatever tribe, and establishing their network of trading posts.

"In fact, there were some tribes of Siculi..."

"Siculi?" I asked, a bit confused.

"Same as Sicels. Anyway, there were some these tribes who inhabited the middle of the Italian peninsula for many years, and during this time they were pushed out of that region by the Ausonians."

"That's a new one. Is that a tribe, the Ausonians," I asked, feverishly writing notes.

"Yes, in a way. They were most populous in a region we now call Lazio and Campania, the central part of the boot, just below the Volsci

Mountains. It seems that they battled with the Siculi in that area, forcing these people to seek an escape. The closest land mass was the island of Lipari, so the Siculi fled there.

"The king of the tribe that expelled the Siculi was Auson, hence the name of his tribe. After a number of years, the Ausonians – who knew of the obsidian on the shores of the Aeolian islands – decided to move some of their tribe there, to an island that was later called Lipari, after Liparus, the son of Auson.

"When was this?" I asked.

"The Siculi landed in, ummm, let me think, somewhere around 1500 B.C."

"Okay. The Ausonians pushed them out of Italy, then invaded them once again on Lipari. Got it," I mumbled. "When did that happen?"

"I think about 1250 B.C. In fact," and Vito chuckled at the thought, "they drove the Siculi out of the Aeolian Islands altogether, pushing them into Sicily. So, the warring Ausonians may have been responsible for sending the Siculi onto the island that was later named after them."

With this last statement, Vito threw his arms up in the air as if in triumph, or maybe in some odd celebration of welcome.

"The Siculi," I began, "they also came down the toe of the boot and over, isn't that correct?"

"Oh, *si*, quite right. That's another story. It's believed that their migration started at the same place, in mid-Italy, and began because of conflict with early Villanovans..."

I held up my hand again. Vito laughed.

"*Si*, another people. The Villanovans were in central Italy and they were the ones who drove those tribes of Siculi south and out of Italy, forcing them to cross the divide at Messina and settle in Sicily."

"So, in addition to the trading people, like the Phoenicians and the Myceneans, the tribes who actually settled in Sicily were the Sicanians, the Elymi, and the Siculi, or Sicels, right?" I asked.

"*Si*. Driven there by expedition, exploration, or conflict with the Ligurians, the Ausonians, and the Villanovans."

"Okay, I think I've got it now."

———

The next morning was unusually chilly for a July day, or maybe I was just accustomed to the tropical weather in Sicily. There had been a light rain falling for much of the night, also unusual since rainfall on the island was rare in the summer. I stepped out of the hotel and into the humid air that resulted from the high temperatures and saturated skies and felt like I needed another – cold – shower to reset my inner thermostat.

I didn't know whether my old friend would bother to come out in this weather, but I found the little table in Café Amadeo very soothing for me. If I wasn't in the library, this corner of the establishment was, to me, the most inviting as it had been my alternate home for these weeks thus far spent in Sicily. So, Vito or not, I planned to go the café, get my morning coffee, and dwell on the things I had learned thus far.

I stepped in through the door and out of the drizzle, shaking the droplets off the umbrella I carried, and slid into my usual spot. I laughed to myself then, too, as I realized that the table was never taken. Perhaps Vito's daily routine had made it obvious to everyone that this table was to be reserved for him; perhaps my added routine reinforced the *prinotazzionu* – reservation – and kept the other customers at bay.

There weren't many tourists in Mazara del Vallo, so those who filled the seats in Café Amadeo would be Mazarans for the most part. On one particular morning, I saw someone who must have been from out of town stop by and start towards this table. The barista intervened and, in broken English – I suppose he realized quickly that the newcomer was American – suggested that the table was taken. Either that or he said the table was broken but, in any case. he pointed to another place the customer could move to. I was still entering the café so there was no one seated there yet, but after diverting the other client, the barista nodded in my direction and then toward the table. I sat down a bit sheepishly.

On this morning, though, the table and three chairs were set as I had always seen them, empty and waiting for me or Vito to approach. I sat down, laid the umbrella at my feet, and listened to the hiss of the espresso machine knowing that my first cup was already being prepared.

I didn't deserve the distinction that Vito had earned in this establishment, but I knew the barista had made a note of my preference and, as with Vito, he didn't wait for me to order to begin the process.

After only a few moments, my old friend appeared in the doorway. He didn't look up as if to find me; he knew where I would be. And if I wasn't already there, he was heading toward that table anyway.

Vito sat down softly, looked in my direction, and said just one word.

"Elymians."

By now I had grown accustomed to his manner. He began conversations with short phrases or, in this case, a single word. But from that root I knew would blossom an entire conversation. So, I waited.

"What do you call them?" he asked.

I knew he was talking about the Elymians, or the Elymi, and frankly it wasn't important what I called them. I wanted to know what he called them. I shrugged my shoulders, casting the question back at him.

Vito sighed, but not in a sense that seemed disappointed. It was more like a deep breath taken in preparation for a long speech.

"The Elymi, or Elyimians, came from..." and he let his voice trail off, nodding his head slowly, peering directly at me, testing me.

"Anatolia. Turkey. Asia Minor," I replied. "You pick."

"Si, from there," he said. "How did they come to Sicily?"

I had to guess, but using what I knew from the Sicani, how they had crossed the gap at Gibraltar and worked their way across the edge of Africa, I assumed the Elymi had taken a similar path from the east, in the opposite direction, through modern-day Egypt to Libya, then across the sea. I said so.

"Quite right," Vito said, sipping at his espresso. "But wrong."

"Okay, which is it?"

"It would be quite right for you to conclude such a thing, but the Sicani came a thousand, maybe two thousand years earlier. What do you think happened between 2500 B.C. and 1200 B.C.?"

I guessed.

"Sailing?"

"*Correttu!*" Vito's enthusiastic reply was a bit over the top, but consistent with his nature.

"Sailing, to most of us, connotes wind and stretched fabric, so that's a bit too far in this case," he continued. "The Elymi, in fact most of their kin in eastern Mediterranean areas, had become adept at managing the seas. Yes, they had harnessed the wind with large sails, but they also equipped their boats with long oars and strong men to pull against the surf when the wind was not there. The Greeks called their craft the *penteconter* and although not all these explorers were Greek, that design was consistent throughout the islands and lands of eastern Mediterranean region.

"The *penteconter* had a tall bow and stern, sometimes carved to imitate a sea monster's head..."

"That sounds like the Viking ships," I suggested.

"Yes, in some ways," Vito replied, "but the similarities in design – the raised bow and stern – were not copied from the Norsemen; the features were probably discovered independently by the seafarers in the Mediterranean and the North Sea from practical experience. Keeping the ends of the boats above the wash of the sea as they propelled forward just made sense.

"Anyway, these *penteconters* would be powered by up to fifty men when the air was calm. A center post would support a single crossbeam, and huge sheets of skin or woven fabric could be pulled up and over the beam, then strapped down at the deck level when the winds were favorable."

"Were these warships?"

"I'm sure they could have been used – and probably were – when open conflict took place on the seas, but most battles between tribes and nations still took place on the ground. Sea battles would come later. Just think about how the Carthaginians bested the Romans on open water when the Romans were still used to fighting in the fields; but let's stick mainly to the boats' use for exploration.

"The Elymi had developed fleets of these vessels following the example of the Phoenicians who used them for trade. The Elymi used them for the same reason, though their trade circles were more regional than the Phoenicians. But when they decided to leave Anatolia, the Elymi had these craft and could cross the seas in less time than it would take to march around the countours of the Levant, Egypt, and then Africa."

"So, they sailed to Sicily?"

"Yes, or sort of hopped there. They went to Crete first, to a port called Knossos. Then they sailed to a place we think was called Euteso, what the Greeks later called Euesperides and what we now call Benghazi. That didn't work out so well, so they launched again..."

"How many boats are we talking about?"

"There was probably a dozen or more at first. The Elymi brought many people over to Sicily, but it was not all at once. The first trip probably opened a seaway that was copied by their countrymen over a century or more. Anyway, they launched again from Euteso, across the sea, and landed in Elyma, also on the coast of North Africa."

"That sounds suspicious," I said, and Vito looked at me in a funny way.

"Why suspicious?"

"The name of the landfall. Why was the name so much like the people?"

"Well, it probably wasn't there yet and they gave it that name. Elyma is what we now call Misrata, in Libya."

"If they named the place, did they stay?"

"Yes, some of them did, and there may still be some Elymian blood in the Libyans. But others moved on, setting sail for Sicily and landing on the western edge of the island."

"When you described the boats, the *penteconter*, you talked about the men who rowed it. But I assume the Elymi were bringing their women with them too, right?"

"Si, there were women too, but not as many as the men."

"Okay, but back to basic biology. We know that growing the population, especially of new settlements, is easier if the women outnumber the men."

"This is true," he replied, "but the Elymi, like most explorers before and after them, assumed there would be female stock at their landing place." Vito said this with a bit of a smile.

"Were there?" I asked. "I mean, female stock on western Sicily?"

"The Sicani were already there, and probably some of the indigenous people."

"But how did the Elymi know that?"

"Just lucky, I suppose," he said with a wink, then took a last sip from his cup and stood to leave. "But really, there had been much seafaring and trade across the Middle Sea by that time. Stories of what to expect no doubt reached back to the places where the ships embarked from."

"But wait," I said, reaching out for his arm. "Why did the Elymi decide to leave Anatolia?"

Vito paused, but remained standing.

"Have you heard of Wilusa?"

"No."

"Troy?"

"Of course. Everyone's heard of Troy."

"Well, Wilusa was a place the archeologists think was built upon ancient Troy. In fact, some of the scientists say that Wilusa is just another name for ancient Troy. And that it was destroyed in battle around 1200 B.C."

"You said the Elymi sailed from Anatolia about that time," I said.

Vito nodded his head.

"Are you saying the Elymians were the Trojans? And that they abandoned that area in defeat after the war?"

"Really?" Vito said with a sly smirk. "What a great theory." Then he walked out of the café.

———

After the morning session with Vito, I nearly ran to the library. I was excited about the idea that the Trojans might have established the great cities of western Sicily. I grew up and went through school thinking that the Trojan War was more myth than reality, but Vito's sly hint convinced me that the people of Trapani – modern-day Drepanon – and the other western Sicilians might trace their lineage back to the brave soldiers of Troy.

"The story of Troy is based on a myth," was the opening of the book I held in my hands. "Not that there was no Troy, and certainly not that there was no Athens. But the war didn't begin with the abduction of Helen or the launching of a thousand ships."

The author of this particular account left no doubt that she was going to challenge the premise of the war, and probably the underlying premise of the existence of Troy. But I knew friends who had gone to the archeological dig at what was purported to be ancient ruins of Troy. My mind wandered and I recalled reading about the life of Jesus, and the debate about whether he was truly a god, or just a man. There had grown a consensus that he actually lived, which settled the question of whether he was, at least, a man. But a god?

Then I came back to Troy and the Trojans. Greek mythology has a dense narrative on the Trojan War, how Paris – a Trojan – took Helen, the wife of Menelaus, king of Sparta, captive, and how the Spartans laid siege to Troy for ten years in retaliation. Among the Trojans to escape the wrath of the Spartans – called Achaeans in this book in my hands – was Aeneas, the son of the goddess Aphrodite who led his band of survivors out of Troy and to Italy.

I slid the book back onto the shelf and withdrew a very old volume, with hardcover and tattered pages, titled, *The Search for the True Troy*. Thumbing through the pages, I wanted to get past the basic history lesson and reach the part where the author, B.J. Antemann, offered his opinion of the historical accuracy of the myth. As with many ancient stories, there was usually a kernel of truth that had been enlarged and embellished over time. Finding the true story, as Antemann claimed to have done, meant peeling back the veneer of exaggeration that accompanied such stories, and revealing the nuggets of truth that lie within.

"Troy was a real city," Antemann said at the beginning of Chapter 37, "we are still searching for the real Trojan War. Troy is now named Hissarlik, a city in Turkey," he continued, "and there were certainly battles and struggles among and between the peoples of the time. But Homer's tale of heroics and majesty, of slaughter and revenge, should probably be filed in the sections of the library devoted to mythology, rather than history."

I looked up from Antemann's book and couldn't help but smile at the fact that his treatise was, in fact, filed under history.

———

The next morning, I was late to my morning session with Vito – overslept, no excuse – but I held out hope that he wouldn't be offended. But habits die hard; after the midday meal, I was drawn back to my usual spot anyway.

Just as I expected, Vito was long gone, but the barista welcomed me with narry a suggestion that I was off schedule.

"*Bon giornu,*" he said with spirit as I walked through the door.

Espressso was always welcome, no matter the time of day, so I slipped into the booth and waited for my shot of java.

"Vito was here this morning," the barista said, "and he looked around while drinking his coffee. As if something was not quite right."

I immediately felt awful. I had established a pattern and my old friend had adapted to it, but I had missed our daily routine and I felt guilty for not being there.

"I'm very sorry," I said, still ashamed.

"It is no problem," the barista said with a wave of the hand. "Vito has been here longer than...well, longer than the café has been here."

"How long is that?" I asked.

"The café?"

"Yes."

"Oh, well, I don't really know," said the barista, looking toward the ceiling to think through it. "Fifty, maybe sixty years?"

"How old is Vito?"

The barista laughed.

"At least a hundred years!"

———

The next morning I was back on schedule. I knew that the library would wait for me, and that I owed it to my old friend to not keep him waiting. I arrived at the café ahead of time, and Vito entered on time, paying no attention to the fact that I was AWOL the day before.

"Phoenicians," he said simply, and with that one word I knew we were back on schedule.

"By the middle of the Twelfth Century B.C., the Phoenicians had developed a farflung trading empire, establishing posts throughout the Aeolian Islands, northeastern Sicily, and as far west as Carthage and the west coast of Sicily," Vito began. "Meanwhile, the Elymian sailors who sailed first across the sea and landed on the western shores of our country had opened their own travel route, though one really intended mainly to bring their people over from Anatolia to Sicily."

"Let's back up," I asked. "Were the two peoples, the Phoenicians and the Elymi, related?"

"No," was his short reply.

"Did they encounter one another, or did they somehow interact in their exploration of Sicily?"

"Exploration. What a fine word," my mentor mused.

"The Phoenicians were circumnavigating the Mediterranean Sea," he continued, "the known world at that time – for the sole purpose of commercial enterprise," he said. "They delivered their goods in exchange for the raw materials and natural resources of our country, and took some of it by...what do you say in America? By 'hook or by crook?'"

"You don't sound like a fan of the Phoenicians," I suggested to Vito.

"No, not a fan, but not a critic either. We should not judge them on their morality, only the success of their trading world."

"And the Elymi?"

"They escaped difficult times in their homeland."

"Troy, you mean." I knew I was trying to fit that into the narrative, but Vito wasn't so easy to fool.

"It seems that it may have been Troy. And it may not have. But what we know is that the Elymi came to western Sicily and established many settlements that are still here today, like Eryx, Egesta, Drepanon, Halyciae, and Entella."

"I recognize some of these," I said checking my notes. "Eryx...that's Erice, right?"

He nodded his head.

"And Egesta is Segesta, Drepanon is Trapani..."

Again, a nod.

"But, I don't know Entella and...and..."

"Halyciae," Vito said. "Entella may be even older than the Elymi, but they are typically credited in the history books with founding it. Now it's called Belice. Halyciae was called both Elima and Halyciae – I think these were two small settlements merged into one – and later known as Alima. Today, the place is known as Salemi."

"The Elymi were busy building," I offered.

"Sì, but their history, such as it was, seems to be somewhat short. At least they left very little record of their actual existence, except for their temples," Vito pointed out. "Most historians and archeologists seem to think that the Elymians were absorbed by the Carthaginians who frequented western Sicily. That may explain how they disappeared from the record, since the Carthaginians had a strong written pedigree and would have rendered their history into writing. As is often said, 'History is written by the winners.'

"One thing we know is that the Elymians brought strong religious traditions with them, and they built a temple on the top of the mountain we call Erice, their Eryx. The Elymi had beliefs similar to the Greeks..."

"Was this tied up somehow with Athens, and its early connection to Anatolia, and Troy?"

"Most definitely," Vito said. "They worshiped a goddess much like the Greek Aphrodite" – Vito's comment brought me back to Antemann's book I had skimmed the day before – "and they venerated the dog. All of this played into the temple in Eryx, built to honor Venus, a goddess of distinctly Greek origin."

I had already been to the top of Erice, and enjoyed wandering among the ruins there, as well as the still-inhabited settlement on the mountain. The crest of the mountain is shrouded in fog sometimes, and the Elymian people thought this was when the gods were engaged in a conclave.

"The churches up there are still held in reverence, although I think the Trapanese – Trapani is at the bottom of Mount Erice – have given up on worshipping the dog," Vito concluded with a smile.

"What about the Phoenicians? What was their role during this period?"

"When the Phoenician trading circuit was at its most robust, they established ports in the Aeolian Islands, on Lipari and Vulcano, mostly to mine the obsidian since that was the only natural resource that flourished on these volcanic islands. But the early Siculi had already settled there, and the arrival of the Phoenicians, even if they were just passing through, set up some conflict. The traders wanted to come and get the obsidian and then deliver it to their markets in Carthage, Drepanon, Siracusa, and Euesperides. The Siculi believed that the obsidian was theirs, and so were the Aeolian Islands."

"So, they fought over it?" I asked.

"Yes, I suppose so. But all we know from that time is the archeological record, since formalized writing was still not in common use. We know that artifacts of Phoenician trade – amphorae, ships' timbers and ballast, and so on – were increasing at this time, and artifacts of the Siculi were decreasing."

"Sounds like the Siculi either died off, were killed, or just moved away."

"Sì, but mostly the latter. Neither the Phoenicians at the time, nor the Siculi were warring types. I believe the Siculi were just overrun by the traders and decided to move on, in this case, to Sicily.

"The original Siculi," I began, somewhat unsure of how to continue, "I thought they came from the toe of Italy."

"That's what most people believe," Vito said, nodding his head, "and I have no reason to doubt that. But there were Siculi on the Aeolian Islands and they, too, fled to Sicily. So places like Messina and Catania on the eastern shore received them, but so did Milazzo. Sorry, Zancle, Katane, and Myla – at that time. Messina, Catania, and Milazzo now."

———

"One of the most important places in Trapani – and Erice – was the Temple of Aphrodite, Roman goddess of love and fertility," Vito said the next morning when I joined him at that café. "Well, not Aphrodite, exactly. Before the Romans adopted this goddess, the Phoenicians called her Astarte, and before that, the Elymi called her Potnia."

"So, Potnia is actually Aphrodite?" I asked.

"Sì, an early form of her," Vito replied.

"And the tradition of Potnia was so essential to the Elymi," he continued, "that they brought her with them from their homeland in Troy, to their new home in western Sicily. And as soon as they landed, the Elymi began making plans to build a temple to their goddess.

"Modern chroniclers like to refer to Potnia, Astarte, and Aphrodite – even Venus – as goddesses of love, but they were actually goddesses of fertility – which, of course, means sex. I think it's more correct to conclude that these early people – people whose children often died young and people who constantly worried about the survival of their tribe – considered sex and fertility to be holy desires. So much so that the temples to these mythical beings were often designed to convey some sexual meaning, like a roofless temple 'open to the gods,' stone altars that were cut in the size and shape of beds, and columns that were – sometimes – rounded at the top to imitate an erect penis."

"Society had already become male-dominant, right?"

At this, Vito couldn't suppress a chuckle.

"Yes, poor things. Men's egos are terribly fragile, so they use their physical dominance to pretend to be superior. But their seed is nothing without the female's ability to conceive and populate the species. This is the reason for primitive peoples' belief in an Earth Mother. Ever heard of an Earth Father? No. And while there are male gods of frightening strength and power – Zeus, Poseidon, Titan, and so on – none of them compare to the goddesses of fertility.

"The early Earth Mother transformed into Potnia, who became Astarte, who became Aphrodite, who became Venus. The Elymian religious cult of fertility and their belief in Potnia was so powerful that the Romans who conquered Sicily centuries later invented their own goddess and called her Venus Erycina."

He stared into my eyes and, as if Vito didn't think I believed him, added, "Look it up."

"But, the temple no longer exists. As much as the conquering Carthaginians and Romans were smitten by the love goddess, they couldn't resist plundering the temple and removing its gold and marble for their own pleasure. The Normans finished the desecration by tearing it down to its footings and building what's now known as the Norman Castle on the spot."

"When was that?" I asked him.

"In the 12th century. Of course, they used the stones from the temple to build the castle."

"Sounds like the temple was quite the place," I added, but I probably sounded too amused. Vito upbraided me for it.

"The myth of Potnia was in many ways a significant thread in the life of primitive peoples. Fertility and sex were more about survival than pleasure," and then I think I saw Vito blush, "although clearly God made it pleasurable to make sure we kept having children."

I didn't want to debate whether it was God or the necessities of biology that made sexual excitement and pleasure the greatest human drive.

"Early societies were always perched on the edge of extinction," he continued, "trying to maintain a net-positive balance in the perpetual struggle between birth and death rates. They weren't scientists in the modern sense of the word, but they probably understood that a downward spiral in this struggle could be hard to turn around. The solution was to produce as many children as possible, watch helplessly as many of them perished, but hope that enough would survive to maintain the tribe.

"The balancing act was especially unique in Sicily. On the one hand, island culture is – by definition – isolated and limiting, since the land area is cut off from the usual roaming hoards on the mainland. On the other hand, Sicily's history was one of constant invasion and conquest. So, whereas their indigenous genetic material was being threatened, the Sicilians were constantly being treated to the infusion of foreign genetic material. The 'invaders' kept the procreative strength vigorous, but they were constantly revising the genetic profile of the tribes in Sicily."

This fact had been clear to me for some time, but Vito described it in unique ways. I knew that the Sicilian "blood" was infused with the genes of many other peoples, from Africa to Europe to the Middle East and farther away. But while the invasions brought more "procreative strength" as Vito described it, it turned the Sicilian blood line into a swimming pool of genetic variation.

———

I spent the next two days in the library since Vito had some appointments. Of course, I started my day at the café where the barista prepared my 'by-now' usual espresso. But he poured it into a small paper to-go cup since – without Vito – he had already assumed that I would not be staying.

My research became more specific and yet more difficult. I was learning far more than I had anticipated when this project began, and my notebook contained more information than was available in the library, even this one in Mazara, the very center of the history I was tracing. Vito's knowledge came from his own studies over the decades, but much of it seemed to come from within. It was as if his knowledge of Sicilian history was an inherited trait, buttressed by his appreciation of Sicilian culture.

On the third day, I returned to Café Amadeo at the usual time, and encountered Vito entering at the same moment. He smiled, tapped the brim of his old hat in recognition, and we proceeded to the booth that was always his – and sometimes mine.

"Carthaginians," he began in his inimitable style. I knew that today's lesson would be focused on the Phoenicians who settled that city on the edge of Africa.

"By the mid-Eighth Century B.C." he continued, "Sicily had become a real destination."

I laughed a little, knowing that Vito also realized the modern meaning behind that declaration. The talk of tourists and well-heeled vacationers who find a spot in the world, flock to it, and make it a destination. But these locations usually pass the mantle on to the next "destination" in a short time, to become last year's hot spot. So thinking of Sicily as "a real destination" in an era of conquest and colonization carried an entirely different meaning.

"The Punics who settled Carthage..." he began, then paused. "They didn't call themselves Phoenicians, you know."

I hadn't thought about that.

"The Punics settled Carthage in – oh – about 814 B.C. and built it into a major regional power. It was called Qart-ḥadašt at the time, but later renamed Carthage. They were a seafaring people, much like the Greeks who roamed the Middle Sea in search of new land and precious trading resources. They came from Lebanon and, as the story goes, they were led by Dido. Sounds like an important explorer, a man of great power, right?"

I nodded, although I didn't know anything about Dido.

"Well, it wasn't a man. Dido, if you can believe the ancient stories, was actually Elissa, the first queen of Carthage. She was the explorer – a woman was the founder of the great city of Carthage."

Vito chuckled at this.

"Remember the Earth Mother and all her offspring?"

I didn't respond. It was a rhetorical comment.

"The Punics continued westward and northward, commanding trading posts as far away as modern-day Spain, and established a settlement in Gadir – today's Cadiz – to trade with a civilization called Tartessos. They also founded cities on western Sicily, absorbing the Elymi people who, apparently, just melted into the newly arriving Punic tribes. The new arrivals made the civilization of Drepanon, Halyciae, and Entella more Carthaginian than Elymi, and the original people began to disappear from the record. We have lost track of the Elymi, significant though they were, and therefore we have lost track of their connection to Troy.

"The Punics' central interest was trading, so a little island just off the coast of western Sicily was very important to them. They took control of it and called it Motya. It was used as a supply depot and trading post with the larger island, and still serves that function today. The Punics also founded Zis, later called Panormus and now known as Palermo, and Kfra, later called Solunto."

"Wait," I said, holding up my left hand while scribbling notes with my right. "Kfra, did you say?" Can you spell that?"

"K-f-r-a."

"That sounds Arabic."

"I don't know the origins of the name...but it was one of the early Punic settlements.

"While the Punics were exploring the west coast of Sicily and building new cities there, the Greeks were exploring the east coast, and building their cities there."

"What about the Sicani, the Siculi," I ventured, "you already said that the Carthig...wait, the Punics absorbed the Elymi, so I guess they are gone."

"Gone, yes, but their genetic material still flows through our veins," Vito replied. He seemed to derive some pleasure in noting that Trojan blood may make up part of his western Sicilian biology.

"So, the Greeks settled in the East?" I said, bringing us back on track.

"Sì," Vito picked up the thread. "They landed on the eastern shore and found comfortable surroundings for new cities there. First they focused their efforts on the southern part of Italy and the islands that surrounded Sicily – like the Aeolians, and Pantelleria and Malta – while they were establishing an important foothold on the eastern shore of Sicily itself. Katane, Syrakosai, and Zancle – I'm sorry – Catania, Siracusa, and Messina were founded during this period.

"But perhaps the Greeks earliest settlement was in Naxos, what the ancients called Nassina. The main currents in the Mediterranean led them naturally to the bay on the edge of this old settlement. The Nassinians had inhabited this part of Sicily for over a thousand years, but their population never increased and they survived on the edge of extinction. When the Greeks arrived, they brought new life to the region, founded their own city Naxos after their origin in Chalkis – also named Naxos – and also created a settlement called Tauro. We now know this as Taormina. It is east of Mount Etna.

"The land was fertile and the Greeks brought grapevines and other perennial crops, but they ran into a bit of conflict with the local Siculi. At first, the Greeks and the original tribes tried to live in peace, then disagreeements arose when the Greeks took more of the arable land away from the Siculi. Ultimately, the new invaders won out, and the Siculi were pushed even more inland in search of farmland and new settlements.

"The Greeks spread into other areas, established Katane as a permanent city, which served as a trading post for the growing commerce between the islands of Greece and what was becoming more commonly referred to as Magna Graecia – Greater Greece – that included southern Italy, Sicily, and the surrounding islands.

"So, although the east and west coasts were fairly well separated – with the Punics dominating the west and the Greeks dominating the east, the Sicani and Siculi were being lost in the battles between these two invasive forces.

"And the Elymi," I tried, with some hope for this forgotten people.

"Sì, well, they might have disappeared by then…but the Sicani and Siculi were being squeezed between the Greeks on one side and the Punics on the other. These two new invaders were more aggressive and powerful, so the original tribes lost ground to them. And, inevitably, as the struggle for land continued, the greater struggle for Sicily itself became paramount. Sicily lay at the center of the Middle Sea, and it would inevitably become the battleground for conflicts that arose between the Greeks and Punics, not to mention the Romans and those who came later."

I continued scribbling notes, but at times thought that my attention would be best spent concentrating on Vito's running commentary.

"And it was in this period that the Punics, who spread their territory along the southern coast of the island, founded an ancient place they called Mazar, the "Rock.""

I wrote this down then paused.

"Wait. Mazar. Is that this city, Mazara del Vallo?"

With a broad grin, Vito replied, "Sì, every bit."

"But you said that the people came to Mazara del Vallo from North Africa."

"And I'm sure the ancient people did, but as with every other settlement, the new arrivals – like the Greeks and the Punics – settled where a small civilization already existed. They all wanted the same things: proximity to water and natural resources, wildlife, farmable land…"

"So you think your ancestors are Punics," I ventured.

"Or north Africans, or the Elymi who intermingled with the Carthaginians, or…"

His voice trailed off but his smile remained.

"We Sicilians are a mix of many races. It's our greatest virtue," Vito said.

735 B.C.E.

735 B.C.E.

SIKANIA

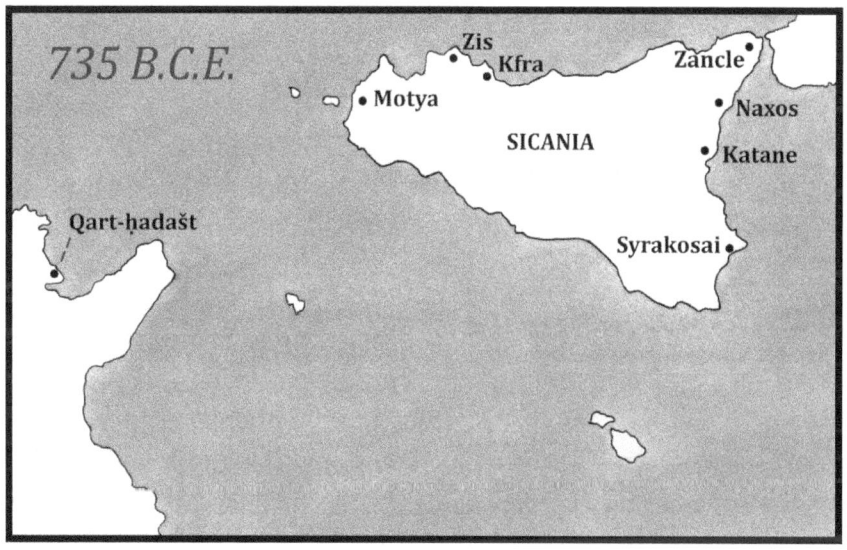

735 B.C.E.
QART-ḤADAŠT

Bomical stood tall on the pier, the sun setting to his left didn't obstruct his surveillance of the ship being unloaded on the water in front of him. A constantly moving line of bare-chested men marched onto and off of the ship, their long black hair tied by twisted braids down to their shoulders, their tunics tucked between their thighs to reduce the drag on their legs as they lifted large sacks and barrels of flour, oil, and other merchants' cargo.

Bomical watched it keenly, appraising the men's work as well as their fitness. There were free men among the slaves, aboriginal Siculi from the island, who were brought in to unload the bounty. The free men worked for wages, and most of them lived here in Qart-ḥadašt, in the squalid quarters inhabited by laborers who traded their sweat and lifetime for a small payoff from the rich merchants. The dark-skinned Siculi had been culled from a large crowd of captured prisoners; the best and strongest survived to work themselves to death while the weak were left to die. These men, these slaves, were the strongest and fittest, but they were also the hardest to control and monitor. The victorious Punics had taken them on from small skirmishes on the mainland of Sicily, and they now served at the whim of the merchant class among this – the greatest trading civilization the world had ever known. The slaves knew their lot, but resisted the masters and merchants, and an uprising was always feared by the moneyed class of Qart-ḥadašt.

The port had grown well since its founding three generations before. The thick walls of the fortress that defined the seaside of this city also served as the foundation from which the merchant class launched the ships to trade their goods with the world, and the bay in which returning ships brought gold, silver, and enormous barrels and crates of the finest treasures of the world. Bomical was one of the city's most powerful shippers, and he knew that this would remain as it was as long as he and the other merchants kept the Greeks in the east from getting a foothold. Either in western Sicily or in Qart-ḥadašt itself. Bomical didn't count on the weak governing class of Qart-ḥadašt; he trusted only the merchant class.

The men continued to march to and from the ship at a steady pace for hours, and Bomical stood on the pier throughout the unloading. He wanted to guard the bounty this ship brought to the port, but he also wanted to judge the men who were working for him. Slave or free, if they looked furtively around or reached into one of the crates, Bomical would be quick to call his officer, Cariamachus, and the man would be whipped and chained. It was best to do this in front of the others; the punishment carried more weight when it affected all the others too.

As the sun fell below the horizon and the light began to fade from the sky, the men were called to a halt.

"Reform," shouted Cariamachus. His voice rose above the clatter of the port at a volume which impressed his master Bomical. "Drop your ropes," he continued, then with a faint note of sympathy in his voice, added, "rest your legs."

This last command was the one that told the men to sit where they were, on the port, dock, or ship, but it was a welcome command. The men knew that it was their last break of the day, and they were to remain seated until the cargo could be counted and inspected. When this was done, they would be released; the free men to their wives, the slaves to their bunks in the flimsy sheds on the outskirts of the port itself.

"It is counted, sir," said Hammen, Bomical's trading agent. The man had walked down all the rows of crates, barrels, and other goods, counted them against the ledger that had been written when the ship took on the cargo, and he compared the two lists to confirm that they were equal.

"All is accounted for," Hammen declared.

At that, Cariamachus cried out that the men should be released. The free men stood and departed in a helter-skelter way; the enslaved workers were stood up by Cariamachus and his soldiers, then marched away to their barracks.

Once the work was concluded and Bomical retired to his home inside the port city's walls, Hammen came to visit. Bowing gently to Bomical's wife, Sophonia, he sat down with his boss to go over the books.

"This is a good year, sir," he began. "We have brought in more than usual, and we have kept the Greek ships at bay."

"How?" asked Bomical. "How were they kept at bay? By threats, by fear, or by luck?"

Hammen laughed lightly at the question, knowing what his master wanted to hear.

"Of course, it is all of these, and more."

"And how is our cargo now? The goods we plan to send to Motya?"

"It is all lined up, master," replied Hammen. "Just as you asked. It is in the warehouse to the west," he continued, waving and pointing his left arm in the direction he intended. "And it is ready to be loaded tomorrow."

"And what about the ship's crew? Are they ready for another voyage?"

"They will be," Hammen said, "after a night of drinking and whoring."

Bomical chuckled at this and looked over at Sophonia. He had met her many years before, when he was a ship's quartermaster and she was one of the lovelies in the port. He had "whored" with her but later fell in love. Hammen's throw-off line about the ships' crews whoring in Qart-ḥadašt reminded Bomical of his own past, and he wondered how many of the young studs running the streets that night would grow mature enough to choose a woman and settle down – before they died from the strain of their lifestyle or they were killed by the evil disease that ate holes in their swords.

"Do they always embark on a new journey drunk and hung over?" he asked Hammen.

"Yes, sire. If they are lucky."

————

When the sun rose the next day, the free men and slaves were gathered again at the dock, and Bomical took up his station at the top of the tower overlooking the port. Cariamachus called the men to order, then lined them up as on the day before, barking out commands that the men had heard before. Cariamachus's words were nearly unintelligible to Bomical at his distance, but the shipper had heard them before and knew from the cadence and sequence of commands what was to come.

After a series of instructions, Cariamachus went silent, stared intently at the lines of laborers as if to strike fear in them, and threw his arm over his head and pointed down the dock along the wood-lined path to the warehouse. He marched the men in two rows toward the cache that awaited their labors, and Bomical stood watching, impressed once again by his officer.

Hammen approached Bomical from behind and took up his position next to the merchant.

"The ship is destined for Motya," he said.

"Yes, I know this," replied Bomical.

"And it is loaded with great treasures and valuable objects of trade."

Bomical wondered why his agent was describing a shipment of goods that he, the shipper, would already be well aware of. He turned slightly to his left and cast his eye on Hammen, willing his agent to continue.

"There are two Greek ships between here and Motya," the agent said.

Bomical turned back around to stare out at the sea.

"Are they traders?" he asked. Bomical didn't like Greek trading vessels in his sea, but he especially didn't like Greek fighting ships.

"Yes, and no," responded Hammen. "One is a trader, one is a warship."

A long silence held the men.

"Where are they?" asked Bomical.

"When our last trader came to port, it was said that the Greeks were on this side of Motya, at the southern point of the great island that protects it from the sea."

"Can our ship get to Motya without trouble?"

Hamman turned away from Bomical and cast his eyes on the sea.

"No," was his simple reply.

Another long silence as the two men considered their options.

"We will send two warships, with Simonire and Pilius in command."

Hammen knew what these commanders meant to Bomical. Simonire was the wisest fighter and knew how to win battles, but Pilius had no mercy. Any captives would be executed, some of them with great cruelty.

"The sea is ours," declared Bomical, then he shrugged and smiled, "at least this part of it. If the Greeks are willing to stay on their side of the island, that is good. If not..." and his voice trailed off.

The trading ship was loaded and, as an afterthought, Bomical ordered another vessel to join the fleet. This smaller boat would be carrying cargo of only a little value, but he was offering it as a decoy to steer the battle toward the weakest sheep in the flock. Bomical and Hammen knew that this might end with the small vessel being destroyed or captured and its crew taken by the Greeks, but it was a ploy to allow the warships to protect the larger vessel and allow it to make Motya. If Simonire and Pilius weren't victorious in sinking the Greek ships, perhaps the Greeks would settle for the small catch and let the greater shipment get through.

When the four ships embarked from Qart-ḥadašt the following morning, there was the large ship with eighty rowers surrounded by the two warships, all trailed by the little vessel carrying what Bomical considered disposable goods. He didn't want to lose any of it, but he also knew that the lead ship was loaded with gold and jewels, and its loss would damn him and his shipping industry. Bomical was willing to lose the small ship – even Simonire and Pilius and their sailors, if need be – to ensure the safe arrival of the great trading ship.

As the bows of the fleet turned northward, Bomical and Hammen stood on the tower looking at the vessels' sterns. At first, they could see the long, thin oars that dipped into the water on each side of the four ships, pulled back and forth in rhythm, until the distance between the port and the ships grew too great to distinguish such fine details.

"Why do the Greeks bring a trading ship?" Bomical asked, although he knew the answer. He merely wanted Hammen to confirm his thought.

"To make trade with the Elymian tribes on the coast, through Drepanon," came the reply.

"Why do the Greeks bring a warship?"

"Because they know that we don't want them to make trade with the Elymian tribes, and because they know we would send warships."

Bomical just stood there, knowing the answers to these questions before they were asked.

———

Simonire was meeting with his lieutenants when a sailor approached them on the deck of the ship. The sound of rushing water was the constant theme in his life, like the splash of the oars as they dug into the waves and pulled the ship forward through the water. But the sailor's quickened breath interrupted Simonire and made him aware that important news was to follow.

"They are ahead," the sailor blurted out. He was a young fellow, although in this line of work, most sailors began their apprenticeship while they were still young. His chin was shiny from sweat and without hair, and the cap that was pulled down over his head bulged where thick curls were bundled.

Simonire didn't need any more information; he knew that this meant the Greeks were in their line of travel, and probably now in their line of sight. The merchant ship was off to his right, and the ship that Pilius commanded on the other side of it, so that the warships hung on either flank of their protectee. Simonire looked over his shoulder at the small "throw-away" merchant ship, shrugged, then signaled to Pilius that he should sail ahead of the merchant and engage the Greeks first. Simonire knew what he was doing; he knew that Pilius's attitude of "take no prisoners" would force the Greeks either to stand and fight, or to flee.

Simonire intended to watch as this developed. If the Greeks fled at the site of Pilius's flag, there would be no encounter. If they did not flee, Simonire would let Pilius stand and fight, and he would guide the merchant ship far to the west, beyond the barrier island that protected Motya's western flank, and swing back around from the north to reach landfall at the trading post on Motya from the north.

On Simonire's ship, the pace of rowing slowed slightly, while the pace on Pilius's ship quickened. The merchant ship remained at their steady pace and, so, fell into a three-ship line with Pilius in front, then the merchant ship, and Simonire taking up the rear. The throw-away merchant ship would take up a position behind Simonire, but its fate was unimportant.

As Pilius drew closer to the Greek warship, he quickened the rowing once more so that his vessel was racing forward. It was an aggressive move intended to summon a response from the Greeks. At first, there was no action on the part of the intelopers, then, as Pilius drew even closer, the Greeks dropped their oars into the water and rowed furiously to the west, turning in a tight arc to swing around Pilius and avoid his oncoming craft.

It was a brilliant move, made all the more effective by Pilius's aggressive play. When the Greek vessel swung to his portside, Pilius was too committed to the assault to easily reduce the speed or peel off in their direction. As a result, the Greek warship slipped past Pilius – who struggled to pull his ship around and re-engage.

Simonire watched all this from a position behind the merchant ship. He had wanted to keep the merchant and the ship's cargo safe between the Punic warships, but with the Greeks' move, now he realized that he was behind the treasure and in a bad position to engage the Greeks' ship before it boarded the merchant ship.

"Call around!" he shouted, a command for all oars to be put to the water and for all sailors to be ready to engage in a battle.

"Pull!" he screamed, "pull!" Simonire was trying to get his oarsmen to quicken their pace and pull along the portside of the merchant vessel that was now threatened by the Greeks. If he could get there first and take up a defensive position between the merchant and the attacker, he hoped to hold off the advance of the Greek marauders until Pilius could come back and join the fight.

"Pull!" he shouted once more. Simonire's oarsmen were tired, but strong, and they did what their captain bade them to do. They pulled, withdrew, and pulled their oars in unison, and they were successful in getting beside the merchant ship before the Greeks could complete their arc and pull alongside.

Moments passed as the crews of each of the ships prepared for battle. The captain of the merchant ship had seen such action before, but still did not comprehend the strategy of the play, or the tactics employed. But he maintained a steady heading as he had been instructed to do before the journey began, trusting in the experience of his naval companions to deliver him safely to Motya.

As the Greek ship completed its wide arc and began to bear down on the Punic flotilla, the commander could see that Simonire had gained the portside of the merchant ship and that Pilius was now closing in on the Greek vessel also. Sensing the overwhelming force that could be used against him, he changed his tactic.

"All on!" the Greek captain shouted, a command to pull all oars in, then added "All port!" to send only the portside oarsmen into action. That effectively turned the Greek ship back away from the Punic flotilla and away from any battle.

Simonire stood on the prow of his vessel and smiled at the evasive action by the Greeks. He looked across the water toward Pilius who, having sensed the same movement from the attackers, had pulled his oars up and slowed his ship.

As the Greek ship sailed away toward the west, the two Punic warships idled near the merchant, and let the small merchant ship gain on them from behind.

"They will not come back," Simonire shouted to Pilius.

"But, where is the Greek merchant ship?" came the reply.

In the action, Simonire had forgotten that the report said there was a Greek merchant ship accompanied by a Greek warship. It appeared that the Greeks had already safely landed their cargo carrier and delivered their goods, at or near Motya. Simonire and Pilius would have some more investigation to do when they gained that port themselves.

735 B.C.E.

SYRAKOSAI

SYRAKOSAI HAD GROWN INTO A MAJOR TRADING POST ON THE eastern edge of Sicily. The Greek explorers brought their culture, their food, and their merchants to this island in the Middle Sea, seeing it as another outpost for Magna Graecia, expanding on their settlements on the mainland of Italy and the surrounding islands.

They came from Corinth, fleeing that city during this time of trouble. Wars were breaking out between the ruling kings of the Bacchiads in their home country and while the stop-and-go revolution carried on for a generation or more, these Corinthian Greeks decided to escape aboard their merchant ships and settle on the edge of the sea, in this area they named Syrakosai. Greek citizens had already established settlements on the island and reports that came back to Corinth were replete with bright news about the climate, the resources, and the opportunities for trade between Greece and what they called Sikania, after the people who had first settled the land.

Photios was the leader of the band to escape but he continued to receive news of the struggles being fought in his homeland. He was relieved when he heard recently that the war was over, the kings had been thrown out of power, and the Corinthians had established a rotating sytem of government that promised a form of democratic rule and more peaceful times.

But Photios and the other Corinthians in this city, including his fellow merchants, Strophios and Hestros, had come to prefer the climate and opportunities that they enjoyed on this island of Sikania. Besides, if they remained where they were, they could still serve as local traders for the Greek ships that sailed toward the island, and they could get rich and fat from the minerals and resources of their new land.

On this particular evening, the three men were dining at Hestros's home, served by his young wife Gaia. She was heavy with child for the fourth time – all of the children had survived, and so Hestros became known as a strong and healthy man – but she navigated the table and men's chairs with ease.

"Is it too much to ask that we be able to trade our goods all around this region, around the islands, including Sikania?" asked Strophios. He was the most aggressive merchant at this table of very aggressive traders, and he believe the world should be open to their market.

"The Sikani would welcome us," he continued, "but…"

"But the Punics would not welcome us," Photios said, completing his statement.

"You sent a ship there already," Gaia interjected. "To the west, to Motya, yes?" She was strong of will, as were most Greek women who had been taught to be equal partners with their husbands. Gaia didn't flinch from offering her own opinion on politics or commerce.

Hestros looked up at her with a smile.

"Yes, we did. In fact, we sent two ships. A trader and a warship."

Gaia regarded her husband for a moment.

"So, you were preparing for battle," she commented with a smile.

"Yes, we were," added Strophios. "But there should be no battle, because…"

"The world should be ours," Hestros said, completing the sentence.

The men laughed, but Gaia took a more measured position.

"As it should be," she said, leaning forward to set a platter of roast pig, olive-marinated grilled peppers, and charred endive on the table. "But the Punics might not agree."

This small group of merchants managed the majority of trading ships in Syrakosai. They knew the Middle Sea from the east in Corinth to the west beyond Sikania. Their ships had steered clear of the vessels from Qart-ḥadašt in recent years, but the encounters became closer and more belligerent over time. Now, every trading ship was accompanied by an armed warship.

Normally, they didn't want to waste resources and insisted that there be at least two trading ships for each warship, but this particular cargo was too valuable and too time sensitive. Photios, Strophios, and Hestros had all invested in the gold that was laid below-decks, and they wanted the warship's captain to remain focused on their plight.

A man appeared at the door of Hestros's house and delivered a message.

"I am from Zancle. I work in your service there at the port."

The three merchants looked up at him but remained silent. There must be a strong reason for his visit, to bring a man all the way from Zancle to Syrakosai.

"We have a messenger who came from Zis, about the shipment."

The man did not mention the cargo; perhaps the secret had been unbroken and he didn't even know what the shipment from Syrakosai had contained.

"It has arrived safely," he said at last and the merchants allowed a short sigh of relief. The interloper's cadence had left them thinking that there was some dire news to deliver.

"However, there is one thing. It is not a problem, but I was asked to report it to you."

The three men at the table turned their chairs toward the man to give him their full attention. Even Gaia stopped and lent the man an ear.

"The warship," he began, "your warship. It sailed behind the cargo ship to protect it in open waters, but when the cargo reached the narrow strait that leads to Motya, the captain of the warship ordered it to turn about. He remained in the strait, idling for over two days."

"Why?" asked Hestros.

"The report is that he was laying in ambush for shippers from Qart-ḥadašt. To seize their vessels."

"That was not his assignment," said Strophios, but he knew this man of lesser rank would not voice an opinion on a captain's assignment.

"Your shipment was delivered," the messenger said, repeating the information these men cared most about. They wouldn't want to hear about the loss of a warship, but they would be enraged if they were told about the loss of their cargo ship.

"What happened to the warship?" asked Photios.

"It has survived," a comment that also sounded ominous, so the man changed his tone. "The Punics sent four ships, one with cargo, two warships to accompany it, and another small ship to trail the flotilla. They were arranged in single file when they approached the strait to Motya.

"With your cargo safely landed at the port in Motya, the captain of the warship ordered his men to lay on the oars to run at the Punic fleet. He intended to split between the warships and ram the shipper."

"To what end?" asked Hestros.

"To send it to the bottom, or so the report goes. He decided that he couldn't defeat the flotilla of four vessels, but he could at least destroy their cargo."

"And risk open warfare?" raged Photios. "And endanger all our future shipments? Was the man insane, or so full of spirits that he couldn't see the problem he has caused?"

The messenger remained silent for a moment, letting the merchants exchange thoughts – and anger – among themselves rather than him wading into their discussion.

"And what of him now?" asked Gaia.

"He remains in Zis, where he has taken up with a woman there."

"He no longer works for us," said Hestros. It was not a statement of discovered fact; it was a declaration that the man no longer works – and never will work – for them in the future.

The merchants returned to their meal, but had not dismissed the messenger, so he stood in the doorway awaiting instructions.

"Just out of curiousity," asked Photios, "did the captain ram the Punic cargo ship?" He was willing to criticize their captain, but he couldn't resist toying with the image of the Punic vessel lunging forward and slipping beneath the waves.

"No, sire, he did not. The Punics had an effective evasive strategy and prevented him from coming around swiftly enough to carry out his planned maneuver. He directed his oarsmen to pull hard to turn and shift their warship away from the encounter." He paused for a moment, then added, "He – the captain – escaped with his crew and sailed all the way to Zis before coming to port. During the night, the captain disappeared into the city while the crew was confined to the ship. They were told the next morning that he had jumped ship."

The messenger knew that the shippers wanted more information on their warship, so he continued.

"The ship's mate took control and is bringing the vessel back to port in Syrakosai. They may arrive in the next day, maybe two."

Hestros waved his hand at the messenger, dismissing him, and the man went out of the door.

"You trusted this captain," Gaia said, brooking no reply.

The men continued with their dinner, although their small talk had been supplanted by this report from the west.

"What should we do?" asked Hestros.

"About the captain?" replied Photios. "Nothing. Let the gods toss him from his next ship and let the sea creatures eat his flesh."

"What about the ship and the crew?" continued Hestros.

"More importantly," interjected Strophios, "what are we going to do with these warships from Qart-ḥadašt?"

Trade wars had been brewing for a dozen years, and the shippers from Syrakosai recognized the peril their vessels were in whenever they sailed far enough west to encounter the Punics. But they also wanted to expand their trade routes and establish ports in the west around Motya,

Drepanon, and Eryx. The Greeks back in Corinth and Athens desired products from western Sikania and even as far away as Gadir, and these men were willing to take additional risks to open sailing routes to these places. They wanted to avoid conflict with the people from Qart-ḥadašt but, if need be, they would fight them for the territory and the riches that could be had on Sikania.

Hestros pushed the chunks of meat and grilled endive around on his plate, then reached for the polished silver goblet for the shiny red wine it held. Drawing a long gulp from the cup, he set it down and was ready to continue.

"Greeks are the better seamen, and we can control our own fate, if we are willing to invest the time and men to be successful."

To these merchants, ships and men were mere objects, resources to be spent, traded, or lost if need be. They were there to serve the interests of the men with money, and Hestros was proposing nothing short of all-out conflict if it was necessary to establish a Greek presence on Sikania, and in the sea that surrounded this great island.

"And are you going to trade the honey, wine, and oil that we produce?" asked Gaia. She knew that western Sikania lacked many of the richest products of the east around Syrakosai – including grapes, figs, pomegranates, and hazelnuts – and she also knew that her husband intended to sell all of this and more to the Elymi in the west. Honey was made wherever bees were kept, but the honey from the bees on the slopes of nearby Inessa – the volcano that spewed fire and lava on a regular basis – was the best honey ever made. It was so good that Gaia and others believed it the best offering to the goddess Aphrodite, who ensured pleasurable sex and healthy children.

Photios was more focused on the products from his sheep and goats. Cheese-making was an art, and he already had several talented artisans in his employ. Photios knew that the cheese made from his herd would bring in many drachmas when sold in the west. And he intended to sell it throughout Sikania, with or without conflict with the Punics.

As if on cue, Gaia delivered a platter of *dulcis in fundo*, a dessert made of honey, nuts, milk, and flour, which she served with fresh bread and fruit, along with a sweet honey-colored wine made from grapes that had been dried on mats and fermented into a luscious elixir.

The men were sated and a bit drunk from the wine, but Gaia couldn't let her husband and their friends leave without serving the favorite finish of Hestros's meal. It was called *tyropatinum* and it was made by combining a sweet soft cheese with honey and raw eggs.

Gaia retired to a comfortable corner of their large house, in the same room as the men to respond to their questions or needs, but far enough away to avoid their conversation. The men had become a bit louder with the consumption of wine, and more boisterous and amused by their own conversation.

Hestros suggested that they move to the stone roof of the home, a flat patio that overlooked the spectacle that Syrakosai had become – the spectacle that men such as these took pride in having built – and, there, he suggested a round of *kottabos*.

"Gaia!" he called. "The disk!"

His wife appeared a few moments later, with another flask of wine in one hand, three silver cups clutched in the other, and a wide, flat bronze disk tucked under her arm. She knew the game and knew what the men planned to do. First, she set the flask and cups down – which the men quickly approached – and then she withdrew the disk from under her arm. Balancing it carefully with both hands, she perched it on the point of a carved stone obelisk near the edge of the roof. Then she withdrew.

Hestros filled each of the cups halfway with wine, and he and his fellows drank all but a sip of the contents. Then, one by one, they took turns flinging the remnants of wine in the cup at the disk, attempting to use the wine dregs to dislodge the disk and make it fall. The disk and obelisk were an arm's length from the edge of the roof so, if it fell as they had planned, the disk would stay on the patio with them for another round. But they paid little attention to the fact that the wine being hurled at the disk would fly past it and over the edge of the roof, splattering people who were below.

After several rounds, which included more drinking and a reluctant withholding of the requisite sip, they continued flinging droplets of wine at the disk balanced precariously on the stone pike across from them.

On some nights, this game might go on for several rounds, with each man keeping score and the final tally deciding the winner. But Hestros and his fellows had already consumed so much wine that they would surrender the game of *kottabos* after the first, successful hit.

Photios raised his hand, using only two fingers to clasp the stem of the goblet. He brought his arm forward and flicked his wrist to send the wine into the air and toward the disk. His aim was good, and only barely missed, but the disk quavered nevertheless. Another shudder that the men also felt under their feet, and the disk tipped and fell to the stone floor in a loud, clattering descent.

The tremble below and the unexplained fall of the disk brought the men to their feet. A rumbling could be heard in the sky to the north. An arrow of red fire split the sky, and a great plume of smoke rose and hid the stars. The earth shuddered again and Gaia ran to the roof seeking her husband. Another shudder of the earth, and an inhuman scream raced through the air and broke the silence of the night.

Hestros grabbed Gaia by the arm and raced down the steps and out onto the street below. He had experienced such earthquakes before, and he knew that they all began with Inessa, the great mountain to the north. Strophios and Photios were right on their heels, also well versed in this drama.

The street below the house was crowded with screaming people, some praying in loud verses, some beseeching the gods to save them. And it was to the gods that Hestros appealed. He knew that the volcano was the work of the god of fire, Hephaestos, and that such things happened when the god was making smoke and fire in his blacksmith's forge. The fact that Hestros believed it was just a workmanlike task of this mighty god – and not the expression of dissatisfaction with the Greeks' behavior – didn't quell his fear or the fear in the heart of Gaia.

The quaking continued in synchrony with the fire that was spitting from the mountain in the distance. From experience, Hestros assumed that Hephaestos would be at his forge for another night or two, so instead of standing petrified in the crowd, he guided Gaia and his guests outside of Syrakosai to a flat pasture in the outskirts of the city. The earthquake and fiery volcanic blasts continued, but the gentle nature and near-silent air of the prairie settled their nerves. They remained there for the remainder of that night and into the next day.

615 B.C.E.

615 B.C.E.

GREEK CITIES ACROSS THE ISLAND

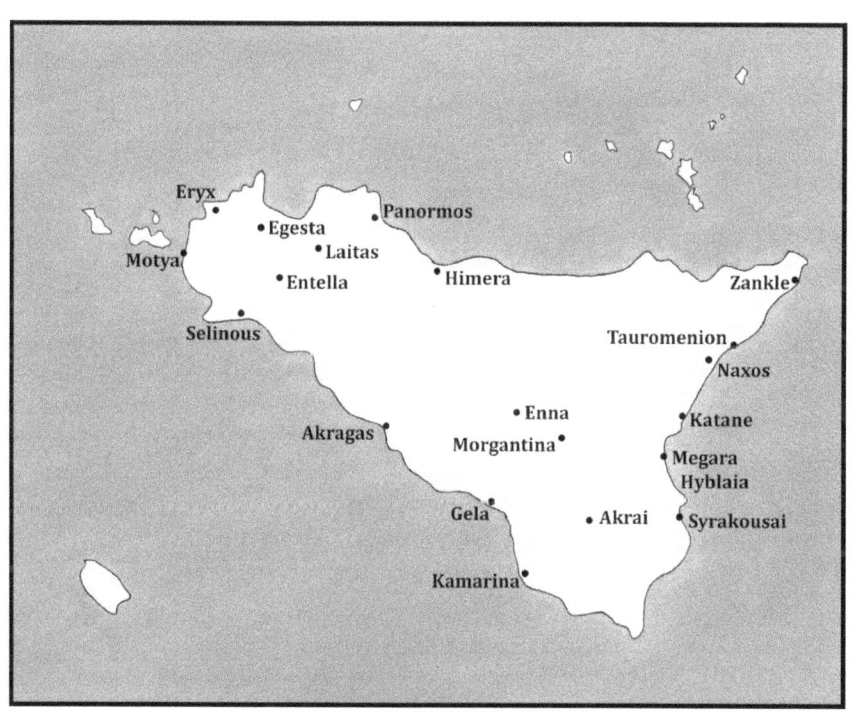

615 B.C.E.
GREEK SETTLEMENTS

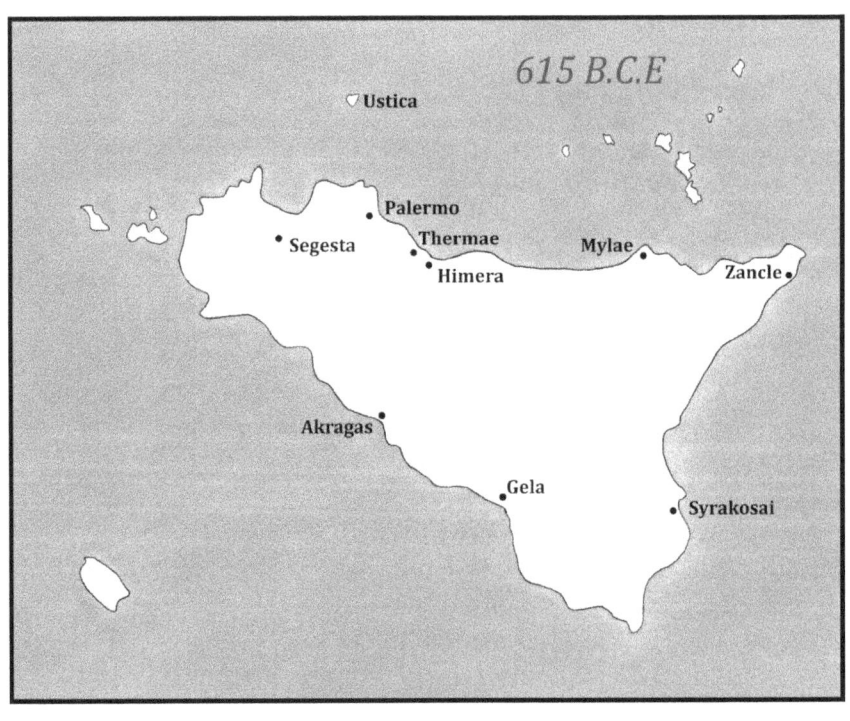

JULY 2018
CAFÉ AMADEO

THE SUN WAS BRIGHT THE FOLLOWING MORNING, AND THE AIR WAS cool. It would warm up by midday, but I had come to enjoy my new routine of walking along the streets of Mazara del Vallo to the Café Amadeo. Vito offered an endless litany of facts and his story-telling expertise made all these ancient details come alive. I could see the cities develop and the people interact. I could easily imagine their struggles and triumphs, how they built their homes and temples, how the social institutions and traditions evolved, even how their food was cooked and tasted.

Sliding into the chair by our corner table, I smiled as the barista delivered my cup of espresso. As soon as I lifted it to my lips, Vito ducked in through the door, his hat askew and his thin gray hair splayed out from under its brim.

"Hellenization," he said.

I knew the Greeks had continued their migration to Sicily, and how the southern regions of the Italian peninsula and this island came to be called Magna Graecia – Greater Greece – and how this ancient society battled with another ancient society of Carthaginians – the Punics as they were known – to control the island and its satellites. It was all about trade at first, but conflicts usually result in winners and losers, and neither of these civilizations was accustomed to losing.

"The Corinthians were not the first Greeks to reach Sicily," Vito began, "but they opened a corridor for others to sail from the eastern Mediterranean to our country.

"Carthage still controlled most of the west, while the Greeks were stretching beyond their eastern cities to establish settlements in the interior of the island. More importantly, they were building cities around the northern and southern coasts. It was a way of pushing the territorial limits, leaning on the boundaries between the two powers and creeping up on Punic strongholds without directly challenging them. At least not yet.

"They moved on old Myla in the northeastern tip of Sicily and renamed it Mylae. It was close enough to Messina – called Zancle back then – to serve as an outpost to extend the trading route for goods received by the Greeks there."

"Just a moment," I begged, as I flipped the pages of my journal. "Wasn't Myla...wait, what did you say about Myla?"

"Myla had been there for a few thousand years, as a small settlement. The early Sicilians recognized it as an important jumping off point for the Aeolian Islands. They would launch from Myla to get to Lipari, mostly for the obsidian."

My page-flipping ended when I found the reference.

"Yes, of course," I said. "The island, the volcano..."

Vito chuckled at the points I was able to remember.

"Si, of course, but much more. A culture persisted at Myla all those centuries until the Greeks from Zancle wanted to move west. Why not merge with an existing culture, they assumed, or at least take advantage of their settlement?

"Then there was Himera, founded around 650 B.C. It's even farther west than Mylae, just about the centerpoint on the northern coast of Sicily. It has a quite colorful history. The tyrant Phalaris ruled it for some time..."

"Wait. A tyrant? What do you mean?"

Vito paused for a moment. He took a sip of his coffee and then set the cup down and leaned back in his chair.

"They were known as 'tyrants,' mostly from Siracusa, but like the other invaders who came before – the Sicani, Elymi, and Siculi – they wanted to stretch their empires away from Siracusa and take control of other cities on the island or form new ones like Himera. But let's save talk of tyrants for later. I want to stick with the spread of Greek culture first."

The barista stepped toward our table bearing a tray of more espresso, a plate of orange slices, and some *cantucci*.

"Phalaris ruled Akragas from 570 to 554 B.C., but he also claimed Himera as his own. He was a bad one."

"What do you mean?"

"Most of the stories paint him as a heartless man, maybe soulless. He seemed to not only employ torture but to enjoy it."

"How's that?"

"He is accused of cannibalism, even eating babies. But his ugliest act was probably the Brazen Bull."

My look of confusion took the place of a spoken question. Vito sipped from his espresso cup and slid an orange slice between his teeth before replying.

"An Athenian sculptor named Perillos invented it for Phalaris. It was a life-size bronze bull, hollow inside, with a hinged door on the side. Victims would be shoved into the bull and locked inside while a fire was set below the beast and stoked to a roaring blaze. The heat of the fire would roast the person inside, and the screams of the burning victim would come out the hollowed nostrils of the animal."

"That's absolutely disgusting," I said in horror.

"Yes, of course it is, and the sculptor Perillos himself was executed in this way."

"Why? He was the man who invented it for Phalaris. What did he do to be executed?"

"Not really sure, at least in the record. But remember, Phalaris enjoyed torture. Why not test the device by roasting the man who invented it?"

"Whew. Can't believe this."

"There was a proper ending, though. Phalaris himself was later executed using this bull."

"Huh," I replied with a satisfied smile. "That sounds like a good use of the thing."

"But, anyway, back to Himera. You see, this city figures very prominently in the history of Sicily, and in the conflict between Greeks and Carthaginians. Various despots and tyrants fought for control of Himera because of its position on the northern coastline of Sikania. In 483 B.C., Terillus was thrown from power by Theron – who was the ruler of Akragas at that time – more on these guys later. As it turned out, Terillus sided with Hamilcar…"

"Wait!" I pleaded, as I furiously wrote down my notes. "I'm trying to keep up with you."

Vito took the plea with pleasure, as he relaxed into his chair and focused on the espresso and cantucci.

"Ready?" he said after a few minutes.

I nodded.

"Hamilcar was a very successful Punic general, a Carthaginian. And Terillus appealed to him to help win back Himera. The Greek hold on that city was symbolic of their expansion throughout Sicily – excuse me, Sikania – and they intended to remain there. Hamilcar's entry into the conflict seemed like a win for Terillus, but, in fact, Hamilcar and his Carthaginian forces had other plans. In the coming months it became obvious that Hamilcar was only cooperating with Terillus in the attack on Himera as a pretext for the Carthaginian conquest of the entire island.

"On hearing news that Theron was under siege, Gelon came from Siracusa…"

"Wait," I said, holding up my left palm as I wrote down this new name with my right. "Who's Gelon?"

"Oh, right, sorry about that. He ruled Siracusa."

"You said that. Was he a tyrant?"

Vito paused for a moment before responding.

"I see we keep tripping over this notion of a tyrant. Let me explain so we can proceed. To Greeks, a tyrant was an absolute ruler, not subject to laws or control by others. It didn't mean that they were murderous or even cruel; just that they were absolute. Now, we will continue.

"Gelon joined Theron to fight for Himera. They represented the Greek side. Hamilcar, a citizen of Carthage, and Terillus, a deposed Greek ruler, represented the Punic side. In the end, the Greeks prevailed, Himera became solidly Greek and – with its position on the central northern coast – it became a powerful instrument for expansion of Magna Graecia.

"Gelon was so overjoyed at the victory that he decided to build the Temple to Athena, honoring his favorite goddess."

"Who is a Greek goddess, right?" I asked.

"Si," confirmed Vito.

"Right there in Himera?"

"Well, no," he added with a chuckle. Gelon understood the importance of construction projects and also understood how his image could improve with a magnificent altar to such a god. So, he chose a spot near Siracusa, his capital, as the site for his Temple of Athena. There was a spot that had been the location for cult practices for centuries..."

"Like?" I asked. I was curious about what cult.

"Use your imagination, Luca! Sicily was rife with cultures and cults. Most of them were polytheistic. In fact, prior to the introduction of Judaism and Christianity, it's safe to say that all Sicilian cults were polytheistic."

"A pagan cult?"

"I didn't mean for you to use THAT much imagination," he replied with a smile. "Anyway, Gelon chose this spot outside of Siracusa to build the Temple to Athena. It was a fantastic structure, with tall, imposing columns squaring off around a holy centerpiece. It stood tall enough to be seen from a great distance and reminded everyone who came into contact with it how powerful Gelon, the tyrant of Siracusa, truly was.

"But let's get back to the battle. Losing the battle of Himera to Gelon and Theron stung the Carthaginians, and the pain did not fade over time. Some decades later, Hannibal Mago..."

"This is the Hannibal of the elephant story, beating the Romans?"

"No, that Hannibal came later. This is Hannibal Mago, Hamilcar's son, who saw it as his mission to avenge his father's defeat in Himera. Hannibal Mago led a Carthaginian expedition to Sicily. Initially, it was portrayed merely as an attempt to support the Punic settlements in the west, around Selinus, but just as his father Hamilcar had done, Hannibal Mago planned a greater invasion of the island. Once he had a foothold in western Sikania, he marched his forces north and south, reaching Himera for a rematch of the great battle fought and lost by his father. He had more success than Hamilcar, beating the Greeks and Himereans who by then had been desserted by their Siracusan supporters. So, the city fell to Hannibal Mago."

"Who was that?" I asked.

"Who? Hannibal Mago?"

"No. Who fell? Who was the Siracusan leader?"

"Hmm," he paused, putting an arthritic finger on his chin to consider my question. "I think it was Dioc..., no, Dioletes. No, Diocles, that's right. Look him up. But let's get back to Himera.

"Hannibal Mago ordered that the city be burned to the ground. He executed thousands of Himerans, some say as a tribute to his father...but I just think he was pissed."

Vito's use of the very American slang made me laugh, and at that he grinned.

"Hannibal Mago destroyed everything that he could of the city, the homes, common buildings, even the temples."

"Did anyone survive?"

"Some, there are no clear records of how many, but some stories tell of Himereans who escaped to Thermae, today's Termini Imerese, just west of the old Himera." Then Vito laughed out loud.

"The Punics thought they were destroying the Greeks and enlarging their Carthaginian Empire."

"Why is that funny?"

"Because the fall of Himera resulted in Greek citizens moving farther west, farther into what Carthage considered its territory. So, the squeeze they put on the Greeks in Himera actually caused more Greek infiltration west into the Carthaginian Empire."

I rendered as much as I could of Vito's comments in my journal, but I had long since learned that his rapid-fire commentary would force me to only capture the names and places, things that I could later research and find in the library.

"Remember that Zis was founded by the Punics, *correttu*?" he asked.

"*Sì*," I replied.

"Well, think of where Zis is on the map. Right there on that promontory on the north coast of Sicily." Vito used his right forefinger to point to a place in the air in front of him, as if he was jabbing at a map that hung in that space before us.

"Now, where is Egesta, or Segesta as we call it today?"

I could only shrug my shoulders, quickly losing the thread in the barrage of facts.

"It's right here," Vito said, raising his left arm and pointing with his arthritic left forefinger at a space west of Zis.

"The Punics settled Zis," he said jabbing his right finger, "but by this time, the Greeks had moved even farther west, to this area," he said, jabbing at that invisible spot with his left hand. "Right in the middle of the region that Carthage thought was theirs.

"At approximately the same time, Ducetius rose to power. He was born in Sicily, but he was a Greek citizen, with Greek training, education, and cultural heritage. He founded the ancient city of Palici..."

"Where was that?"

"I'm getting to that," Vito responded. Ducetius sought to control the inland areas of Sicily, and he founded the city I just mentioned, Palici, west of Katane. Gelon and Hiero..."

"Another tyrant?"

"Who?"

"Hiero. I haven't heard his name yet."

"Sì, Hiero ruled Syrakosai at the time when Gelon ruled Agrigento and Gelo. As Ducetius's power spread, these other tyrants began to see it as a threat to their empires, so they countered. Again, remember, these are conflicts only among the Greeks, but these conflicts were a direct result of the push to hellenize Sicily and oust the Carthaginians. The pushing and shoving going on in eastern Sicily had spread to central Sicily and threatened to spread to western Sicily, where the Punics watched and waited. The turmoil on their eastern boundary of their western territory was becoming a true danger to the Carthaginian settlements on the island.

"At the end of the Fifth Century B.C., the Carthaginians tried to bolster their defenses in the west. They brought in more soldiers, continued to destroy Greek towns like Himera which they thought posed a threat, and moved on Selinus, Akragas, Gelo, and other cities to the east. The Carthaginians even set up a permanent military installation at Zis – Palermo – to serve as their military command post.

"The result of all this build-up was that Carthage controlled most of the Mediterranean coast between their home in north Africa and the western edge of Sicily. And by commanding the seas between Carthage and the southwestern tip of Sicily, they could prevent the Greeks from sailing beyond this island in the middle of the Mediterranean. As a result, the Carthaginians could control every trade route west, including those to modern Morocco and the Iberian Peninsula. Not inconsequentially, this command also prevented non-Carthaginian fleets from reaching Gibraltar where they could gain access to the Atlantic Ocean. The alternative route was to sail around the east and north of the Sicily – through the dangerous Strait of Messina – and curve through the Aeolian Islands.

"The Greeks and Carthaginians had laid down roots in their strongholds and established firm Greek and Carthaginian empires on Sicily, but they would nevertheless continue to fight for territory for years to come."

"Until the Punic Wars?"

"No, the Greek-Carthage conflicts ended before then. The Punic Wars were fought between Rome and Carthage. Do you know about Ustica?"

"I don't think we've talked about it yet," I responded.

"Ustica is an island off the north coast of Sicily. It was named Ustica later by the Romans. In the time of the Carthaginian wars with the Greeks, the island was named Osteodes, which means ossuary or burial ground. It was given that name because it was where thousands of Carthaginian mutineers were shipped – without provisions – to die of hunger."

"That's grim," I replied.

"It's the price of war, some would say.

"Despite all these confrontations and border challenges, the hellenization of Sicily proceeded with great success, during and after these wars with the Carthaginians," Vito continued. "The Greeks came to the island for its resources, but also because the population of Greece itself was growing and – as mostly a collection of small islands itself – the Greek coalition of city states needed to grow beyond its own borders and find land for its people. Sicily was about ten to twelve days sail from mainland Greece, which didn't mean it was nearby, but the arable land and prosperous fields of wheat and other crops enticed the new arrivals to establish trading systems with their homeland to ship grain and other foodstuffs to Athens and surrounding cities."

He paused for a moment.

"But this island is where one of the most important historical events took place," he said, with a note of mystery.

"Another war on the high seas?" I asked.

"No," Vito smiled, "writing. Trade over great distances requires better record-keeping. If you were selling something to someone in the marketplace, you would haggle over price face to face, and the exchange would take place. But if you're selling shiploads of crops, grain, legumes, wine, and so on, with people who are two weeks travel from you, you would be expected to log all the items, establish prices, and communicate your intention, right?"

I nodded.

"The Greeks had a system of writing," I interjected.

"At the time, it was not really an alphabet. The original Greek writing was more pictorial where images called ideographs represented objects or concepts. The Phoenicians had already developed an alphabet that used symbols to indicate sounds, instead of things."

I had to ponder that for a moment.

"So, the first writing was a stream of pictures," I began slowly, "like if I drew a man, then a spear, then an animal..."

"It would communicate that a man had killed an animal with a spear."

"Right," I agreed, but added quickly, "but the Phoenicians created symbols for each sound, so the symbol for "a" or "s" could be used repeatedly in different contexts to string together enough symbols to communicate an entire thought."

"*Certu*," said Vito – certainly. "But the sounds were more like syllabic sounds at this point, something like 'ar' or 'tist' or 'oyl.' Instead of drawing a man with a brush and clay pot, they could combine these symbols to write 'artist oil.'"

I felt like writing was being invented as I sat there.

"The Greeks adopted the Phoenician alphabet and symbols, which over time evolved from sounds to morphemes..."

"What's that? What's a morpheme?"

"It's the smallest unit of sound, or the building block of modern language. The pictures or pictographs were broken down into syllabic sound units, which yielded to morphemes – something like what we call letters – and the Greeks adopted this system of writing. It was taking place in mainland Greece, of course, but the far-flung trading posts of the Greek Empire required that a consistent and reliable system of communication exist so that goods and services..."

"Wait. What's a service that can be traded long distance?" I asked.

"Not all things traded were grain, legumes, and wine. Sometimes women went with the sailing ships."

Vito seemed to recognize the social importance of what he was saying, but also seemed unperturbed by it.

"We can – we should, in this day – refuse to accept wife selling and the treatment of young women as property, but we can't impose this value on the people who lived two thousand years ago."

"Okay," I said, after a moment. "Back to trade and the alphabet."

"The new alphabet allowed the traders to communicate their list of products, values, and intended price over long distances, so we might conclude that the hellenization of Sicily and the sprawling Greek trading empire led to the development and acceptance of the writing systems that we use today."

———

I spent most of my days wandering around Mazara del Vallo. My original plan when coming to Sicily was to rent a car and drive along the coast, first across the northern border of the island, all the way around the northeastern tip near Messina, then clockwise down toward Catania, Siracusa, and Noto, around the southern coastline and back. I knew that I should visit some of the interior cities – Sicily isn't just a coastal civilization – but those would have to wait.

In fact, all of my plans to drive around the island and visit places like the Temple of Segesta, the volcano at Mount Etna, and the beaches of Taormina were put on hold since meeting Vito Trovato. He kept me in rapt attention with his colorful and detailed knowledge of Sicily from the most ancient times to the present. So, instead of a rambling tour by road, I kept my lodgings in this port city, meeting with my mentor each morning, studying in the library in the afternoon, and enjoying the fresh air and nightlife of Mazara del Vallo each evening.

It was on one particular evening when I was strolling past a café that I had frequented before, that I heard a familiar voice.

"Tyrants."

There was no mistaking who the voice belonged to, but it was out of the normal context, and I admit that it startled me at first. I turned toward the voice and I saw Vito sitting at a café table, a not-so-full bottle of wine in front of him, and three glasses. He had his own glass tipped to his lips, but there were two more that rested half empty on either side of him.

I approached him and, with a wave of his hand, was invited to sit down. I sat across the table, leaving the two unattended wine glasses on my left and right, and leaned forward on the table.

"I am so pleased to see you here," I began. I was slow to engage because I didn't know how to approach our usual subject in a setting so different from Café Amadeo. Just then, a young man and woman came to table, took up the two remaining seats and greeted me.

"Hello, I am Santo," said the man, offering his hand to shake.

"And I am Emilia," said the woman, who also offered her hand.

"You know our Professore Trovato, no?" said Santo.

"Sì," I replied, but then I realized that I had not yet thought of Vito as a professor. How could I have missed that. In fact, I sat there in a bit of a stupor, thinking about how I had spent the last two weeks of mornings with him, learning more in short morning conversations than I had absorbed from my first two years of university education, and had not bothered to find out more about the man I now considered my teacher.

"Vito has been teaching me the history of Sicily," I said.

Both Santo and Emilia rolled their eyes, and Vito's eyes shown bright with glee.

"He'll never stop talking," Emilia warned me, patting me on the arm.

"But listen carefully," added Santo. "He doesn't like to slow down or repeat something he has said."

I smiled slowly, peering across the table at Vito and nodding my head. I had discovered in that moment that, first, my teacher was in fact a teacher and, second, that while his students seemed to love and revere him, they too agreed that he could be a lot to handle.

Santo and Emilia excused themselves and wished me a *'bona sira,'* – the Sicilian pronunciation was obvious – then walked into the noisy crowd and left me alone with Vito.

Vito and I smiled at each other, then he spoke.

"Tyrants."

I nodded my head. Fortunately, I had my ever-ready notebook in my pants pocket.

"First, I must repeat what we talked about in passing earlier today. Tyrant was a word for rulers in Sicily. Although the Greek islands didn't have tyrants, the Greek rulers – and some non-Greek rulers – in Sicily were considered by that term. It wasn't pejorative; it didn't mean they were cruel, although the exercise of absolute power sometimes required demonstrations of cruelty to keep their people in line. The term simply refers to the powerful leaders who, perhaps, founded cities or kept them under their thumbs after they were founded. By the way, the Greeks so fervently pursued new settlements that they gave a name to the man who did this. They called him an *oecist.*"

Not knowing what to do with this tidbit, I wrote it down anyway.

"The period of Greek hellenization of Sicily also happened to be the age of tyrants. Of couse, the two would go together."

I wasn't so sure of the "of course" part but remained silent.

"You see, the Greeks who came to our island saw its potential, and they spread their influence across the coastlines, into the interior and up the mountains like Etna. With such a vast and largely unclaimed territory, the man who commanded the strongest army or held the greatest wealth could secure leadership of his region. And, as you know, greedy men are seldom satisfied with what they can grab in one swipe. They usually want more.

"So, tyrants like Gelon and Phalaris – we talked about them this morning, right?"

We had, but Vito's slippage of memory both surprised me and made me like him more.

"These guys couldn't be content with Gelo, Akragas, Syrakosai – even with cities as far away as Himera. Meanwhile, they always had to watch their flanks. Scythes – tyrant of Zancle, on the northeastern tip of Sicily – coveted the area around Etna and Katane, and probably farther south. Theron and Terillus we've talked about, but don't forget that they were hoping to expand their empires at the expense of some tyrant who didn't pay enough attention to their motives.

"There was a succession of tyrants battling over Siracusa – sorry, Syrakosai – including Dion who ruled for forty years at the beginning of the Fourth Century B.C. He was succeeded by his son, Dionysius II who lasted twenty some years but Timoleon stepped in to return democratic rule to the city – not what you think of as democracy, but close enough – but his efforts stalled when Agathocles took over as tyrant and lasted about thirty years."

"Were all the tyrants in Syrakosai?" I asked.

"No. That was the most powerful city on Sicily at the time, so control of it required an especially aggressive form of leadership, so tyrannical rule fit the bill.

"They had many techniques at their disposal. Inter-marriage worked well..."

"Was this related in some way to the bride-selling that you talked about earlier?" I asked.

Vito drew on his wine glass and looked at me over its rim. Setting the glass back on the table, he continued.

"Whether we like it or not, 'bride-selling' as you've termed it has been a feature of advanced civilizations for thousands of years. Oh, no..." he said in protest, lifting his right hand slightly above the table level, "it's terrible. Truly. I don't mean to make light of treating women like chattel. But if we want to understand history, we can't just criticize it. We have to understand it in the context of its time."

He took another sip of wine and stared back at me.

"Two hundred years from now, thanks to the evolution of learning, a child will be able to absorb more scientific information than all of what is known today, in the entire universe, all by the age of fourteen. All because teaching and learning techniques will evolve beyond the imagination today."

I didn't know where he got that information, but I held my tongue.

"And if that child tells your great, great, great grandson that requiring him to be sent to school is like being held in bondage, will that make you – Luca – wrong today?"

"I would have to say that requiring a pubescent boy to attend school is not the same as installing a pubescent girl into sexual-slavery, marriage or not. They're not the same."

Vito sat back and nodded his head.

"That sounds a lot like what our great, great, great grandparents said of their social institutions two hundred years ago."

He sat forward and raised his wine glass again, tipping it in my direction, and continued.

"In any case, we're talking about tyrants. Gelon and Theron married into each others' families, and Anaxilas of Rhegion married Terillus's daughter."

"That's the same Terillus from Himera?"

"The same. But they didn't all intermarry. Another option was ethnic genocide, or enslavement. The point was to eliminate resistance, but the tyrants were short-sighted. They believed that their power would continue, and that the forces that protected them would be retained, and that the people would not rise up."

"Did the people rise up?"

"Sì. There were revolts that challenged most of the tyrants' authority. Even the slaves rebelled."

"When?"

"That's a long story. You've heard about Spartacus?"

"Yes, of course."

"Well," Vito laughed as he sipped his wine. "It's not about him." And he laughed again.

"But we'll get to the slave revolts tomorrow."

Vito and I sat for a while in silence, enjoying the crisp evening air and the slowly emptying bottle of Nero d'Avola on the table. He lifted the carafe, then saw that the level had reached an unacceptable level and held the bottle aloft. He didn't turn to see if the bartender or waiter were watching; it seemed that Vito was a singular personage in Mazara del Vallo, and the barista and bartenders all knew him and his gestures.

And just as I looked around to see if my mentor's non-verbal gesture had gotten any traction, a young man with a white towel slung casually over his shoulder approached our table. He was holding a bottle of the same type of wine, and a plate of cheese and bread that was so fresh that the steam still rose from the crackling crust of the loaf.

"Scientists," Vito said. "Do you have any idea how many scientists were born or lived here?"

I could detect a level of amazement even in the normally mild tone of my mentor's voice.

"Plato, for one," he began.

"Wait. Plato was a Greek."

"Of course, he was. So were tens of thousands of other people who lived on the island of Sicily."

"You'll have to explain yourself better," I said. "Do you believe that Plato was a Sicilian?"

"Oh, no. He was born in Athens, and he died in Athens. But he visited Sicily and considered it to be a magnificent land. It is said that he used it as the backdrop for his book, *Republic,* one of history's greatest rebuttals of totalitarianism."

Vito nodded, as if to give credence to his last statement, then he pulled the new bottle toward him and filled his glass.

"But the tyrants of the time didn't look kindly on Plato's thesis. According to some sources, he was sold into slavery by Dionysius..."

"The tyrant of Syrakosai?"

"*Correttu.*"

"Archimedes was born in Siracusa, the mathematician who discovered calculus, and the way to determine the volume of an object with an irregular shape..."

"I think I know that story," I said.

"Of course. All schoolboys have heard it. The tyrant of Siracuse, Hiero II, doubted the weight of a crown he had had crafted for him. One day, while taking a bath, Archimedes noticed that the water in the tub would spill over its edges equal to the volume of his body, or any other object placed in the water. From this, he was able to quantify the volume of Hiero's crown.

"But there's more," he continued. "What about the screw?"

I knew of Archimedes's screw. It was the most efficient device for moving water upwards to a new level. With his invention, the water in a river or stream could be delivered to another channel above – the principle behind water movement in the aqueduct system.

"By the way," Vito said, "do you know how Archimedes died?"

I had some vague memory but wasn't sure.

"The king of Siracusa at the time of the Second Punic War kept Archimedes busy designing war machines to fight the Romans. He was a mechanical genius, after all, and the Siracusans were attempting to thwart the Roman advance on their city. When the aggressors were approaching the walls, the Roman commander, who was very impressed with Archimedes' inventions, ordered that he be spared and brought to the Roman camp for interrogation. Against that command, however, an over-zealous Roman soldier cut the scientist down.

"And then there was Empedocles. He was born in Akragas, was considered a great philosopher, and wrote and taught extensively on what we now call cosmogenesis."

"Sounds like the origins of the cosmos," I offered.

"Quite right. He was the first to describe in writing the four basic elements of nature: earth, water, air, and fire. Speaking of fire, Empedocles met an untimely end."

"How do you mean?"

"He climbed to the top of Mount Etna to inspect the volcano. Depending on your sources, he either slipped or was pushed but, in any case, he fell into the cauldron and died there.

"Aeschylus was a dramatist. He was born in Greece but spent most of his life in Sicily and is considered the father of Greek tragedy. He died in Gela.

"Gorgias, a philosopher and writer, lived in eastern Sicily. And Timaeus, an historian and philosopher, was born in Taormenium. He was exiled from Sicily by Agathocles but returned late in life and died here."

"Were there any more?"

"Many more, scientists, artists, composers – think of Pirandello – but they came much later."

Vito sipped from his wine glass, emptied it into his mouth, then stood to leave. He braced himself on the back of the chair, a move not caused by consumption of wine as much as his advanced age. In the café each morning, I watched him come to table with measured steps, but he seemed fine. By the end of the day, however, he seemed older than usual.

"So, Luca, I bid you good night." And with a finger tapping the brim of his hat, he walked into the piazza at the edge of the bar and disappeared into the crowd.

WAR AND DISASTER

413 B.C.E.

HARBOR OF SIRACUSA

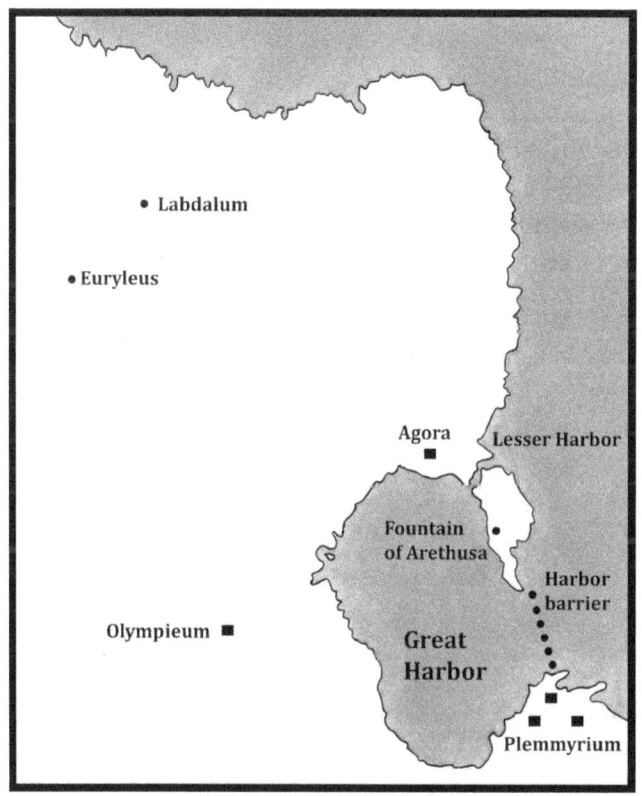

413 B.C.E.
SIRACUSA

"THEY HAVE BEEN HERE LONG," SAID THAESTUS. HE LEANED ON the rough-cut stone at the top of the walls that surrounded the military port of Siracusa. It was deep into the night and only the stars that escaped the thin veil of clouds were visible above. The air was warm and there was no wind; it all contributed to the feeling of suspended tension in the world about him.

Thaestus and Dionodes were soldiers commanded by Gylippus, the Spartan general who had come to defend Siracusa against the attack of the Hoplites and archers from Athens. The two men wore uniforms required by their commander which, by itself, was an improvement in the military order from before the time the Spartan had arrived. Gylippus believed that order and obedience were required for an army to prevail, and so he had the people of Siracusa make uniforms for his men that fit the general's notion of military clothing. The soft tunic and cushioned shoulder pads were comfortable; they were intended to protect the men's skin from the weight and hard surfaces of the torso armor and arm plating that Gylippus required of all his men.

Here, on the parapet, far from the enemy ships in the harbor below, the armor wouldn't have helped, but all soldiers were dressed out the same. The only difference would be for the sailors, whose duties included rope climbing and sail management, tasks that precluded heavy armor and, not incidentally, left them more vulnerable to a sharpened arrow in an attack.

"These Athenians," complained Dionodes, pointing to the aggregating flotilla below, "they remain in our harbor, gathering their ships and men. Are we going to let them be?"

"The commander tells us not to strike yet," replied Thaestus. "It is not time."

But the mysteries of military strategy eluded both men. Their elevated position allowed them to look down on the Athenian ships in their harbor, which meant that they should have the advantage in attacking the alien fleet with their arrows. But Gylippus called for patience. So, Thaestus and Dionodes waited through their night shift.

When daylight appeared and the sun blinded them from the east, it was hard to make out the shapes of the ships in the harbor in that direction. The weary men accepted their replacements on the wall's fortifications, descending the stone steps to the courtyard below and retiring to their homes, a warm fire, and a friendly wife. The Siracusans had built an empire in this port city, and they enjoyed a span of time without conflict, so even the soldiers had come to enjoy life as normal citizens of the city.

Their replacements, Phaletus and Girius, took up their position on the rampart. Phaletus cupped his right hand over his brow to shield his eyes from the rising sun and surveyed the harbor below. Girius also shielded his eyes and used his index finger to tap out the number of ships down below, then announced his conclusion.

"Each of us, the Siracusans and Athenians, we have an equal number of ships."

Phaletus had come to the same conclusion, but he remarked on the vast number of vessels, and how their total count filled the harbor to capacity and beyond.

"How can so many ships do battle? It looks more like a gathering of merchants, peaceful merchants, than a siege by the Athenians."

His assessment was right on point. Although the Athenian navy gathered its forces and the Siracusan army and navy assembled sufficient resources to equal their attackers, the conclave looked more like a peaceful draw rather than the beginnings of a violent assault.

"If the Athenians win the contest..." began Phaletus, but Girius cut him off.

"They cannot. We are stronger and this is our land." Then, pausing for emphasis, he added, "And, also, if the Athenians win, we all die," Girius added. "And I don't plan to die. At least not here, not until the gods call me."

Nicias, the Athenian commander of the invading navy in the harbor, had bolstered his forces on the expedition to Sikania, until he had over one hundred ships – triremes with three decks of rowers for power and speed – seven hundred sailors trained to fight, and the support of one thousand Hoplites with layers of armor from shoulder to knee, and a lance and shield for close-in combat. He was emboldened to sail into the harbor of Siracusa, believing that his force would be able to overcome the men of Gylippus and he could claim this great city and port on the east coast of Sicily for Athens. These were challenging times for his homeland; threats from the Spartans and other Greek cities and a squeeze on foodstuffs and other necessary items, left him – Nicias – in the role not only of protector of the empire but of guide and god. If he could conquer Siracusa and, with it, gain access to the grain and goods of the island, he would save his country from other perils and be hailed as a hero at home.

On the opposite side was Gylippus. He had had his victories and defeats and he was, frankly, not well liked at home in Sparta. He was tasked with defending Siracusa from all comers, particularly the Athenian forces who had displayed clear designs for conquest in Sikania for a dozen years. If he was successful, Gylippus could stop Athens in their tracks and not only save Siracusa but also halt the advance of the Athenian expedition into Sicily, its hinterland as well as its coastline.

Gylippus's strategy was one of waiting. He had sent a navy out off the east coast of Sicily to engage the Athenians before they moved closer to the city, but that strategy had failed. He then ordered the fleet and soldiers back into the harbor where they waited until the right moment to counter Nicias's moves.

Meanwhile, the eerie sight of a lunar eclipse that swept across the southern border of the island of Sikania had paralyzed Nicias in his approach to Siracusa. He consulted the priests for their reading of the event, and the holy men advised that he hold off on attacking Siracusa for twenty-seven days. He followed their advice, but that gave the Syracusans time to bring in more ships and soldiers.

Phaletus kept his attention on the ships below and focused even more when he sensed some movement. His position allowed him to see the action, but not to engage it. Girius was distracted for a moment with the need to urinate, which he did over the wall and down the cold stone of the fortifications below.

"They are moving about," Phaletus said. The subtle actions by the Athenian ships were too slow and subtle at this point for him to decipher an intent. But the forces under Gylippus reacted, whether under command or instinctively. The movement of the sailing ships far below him seemed like a dance carried out in slow motion. He called Girius's attention to it, and they stood watching while the orchestrated actions of the Athenians and Siracusans proceeded.

Within minutes, one of their ships landed a glancing blow on the bow of an Athenian ship. The collision pitched both vessels sideways and away from each other, but Phaletus noticed the splintered wooden hull of the Athenian ship had sustained greater damage than was done to the vessel from Siracusa. In a short time, all the boats had come into motion, some coordinated with fellow ships by their side, and some that seemed random and individualistic. Girius and Phaletus leaned on the stone wall to see the naval battle in greater detail. From their vantage point, it seemed more like a game, but they had fought in battles before and they were keenly aware of the loss of blood and life taking place far below their position that was a part of every such contest.

"That's it!" shouted Girius, but he suddenly realized his display of enthusiasm and looked toward, then away from, Phaletus in embarrassment.

Small fires could be seen on the decks of some ships, no doubt set by catapulting small smudge pots of grease or glowing embers across the watery divide between combatants. Captain's orders rent the air and traveled easily to the sentries on their post above it all, penetrating the general cacophony of shouts from men fighting or dying below.

Now and then, the hull of a great ship would pitch and show its keel just before capsizing. Or the flaming remnants of a burning sail would illuminate a mast just before it plunged into the sea. Clattering sounds of swords and armor punctuated the battle noise and sounds of a death rattle choked in the throats of the dying.

The battle grew in intensity and crews from each ship threw grappling hooks onto the decks of their enemy, pulling on the ropes to draw the attacking vessel closer and allow them to board. Hand-to-hand combat ensued, but the sailors – though hardened by battles fought for years – were not provisioned as soldiers. They had no armor and little talent handling spears and swords in close-in fighting.

One sailor was driven against the rail on the side of his ship, his attacker pushing on the shaft of a spear and driving the head of the weapon deeper into his victim. As the stricken man grasped at the spear that had crushed his ribs and opened a bloody wound in his chest, his feet slipped on the oily, bloody deck and he went overboard, just as the spearman sucked the vicious weapon backward to save it from following the man into the water.

The Athenians fought well, losing only a few ships and delivering fatal blows to many more Siracusan ships and soldiers. But then the action slowed and the combatants separated. But Nicias's delay in provisioning his ships – thanks to the priests' advice concerning the omen from the eclipse – had let Gylippus bring in enough troops and ships to seal off the harbor and to trap the Athenian ships inside.

So, the survival of the Athenians required that they fight it out in the harbor or land their troops and march inland.

"The triremes of Athens are failing," cried Phaletus, drawing Girius's attention back to the harbor.

"That one's sinking," Girius said, pointing to the stricken Athenian ship in the harbor.

Other Athenian ships were rammed, and they slipped sideways toward the waterline. Still other vessels beached on the shores of the harbor to allow the sailors to slip onto the sands and push toward safety on land.

About then, Thaestus and Dionedes appeared at the portal of the ramparts, out of breath and panting, but directing their words to Girius and Phaletus.

"We are told to go to the sand, to the Athenians landing below," blurted Thaestus between breaths.

Girius and Phaletus stared back at their fellow soldiers but they didn't move.

"We must go," emphasized Dionedes. "The Athenians have landed and they're trying to escape from the harbor onto the land beyond Siracusa."

Girius reached for his spear and helmet and ran to his friends standing in the doorway. Phaletus didn't budge.

"Who gives these instructions?" he asked. There was some insistence and rebellion in his voice.

"It comes from Gylippus," said Thaestus. "We can catch the Athenians and strike them down. This is our chance. They are on the run."

Still, Phaletus didn't move. Dionedes shook his head and threw his arm back over his head, indicating to Girius and Thaestus that they must go, even if Phaletus refused.

As the men disappeared through the doorway, Dionedes looked back at his recalcitrant comrade.

"Apollo will destroy you," he said, then turned into the darkness of the portal and disappeared.

The Siracusans assembled on the plain below and rushed after the fleeing Athenians. Nicias's comrades bolted from their ships and moved in disorganized fashion toward the land beyond the port of Siracusa. Once on land, they encountered a number of Siracusan soldiers and those loyal to Gylippus, who pestered the Athenians with arrows, rocks, and spears. Scores of the enemy were killed, many more captured.

Phaletus finally descended from his post on the ramparts of the Sircusan fort, but instead of joining his fellows in pursuit of the Athenians, he returned home to his wife, Lydia.

"How have you fared?" she asked her husband when he stooped through the doorway into their home. Lydia had heard the fighting but had no knowledge of its meaning or course.

"It is done," Phaletus said. "The battle was waged, but it is done." And he began to disarm himself of his soldier's uniform and he donned a long, woven tunic in its place.

He told Lydia nothing of the destruction of ships in the harbor but, more importantly, he said nothing of the flight of the Athenian soldiers and his commander's order to assemble and chase them.

The Siracusans prevented the sack of their city that day. Gylippus was so successful that he called for the uniting of the many Sicilian cities around the eastern and southern parts of the island, a suggestion that was readily accepted by the surviving Sicilians.

The Athenians did not fare well at all, losing many men and ships on a day celebrated by their Siracusan enemy. Many were killed in the engagement and thousands were sold into slavery. The captives who were not enslaved were sent off to the stone quarries outside of Siracusa where they died off from disease or simple starvation.

Athenian general Nicias was captured along with his men. As the leader of the invasion, he was executed by the Siracusans, despite Gylippus's efforts to save him.

309 B.C.E.

SIRACUSA, THIRD SICILIAN WAR

THE PEOPLE OF SIRACUSA HAD KNOWN NOTHING BUT WAR FOR many generations. The Greeks that built up their city were threatened by Athenians sailing from the homeland to take control of the port. Although the invaders were repulsed, a string of tyrants from Siracusa itself and from nearby Akragas continued to wage wars around the island, sparking fierce conflict from the people they invaded and turning the battles back on the Siracusans.

As Phaestus awoke in his bed in Siracuse, he assumed that the Carthaginian siege of the city was still on. It put pressure on him and his fellow citizens, a pressure that Hamilcar, the Carthaginian general, fully intended, and Phaestus wondered how much longer they could hold out. Their own general, Agathocles, decided not to challenge Hamilcar directly. Instead, he commanded a force to attack Carthage. The plan was to put equal pressure on Hamilcar's homeland and draw him and his army back to North Africa and weaken the Carthaginian grip on Siracusa.

To finance this venture, Agathocles took a number of steps that were common among tyrants. First, he drafted men from families left back in the city to serve as soldiers, to ensure that those who remained behind didn't dare rebel against his effort. Then he took jewelry and gifts from the families, even from the shrines to their gods, and converted them to his purpose. He had one last strategy that was as diabolical as any he had ever attempted: He granted the richest families in Siracusa safe passage out of the town to avoid the war, but then Agathocles's soldiers fell upon them and killed them outside the city's walls and confiscated their money and possessions.

"Insane," was Gesuta's one-word description of the Siracusan strategy. She was Phaestus's wife and saw no reason to hold her tongue.

"We are stuck here in this city," she complained, "captives of the beasts from Carthage, and he took our army on a wild chase to another country? What are we to do, left here on our own, with our fields in the hands of the enemy and our supplies dwindling?"

In fact, Agathocles's move did have a positive affect. Fearing the loss of his capital while he waged war on Sicily, Hamilcar split his force and sent some of the soldiers back home to defend it.

"He tried to storm our walls," Phaestus said, "but you know it didn't work."

He was referring to an attempt by the remaining Carthaginian attacking force in the previous year, an attempt to assault the walls of Siracusa, an attempt that failed.

"I am told by Hemestra that they've blocked our port. How are we going to receive the trading ships?" she asked.

"We have time, yet. Our army..."

"Our army is in siege of Carthage!" she shouted.

Phaestus decided not to argue further. His wife was informed and knew the risks they faced, but she was also on edge by now. And he wondered what their life would be like – theirs and their children's lives – if Hamilcar came back and attacked the city.

The day wore on like so many before it. Sieges were odd things. It was a good tactic over a long period of time, but an army that laid siege to a fortified city must have the patience, supplies, and resolve to remain bivouacked on the outskirts for months or years to come. On this morning, the Carthaginian army had been camped outside of Siracusa already for three years and, except for their failed attempt to storm the walls in the previous season, most of the confrontation was one of waiting.

The strategy contained two important elements, however. A blockade of the port would deprive the Siracusans of goods that might leave or come in, while a land siege opposite the portside of the city would preclude escape or interactions with the lands beyond Siracusa. While this posed a logistical threat to the people, another more potent element was also at play.

The Siracusans, as Gesuta had demonstrated, were falling prey to the stress of imprisonment. Without the ability to move about, to come and go with trading partners, or to visit the fertile lands outside of Siracusa where their farmland was, the people were becoming progressively more agitated about their situation.

The stress threw them into open conflict with city leaders, even among themselves. Each had a different impression of their plight, and each had a different answer as to how to resolve it.

Gesuta argued with her husband, Hemestra argued with her own, and when people gathered in the market with its dwindling foodstuffs, they complained about their situation the next day, and the next. Water was not a problem since they still controlled the harbor, and the people had adapted to growing some small edible plants in the earth around their homes. There would be no more meat since the livestock had been exhausted by then, and precious little seafood, limited to that which drifted into their harbor from the open sea.

Nicostros was a skilled blacksmith and he continued making weapons and tools during the siege with the supplies of metal that were still available. He was Hemestra's husband and she was reassured that, with his profession, as long as there was war there would always be a need for his services.

Dariana stood over her stand at the fish market. She haggled over price with the best of them, prices that had gone up in the previous year as supplies had been reduced by the siege. Temula, her daughter, helped out but, as a mere child, she displayed less anxiety than her mother from day to day. In fact, the little child liked how more people gathered in the market than in the past years; more gathering there to trade news of the siege instead of going out on fishing boats or into the field to work the farms.

Demosthenes was a city elder. He had spent less time in public because the conversation always centered around the threat posed by the Carthaginians, and why Agathocles and the leaders of the city couldn't defeat the siege. His wife, Aloria, was more gregarious and didn't like staying holed up in the large house they occupied on the hill inside the city. Against Demosthenes' advice, she spent much of her day circulating with the other Siracusans, and she was often pulled into general criticism of the government's inaction, which necessarily included criticism of Demosthenes himself.

"Stay out of it," he had warned her.

"What? The market?" was her snide reply. Aloria knew he meant the conversations and critiques of his performance, but she, too, was falling victim to the sustained stress of being bottled up in the city for over two years.

"You know what I mean," he nearly shouted. "I order you to remain in our house and avoid contact with the people of Siracusa."

Aloria didn't bother to vocalize her reply, but she huffed at him to make it clear that she had no intention of following his command.

And, so it went, day after day, with tense debates in the marketplace, arguments in the homes, and divided loyalties throughout the city under siege.

Late that evening, there was a commotion in the square and a sudden increase in the conversation volume. Aloria whispered among her friends in hushed talk, and Demosthenes appeared at the edge of the crowd. He wedged his way into Aloria's circle and pushed her away.

"Go back to your home," he ordered. When she paused, he swiped at her with the back of his hand.

"I said go, and do not come here again!"

Demosthenes was known to be patient and respectful of his wife, so this turn in his behavior convinced the gathering crowd that something was afoot.

"Where are they?" one woman called out, and Demosthenes turned in her direction.

"Where are the boats?" asked another.

"I have seen them," answered Diodorus. He was an armor-clad soldier, and he stepped into the circle of the growing crowd.

"There are no boats," declared Demosthenes. "We have kept the Carthaginian boats out. See for yourself," he said, pointing his right hand in the general direction of the harbor.

"Those are not the boats we're talking about," came a retort from the crowd.

Demosthenes stood silent for a moment, glaring at the crowd, trying to conjure up his next words.

"They've burned our boats down to the water's edge," came another shout from the crowd.

Word had come to the city leaders that Agathocles's boats were attacked on their voyage to Carthage and had all been burned. Hamilcar had their charred hulls towed back to Siracusa and pushed them into the harbor, warning the city's resistance that this is what will become of Siracusa if they didn't surrender.

"I have seen them," repeated the soldier. "I have been to the harbor. The boats we sent to raid Carthage have been destroyed, and all we have left are the burned planks that once carried our brave soldiers across the sea."

Just then, a messenger came for Demosthenes.

"Antander calls you, sire."

Antander was the brother of their king, Agathocles.

———

The Siracusan assembly of elders had gathered by the time Demosthenes arrived. He was the last to enter the room where the men sat in a circle around Antander. It was an eerie scene. Demosthenes noted that although there a hush over the group, there were avid arguments and finger-pointing going on in small groups of three and four men.

Antander was biding his time and letting the men exhaust their debates. When Demosthenes stepped up to him, the king's brother called for silence.

"There is a man who wants us to surrender," he began.

At first, Demosthenes thought Antander had called him up to accuse him.

"But, no, sire..." he protested. But all the elders in the room knew that it would not be Demosthenes.

They looked from right to left, although with some reservation because they each believed that Antander could be calling them out, having shared the same idea.

"Constantus," Antander finally said, and he glared at the man. "Why would you have us surrender?"

Constantus was not anxious to enter the argument, and less anxious to be pointed out as the leader of the plan to surrender to the Carthaginians.

"We are all doomed," he said at last. "We are under siege, our food is running out, and our army was sent on a mission that killed them all and destroyed our navy. What do we have left to protect? If you say our lives, then I say our lives can only be protected by letting Hamilcar take the town."

"Whose lives are you referring to?" asked Demosthenes. "Your own? Your family? Your friends?"

Constantus was slow to respond.

"Your friends might be spared by Hamilcar, but you will not be. And if you wife is spared it is only because Hamilcar's men would like to use her for their pleasure before throwing her defiled body off the cliff to the rocks below."

"Take him," Antander said, indicating to the soldiers attending the assembly that they should arrest Constantus.

When the man had been taken from the chamber, Antander restored order.

"There will be no surrender."

———

Late that night, another messenger came to Demosthenes, calling him to go see Antander, even in the dark hours before the sun came up.

"It is urgent," said the messenger, who then turned and hurried out of Demosthenes's home.

When he arrived at Antander's place, he was let in by a dark-skinned slave. Demosthenes knew this man; he had been captured in a previous invasion of Africa and was one of many brought back to Siracusa to serve out their lives in captivity.

"They are preparing to storm the walls again," said Antander. "I have word from our comamnders that they have seen the dirty Punics massing in the regions near our city."

"What should we do?" Demosthenes had his own ideas, but in this hierarchical society, you always waited for the highest bred to offer an opinion first.

"I have already done it. I have sent our soldiers to Euralys to defend it first."

Euralys was a fortress west of Sircusa and an important first line of defense against attack by land forces. Demosthenes knew that the men sent there would probably die, but their death would inflict losses on the other side and possibly slow the Carthaginians enough to have them retreat.

"There will be many soldiers and archers, even some of the new catapults to hurl stones at the invaders. They will be repulsed," said the king's brother.

Antander spoke with the confidence of a leader; but as Demosthenes sometimes thought, a clueless leader. He knew that the Carthaginians had brought ten times the soldiers and archers that Siracusa had at their disposal. Winning against that enemy would require help from the gods.

To that end, Demosthenes excused himself and prepared to return home and offer tidings to the gods.

The Carthaginian forces threw themselves at Euralys and killed many of the Siracusan soldiers, but they also sustained heavy losses themselves. After the fortress was taken, Hamilcar moved his men forward to storm the walls of the city itself.

Perhaps it was Demosthenes's offering to the gods, but Hamilcar's first assault on the walls of Siracusa failed. Sensing the loss of life and capital, and now worried from the messages coming from Carthage about Agathocles' attack there, Hamilcar siphoned off thousands of his own soldiers to return to Africa to defend their homeland. But he remained to continue his assault on Euralys. It would prove to be a defining moment, and a critical mistake.

Late one night, Hamilcar – aided by a Siracusan traitor, Deinocrates – attacked the city once again. The access road was narrow and various tribes of locals along the way were mistaken for Siracusan forces. When the survivors of Euralys noticed the new attack, they mounted an offensive that appeared, in the darkness, to be much stronger than it was.

Thinking that they were overmatched, the Carthaginians panicked and fell into disarray. Hamilcar proudly took his stand but was captured.

The following day, the Carthaginian general was tortured by the city's residents, and then executed. Despite the siege and the patience it required, the invading forces were repelled by this victory and Siracusa stood.

265 B.C.E.

ROMAN CITIES IN SICILY

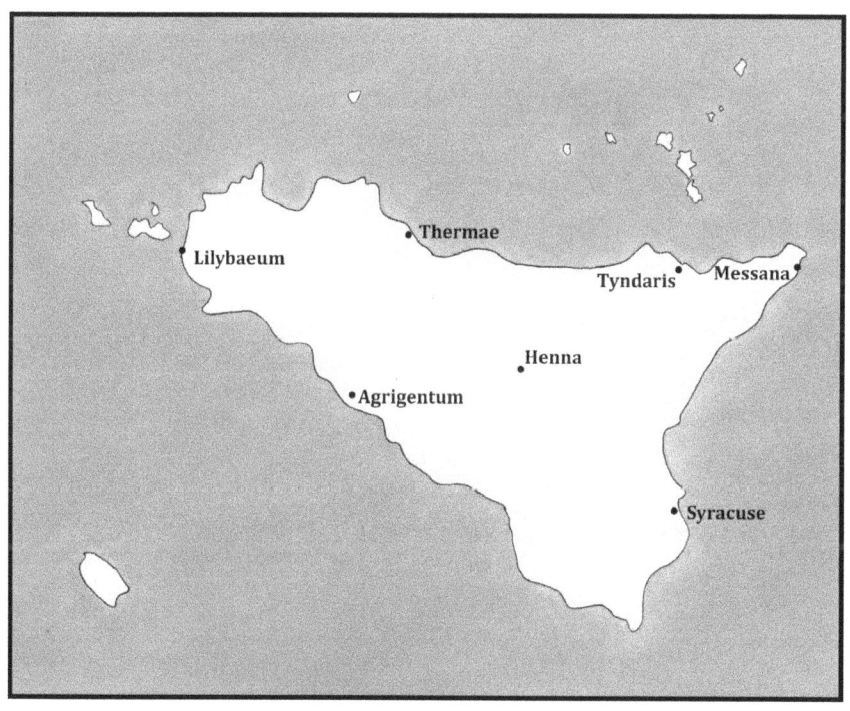

265 B.C.E.

CARTHAGINIANS IN SICILY

,

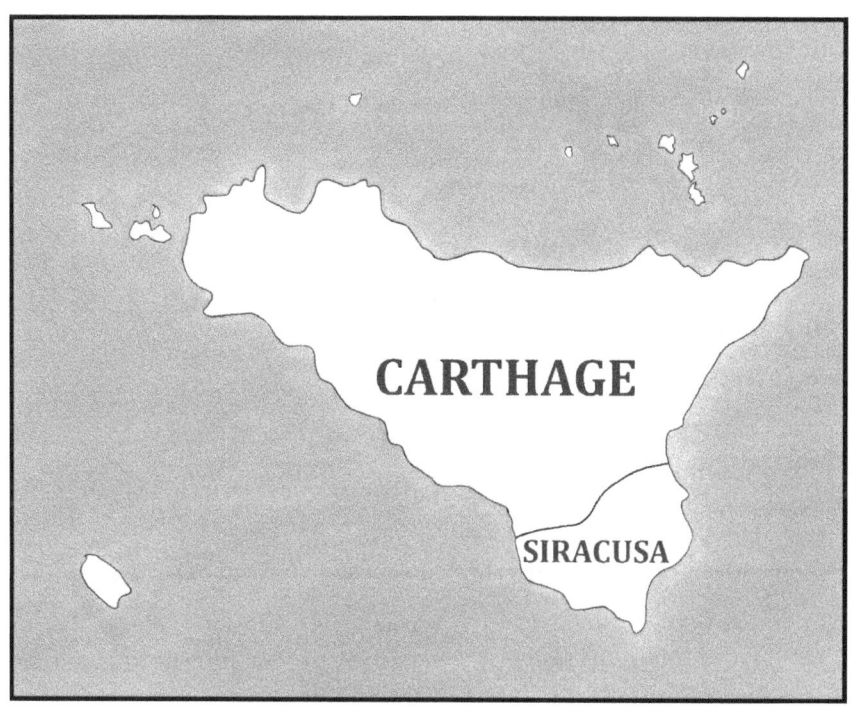

250 B.C.E.

MESSANA

ANTILIUS HAD HIS RIGHT FOOT PROPPED UP ON THE PLATFORM IN the bow of the trireme. He felt the gentle rolling of the ship as it floated over each wave, and he heard the slap of the oars as they splashed into the water in rhythm from all three levels of the ship. He let out a sigh, wondered about his wife and children at home, and returned his attention to the work at hand.

Antilius commanded this Roman trireme. They had embarked from Latium, the region south of Rome, to engage the Carthaginians who controlled the port of Messana on Trinacrium, the Roman's name for Sikania. Other boats led by Roman generals Stario and Philippus were following closely and, together with smaller, swifter craft, they represented the leading edge of another Roman assault on the Carthaginian control of the island.

This war between Carthage and Rome was waged for control of the Mediterranean Sea. Unfortunately for the Romans, it was being fought on the open seas, where they were short on experience and weapons. The Romans had been conducting a successful campaign to spread their power throughout the peninsula of Italy, in southern Europe, and even across parts of the eastern Mediterranean region, but these conquests were achieved with land forces. Here, as he sailed to Messana, Antilius wondered how he was going to win a naval war like none he had ever fought before. There would be occasional conflict on the shores of Trinacrium as well as on the "toe" of the Italian peninsula and also on the shores of Libya and Carthage, but he knew that victory must be claimed on the high seas before control of the Mediterranean would be in his hands.

The Mamertines of Messana had been hired as mercenaries by Agathocles, who decades earlier proclaimed himself King of Siracusa but had designs on also controlling the critical port city of Messana. The mercenaries traded the tranquility of their home in Campania for excitement, war, and bloodshed, happily accepting the offer of Agathocles to go into battle and attack the port city for the king who, nevertheless, remained in his southern city of Siracusa. He died before the Mamertines could capture Messana, and his death left them unemployed and lacking sufficient excitement to keep them from rioting amongst themselves. To satisfy their various hungers, the Mamertines went anyway to Messana and allied themselves with the Carthaginians who controlled the city at that time. In doing so, this new band of invaders transferred their allegiance to Carthage while in Messana. Not content in any peaceful situation for very long, the Mamertines once again rioted, killing the male inhabitants of Messana and dividing up their women and property among themselves.

Hiero II, then the dictator of Siracusa, watched the goings on in the northern region with great interest. He drew up an army, led them to the outskirts of Messana, and engaged the Mamertines for control of northeastern Sicily. The initial battle took place when Hiero II threw his first line of soldiers at the enemy, knowing that they would be overcome and probably slain by the merciless Mamertines. But Hiero II had bigger plans, and using these castaway soldiers allowed him to sap the enemy's resources and will. When the armies met again in open field battle, the Siracusans easily conquered the faithless Mamertines, who then slinked back to the confines of Messana for protection.

Sensing his opportunity, Hiero II pushed forward toward Messana but, by then, the Mamertines had been reinforced by Carthaginians who had been at war with the Siracusans for a very long time. When Hiero's army paused in an attempt to assess the strength of the Carthaginian force, the Mamertines turned on their own protectors – the Carthaginians – and asked for help from the growing Roman army that was just now descending the peninsula and conquering all in its wake. With constant fighting and switching of allegiances between these warring parties, control of the eastern half of the island was constantly in flux.

Antilius was part of a garrison of Roman soldiers sent to support the Mamertines in Messana. It was, from the first, an odd partnership. The Mamertines had forsaken their alliance with Carthage in favor of Rome, and Rome had demurred initially, not wanting to antagonize the Carthaginians.

Meanwhile, the Siracusans under Hiero II sensed an advantage. Carthage was enraged by the Mamertine betrayal and Rome's entrance in a wartime alliance, so Hiero chose to ally Siracusa with his long-time enemy, Carthage.

"All up," called Antilius as the trireme he commanded approached the shores of Trinacrium.

"All up," he called out again, standing stoutly on the prow of the boat and waving his arm so that Stario and Philippus could see his intent. He was commanding the oarsmen on the three levels of the trireme to lift their oars and idle in the water, bringing the fleet to a halt just outside of Messana. From there, he would send scouting boats ashore and assess the situation before committing his warships to an unknown environment.

The small boats were let down and the sailors pulled against the oars to bring them around and away from the trireme.

"Off," Antilius commanded, the one-word call to lower the sail. When the boom of his ship was lowered and the sail furled, the other boats followed suit.

The triad of warships idled in the waters off the port of Messana until nightfall. The scout boats were under strict orders to return before dark because, if they stayed overnight, they could be taken by the enemy without Antilius knowing their fate or the meaning of their loss. If they returned, he could believe their report; if their return waited until morning, it could be that they were being used as captives and informants for the enemy on the shore.

As the sun set off the water line in the far distance, small boats could be seen in the soft light of the lanterns hung from their bow. They were seen plying the waters back to Antilius's fleet. Once the men were lifted back onto the ship's deck, they made their report.

"Kiokis, the Mamertine leader, welcomes you, my lord. He sends warm wishes from his city, Messana, from the soldiers that he commands there, and says that these soldiers would be under your command. He wishes to meet with you when morning comes."

Antilius took this news well. It is what he expected, and the tone seemed appropriate. He would be willing to meet with this Kiokis on the next day.

The fleet of Roman triremes spent the night bobbing on the waters just beyond the Strait of Messana. The men were comfortable aboard ship, in circumstances they had come to appreciate but, as soldiers of the land, they longed for solid earth under their feet.

In the morning, Stario rowed over to Antilius's boat to join him on the landing party. It would be better to show that two Roman commanders were there to greet the Mamertines while letting them know that other skilled and brave commanders stood watch on the ships left on the waves.

Kiokis offered Antilius control of his army if he would commit Rome to protecting the city of Messana from encroachment by Hiero II and their new ally, the Carthaginians.

"This city is now a Roman colony," declared Antilius, "and as such it is under our protection. We will ensure that your people and possessions are not compromised by the barbarians from the south."

They remained in Messana several days before hostilities broke out. As superior sailors, Carthage wanted to fight the battle on the open seas, which was not usual for the Siracusans from the southern tip of Trinacrium. However, Antilius debated engaging the enemy on their terms. The Roman army was a land force. It had few ships, despite the triremes that he brought down to Messana. And their military strategies were based on land fighting. He had to consider a way to fight the Carthaginians on land, or how to simulate fighting them on land.

Instead of ramming and maneuvering on the high seas for advantage – which Antilius was certain would give the advantage to the enemy, Antilius devised a strategy that would force the ships to couple, or be strung together, to ensure a pitched battle in hand-to-hand combat.

He had discussed this strategy before leaving Italy and an inventor there had outfitted his vessels with a *corvus*, a wooden bridge that was hinged so that it could swing horizontally out from the Roman boat toward an attacking ship. The *corvus* came with a spike on the outside swinging edge which, when the bridge was dropped suddenly on the deck of the other boat, would impale itself in the wooden planks. In this way, the Roman soldiers-turned-sailors could revert to fighting face-to-face, as they would do in a land battle.

Antilius and his other commanders had not tried the device yet, at least not on an enemy warship, so this would be their first true test.

Days went by and the soldiers continued training on shore. During that time, they spent some hours each day swinging the *corvus* back and forth, testing its features and learning not to drop the weight of the heavy wooden apparatus onto their own deck. There it would remain impaled on their own vessel and lost to the battle.

When the sea war began, the Carthaginian navy rightly expected to handle the novice Romans in strategy and tactics. At first, they were successful in turning Roman ships about, ramming them with the armored prows of their boats, and grappling onto the Roman vessels that they chose to board. The battles that stretched out over days and weeks went poorly for the Roman forces.

When the seas were calm, however, and the Roman soldiers had gained their sea legs, their movements were more fluid. They had come to understand the Carthaginians' strategy and how to counteract it. But foremost in the change of tide for the battles was the use of the *corvus*. With it, instead of fending off the Carthaginian attack by grappling, the Romans could sail beside the enemy vessel and execute the swinging motion of the device. At first, the Carthaginian navy didn't quite know how to handle this new problem. Unlike their grappling, which was a loose, rope-led connection, the Roman device locked the two ships together in a death-grip and was wide enough for Romans armed with lances to sprint across the bridge onto the Carthaginian boats.

Antilius had fought through the early battles before ordering the use of the *corvus*. Philippus had been calling for it, as his ship suffered damage equal to that which doomed the smaller Roman and Mamertine craft in the waters, and he wanted to engage the enemy face to face. When Antilius authorized the deployment of the *corvus*, Philippus gave out an order that sounded more like a primal scream.

"Load!" he shouted to his men. "Load and board!" He wanted the *corvus* swung out and dropped onto the nearest Carthaginian craft, and he called for boarding before the device was even in place. Philippus had earned his reputation in the bloody battles of southern Italy, charging into the teeth of the enemy, and grappling with them in mortal combat. He had never left it to his men to wage the battle; Philippus had always been in the vanguard, hand held high, brandishing his infamous shiny half-sword that was called *La Macchina* by his army – the machine by which their leader sent the enemy to hell.

So, when the *corvus* of his great trireme swung out from the ship, Philippus himself was standing on the first step of the bridge, ready to charge as soon as the spike bit into the deck of the Carthaginian vessel. With a thunk and the cracking sound of deck boards shattering under its weight, Philippus once again raised *La Macchina* above his head and leaped upon the bridge and, in one bound, onto the enemy ship. Once there, his practiced slashing motions cut through the unprepared Carthaginian sailors. They had grappled onto their adversary's vessels before, but their tactics involved cutting sails and puncturing the hulls of the ships they fought. They were not accustomed to the almost maniacal plunging attack of this madman.

Carthaginians were cut to pieces, some tossed overboard into the flames that covered the water from burning sails, and some were run through with the lances of Philippus's men. The engagement quickly turned into a rout, and as soon as his men could disengage the *corvus*, the captain went in search of another enemy vessel to destroy.

218 B.C.E.

SECOND PUNIC WAR

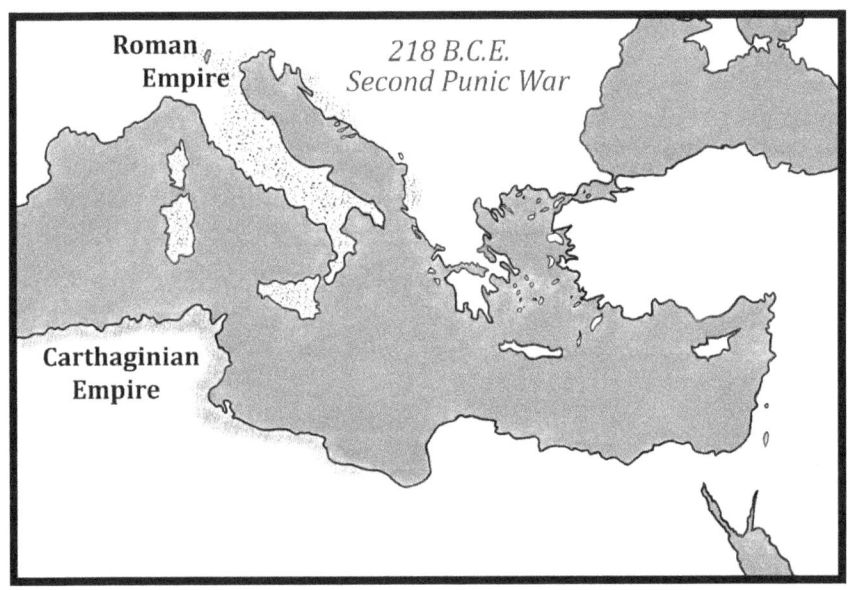

213 B.C.E.

ENNA

The people stood on the parapets of their city in Enna, built on this high plateau for security. The city had been there for many generations, and the Ennaeans felt safe from the wars being fought in the fields below them and the port cities on the long coastline of their country, Trinacrium.

They had come to accept the Roman name for their country but the Ennaeans were still reluctant to yield to the empire of Rome. Gulian, the primary city elder, cautioned against surrender. He knew that many of the cities on his island had succumbed and pledged their loyalty to Carthage, and he feared that the same would happen to his beloved city. Pinarius, the governor of Enna, was a coward and Gulian knew that he must marshall the forces of his local townsmen to foreswear allegiance to Rome, maintaining their independence from the assault the Roman Republic was perpetrating across his country.

Enna was uniquely safe from the hostilities that waged below. Romans had fought Carthaginians for many years by this time, and Gulian knew that the first engagement that resulted in Rome's victory of Carthage on the seas around Trinacrium could be used as a starting point for an extended expedition into the interior of the island. Gulian met with his advisor, Laurentiis, to discuss plans to thwart the Roman march on Enna.

"They are here, among us," he said.

"Not among us, not yet," answered Laurentiis. "The Romans have won over many cities that surround Enna and will continue with their plans. But our city is safe. Our ancestors built this city upon the mountain, we are above the fields and hard to reach."

"We come up and down, when we farm the fields below," Gulian cautioned.

"True, but the paths are narrow," Laurentiis said, then he laughed. "Even our farmers complain that the paths up to Enna are too hard to manage."

"So, we grow our crops up here," Gulian noted. "On the plateau."

"Exactly. And this is why we will be able to continue to feed our people. There is nothing to worry about. We Ennaeans are Roman subjects, and the soldiers housed among us will protect us from the Carthaginian hordes who are threatening the valley below us."

"You do not fear treason?"

"Why treason?" Laurentiis asked. "Do you think any of our people would go to the enemy? We are Roman..."

"Yes," interrupted Gulian, "but we are not really Roman. We have accepted their rule and sought their protection. And we hope that the Romans themselves will not turn on us."

Laurentiis considered the comment, shrugged his shoulders, and moved on.

The people of the city of Enna, like Gulian, feared that the defection of citizens and cities surrounding them in Trinacrium would bolt from Roman rule and side with the Carthaginians. Because of their isolated status on the top of this plateau, the Ennaeans did not have enough contact with their neighboring settlements to know the reasons for them to transfer their loyalty to the people from the great continent to the south. And yet, this same separation made them wonder whether they were not in error, themselves, and whether the nearby cities and towns had more information about the course of the hostilities.

In these days, the safest route was to follow the most potent party. If that was your own, so be it. If not, changing sides to stay alive was a proper alternative.

Later in the evening, Gulian and Laurentiis were called to visit Pinarius. The governor had been contemplating the same things and wanted to know what his council elders thought.

"We are safe," Laurentiis began, repeating the reassurances that he had given his friend, Gulian.

"But the towns below, even Morgantina – and I have information from my family living there – have switched sides to Carthage."

"We have a Roman garrison here," cautioned Gulian. "Do you really think that we would – that we could – throw the city to Carthage?"

Pinarius was quiet for a moment, then he walked across the wide room toward the large oak table that was set in the open terrazza. He approached the dining table that his wife, Assentia, has just cleared and set with a wine bottle and three silver cups.

Pouring a full cup of wine for himself, he drained it easily. Then Pinarius stood looking out on the city of Enna, the civilization that he was responsible for, and which he had lost hope of keeping.

Turning toward his visitors, Pinarius lifted the bottle in a sign of offering.

Gulian and Laurentiis accepted the unspoken gesture and approached the table. They, too, poured generous portions of the deeply colored red wine for themselves, drained their cups and looked out upon Enna. For a moment longer, the three men were silent.

"What do you believe?" asked Pinarius.

The two men didn't know what the question really meant. Was the governor asking what they believed from the gods, what they believed as men who led the Ennaeans, or what they believed their chances were of surviving the war raging between the Roman legions and the Carthaginian forces below.

"The people of Enna don't want to fight a war that they didn't start," offered Gulian. "They will fight for their families, but it is not clear to them why they should side with the Romans or the Punics."

"Perhaps, with the protection of the Romans, we can wait it out," suggested Laurentiis.

"Wars go on for many years," came the voice of Assentia, as she reentered the room. "Men kill men, and they rape women. That's what they do. Why should we think the conflict we have right now would not go on longer than we can survive?"

Pinarius and his two visitors had turned to listen to the words of the governor's wife. She held extreme views, pessimistic views that suggested that the war would claim many Ennaeans regardless of what action they took. The men preferred to look for action, for solutions, although in their hearts they knew that fighting men seldom knew when to stand down, and commanding generals were always looking for another battle to fight.

After finishing off another bottle of the governor's wine – it was better than they were accustomed to – Gulian and Laurentiis excused themselves and returned to the main piazza in Enna.

"Do you really think the Ennaeans will stand and fight?" asked Gulian.

"I didn't say they would stand and fight. I said I didn't expect them to change sides. Right now, we're on the side of Rome. That's fine with me. If we had been on the side of Carthage, that would have been fine with me also."

"I worry about Assentia," Gulian continued.

"Assentia? She's a woman!" replied Laurentiis.

At first, Gulian was surprised that his friend would dismiss the governor's wife so casually. Then he laughed, realizing that Laurentiis was being facetious.

"Yes, I know," Gulian said, laughing and casting his gaze down to the ground. "The women don't tell us what to do, do they?"

Pinarius didn't sleep well that night. He had dreams that bordered on nightmares. Most people of this time were convinced that dreams foretold soon-to-be realized experiences, and high-ranking officials believed in the interpretation of dreams the most. Pinarius, like his fellow governors or tyrants, was certain that a dream was a message from the gods, and that the thoughts and actions that were displayed in his state of sleep were warnings about the future.

Assentia had tossed and turned with her husband's restless sleep all night, but then Pinarius finally relaxed, so did she. In the middle of the night, he fell into a deep sleep.

It was just before dawn when he shot into a sitting position, eyes full wide, and his consciousness on high alert. He was in that twilight between sleep and wakefulness when every image of his subconscious seemed abundantly real to his conscious mind.

"Fire! Terror!" he uttered. It came out as a silent scream, so terrifying that Pinarius's voice couldn't even raise its volume, in fear of its relevance.

It took only a moment for Assentia to awake; seeing her husband bolt upright in their bed set her nerves on edge. But she was quicker to consciousness than he was.

"You're destroying Enna," she whined. "This is your city and you're waiting idly by while the Punics attack our neighbors."

Pinarius was still sitting paralyzed in his half-conscious state.

"If you don't act, all will be lost," she continued. "You're the governor," she said, as if her husband was in a state that would allow him to comprehend her every statement.

"You know what they do with governors, don't you?" she said, rhetorically. "They pitch them over the walls. And you know what they do with governors' wives, don't you?"

By that point, Pinarius's dreams were beginning to fade and all he could focus on were Assentia's words.

"Yes, I know," he replied.

But he noticed a change in Assentia's voice when she indicated a woman's peril at the hands of the enemy. Pinarius had not been an attentive lover for some time, and he wondered whether his wife – who was still young and adorned with the jewels that were the result of his governorship – would be in search of another man to please her. Even an enemy soldier.

Pinarius swatted his arm at her in anger, although he had no obvious reason to do so. Then he rose from their bed and wandered toward the table in the great room where a half-empty bottle of wine remained.

———

In the morning, Pinarius was walking through the piazza in Enna when he realized that the crowd around him was quiet. It was like a silent wave that followed him through the throngs. There was conversation murmured ahead of his path, in small clutches of citizens quietly debating their security, and there were whispered conversations behind him as he moved forward.

"It is good to see you, sire," said one man. "How have the gods treated you?"

This was a not uncommon phrase among the people. They believed the gods controlled their lives and dictated their future; in fact, the awareness of fate was a routine feature of their lives. When a man asked his governor how the gods had treated him, he was truly interested in the communication between the heavens and earth, and whether the deities still favored their governor and, therefore, the people of Enna.

"Well, thank you. They have treated me well," said Pinarius, although the gut-level fear that his dreams inspired was still gnawing at him.

"Arturus," the governor said with delight. "How are you today?"

Pinarius had spotted the Roman commander in the square and wanted to shift his attention from the common Ennaean man who questioned him to the one who ruled the military garrison in the town.

"I am well," sire, replied Arturus.

The Roman soldiers had served easy duty in Enna. There was little expected of them except to maintain the peace. And, in a city built upon a high mountain such as Enna, with little real concern of attack by outsiders, Arturus's men had come to think of this assignment as a vacation.

"It is good, no?" asked Pinarius.

Arturus had come to understand the governor and his insecurities. Pinarius was constantly worried about the situation in his city. But Arturus also understood that the governor's concerns were less with the daily security of the Ennaeans and more with the thing his wife called out: the possibility that Pinarius himself would be pitched over the ramparts to be shattered on the rocks below.

In fact, Arturus had come to think of that more often, and also to think of the kind of man the governor's wife would need when the old man was gone.

"It is good," was Arturus's simple reply.

"The Romans are well fed, yes?"

"Of course," Arturus said. Of course, his soldiers would be well fed. They're Romans. And if the Ennaeans – or any other conquered citizens – didn't accommodate the legions of soldiers, the Romans would simply take what they wanted.

Later that evening, Pinarius called Gulian and Laurentiis to his home again to discuss the future of Enna. He wanted to know whether these men wanted to remain with Rome, or switch sides to Carthage.

"We spoke of this last evening," said Gulian. "Why are you not convinced?"

In fact, Pinarius was testing these city leaders. He feared that someone in Enna would betray him and turn the entire city over to the Carthaginians. So, he pestered Gulian and Laurentiis with questions.

"Enna is mine, and you serve me," he said.

Gulian and Laurentiis nodded ascent.

"And Enna is garrisoned to Roman troops."

Again, they nodded.

"And if the Punics try to take the town...well, we are well equipped to put them off, no?"

"Enna will not fall," said Gulian, "unless it is betrayed from within."

This conversation went on deep into the night and, as the wine bottles were emptied, the fear in Pinarius heart rose equal to the confidence in the minds of Gulian and Laurentiis. When the men tired of the two-sided debate, they retired to their own homes.

———

On the next day, Pinarius called Arturus to his home. The Roman commander called at the door and was greeted by Assentia. She lowered her eyes and smiled demurely at the handsome man at her door.

The subtle flirtation was missed by Pinarius who was absorbed in his thoughts about Enna, his security, and what he should do to avoid a Carthaginian attack.

"I want your advice," he asked Arturus, as the general stepped into the house.

"On what, sire?" came the reply, but Arturus's voice didn't hold the respect that the term 'sire' intended.

"I believe Enna will fall," Pinarius told the Roman.

"And you believe this, why?"

"If you believe that," Asssentia said, interrupting the men's conversation, "you had better make provisions for your wife." At that she turned her gaze toward Arturus.

Pinarius was not dissuaded by her comment, and he continued.

"If we are to fall, how can you Romans help us?"

Arturus considered the request and thought it odd. When an armed commander with trained soldiers under his lead is asked what he can do to help someone, his immediate thought is to sweep the man from control and take all that he has. Smiling slyly, Arturus returned Assentia's gaze, and considered that very reply to Pinarius.

"I will take care of this," he told Pinarius. And, then, pondering his next move, he added this.

"I want to address all Ennaeans. Could you gather them in the theatre in the center of Enna, so that I can tell them what I need for them to do?"

"Yes," said Pinarius. I will arrange for that this afternoon. They will be pleased to hear from their protector."

And the word went out. Pinarius instructed all of the people of Enna to assemble in the theatre to hear from Arturus, exalted leader of the Roman troops quartered in their town. At sunset, the churches, homes, and marketplace were emptied, as streams of people walked toward the assembly point. Great talk permeated their congregation as so many of the Ennaeans had wondered how the struggles in the valleys that surrounded the city would affect them.

There was a general hum among the people assembled in the theatre that evening. Then, Arturus strode into the center of the arena as his soldiers guarded the perimeter of the building. He invited Pinarius into the spotlight with him, then nodded to Assentia in the first row of people gathered there. Arturus raised his right hand, and then clenched his fist.

With this gesture, the armed soldiers that had encircled the theatre fell upon the people sitting there. First, they slew all the men and any women who resisted their efforts. Then they cut down the young boys and tossed the young girls into the pit in the center of the theatre to be captured by another squadron of soldiers waiting for the pubescent girls to be delivered.

Their blood was shed and hundreds of Ennaeans were slaughtered. Assentia was grabbed by two Roman soldiers and dragged out of the arena to safety. She watched over her shoulder as Arturus drew a sharpened blade across Pinarius's throat.

By nightfall, it was over. Enna had already been under the control of the Roman legion that had occupied it, but now it was fully in its command.

JULY 2018
CAFÉ AMADEO

"There were three," Vito said, even before I had sat down.

"Three what?"

"Wars."

I immediately thought of the Punic Wars, of which there were three, and the Servile Wars, of which there were three, but I didn't know where Vito was going with this.

"What wars?"

Vito sat back into the chair. His slight build and height always reminded me a gray-haired gnome as he settled back into the cushion of his chair. But then he smiled and nodded, and I knew it was time to begin.

"They're called the Sicilian Wars, and they took up most of the Fifth and Fourth centuries B.C."

"These were not related to the battles with the Carthaginians, or with the enslavement by Rome's victors, were they?" I asked.

"Well, a bit. The Punic Wars pitted Carthage's power at home and on the island of Sicily against a growing threat from the Roman expeditions. They occurred later, in the Third and Second centuries B.C. We'll talk about that in due time.

"The Sicilian Wars came first, after Carthage had taken control of much of the island and matched the Carthaginians against the Greco-Sicilian cities in the east. At stake was not only the island, but control of the western Mediterranean."

"Isn't that what the battle of Himera was about?"

"*Esattumente.* That was the first, about 480 B.C."

"The first what?"

"The First Sicilian War!"

"Sorry, but there are so many wars that I'm getting confused."

Vito nodded with an understanding gesture.

"*Sì*, you are so right. There were so many wars in my country that everyone gets confused. In fact, it was around the Fifth Century B.C. that the invasions and counter-thrusts began in earnest."

"And after the First Sicilian War, there were more?" I asked.

"There were more. Now that we look back on this, we call them the First, Second, and Third Sicilian Wars. They were fought between the Greeks in the east and Carthage in the west of Sicily. But the combatants didn't know that the struggle to control Himera – way back in 480 B.C. and won by the Greeks – would still be contested in 415 or 410 B.C. So, they didn't know it was the 'first' Sicilian War."

"What of the second?"

"We need to set the stage," Vito intoned, then sipped from his coffee and bit off some of the *cantucci*.

"From 480 B.C. until about 415 B.C., the Greeks spread their influence around the island, moving westward and setting up colonies and trading posts on the northern and southern coastlines, all the while pushing the Carthaginians back into a smaller and smaller piece of the island along the western edge. Carthage was busy building their outposts in North Africa and developing successful agriculture in the fertile edge of that continent. They hadn't given up on winning territory in Sicily, but they took the Greek aggression in stride. At least, that was how it appeared.

"The Carthaginians were also waiting. Perhaps they could tell that the various segments of the Greek community were at odds..."

"Why is that?" I said, interrupting Vito, realizing that I was going to lose the thread if I didn't stay up with the constantly changing alliances and confrontations.

Vito only smiled, and I could tell from the twinkle in his eye that he was about to tell me.

"The Greeks who came to Sicily represented – for the most part – two types. The Ionian Greeks had fostered good relations with the indigenous Elymi and occupied Segesta. The Dorian Greeks occupied Selinus, and the two were often at odds with each other."

"Why?"

"We don't have much specific information, but it seemed to come mostly from the fight for land. Around 416 B.C., the Selinians expanded toward Segesta, ultimately defeating the Segestans in open conflict. I suppose that victory wasn't enough to convince the Segestans to stand down, because another war broke out between the cities in 411 B.C., and once again Selinus was victorious. Not to be outdone, the leaders in Segesta called in the Carthaginians and, with their help in 410 B.C., drove the Selinians from their city and reclaimed the land.

"Meanwhile, you've got the Athenians attacking Siracusa in 413 B.C...."

"Yes, I remember that. The Athenian force was defeated."

"*Certu*, and this convinced the Siracusans that they were strong enough to fight for, and win, new territory to the west.

"So, back out west, Hannibal Mago brought his army from Carthage to fight on the side of the Segestans in 409 B.C. Some historians call this the Carthaginian Invasion – which, in a sense, it was – but the books generally refer to this as the Second Sicilian War. Hannibal Mago and his massive force defeated Selinus. He then marched on Himera and destroyed it. Here's where it gets interesting.

"The emboldened Siracusans went to defend Himera and keep it in Greek hands, but the Carthaginian invasion was too strong. They pushed the Siracusan force back, claimed Himera, and burned it down again. This signaled the beginning of Carthaginian expansion throughout Sicily.

"Battles raged for many years before, ultimately, Carthaginian general Himilco captured Akragas, then Gela, Camarina, and other cities previously controlled by the Siracusans. In fact, Himilco's conquests grew so much that he continually threatened Siracuse itself. By 398 B.C., Carthage's dominion of Sicily was at its peak.

"All this fighting – including forces from North Africa, mainland Greece, indigenous Sicilians, and the immigrants from Carthage and the Greek colonies – were just a clue to what would ensue on this island."

"Was that the Second Sicilian War?" I asked.

"Yes. It was the beginning of a nearly century-long fight that would shape the political and military contours of our country and lead to the Punic Wars."

"How so?"

"Remember, the Sicilian Wars were mainly fought between the Greeks and Carthaginians," Vito explained. "The Punic Wars were fought later, between the Carthaginians and the new Roman Republic."

I nodded.

"So," he continued, "who do you think won the Sicilian Wars for control of the island?"

"It had to be Carthage, the last army standing to contest with Rome for control of Sicily."

Vito gave me an approving nod.

"That's how you learn history, by connecting the dots, not memorizing dates," he concluded. Then he lifted his espresso cup to his lips and drained it. As Vito stood to go, he tipped his hat to me, then scooped up two more *cantucci* before leaving.

———

The next time we met, Vito was quick with a joke.

"It's a good thing Antander didn't cave in to the threat and surrender Siracusa," he began before I could even sit down. "Those were Hamilcar's boats that he put to the torch, burning the old craft to the waterline and pretending that he had conquered Agathocles's party and destroyed their navy.

"In fact, Agathocles prevailed and returned to Sicily a victor.

"Punics," Vito said, as I slid into the chair beside him.

By now, I was able to laugh. I was still highly impressed with his knowledge and grasp of history, but I was no longer in awe of him. Well, that might not be entirely true. I was still in awe of Vito, but I was no longer afraid of him.

So, I laughed.

"Punics," I replied, copying his manner of using single words to introduce new topics.

"How long did that label stick?" I asked.

"I don't know. When did it begin?" came his reply. Frankly, I hated it when someone answered a question with a question, but I was willing to give Vito some leeway.

"I don't know," I began, then chided him. "That's what you're here for."

For a second, I wondered if I hadn't violated my role. I suddenly realized that I had become too familiar with Vito and might have ventured into a space that wasn't appropriate. But then he smiled.

"Punic is the Roman term – *punicus* – the Latin word for Phoenician," he began. "The Phoenicians were the first to sail from the eastern part of the Mediterranean – at least the first to make something of their voyages – and so Punic, the Latin name, came to be known as those who settled in Carthage."

"Why do why call them the Punic Wars?"

"Because it was a war with the Punics!" said Vito. He was so pleased with his own simplication of the answer that he didn't immediately correct and supplement it. But then…

"Of course, the name 'Punic Wars' didn't come about until later historians tried to capture it in a chronological sequence. You see, there was nearly an unbroken string of wars fought on Sicily throughout the last five centuries before Christ. They were so frequent, and so often overlapped, that the people who fought them didn't care what they were named, they just wanted them to end.

"What did people call the war that terrorized the entire world from 1914 until 1917?"

"The Great War, I suppose," I offered. "Some liked to call it the war to end all wars."

"Si, but they didn't call it World War I until there was another war to group it with, World War II. It was the same with the Punic Wars and the Servile Wars. Endless conflict doesn't break nicely along the perforated edges of history. Some run right into the other."

"There was a Third Punic War, right?"

"Si, but by then – it began in 149 B.C. and only lasted three years, not as long as the first two – ummm, where was I?"

I thought it amusing that Vito's rapid-fire recollection of facts could sometimes leave even him confused about what he was saying.

"The Third Punic War. 149 B.C."

"*Corettu*, 149 B.C. Well, by that time, the Romans had successfully marched across Sicily and had taken over most of the island. The Third Punic War was fought mostly in Carthage and along the coast of Africa where the Carthaginians reigned. We Sicilians remained subjects of the Roman army, but otherwise didn't have much of a play in the hostilities going on in Carthage.

"The Romans laid siege to that city and, after vanquishing the enemy, razed the walls of Carthage, annihilated the population, and destroyed most of the evidence that the Punics had even existed."

"What was the cause of the hostilities?" I asked.

"Sometimes, as with many aggressive nations, the causes can be minor, and often overlooked. But not here. Here there are two major reasons. The peace treaty signed between Carthage and Rome at the end of the Second Punic War required that the defeated people had to pay Rome a large amount of money every year for fifty years. That would be starting from about 201 B.C. Carthage did so, grudgingly, but by around 151 B.C., they came to the conclusion that their debt was paid.

"Rome wasn't that easy to convince. They had grown accustomed to receiving this tax from the Carthaginians for longer than most of the Roman people had lived. In other words, they thought the tithe on Carthage was a permanent feature.

"Plus, Carthage had developed successful farmland around its territories – also in Sicily, but I'll get to that later – and as the Roman population grew, they depended more and more on imported food. So, when Carthage decided to stop the payments and resist Rome's insistence on renewing the imports, they were doomed. The Roman Senate, led by Cato the Elder, would not allow Carthage to escape their grip so easily, so they sent an army and navy there to destroy the city and its people and take over the land."

"What of the taxes that Carthage had ended?" I asked. "Destroying the city wouldn't recover that money."

"Sometimes, with aggressive nations like ancient Rome, reason takes a back seat to rage."

———

We finished our coffee and I bid Vito goodbye. I wanted to hurry to the library to research the Punic Wars and get more detail on what he had told me. When I was about halfway there, I remembered that Vito had talked about Sicily as a source of grain for Rome and wished that I had asked him more about that.

I pulled an armful of books from the shelf in the quiet of the library and settled into a chair set askew of a large table. The large window beside the table would provide ample light and, since it was only about ten o'clock in the morning, I knew that I had plenty of opportunity to read and take notes.

Everything that Vito had told me checked out, not that I doubted it. Even his description of the reasons for the Third Punic War were corroborated in the history books I flipped through. I paused and smiled, though, as I recalled what a history professor had once told me.

"History is written by the victors," he said.

Of course, the losers of most wars had too little left after the conflict to influence the narrative that captured the time, so the victors would control the logic and justification – not to mention celebrate the bravery – of the war. So, I looked once more through the books piled at my elbow and tried to take that into consideration when I thought about the defeated Punics, not to mention my own distant ancestors on the island of Sicily and how they would have described this period when the Roman Republic, at its peak strength, was tearing across their country and taking their women, their resources, and their towns.

———

That evening, I returned to the bar where I had seen Vito the other evening. I wandered through the crowd but didn't see him anywhere. Just as I was about the leave, I bumped into Santo and Emilia walking arm in arm.

"*Ciao, Luca,*" Santo said with a smiling voice. "*Comu si senti?*" – how are you? I noticed the Sicilian dialect and tried to respond in kind.

"*Sugnu bonu, grazii,*" I replied, doing my best to say, "I am well."

"You're looking for Vito, no?" said Emilia.

At that, Santo cocked his head toward the bar where a clutch of sports fans – with the elfish Vito in the center – was cheering on the blue-and-yellow-clad soccer team, *Mazara Calcio*.

I approached the little crowd that was elbow to elbow at the bar but couldn't get much closer than the third rank from the front. There was much shouting and jeering at the officials' calls, but during one brief period of relative quiet, I heard:

"Eunus." I had never heard the name before but assumed that it had nothing to do with *futbol*. Besides, I recognized the thin, raspy voice was Vito's. As I moved to another angle to see him clearly, I noticed Vito's clear eyes staring back at me between the broad-shouldered Sicilians around him.

With a slight jab of his right elbow, he parted the crowd much as I would have expected Moses to part the Red Sea and hopped down from the bar stool.

"They're losing," he said. "So, we should have some wine and talk." At that he guided me toward a table at the corner of the narrow patio that surrounded the bar. I don't know how this particular table was empty given the throng of people at the bar, but I suspected by now that Mazara del Vallo reserved many such territories for this honored citizen.

———

"Eunus. Ever hear of him?" Vito asked me as we settled into our chairs.

I shook my head.

"Slaves. I know you've heard of them."

"Well, of course I have. But in what context?"

"As the Romans conquered all the regions of Sicily, North Africa, and other parts of the Mediterranean, as far east as Syria and Lebanon, they enslaved many of the men who survived death on the battlefield. These slaves were mostly employed to do the Romans' bidding where they lived, but it was not unusual for the victors to fill ships below decks with these men. They were strong enough to work as slaves, so they should be strong enough to survive the sea voyage to wherever the Romans wanted to send them."

"Sounds a lot like the American slave trade," I commented.

"Si, and as horrible as the American history is on this topic, they didn't invent slavery, or the shipment of slaves.

"Anyway, the Romans made great use of all these captured people – and although I said men, many women and young girls were enslaved, too. They were put to other purposes, though. The men were assembled and shipped away, and their captors generally tried to mix the groups up so that there was less cultural and social identity in each grouping. Of those who stayed, many worked tirelessly in quarries, salt fields, and in construction of the new arenas and temples the Romans prized so much.

"Many were shipped to other shores, and tens of thousands landed in Sicily."

"Was there a particular reason for that?" I asked.

"Yes, and no. There were probably as many slaves sent to various parts of the world but we, here, count only those who came to Sicily. However, this island was already considered the granary of the Roman Republic, whose fertile fields and mixed soils – including volcanic soil..." and I noticed a grin stretch across his face at the mention of volcanoes, "whose fertile fields could produce millions of baskets of grain that the Romans would ship to their people on the mainland. So, Sicily was a likely place to grow slavery.

"There was another thing happening at the same time. As the Roman armies swept across our country, they claimed lands and then resold huge parcels to rich Romans who were descending on Sicily to claim this valuable real estate. Those who had not yet been enslaved found themselves in a precarious position, evicted by the Roman elite who claimed the land, or forced into labor on the lands they once held as owners. Needless to say, these years of confiscation and enslavement didn't endear the conquering army to the people of Sicily.

The waiter brought a bottle of Nero d'Avola, apparently Vito's favorite since he didn't have to speak up to order it. He set two glass tumblers beside it, and then put a tall glass filled with *grissini* – breadsticks – on the table and walked away.

"The people of Trinacrium, as the Romans had dubbed the island, were not happy. The slaves resisted their condition and the formerly landed farmers resisted the confiscation of their property. There were Romans here to manage things, but there was still a simmering rage among the locals as to what had become of their country.

"You remember Enna, yes?" Vito asked.

I nodded.

"And you will probably recall that Arturus and his men slaughtered the Ennaeans, mostly the men, and enslaved the women."

Again, I nodded.

"His – Arturus's – sudden usurpation of power required that they annihilate the Ennaean men. There was no time to negotiate. So, at the end of the takeover, he found himself in command of a town where there were lots of women and very few men."

"So, what did he do?" I ventured.

"He arranged to have slaves brought into Enna. He needed the labor to continue with the work of the town. So, foreign slaves were imported, including a man named Eunus."

"He's the guy you mentioned when we first sat down. Who was he?"

"He was from Syria, a tall strong man whose physique pointed to him as a natural leader. But he had certain other qualities. He was a poet and magician and he was often called in to entertain the Roman leadership during their festivals and parties. He spoke candidly, spinning tales, even telling apocryphal stories about how the tide would turn, and how the enslaved people would overthrow the rulers. At this, the Romans only laughed."

"Did they think he was crazy?" I asked.

"Perhaps. One of his magic tricks was breathing fire, probably done in much the same way as crazy college kids do today, with lighter fluid and a match, although Eunus would have had to use a simpler combustible liquid. So, yes, the Romans probably thought he was crazy. But, also, I think the soldiers and their commanders were so confident of Roman power that they couldn't believe any yarn about slaves overthrowing their masters.

"Well, the fire that Eunus breathed kindled a flame that would do just that."

SLAVE WARS

134 - 100 B.C.E.

134 B.C.E.

ENNA

He stepped lightly across the narrow edge of the proscenium that separated the entertainers from the Romans who gorged on fattened lamb, roast pig, and wine. Eunus was a foreigner in this land, having been chained and dragged here from his homeland to work in the Romans' quarry. On this particular evening, like many before it, he was made to play a jester, a chattering fool with a mouth full of rhymes and falsehoods, to bring laughter to the lazy leaders who had taken control of Enna many years before.

Eunus stood taller than most of the foreigners who controlled this town and others across Trinacrium. Because of this, he inspired awe in some, but most of the Roman legions considered him nothing more than a tall clown, a simpleton who spouted nonsense in exchange for a leftover hamhock at the end of his performance.

"She calls me to her," he said, beginning another of his soliloquys, "and speaks to me in her soft voice."

The Romans, drunk on too much wine, listened in whenever Eunus told these fantastical stories of his goddess Atargatis. She was the goddess of fertility, much like the Roman Aphrodite, and the poet on the stage claimed to have private conversations with her. Some of the Romans believed him, others did not. But they all enjoyed the imaginative way Eunus would describe his dialogue with the deity.

"She has lighted the way for me," the slave said, as he exhaled mightily and a burst of yellow flame shot from his lips, "and she has called me to her. Soon, I will be lying by her side, cupping her breasts, and breathing in the scent of her body."

His descriptions made the room fall quiet, and the Romans leaned forward on their couches.

"Atargatis whispers in my ears..." but he projected his voice so that his whisper could be heard by all the men present, "...that I am the one, and the black will become white, and the slave shall become master."

He spun halfway around on his heel, swung his arm out again as if beseeching the audience to bear witness.

"She reaches for my hardened weapon and pulls it toward her and brings me down between her legs and holds me until I am satisfied."

The quiet in the room was broken only by a sigh from the back. And Eunus smiled.

"Atargatis tells me that I will rise up from the warmth of her legs and raise up an army. And this army will be my legacy, and this army will bring down the most powerful on earth."

Eunus stood up straight, smiled at the assembly of Romans, and bowed at the waist.

There was a subtle hum of conversation in the room, then it broke out into laughter and applause.

The slave bowed again in mock appreciation for his masters' acclaim. In his heart, he knew that what Atargatis whispered in his ear would come true.

A guard returned Eunus to his cell in the stone buildings that edged up to Enna's fortifications. Most of the slaves were kept below ground, where Eunus began his enslavement in this city. He was rewarded for his entertainment value by not having to live like a mole, and his above-ground dwelling contributed to the respect that the other slaves held for him.

Enna's position at the top of a mighty plateau, and its narrow, twisting paths down to the valley below, made it nearly impregnable. Armies could not scale the cliffs, and even slaves attempting to retreat from the great heights more often fell to their deaths in their hurried retreat. Few attempted escape; even Eunus's proximity to the outer wall of Enna was not thought to encourage a flight to freedom.

But many of the slaves in Enna had been collected from the same region of conflict, and they enjoyed a common language. So, rumors and plans passed easily among the slave compound and there were frequent conversations about insurrection. Unlike the indigenous Trinacrians who had been divested of their property, these imported slaves had nothing here, so their risk of being exposed was a fair gamble given that they had already lost everything.

Stories reached the Ennaean slaves from outside, stories of unrest and similar grudges. These rumors convinced Eunus that a slave rebellion could be successful. Over the course of several months, he and Cleon, another slave taken from his homeland in Anatolia, continued to fan the flames of revolt. The slaves of Enna were encouraged to continue in their roles so as not to raise suspicion, but they gathered tools as they could, turning shovels and pick-axes into weapons, and preparing for the right moment to rise up against the Roman oppressors.

The timing of the revolt might have been accidental, in the end. Eunus was still preparing his erstwhile army when news of a conflict between slaves and owners near Morgantina was received in Enna. After another appearance for entertainment that evening in the consul's house, he told the guard accompanying him that he wanted to retire in the quarters with the rest of the slaves.

"Why? What are you doing?" came the skeptical reply.

Eunus had thought through this already and gave his practiced actor's reply. Raising his eyebrows and curling his mouth into a twisted smile, he responded.

"I have a friend down there that I want to spend the night with."

The Roman laughed.

"Is it a girl or a boy?" he asked derisively.

Eunus passed off the comment with a shrug of his shoulders and was allowed to enter the slave quarters belowground.

When the guard withdrew, Eunus gathered his followers around him and passed on what he had heard about the rebellion outside of Enna.

"They are fighting the Romans as we speak," he said.

"Who?"

"The slaves. I don't know who, but they are slaves."

"Can they win?" asked another.

"Certainly, if they keep Atargatis in their thoughts. And so can we," he assured them.

Throughout the night, they argued about the progress and whether they were prepared. Many slaves who had avidly helped in collection of weapons were now reluctant. They were now face to face with a violent assault on the armed and well-trained Roman military, and fear captured them.

But others were bolder, and Eunus kept talking to them for hours, convincing the crowd of slaves bunched under the dim light of the lanterns that hung from the ceiling of the cave. By morning, about four hundred of the Ennaean slaves had committed to attack the Romans. They needed a plan, so Eunus sat with his closest advisors to plot strategy. After a few hours of restless sleep, the men awoke to a new day, with the prospect that by nightfall, they would reside above the ground and even in the Romans' gilded homes.

The day passed as they planned, without much activity and little or no resistance. Eunus and Cleon, his military aide, had taught their fellows that surprise was critical, especially if the surprise came at nightfall when the Romans' bellies were full and their wits sotted with wine.

And so it went.

As the sun set and the Romans' milled about Enna preparing to return to their homes, the slave revolt unfolded. Eunus and his closest confidantes had purposely spread out among the slave quarters so they could lead each group in the assault. These men were prepared to die at the point of the attack if necessary, but Eunus also knew that if leadership failed, the men's will would fade.

When a string of hand-held lanterns lit a jagged path through the center of Enna, showing the way for the Roman soldiers to find their homes, the slaves sprang upon them. Clear-eyed and sober, the men led by Eunus and his lieutenants cut down the soldiers with axes and shovels, using sharpened knives in hand-to-hand combat. The noise rose from the central square and roused the Roman officers who had already retired for the night.

But Eunus was prepared for this. He told the house slaves to remain close by the officers' homes after their duties were served, on a pretense of straightening up and preparing the house for the next day. When the officers rose from their beds, the slaves fell upon them, cutting throats or thrusting spears through their bodies. As the officers were cut down, their bodies were tossed out of windows onto the city streets, a stark warning to Roman soldiers below who were fighting not only the slaves but also their own fear. The sight of slaughtered Roman leaders' bodies tumbling out of windows and falling in a broken heap at their feet set the soldiers' fears on high alert. The Romans might have put down the slave revolt, but Eunus's plan to decapitate the Roman army rather than simply take the leaders prisoner was wise and deflated the soldiers' resolve.

The combat ensued for several hours but, before dawn, Eunus had taken up residence in the Roman general's quarters and claimed victory.

"Go out," he commanded his followers in the morning. "You are now free to go out and tell our comrades throughout Trinacrium that they are, and should be, free."

———

Over the coming months, Cleon led his army of freed slaves into the various cities and towns of Sicily while Eunus preached solidarity and continued to battle the small contingents of Roman soldiers that still occupied the country. Their army of four hundred slaves in Enna united with other slave armies, to the point that the rebellious tide reached seventy thousand and occupied every corner of Trinacrium. They killed

Roman soldiers when they could, confiscated their property, and took their women.

In the meantime, Eunus declared that his new title would be King Antiochus and that he would rule the island country from his home in Enna, the nearly impregnable fortress at the top of the mountain. Cleon marched out and, with his forces, captured Agrigentum, Katane, and Tauromenium, with a plan to control the entire island in a matter of months and drive the occupying Roman Republic out for good.

News of the slave rebellion reached Rome, where the high officials doubted the truth of the claims, but also doubted the virility of the Roman detachment that had been defeated in Enna. The following year, they sent Lucius Calpurnius Piso to blockade Enna and defeat Eunus where he lived. They recognized the difficulty of claiming the mountain fortress, especially considering the few, and narrow, passages to the top, so Piso adopted a siege strategy. When armed conflict arose, the Romans had new weapons at their disposal. They made good use of an improved catapult which was capable of launching large rocks far into the air. Their infantry also had invented the *amentum* – a leather strap they could attach to the back end of a javelin and allow the soldier to launch the weapon farther and higher.

The siege wore on for months but the slaves in Enna survived thanks to their own distinct advantages. First, the former Roman occupiers had stored more food and dry goods than they deserved, pillaging the surrounding villages during their stay in Enna, and this store now would serve the slaves for a very long time. In addition, the slaves were familiar with farming small plots and could use the seeds of some plants to generate new ones within the walls of Enna. Lastly, there were several natural streams that poured from fissues in the rock surrounding Enna. Eunus had his men build devices for capturing that water and refilling the cisterns that had long served the Ennaean people.

Ultimately, Rome grew tired of Piso's inaction and replaced him with Publius Rupilius whose military strategy was more aggressive. Rupilius ordered charges up the hill at the expense of the foot soldiers who went first. The general didn't care about the lives of these inconsequential men. His plan, and command, was to defeat Eunus, reclaim Enna, and execute the slaves or return them to their previous condition.

After many weeks of activity, Rupilius's series of attacks weakened the defense of Enna. Eunus led his men in a daring escape down one face of the mountain, intending to link up with other slave armies below, but he was captured. Many of his men died and some were taken into custody, but Eunus was held prisoner, saved by Rupilius's orders, and put into chains in Morgantina, a neighboring city whose slave rebellion had also been recently defeated.

Rupilius reported his victories to Rome and planned to bring Eunus there to parade him before the Roman people, but the slave leader died in captivity before Rupilius could carry out this plan. In fact, when Publius Rupilius returned himself to Rome, expecting a grand reception for putting down the slave rebellion in Sicily, he was treated to no such honor.

"He killed a bunch of slaves," said one bent and gray-haired Roman official. "I could have done that."

122 B.C.E.

AETNA

Eschypius sat at his desk enjoying the sunlight streaming in through the window. This was the most comfortable place for him, a cushioned chair for his aging muscles set at a table positioned in front of a broad window to the outside. He had chosen this spot in his home in Catania when he first moved here from Athens. It was perfectly positioned on this rise to see the marketplace and common areas of Catania below, and it faced north toward the majestic mountain, Aetna.

His servant had originally thought he would prefer another room, one that faced east toward the rising sun, but the light there was too bright.

"Besides," Eschypius told her, "the light would fade when the sun arced over the house and disappeared in the opposite direction.

He pointed to this other room, one that looked north and away from the sunrise, and one which would benefit from bright natural light for more hours of the day.

More hours for him to work on his mathematics and on the drawings of the little machines he was inventing. And it was just so, this morning, as he leaned on his left elbow on the drawing table, his right hand delicately clutching a quill. He had already rendered a number of lines and curves on the parchment before him as the image of a tension machine began to emerge from the paper. It would be a spring-loaded pulley, one designed to reduce the effort required to raise large weights, reduce them enough that a single man could lift a Roman catapult like the one that stood unused in the square below him. Eschypius had measured the catapult in minute detail on the preceding days – activities that drew the attention of the Roman legions holding the town of Catania – but he was thought to be an innocuous old man, so they let him be.

As he gazed down at the catapult, he also took in the cloudless blue sky above. The azure brilliance on that morning, combined with the green hills and dusty valleys that stretched off to the horizon seemed to Eschypius to be the work of some great artist who wielded the elements of nature like a painter's palette.

He bent down over his work again, added some cross-hatching strokes to indicate a deepened groove in the side of the machine, then a few quick curved lines to suggest movement. Then Eschypius stopped. He swept his eyes left to right on the page and tried to imagine the device at work. The inventor in him found that the only sure way to design something with moving parts was to look at the drawings and then allow his imagination to see them in motion. Once, twice, and a third time, Eschypius swept his gaze from left to right, the direction that the machine would take as it was put to movement, and he could almost see it lift off the page and carry out his unspoken commands.

He laid the page back down on the drawing table and rested his hands. Using his left thumb and forefinger, he massaged the bulky muscle at the base of his right thumb, the muscle and joint that always tightened up when he spent too long at the drawing table. Pushing and stroking the joint unconsciously, he looked out of his window toward the north.

Eschypius noticed a thin reed of grey smoke rising from the peak of Aetna. Then there was a puff of smoke, and the thin reed resumed. The puff that interrupted this trail of grey cloud rose into the sky as if it was climbing a ladder of smoke, reaching the apex of the column and then spreading out left and right. As he watched this unfold, another puff was emitted from Aetna's highest part, bigger than the first, and it climbed the ladder of the reed of smoke just as its predecessor had.

Eschypius drew another piece of parchment from the shelf below his drawing table. It already was crowded with preliminary drawings of his pulley system; most of the paper available to him was already filled with earlier imaginings of the artist scientist. He pushed the parchment farther away from him so that his hands rested comfortably on the lower edges, and then picked up his quill. The muscle in his right hand still ached but Eschypius chose to ignore it for now.

Once fully set up, the artist looked back out the window toward Aetna in the distance. While he was preparing his drawing paper, the cloud of smoke had grown higher, and the puffs had migrated outward from the column. It took on an appearance of a stone pine tree that he had seen here and in southern Italy. This type of tree had a long slender trunk, seldom divided into parallel trunks so that it looked like a stone column standing upright. The branches grew from the head of the tree and not often from the lower levels of the trunk, so that the whole effect was a t-shaped tree. Eschypius immediately thought of this tree when he tried to copy the growing cloud of smoke above Aetna, and he let his right hand follow this image as he drew the scene before him.

The system of cloud column and canopy continued to grow in height and width, forcing Eschypius to abandon his earlier sketch and create another drawing squeezed into another corner of the parchment. Distant sounds from the mountain were now being heard by the Catanians below and people were coming out of their homes and gathering in the common areas and streets. From his elevated perch, Eschypius could see the action directly, although the people below caught only the tops of the smoke that rose above building height, smoke that was beginning to stretch out across the horizon in the north. He continued to draw the image in detail, and even added z-shaped lines when he witnessed lightning bolts that shot from the peak of Aetna. The booms that he had heard over the last few minutes grew in frequency and volume, and there was another sound now accompanying the explosions taking place on the mountain.

The booms he heard at first were emitted from the now-red hot opening that the volcano was exposing on the peak, but louder, closer booms sounded different. With his failing eyesight, Eschypius saw very little detail of movement from Aetna itself – except for the fire and scorching lava that was beginning to pour down the slopes of the mountain. But he was seeing large rocks and boulders – some as big as the catapult he had so carefully measured – fall into the near valley, with some reaching as far as Catania itself. Eschypius thought hard about the different sounds – one indicating an explosion that sent the rock up from the volcano and the other which sounded when the rock landed on earth – and he tried to use these different sounds rather than his eyesight to calculate the rate of fall and the nearness of the hits.

He calculated that most of the biggest explosions sent up large boulders that could not fly that far, boulders that landed in a spectacular splash on the slow-moving rivers of lava that were streaming down the slopes of Aetna and onto large portions of the valley at its feet. Smaller explosions sent up a spray of rocks that flew through the air, some reaching Catania, and were now crashing down on the people and their homes. The crowd gathered below scattered in all directions, but no one knew the way to safety. Some returned to their homes, probably to retrieve little children or other valuables; many raced away from the direction of Aetna and toward the southern portion of the city, as if even this slightly greater distance would protect them.

Eschypius continued to draw his images as fiery rocks streaked across the sky. The smoke trails these missiles left behind smelled of sulphur and were beginning to fill the blue sky with the ugly grey haze that hangs over a massive fire.

A brilliantly red rock was heading straight at Eschypius's home at that moment. By that time, his servant had come to his room to seek answers and comfort as it seemed the world was coming to an end. She stood at his shoulder when this new missile could be seen in a direct line toward them, and she turned and ran from the room. Eschypius did not move. He knew enough about mathematics and had, thus far, studied enough of the rocks spewed that morning from the volcano that he could imagine the path of this rock and concluded that it would fall far short of his abode.

Eschypius was right. The burning, steaming rock fell in the square below his window, so he continued to chronicle the events of the day with his sketches.

Other rocks began to fall on Catania as the river of lava slowly claimed the land in the valley and moved toward their town. Houses were on fire, having been set ablaze by the hot rocks raining down on them from the sky.

At one point, Eschypius noticed one of the missiles arc barely over his head, and he knew in that moment that its vector would not clear his home. Just as he thought, he heard a crash above him and smelled the fire set by the rock landing on his wooden roof.

His servant returned – which surprised Eschypius; he was sure she had fled the city – and urged him to abandon his study. The artist refused at first, but when another rock was seen heading directly toward them, he quickly reconsidered and followed the servant out the door.

In a panic, Eschypius stopped in the portal and spun back around. He had forgotten the drawings he had made to track these events, so he ran back to the table to gather them. The servant ran after him, holding onto his elbow, and then dragged Eschypius from the room.

He looked over his shoulder at the path of the rock and saw that it missed his home. Relaxing for only a moment, he turned to his servant.

"We can be safe here. I should stay."

She did not even answer. She just grabbed onto the old man's elbow with both hands and dragged him from the home and into the street below.

Most of the Catanians evacuated the city over the next few hours; those who lagged were killed by fire or falling rocks. Beyond the city walls they could survey the damage throughout the region. Their farms, which lay in traditional fashion as a tapestry around the city, were being ravaged by fire and lava. The buildings in the city they had just left were being crushed or tossed sideways by the force of Aetna's eruption. And the sky was filled with smoke and the acrid smell of the devil's workshop.

102 B.C.E.

TRIOCALA

T HERE WAS A GENERAL COMMOTION IN THE CROWDED QUARTERS OF slaves turned rebels in the city of Triocala. Salvius had led his rebellious army against the might of Rome, faltering at some points but maintaining a faithful following throughout.

From the beginning of the uprising several seasons ago, he – now known as Tryphon – had commanded a growing army of former slaves. The power that led Rome to enslave them was not recognized by the men taken from conquered territories, and they remain in bondage only because the Roman legions forced them into it. The ranks of the slaves were further enlarged by a corrupt system of tax collection, a system that caught many faithful Italians in its web as well as many foreigners and cast them into servitude in Sicily.

Gaius Marius, a Roman consul, was assembling his army to fight the Celts in Gaul. To do so, he counted on Roman allies throughout southern Europe to supply funds and men, but these people resisted him. He then turned to the slave system in Sicily and declared that those loyal to Rome should be freed, which meant most of the men taken from mainland Italy who were held in bondage. But many non-Italian slaves thought that the emancipation of the Italians from their ranks meant that they, too, had been emancipated. The truth was more complicated.

Publius Licinius Nerva, the governor of Sicily, was then in a tight spot. He set up a program to review all applications for freedom, decide whom among the slave population were Italians, then free them while keeping the non-Italian slaves in chains. After eight hundred or so slaves were set free, those who remained rebelled against Nerva and the Roman system that held them. They quit their slave masters and left for lives on their own.

Nerva was criticized from all sides – by Marius for an inefficient system that slowed the recruitment of his army, by the landowners who didn't have the labor to maintain their farms, and by the slaves who insisted on their freedom. Nerva's system collapsed under the load of applications and, frustrated, he ordered all erstwhile slaves to return to their masters.

Not surprisingly, the rebellion grew under these circumstances.

Tryphon watched all this and the angry protest by the enslaved men was exactly what he wanted. He enlisted a large contingent of slaves who would not buckle under Nerva's decree to return to slavery, and he received help from Athenion, another slave respected by the masses, who mounted an army of slaves to resist the move to put them back into bondage.

Meanwhile, the rulers in Rome followed the progress of events in Sicily and could see that their tenuous hold over the island was slipping. Having lost faith in Nerva, they replaced him with a much more aggressive consul, Lucius Licinius Lucullus, to quell the revolt. Nerva was a governor; Lucullus was a military man. The new Roman leader in Sicily met the slaves' demands with edicts of his own, then ordered that resistance would be met with a ferocious response. The simmering anger on both sides continued to build.

It was not long before Tryphon and his slave army would meet the Romans in battle. He had wanted to garrison his army in Triocalla and strengthen his defense of the city against a Roman attack. There would be the slaves' stand against the mighty Roman Republic; but Athenion disagreed with the tactic. He convinced the self-proclaimed king of the slaves that his forces were great and that he should prepare to meet Lucullus in battle.

The date was set, and the place would be the fields around Scirthaea. The slaves outnumbered their aggressors nearly three to one but the

Romans were more experienced and better equipped for these contests. The battle waged for days and was heading toward a draw, but suddenly Athenion was cut down in hand-to-hand combat. He was bleeding badly but realized that his only survival was to feign death and, thereby, escape execution right there on the battlefield. The ruse tricked the Romans who ignored him, but it also tricked his own men. Thinking that their leader had perished, his army of slaves fled the scene and, in their disorganized retreat, drew forces from Tryphon with them.

The slave army of both Tryphon and Athenion retreated from the battlefield to Triocala, Athenion limping back himself after the field was nearly cleared. But Tryphon hoped to withstand the siege of Lucullus and prevail.

For nearly a year, Lucullus remained on the outskirts of Triocala, in siege, but without progress. The stand-off discouraged Rome and caused many of Lucullus's supporters to desert him. Once his support and advocates in Rome were lost, the assembly decided to replace Lucullus with Gaius Servilius, a consul in Rome and a ruthless commander, to vanquish the slaves.

Being replaced by this man didn't please Lucullus, who continued to argue that he had exploited every advantage and was on a path to success. Unable to convince the Roman leaders, and angry that he was being replaced, he chose to destroy all of his siege equipment around Triocala to prevent Servilius from benefitting from his efforts.

Servilius took over despite having to rebuild the offensive and he reported treasonous actions of Lucullus to the Roman consuls back home. Charges would be filed against him, but for now Servilius had to find a way to be successful and avoid the same judgment that was levied on his predecessor.

After another year of siege, Servilius was still unable to quell the rebellion and bring the slaves back to their masters, so Rome replaced him too. In came Manius Aquilius, who was a follower of Gaius Marius and, not surprisingly, promoted by Marius to this new post. By now, the export of grain from Sicily to Rome had slowed to the point that bread and other important foodstuffs were being cut off, creating a food shortage and overall discontent on the part of the Roman citizenry.

True to the faith that Marius put in him, Manius Aquilius finally put down the revolt the following year and returned to a hero's welcome in Rome.

The two slave revolts on the island of Sicily spawned other rebellions on the mainland, but they all ended with mass executions of slaves who participated in them. Rome intended to crush any desire of slaves to force emancipation, and worse treatment awaited any future uprising.

JULY 2018
CAFÉ AMADEO

"They lost," Vito said.

"The slaves?"

"Sì. It wasn't until 100 B.C. that the Romans got control of the situation. Manius Aquilius, who replaced Gaius Servilius, broke the resistance and sent the slaves back to the landowners. The campaign included much bloodshed, and many terrible deaths preceded by torture, to demonstrate to the lingering rebels that they should relent and return to their duties.

"Although the general governing philosophy of Rome was very complex, there was a consistent theme that repeated itself whenever they conquered new territory. They used force to put down resistance, but after the people surrendered and gave in, the Romans preferred to let them be. They taxed their products, their farms and their people, but the new rulers mostly let the existing systems of government in each territory remain. There were some local Roman governors who might have objected to the gods of the conquered people, but even these tended to escape Roman objection.

"So the people were left to choose between continued armed resistance in which more of them would be crucified or imprisoned, or accept the Roman rule and live in a condition of relatively peaceful domination."

We were once more sitting in Café Amadeo, enjoying our morning espresso and rolls. Originally, I had planned to leave Mazara del Vallo the following day, and had told Vito about my plans. We sat in silence for a while after his description of the slave wars. I knew there were more; in fact, the most famous slave war led by Spartacus was inspired by Eunus and Salvius, but it was fought on the mainland near Rome and was put down with more vicious treatment than the rebellions by the slaves in Sicily.

I thought about the month that I had spent in Vito's tutelage. I had come to this land to learn about World War II and its impact on my family's homeland. I began in that way, until my very first morning with Vito, when the kindly gentleman guided me back in time to a point thousands of years past, and then guided me slowly, carefully, forward through the migrations, invasions, and evolutions of this country.

Sipping the last from my coffee cup, I realized that in this time together, I had only covered the time before Christ, thousands of years yes, but I still hadn't gotten to the waves of invasions since that time, the Roman era, the Goths and Visigoths, the Vandals sack of Rome, the Byzantine and Arab periods, even the Vikings, British, French, and Spaniards. And all these happened centuries before my original starting point of World War II.

"I don't think I'll go," I said to Vito.

"Go where?"

I knew he knew what I meant; he was playing with me. But his smile was thinner than usual and his eyes showed a bit of sadness.

"I don't think I'll leave," I repeated. "I have so much to learn."

Vito looked at me and smiled a tiny smile. Then he sipped from his espresso and said only one word.

"Romans."

And I knew that I would remain on Sicily – and that we were about to resume my education.

ANCIENT PLACE NAMES AND APPROXIMATE ERA WHEN THEY FIRST APPEARED

(NOTE: FICTIONAL NAMES APPEAR IN ITALICS)

Far Ancient Times	Ancient Times	c. 1500 BCE	c. 1000 BCE	c. 500 BCE	c. Year 0	c. 500 CE	c. 1000 CE	c. 1500 CE	Current
	Ankara	*Akra*				Aggyrium		San Filippo d'Argirio	Aggira
				Acragas	Agrigentum		Girgenti		Agrigento
					Hippo Regius				Annaba
	Letopolis	Khem							Ausim (Egypt)
			Entella						Belice
		Eutesо		Euesperides					Benghazi (Libya)
					Brundisium				Brindisi
		Gadir							Cadiz (Spain)
	Italoi				Bruttium				Calabria
						Qal'at a fimi			Calatafimi-Segesta
				Triocalla					Caltabellotta
				Capeva					Capua
	Casello	*Casegno*							Castellaro Vecchio
							Castello de Hauteville		Castello Aragonese
				Katane					Catania
				Cephaloedium			Gafludi		Cefalù
			Centuripa	Kentoripa				Centorbi	Centuripe
	Kaptara	*Keftiu*							Crete
						Adrianople			Edirne (Turkey)
			Hemna	Hennaion		Henna	Kasr'Ianni	Castrogiovanni	Enna
			Eryx				Cebel Hamid	Monte San Giuliano	Erice
			Inessa	Aetna					Etna
Fave	*Aballa*								Favignana
								Île Julia (in 1831)	Ferdinanda
	Sypho	*Sintelia*		Gela			Terranova		Gela
		Knossos							Heraklion (Crete)
		Troy							Hissarlik (Turkey)
					Ietas				Iaitas
				Byzantium		Constantinople			Istanbul
		Oenotria							Italia

						Shalem	Yerushalayim			Jerusalem
Fansa			Lentinoi	Lefansu						Lentini
	Bevira				Phorbantia					Levanzo
					Phintius					Licata
			Maia						Lemusa	Linosa (island)
						Melita				Malta
Tirsa						Algusa				Marettimo
					Lilybaeum			Mars-al-Allah		Marsala
					Massalia					Marseille
Maxra			Mazar					Mazara[1]		Mazara del Vallo
					Maleth	Melite		al Madinah		Mdina (Malta)
			The Great Sea	Syrian Sea	Mare Nostrum				Bahr-i Sefid	Mediterranean Sea
					Zancle	Messana				Messina
		Myla	Mylae							Milazzo
							Miniu			Mineo
			Elyma							Misrata (Libya)
					Hyblaean Mountains					Monti Iblei
			Motya					San Pantaleo		Motya (Mozzia to Sicilians)
		Nassina								Naxos
		Picta								Nebrodi Mountains
			Netumo			Netum				Noto
Manta			Zis		Panormus		Bal'harm			Palermo
		Pantea	Euonymos		Hycesia					Panarea (island)
		Picta					Bint al-Riyäh	Cossyra		Pantelleria
										Peloritans Mtns
									Piana dei Greci	Piana degli Albanesi
									Piazza	Piazza Armerina
						Rhegium		Riväh		Reggio Calabria
			Elima		Halyciae		Alicia	Salam		Salemi
					Didyme		Salam			Salina (island)
	Precipio						San Filadelfio			San Fratello
	Thera	Akrotiri								Santorini (island)
	Rivesa				Thermae			as-Saqqah		Sciacca
		Gania	Egesta				Syac			Segesta
					Selinus					Selinunte
Gania	Dian		Sikania		Trinacrium					Sicily

[1] "del Vallo" added in 19th century

Stentinello	Kfra	Syrakosai	Siracusa	Siracusae		Siracusa
						Solunto
		Pillars of Hercules				Strait of Gibraltar
		Strongulē				Stromboli
					Bilad al-Sham	Syria
					Tingis	Tangiers (Morocco)
		Tauro	Tauromenium			Taormina
		Taranto	Tarantum			Taranto
		Himera	Thermae			Termini Imerese
		Heracleion				Thonis (Egypt)
Pani	Drepanon	Drepanum				Trapani
Adda		Oea	Regio Syrtica	Regio Tripolitana		Tripoli (Libya)
		Qart-badašt	Cathago	Carthage		Tunis (Tunisia)
				Ifriqiya		Tunisia
			Tyndaris			Tyndaris
Wallee			Osteodos			Ustica
Vera			Therassia			Vulcano

List of Characters

(Note: Fictional names appear in Italics)

1943 – North Africa

Vito Trovato

2018 – Mazara del Vallo

Vito Trovato
Luca Siragusa
Santo
Emilia
Antonio

9230 B.C.E. – Fansu

Anu (later Anutu) – male, Baia's man
Baia – female, Anutu's woman
unnamed boy (later Anu) – male toddler, Anutu and Baia's son
unnamed infant – female, Anutu and Baia's daughter
Lotya – male, Nanda's man
Nanda – female, Lotya's woman
unnamed girl – Lotya and Nanda's daughter
Tano – male, Folu's man
Folu – female, Tano's woman
Neeri - female
Farutu – old male
Seeta – old female, shaman

7810 B.C.E. - Adda

Addians:

Palo – male, Sari's man, hunter and shepherd
Sari – Palo's woman
Eliu – son of Palo and Sari

Sinsa – daughter of Palo and Sari
Lefu – male, Bele's man, fisherman
Bele – Lefu's woman
Femo – male elder, Opra's man
Opra – female, Femo's woman
Rota – female elder, shaman of the tribe

Masrians

Kamo – male, leader of the Masrians, Lotu's man
Lotu – female, Kamo's woman
Lilia – young female, Kamo's daughter
Tira – female, Papia's woman
Papia – male, Tira's man

4870 B.C.E. – Gibraltar

Tomas – male, Villa's man
Villa – female, Tomas's woman
Simpo – male, Vastra's man
Vastra – female, Simpo's woman
Anxio – young boy, Simpo and Vastra's son
Keto – young girl, Simpo and Vastra's daughter, between ages of
Anxio and Suraisa
Suraisa – young girl, Simpo and Vastra's daughter
Chandra – male, Lila's man
Lila – female, Chandra's woman

4350 B.C.E. – Ankara

Telia – male, Sapira's man
Sapira – female, Telia's woman
Keeta – young female, Sapira and Telia's daughter
Nessie – female, Kropia's woman
Kropia – male, Nessie's man
Barla – female, Fante's woman
Fante – male, Barla's man
Lano – female, Cheechia's woman
Cheechia – female, Lano's woman

Alia – older female
Pali – young male, Alia's apprentice

3950 B.C.E.

Myla

    Xappo – male, Fina's man
    Fina – female, Xappo's woman

Casello

    Roaro – male, Mina's man
    Mina – female, Roaro's woman
    Soluri – young male, Roaro and Mina's son
    Chinsi – adolescent female, Roaro and Mina's daughter
    Donota – infant male, Roaro and Mina's son

Ankara

    Nefa – male, Bari's man
    Bari – female, Nefa's woman
    Papu – male, Sincia's man
    Sincia – female, Papu's woman
    Lalana – female, Papu and Sincia's daughter
    Insta – male, Hamu's man
    Hamu – female, Insta's woman
    Chaka – male, Fintala's man
    Fintala – female, Chaka's woman
    Mina – young girl, Chaka and Fintala's daughter
    Chilia with new baby
    Camio – male
    Adeto – male

2575 B.C.E. - Dian

    Nassina
    Dravo – male, Enna's man
    Enna – female, originally from Myla, Dravo's woman

Delallo – male, Linate's man
Linate – female, Delallo's woman
Wanto – male, Fippa's man
Fippa – female, Wanto's woman
Berari – male, Zinia's man
Zinia – female, Berari's woman
Chala – young girl, Berari and Zinia's daughter

Sypho
Santo – male
Xinta – male

Kronio
Dala – male, Resta's husband and leader in Kronio
Resta – female, Dala's wife
Lefanu – female, to become Xinta's wife
Alio – male, Kinta's husband, a metalworker
Kinta – female, Alio's wife

Myla
Strano – male, brother of Enna (from Nassina), Lilia's man
Lilia – female, Strano's woman
Tifo – male, Ridolfa's man
Ridolfa – female, Tifo's woman
Genio – young male, Tifo and Ridolfa's son

1510 B.C.E.

Rivesa

Aloxa – male, Rota's husband
Rota – female, Aloxa's wife (originally from Akra)
Parapio – male toddler, son of Aloxa and Rota
Tlana – Rota's god of the animal food
Untala – male, Scripa's husband
Scripa – female, Untala's wife (originally from Akra)
Poppo – male, Gia's husband
Gia – female, Poppo's wife
Befalo – adult male, son of Poppo and Gia

Akra

> *Laru – female, Taania's wife, Rota's mother*
> *Taania – male, Laru's husband, Rota's father*
> *Chia – adult female, Taania and Laru's daughter, Abele's wife*
> *Abele – male, Chia's husband*
> *Sorna and Alifa – children of Chia and Abele*

1178 B.C.E.

> *Ephso – male, commander of the Elymian flotilla*
> *Gorgidas – male, expert in farming*
> *Heliocles – male,*
> *Alcon – male, Gala's husband*
> *Gala – female, Alcon's wife*
> *Antemion – male*
> *Eurytos – male,*
> *Leodes – male, Calliope's husband*
> *Calliope – female, Leodes' wife*

1120 B.C.E., Eryx

> Potnia – goddess of love (actual)
> *Phinoto – high priest at Potnia's temple*
> *Kitro – male, Sicani slave*
> *Phenandia – male, Sicani slave*
> *Crispo – male, Elymi builder*
> *Renata – male, Elymi builder*
> *Scylla – female, priestess at Potnia's temple*

735 B.C.E.

Qart-ḥadašt

> *Bomical – male, merchant, Sophonia's husband*
> *Sophonia – female, Bomical's wife*
> *Cariamachus – male, Bomical's officer*
> *Hammen, male, Bomical's trading agent*
> *Simonire – male, ship captain*

431

Pilius – male, ship captain

Greeks

Photios – male, merchant, leader of a band

Corinthian Greeks

Strophios – male, merchant
Hestros – male, merchant, Gaia's husband
Gaia – female, Hestros' wife

413 B.C.E., Siracusa

Siracusans (on land)

Gylippus – male, Spartan general (actual)
Thaestus – male, soldier
Dionodes – male, soldier
Phaletus – male, soldier, Lydia's husband
Girius – male, soldier
Lydia – female, Phaletus's wife

Athenians (on ship)

Nicias (actual)

309 B.C.E., Siracusa

Phaestus – male, Gesuta's husband
Gesuta – female, Phaestus's wife
Hemestra – female, Nicostros's wife
Nicostros – male, blacksmith, Hemestra's husband
Dariana – female, fishmonger
Temula – female, Dariana's daughter
Demosthenes – male, city elder, Aloria's husband
Aloria – female, Demosthenes's wife
Antander – male, brother of the king, Agathocles (actual)
Constantus – male, proposed surrendering to the Carthaginians

Deinocrates – male, Siracusan traitor

250 B.C.E., Messana

Romans

> *Antilius – male, captain of a Roman trireme*
> *Stario – male, Roman general*
> *Philippus – male, Roman general*

Mamertines

> *Kiokis – male, leader of the Mamertines*

213 B.C.E.

> *Enna*
> *Gulian – male, primary city elder*
> *Pinarius – male, governor of Enna*
> *Assentia – female, Pinarius' wife*
> *Laurentiis – male, Gulian's advisor*
> *Arturus – male, Roman commander*

134 B.C.E., Enna

> Romans
> Lucius Calpurnius Piso, Consul (actual)
> Publius Rupilius, Consul (actual)
>
> Slaves
> Eunus – slave leader, also known as King Antiochus (actual)
> Cleon – slave leader (actual)

122 B.C.E., Aetna

> *Eschypius – artist, scientist*

102 B.C.E., Triocala

Romans
Gaius Marius – Roman consul (actual)
Publius Licinius Nerva – governor of Sicily (actual)
Lucius Licinius Lucullus – replaced Nerva (actual)
Gaius Servilius – Roman consul (actual)
Manius Aquilius, Roman consul (actual)

Slaves

Salvius – slave leader, also known as Tryphon (actual)
Athenion – slave leader (actual)

VOCABULARY

The following terms and words have been used throughout the book and are listed here for the readers' benefit.

(**Note**: *Fictional words appear in Italics*)

Word	Translation
ager publicus	public land
allaghia	6th century Byzantine cavalry
allu	garlic
almogavars	lightly clothed but armed soldiers from Iberia who fought for Peter of Aragon
alod	in feudalism, an allowance for land owners to keep their land if owned before the feudal system was imposed
anusim	anyone forcibly converted to Christianity; see neofiti
As-Salamu Alaykum	Arabic for "I will be with you"
bacu	abacus
Bagno Ebraico	Hebrew Bath; Roman and Siracusan name for the Great Mikveh of Siracuse
baldric	a leather strap bound around the chest and shoulders; used to carry weaponry, especially to sheathe a sword
bandon (pl. banda)	6th century Byzantine army detachment; approximately 150 men
bireme	two-decked ship, each deck with its own set of oarsmen
bon sira	good evening
boviu	cow
brit	beer
bucellarii	armed soldiers in a private army
Calic' Bellu	name of tavern in Siracusae, 535 C.E. (translates to "Cup of War")
cameriere	waiter
cantucci	little biscuits, like biscotti
cassata	cake
cataphract	armed and armored man on horseback; also the armored horse itself
catepano	referred to person in charge in a Byzantine army, "the one placed at the top"
cheeka (see gira)	Masrian word for spring onion
ciciri	chickpeas
coniglio	rabbit
contadini	peasants, farm workers, and miners
corvus	wooden bridge hinged to a ship that could swing out and couple with another vessel to allow boarding
cubit	Roman unit of measurement, equal to one and one-half feet
denarius (pl. denari)	Roman unit of money
dhimmi	Jew or Christian in a Muslim society
dolmen	primitive stone constructions, usually a simply arrangement of two or more vertical members spanned by one horizontal member above
dulcis in fundo	dessert made of honey, nuts, milk, and flour
Elymi (a.k.a., Elymians)	tribe from Anatolia to migrate to Sicily
Fasci dei Lavoratori	see Fasci Siciliani

Fasci Siciliani	protest movement in 1890s in Sicily, arguing for workers' rights; a.k.a., Fasci dei Lavoratori
feudi	parcels of land distributed by the king in a feudal society
gebbiu	cistern, from Arab word *giebja*
ghulam	soldier slave
gira (see cheeka)	Addian word for spring onion
hecatontarch	Byzantine leader of the cavalry
hijab	Muslim dress for women, covering all but the face
Hoplites	citizen-soldiers of Ancient Greece
infama	lowest class of Romans, just above slaves; also used to refer to prostitutes
In shā'a llāh	As Allah wills it
isolani	islanders
jizya	a tax on all non-Muslims (see zakat)
kanat	Arab irrigation system of tunnels under Palermo
kasbah	marketplace, from the Arab word
keyla	olive tree
kottabos	a drinking game in which the celebrants would fling the remnants of wine from their goblets at a disk trying to dislodge it from its perch
koursorses	Byzantine cavalry
lateen-rig	a triangular sail set on a single mast
latifundia	systems of farms
lazzaroni	poorest class of people in 18th century Naples
lochagiai	6th century Byzantine infantry
Magreb	region of North Africa
mal del stomaco	stomach ache
mangonel	a type of traction trebuchet
Mare Nostrum	Roman name for the Mediterranean Sea
mattanza	circling a school of fish with boats, then closing the circle until the fish could be clubbed and brought aboard
minieru	mine (Italians would say miniera)
moirai	6th century Byzantine division of soldiers
Naxians	people from Naxos
neofiti	the word in Sicily for the anusim, or Jews converted to Christianity
Notinesi	people from Noto
oecist	Greek term for someone who founds a city or settlement
oinos	wine, word used by the Greeks by 750 B.C.E.
pazzu	crazy, wild (Italians would say pazzo)
pecore	sheep
pistola, pistole (pl.) (sometimes pistolese)	pistol, pistols
pistolese	soldier with a pistol
pizzu	bribe (Italians would say pizzo)
pomolo	lentils
poncho	*Posidonia oceanica*, Mediterranean marine plant, also known as Neptune Grass
Potnia	Elymian goddess of love and fertility; same as Phoenicians' Astarte and Roman Aprhodite (and Venus Erycina)
pugio	small dagger worn by Roman soldiers

qadi	judge in an Islamic Shari'a court
qanāt	water management system employed in Bal'harm (Palermo)
rashidun	elite Muslim soldier in Middle Ages
rishta	noodle-like pasta introduced to Sicily by Muslims
seah	a unit of volume used by Jews, roughly equivalent to 15 liters
seeio	hello
shatranj	early Persian name for the game of chess; the name persisted into the era when it was introduced to Europe in the 13th century
Sicanians (a.k.a., Sicans)	first tribe to settle in Sicily
Sicels (a.k.a. Siculi)	tribe from mainland Italy to migrate to Sicily
sida	obsidian (before 3950 B.C.E.)
sidia	obsidian (after 3950 B.C.E.)
skutatoi	6th century Byzantine archers
strategos	general (or commander) in the Byzantine army
sūrah	chapters of the Quran
Svevi	Swabians
tartrae	truffles
tercio, tercie	Spanish infantry
Tercio de Sicilia	Charles V's infantry in Sicily
tevilah	Hebrew word for full immersion, as in a mikveh
tina	wine
toma / tomae	olive / olives
tourmarch	Byzantine leader of an infantry
trichiagon	tarragon
trireme	three-decked ship, each deck with its own set of oarsmen
tumarch	leader of infantry in the Byzantine army
tyropatinum	tyropita, sweet soft cheese with honey and raw eggs
wāli	Muslim governor
yero	bitter vetch
zagara	blossom, from Arab word *zahra*
zakat	a tax required under Islamic law to aid the needy; in some areas like the Maghreb, the zakat is supplemented by the jizya (see)
zibbibbu	raisins, from Arab word *zbib*

WARS IN LAST HALF OF FIRST MILLENNIUM B.C.E.

- First Sicilian War, 480 B.C.E.
- Segesta-Selinus Conflict, 416 B.C.E.
- Athenian Invasion of Siracusa, 415-413 B.C.E.
- Second Segesta-Selinus Conflict, 411 B.C.E.
- Second Sicilian War, 410-340 B.C.E., a.k.a., Carthaginian Invasion
- Third Sicilian War, 315-307 B.C.E. (of which the Siege of Siracusa (311-309 B.C.E.) was most significant)
- Pyrrhic War, 280-265 B.C.E., which led to the Punic Wars
- First Punic War, 264-241 B.C.E.
- Second Punic War, 218-201 B.C.E.
- Third Punic War, 149-146 B.C.E.
- First Slave War, 135-132 B.C.E.
- Second Slave War, 104-100 B.C.E.
- Third Slave War, 73-71 B.C.E. (led by Spartacus on mainland Italy, therefore not related to Sicily)

ACKNOWLEDGMENTS

A writer's world is inhabited by many beings. Some are imaginary, like the muse whispering in our ears – both distracting and inspirational in equal measure. Some are the spirits who come back to us from distant memories, or the phantoms who materialize from the shadow of our fears. Some are the real, flesh-and-blood people who come and go in our lives, and who stay and persevere throughout the insanity of the creative processs. The sane and encouraging influence in mine was that of my wife, Linda. The literal "push-in-the-back" came from my good friend Don Oldenburg, who after I had been researching this for several years admonished me that "sooner or later, you have to start writing." And the drive to complete the work came from the memory of my father and the encouraging presence of my daughter, both Sicilians connected by me.

Although *The Sicily Chronicles* is a work of historical fiction, the story it tells would not have been possible without the research and insights of numerous historians, sociologists, archeologists, anthropologists, and other writers. From their works I have been able to construct a plausible, sensible, and detailed chronology of Sicily, from ancient times to the present day.

Great thanks and respect are due to hundreds of diverse sources, but the following references are among the most influential in the research I have conducted over the years.

Abulafia, David, *The Great Sea: A Human History of the Mediterranean,* Oxford University Press (Oxford, 2011)

Attenborough, Richard, *The First Eden,* Little, Brown (1987)

Benjamin, Sandra, *Sicily: Three Thousand Years of Human History,* Steerforth (New Hampshire, 2006)

Booms, Dirk, and Higgs, Peter, *Sicily: Culture and Conquest,* The British Museum (2016)

Brownworth, Lars, *Lost to the West: The Forgotten Byzantine Empire That Rescued Western Civilization,* Broadway Books (New York, 2009)

Cline, Eric H., *1177 B.C.: The Year Civilization Collapsed,* Princeton University Press (Princeton, 2014)

Cook, Michael, *A Brief History of the Human Race,* W.W. Norton (New York, 2003)

Crowley, Roger, *Empires of the Sea: The Siege of Malta, the Battle of Lepanto, and the Contest for the Center of the World,* Random House (New York, 2009)

Cunliffe, Barry, *Europe Between the Oceans: 9000 BC to 1000 AD,* Yale University Press (2011)

de Souza, Philip (ed.), *The Ancient World at War,* Thames & Hudson (London, 2008)

Dickson, D. Bruce, *The Dawn of Belief: Religion in the Upper Paleolithic of Southwestern Europe,*

University of Arizona Press (1990)

Farrell, Joseph, *Sicily: A Cultural History,* Interlink Pub Group (Massachusetts, 2014)

Keahey, John, *Seeking Sicily: A Cultural Journey Through Myth and Reality in the Heart of the Mediterranean,* St. Martin's Press (New York, 2011)

Lacey, Robert and Danziger, Danny, *The Year 1000: What Life was Like at the Turn of the First Millennium,* Little, Brown, and Company (Boston, 1999)

Linder, Douglas O., "Famous Trials: Gaius Verres Trial (70 B.C.), Mendola, Louis, *The Peoples of Sicily: A Multicultural Legacy,* Trinacria Editions (2014)

Mendola, Louis and Alio, Jacqueline, *Norman-Arab-Byzantine Palermo, Monreale & Cefalù,* Trinacria Editions (New York, 2017)

Miles, Richard, *Carthage Must be Destroyed: The Rise and Fall of an Ancient Civilization,* Penguin (London, 2010)

Mitchener, James A., *The Source,* Dial Press Trade Paperback (reprint, 2002)

Nesto, Bill, and di Savino, Frances, *The World of Sicilian Wine,* University of California Press (Berkeley, 2013)

Norwich, John Julius, *Sicily: An Island at the Crossroads of History,* Random House (2015)

Piccolo, Salvatore, *Ancient Stones: The Prehistoric Dolmens of Sicily,* Brazen Head (London, 2013)

Privitera, Joseph F., *Sicily: An Illustrated History,* Hippocrene Books (New York, 2002)

Robb, John, *The Early Mediterranean Village: Agency, Material Culture, and Social Change Neolithic Italy,* Cambridge University Press (2007)

Runciman, Steven, *The Sicilian Vespers: A History of the Mediterranean World in the Later Thirteenth Century,* Cambridge University Press (1958)

Sammartino, Peter, and Roberts, William, *Sicily: An Informal History,* Cornwall Books (1992)

Simeti, Mary Taylor, *On Persephone's Island: A Sicilian Journal,* Vintage (New York, 1995)

Simeti, Mary Taylor, *Pomp and Sustenance: Twenty-Five Centuries of Sicilian Food,* Henry Holt (New York, 1991)

Toussaint-Samat, Maguelonne, *History of Food*, Blackwell Publishers (1992)

White, Randall, *Dark Caves, Bright Visions: Life in Ice Age Europe*, W.W. Norton (New York, 1986)

Useful websites:

www.bestofsicily.com

www.sicilybella.com

http://www.wondersofsicily.com/

http://www.italythisway.com/

www.timesofsicily.com

Dear reader,

We hope you enjoyed reading *Islands of Fire*. Please take a moment to leave a review, even if it's a short one. Your opinion is important to us.

Discover more books by Dick Rosano at https://www.nextchapter.pub/authors/author-dick-rosano

Want to know when one of our books is free or discounted? Join the newsletter at http://eepurl.com/bqqB3H

Best regards,

Dick Rosano and the Next Chapter Team

The story continues in:
Crossroads of the Mediterranean by Dick Rosano
To read the first chapter for free, please head to:
https://www.nextchapter.pub/books/crossroads-of-the-mediterranean

ABOUT THE AUTHOR

Dick Rosano's columns have appeared for many years in The Washington Post and other national publications. His series of novels set in Italy capture the beauty of the country, the flavors of the cuisine, and the history and traditions of the people. He has traveled the world but Italy is his ancestral home and the insights he lends to his books bring the characters to life, the cities and countryside into focus, and the culture into high relief.

Whether it's the political drama of The Vienna Connection, the workings of a family winery in A Death in Tuscany, the azure sky and Mediterranean vistas in A Love Lost in Positano, the intrigue in Hunting Truffles, or the bitter conflict of Nazi occupation in The Secret Altamura, Rosano puts the life and times of Italy into your hands.

OTHER BOOKS BY DICK ROSANO

Sicily: Crossroads of the Mediterranean – An historical novel of the island at the center of Western Civilization from the time of Julius Caesar until the present day.

A Death in Tuscany – A young man mourns the suspicious death of his grandfather while preparing to take the reins of his family's winery in Tuscany.

The Secret of Altamura: Nazi Crimes, Italian Treasure – Secrets hidden from the Nazis in 1943 are still sought by an art collector in modern days. But evil stalks all those who try to reveal it.

The Vienna Connection: Hidden stories connect the American establishment to suspicious activity in Vienna, Austria, and Darren Priest is called back from retirement to unravel them.

Hunting Truffles – The slain bodies of truffle hunters show up, but the truffle harvest itself has been stolen.

Wine Heritage: The Story of Italian American Vintners – Centuries of Italian immigration to America laid the groundwork for the American wine revolution of the 20ᵗʰ century.

OTHER BOOKS BY D.P. ROSANO

A Love Lost in Positano – A war-weary State Department translator falls for a woman under the blue skies of the Mediterranean, then she disappears.

Vivaldi's Girls – The young red-haired prodigy could make women swoon with the sweeping grandeur of his violin performances – even more so after he traded in his priest's robes for the dashing attire of a rich and notorious celebrity.

To Rome, With Love – Some memories are never forgotten. As Tamara discovers the charms of Rome in the arms of her first love the sights, food, and wine sweep her away.

Lightning Source UK Ltd.
Milton Keynes UK
UKHW012143120421
381888UK00008B/665/J

9 781034 754077